34320000109834

D0016542

LoveMurder

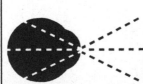

LOVEMURDER

SAUL BLACK

THORNDIKE PRESS
A part of Gale, a Cengage Company

GALE
A Cengage Company

Farmington Hills, Mich • San Francisco • New York • Waterville, Maine
Meriden, Conn • Mason, Ohio • Chicago

LIBRARY OF CONGRESS CIP DATA ON FILE.
CATALOGUING IN PUBLICATION FOR THIS BOOK
IS AVAILABLE FROM THE LIBRARY OF CONGRESS

ISBN-13: 978-1-4328-4521-6 (hardcover)
ISBN-10: 1-4328-4521-7 (hardcover)

Published in 2018 by arrangement with Macmillan Publishing Group, LLC/St. Martin's Press

Printed in Mexico
1 2 3 4 5 6 7 22 21 20 19 18

ACKNOWLEDGMENTS

For the sustaining mix of professional support, friendship, hospitality, and occasional gratis psychotherapy my thanks to: Jonny Geller, Jane Gelfman, Bill Massey, Charlie Spicer, Kim Teasdale, Stephen Coates, Nicola Stewart, Mike Loteryman, Anna Baker Jones, Peter Sollett, Eva Vives, Susanna Moore, Louise Maker, Marina Hardiman, Lydia Hardiman, Alice Naylor, Sarah Williams, Ben Ball, Tracy Ryan, Emma Jane Unsworth, Rachel Willis, Rene Unischewski, Joanna Yeldham, April Osborn, Bethany Reis, and Henrietta Rose-Innes. For unpaid editorial labors, I'm especially grateful to Mark Duncan, and for taking the time to answer my legal queries, Evan Marshall. As always, a big hats-off to my dear Ma and Pa.

Between them, Jonathan Field and Vicky Hutchinson made an incalculably generous

contribution to the completion of this novel.
I am forever in their debt.

PROLOGUE

May 2009

Exquisitely beautiful Katherine Glass was the most hated woman in America, and on a wet Tuesday afternoon in May 2009, San Francisco homicide detective Valerie Hart sat in the Bryant Street courtroom staring at the back of her infamous blond head. The verdicts had just been delivered, and now, despite Justice Amanda Delgado's gavel-whacking and repeated calls for order, the place sounded like a cocktail party at its thudding zenith. Six charges of Murder One. Guilty, six for six. The public gallery was in an ecstasy of self-righteous titillation. Faces were greedy and alive. *Serves the bitch right. Pure. Fucking. Evil.*

"Order," Justice Delgado drawled, for the fourth time. "Order!" Delgado, a whittled Latina in her early fifties, had a small coltish face long past surprise, but Valerie had watched its jaded composure fracture through the course of the trial. Like the jury, Delgado had seen the videos that convicted Katherine Glass. So, too, obviously, had Valerie. The images were with her now for the rest of her life. The images were with all of them.

"Order!"

Valerie released a breath she hadn't been aware of holding. Her body's tension remained. No relief. Granted, she'd caught Katherine Glass. Granted, Katherine Glass was being removed from the equation.

But Katherine Glass was, as everyone knew, only *half* the equation.

The videos had a costar. Katherine's masked male lover, director, choreographer, soulmate, and partner in extraordinary crime. Despite the months of investigation and everything Katherine had given them, he was still out there. He was still unknown, untouched, and almost certainly undeterred. Six women were dead and he was still — the word sent a neural charge of weakness down Valerie's abdomen — *free.*

Meanwhile, white and golden and jewel-eyed Katherine Glass, *not* free, stood motionless in the dock. Her blond hair was pulled back in its signature tight ponytail. If she was suffering there was no outward sign of it. Not that the verdict could have surprised her, Valerie knew. The trial's issue had been whether the defendant was — fuck the clinical niceties — completely out of her mind. The quaint moral reflex said she couldn't, given what she'd done, be considered otherwise. Her actions *guaranteed* her madness. But this was the twenty-first century. The binary certainties were gone. The world had gotten used to the idea that you could be in all respects rational, sound, intelligent, *normal* — except for your delight in doing the things Katherine and her lover had done. The world could no longer pretend the words "human" and "monster" referred to two different species. Monstrosity was just another human option, like vegetarianism or Tai Chi.

Naturally, Katherine's defense had gone through the motions. Psychological disorder and diminished responsibility. No one had bought it. No one was ever going to buy it. The collective will craved raw vengeance. If Katherine had been plain, Valerie thought, she might have had a chance. But looking the way she did, it was a fait accompli. *The New York Times* had indulged itself with a description of her as "a living koan of corruption and beauty." A *Chronicle* editorial with literary ambitions had called her "the grotesque and compelling offspring of

Aphrodite and Lucifer." The *National Enquirer,* true to its readership, had dubbed her "The Sex-Angel of Death," while Twitter had, among its countless inanities, supplied: "Katherine Glass makes Helen of Troy look like a fucking bag of chisels." She might be the most hated woman in America, but the hatred was swimming in desire, and that fact, more than her crimes, meant she had to be destroyed.

Which would, Valerie knew, give Justice Delgado a major headache between now and sentencing. Since 2006, when a district judge had halted executions in California after finding flaws in the lethal injection process, undischarged executions had stacked up like airplanes over a jammed airport. The judicial review of the allegedly improved death-kit was taking forever, and in any case the legal battles between prisoners' lawyers and the state's attorney general just kept going. In effect, there was a moratorium on killing death row inmates, and, by unspoken extension, on issuing death sentences. Katherine Glass would be locked up for the rest of her life, but for the baying majority that wouldn't be enough. Nothing short of death would do.

Valerie got to her feet and headed through the warm crowd to the double oak doors at the rear of the courtroom. The trial had drained her, and the hours of interviews with Katherine Glass had left dirty marks on her that would never fade. What she wanted now was to get out into the damp San Francisco air, light a Marlboro, walk the two blocks to the nearest bar, and order herself a triple vodka and tonic. Followed by at least three more of the same, since she had the day off. But at the exit, an impulse forced her to turn and look back.

Katherine was still on her feet, cuffed and guard-flanked. Valerie thought of the videos, the weeping victims, the calibrated escalation of their suffering, the calculated false endings and postponements, the begging, the manifest subtlety Katherine and her lover brought to what they were doing, the mordant humor they shared — and the strange, screen-captured deflation between them when the moment came at last, and the victim's life was gone, and there was nothing more they could do for their pleasure. She thought of all the conversations she'd had with Katherine, separated from the woman's concussive physical beauty by only the width of the table in the interview room, Katherine with the lovely white hands and calm mouth and omniscient green eyes (bitch eyes, as Will had described them) speaking with quiet, articulate precision, as if she were in possession of a wisdom toward which the rest of humanity was lumbering with laughable slowness.

Don't look at her. Turn and walk away.

But as she hesitated Katherine Glass turned and looked at her — and smiled.

1

July 2015
"This is the thing you've been dreading," Nick Blaskovitch called from the locker room showers at the Bay Club. "The great shift in the balance of power. Like all dreaded things it's probably come as a relief. It's okay to cry, by the way."

"Look, I had an off day," Eugene Trent replied from the bench, where he sat in his white Calvins, drying his toes. Nick had just beaten him at squash for the first time since they'd begun playing, eighteen months ago.

"I'm exhausted from screwing all night," Eugene said. "Not a problem *you* have, obviously — which is the real story here, by the way. Today was just you channeling your jealousy and rage. That gave you an edge against a sex-weakened opponent, but you're deluded if you think it was anything more than a glitch. In fact it was a cruel glimpse of something you'll never experi-

13

ence again."

"It was so obviously psychological," Nick said. "I could feel it in you: you've exhausted your repertoire. You know you're not going to get any better. Whereas I" — he shut off the water and reached for his towel — "am still expanding mine. I am still . . . *ascending.*"

"Don't talk to me about repertoire," Eugene said. "This girl last night was twenty-seven, and she stuck her finger in her ass. *Her* ass, mind you, not mine. I'm just saying: these things take their toll."

Their postmatch ritual was two beers apiece in the club bar. After the depletions of the gladiatorial squash court, two was enough to give Nick a pleasant buzz. More than two and he wouldn't be able to drive home.

"Seriously," Eugene said, "these girls today . . . I don't know what's happened. I mean, okay, she's got thirteen years on me, and what the fuck do I know, et cetera, but it's like a whole porn generation thing. I don't like it. *I* want to be the corrupting influence, you know? I want to *talk a girl into* putting her finger in her ass. I'm a traditionalist. In fact, when it comes to filth, I'm a romantic."

This, too, was ritualized, Eugene's long-suffering satyr to Nick's settled monogamist. Nick and Valerie had been together (second time around) for just over two years, ever since he'd come back to San Francisco and the department's computer forensics unit.

"I know you think I want what you've got," Nick said. "But the truth is you have to think that, because *you* want what *I've* got."

"Eventually," Eugene said. "Of course, *eventually.* But not now. Now I'm in my prime. It's a sin against masculinity to waste your prime. Be honest: What are you guys down to now? Once a week? Twice a month?"

"Just pick a number that makes you feel better about dying old and alone."

"What's so terrible about dying old and alone? I'll get a dog. I'll get a maid. I can imagine a quite beautiful relationship with a maid. Like Philip Roth but with tenderness."

It was an odd friendship between them, Nick thought, formed from the sort of accident you imagined the hyperscheduled twenty-first century no longer had to offer. Nick's game was racquetball, and his usual opponent was Valerie's partner, Detective Will Fraser. But five minutes into a game a year and a half ago Will had pulled a calf muscle, and they'd had to retire to the bar. Eugene, whom they recognized as a fellow regular, had been stood up by his squash opponent and, as he had a spare racquet, had asked Nick if he felt like giving it a try. Since then, they'd been playing every two or three weeks. Eugene was one of those nuts who felt he had to balance his Caligulan excesses with a superhuman fitness regimen. The early games had seen Nick struggling to get through without having a nosebleed or throwing up, but his natural talent for racquet sports (and what Eugene referred to as his "devious mongrel style") had, over time, closed the gap between them. Hence today's milestone victory. The loser in all this was Will Fraser. The squash had so improved Nick's racquetball that Will hadn't won a game in months. Meanwhile Nick was in the best physical shape of his life. Valerie, running her hands over his lean muscles, had joked: "Are you sure this is just the squash? I mean, you're not working up to telling me you're gay, right?"

"I assume you're seeing her again?" Nick said to Eugene. "She sounds perfect for you."

"That's what I thought," Eugene said. "But this morning she was up and dressed

16

while I was still in fucking REM sleep. If I hadn't heard the door open she'd have been out of there without me knowing. As it was, I'm like, hey, what's the rush? Come back to bed. I know a great place for breakfast. She looked at me like I was retarded."

"Maybe she sensed your confusion when she stuck her finger in her ass?"

"Don't joke about it. I was hurt. I thought there was a real connection. We fell asleep with our arms around each other, for Christ's sake. I gave her a *foot* massage."

Nick smiled. He took these tales of sexual conquest with a pinch of salt, but this time Eugene looked genuinely wounded.

"You know what she said to me?" Eugene said, his shoulders slumped. "She said: 'You're sweet.' Sweet! She didn't even leave her number. I mean, she could've left me a *fake* number at least. That's what a civilized person would do."

"What's it like, knowing you've been a sexual disappointment?"

"It's not easy. I'm not used to it. After she'd gone, I sat down in the shower. You don't sit down in the shower unless you're really upset."

They walked out to the parking lot together. It was a warm bright day, with a breeze bringing the fresh salt smell of the

17

bay. Nick rarely took the risk of noticing his own happiness but occasionally a flash got through. He felt it now, via the sunlit cars and the rough scent of the ocean and his body's honest exhaustion and the gentle influence of the beer. These things had power again, now that he had Valerie, now that he had (this was the flash that shocked him with a sort of delighted absurdity) *love.*

"So what have you guys got planned for the weekend?" Eugene said. "No, wait, let me guess: You're going to watch TV together. Pair up the odd socks. Bleach the toilet."

"Actually, we're going upstate," Nick said. "Wineries and a great little hotel in Calistoga. Then the beach."

"What, cops get weekends off now?"

"Once every decade."

"This is what I'm paying my taxes for? Who's going to catch all the murderers while your lady's having her mimosas on the beach?"

"What can I tell you? Lock your windows and doors."

They made a loose date to play again in a couple of weeks, then headed to their vehicles.

"Hey," Nick called over his shoulder.

Eugene stopped. "What?"

18

"Good luck at the STD clinic."

Eugene opened his mouth for a reply but was distracted by a stunning red-haired girl emerging from a bottle-green Jaguar convertible. Sunlight glowed on her bare legs and shoulders. Eugene looked at Nick: See? All this is still available to me.

Nick, shaking his head, turned and walked away. *Wineries and a great little hotel in Calistoga. Then the beach.* What he hadn't added was: *Oh yeah, and I'm going to ask Valerie to marry me.* Not because he dreaded Eugene's astonishment (in fact he was looking forward to it, to seeing Eugene's face caught between outrage and envy; he would break the news next game, just as Eugene released the ball to serve) but because it offended something in him to speak of it to anyone. He *hadn't* spoken of it to anyone. He'd simply been walking around for a weird indeterminate time with the vague feeling that he was going to propose, until, a few weeks ago, the vague feeling had stopped being vague and become the central certainty of his life. It had happened, this epiphany, when he'd been on one of his occasional solitary afternoon hikes in Cascade Canyon, where he used to go with his father as a boy. Love (you had to laugh; *he* laughed, at himself) simplified aesthetics.

He'd found himself wanting elemental things: sky, rock, trees, water. He felt archetypal: a Man who had found his Woman. He knew this idiom was ridiculous, but he was helpless. Whether he liked it or not this was a great benign, almost comical truth into which he had been released, like a horse into a field of delicious grass. He supposed it had been this way for prehistoric people, this primal recognition. To him the necessity of Valerie was a fact like the heat of a flame or the sweetness of honey. It was a wonderful thing to have been confronted by something against which there was no argument, however embarrassed he would be to explain it if someone asked. So he'd spent the day walking, and each time he put one foot in front of the other it confirmed him.

You're going to marry Valerie.

Well, now that you mention it, yes, I believe I am.

Then get a ring, dumbass.

Okay.

So he had. It had taken a while. A farcical while, in fact. Valerie wore only one ring (not on her wedding finger), which was one of a pair her parents had had made for her and her older sister, Cassie, and presented to each of them when they'd turned eighteen. She wore only this one ring (silver and amethyst), but she had a dozen or more in the jewelry box on her dresser. *Hey, how come you never wear any of these?* He'd waited until they were both slightly drunk, then got her to try them on, one by one. He took note of the ring that fit her wedding finger and used it to size the Actual Ring a few days later. With which he was going to present her (*probably* not down on one knee, which would make her think he'd lost his mind, but there was no telling what his life would spring on him at the last minute) this weekend at the Calistoga bed-and-breakfast just before bed. Oddly, he liked the idea of proposing to her while she was standing, naked, brushing her teeth. He wanted to watch her face reacting in the semi-fogged mirror. He liked the thought of her, dark eyes wide and mouth foamy with toothpaste, decoding what he'd just said, letting it sink in, spitting out toothpaste, then saying: yes. He knew she would say yes. They'd never discussed marriage. But there it was: he would ask her and she would say yes. It wasn't arrogance on his part. It was just pure revealed knowledge.

He started the car, put on his sunglasses, and eased the vehicle out of the lot. He had a couple of hours before Valerie got home, during which he planned to look up possible honeymoon destinations. He didn't care where they went. He only knew that he wanted to see her lying in a hammock drinking an elaborate cocktail, her hands and ankles gleaming with sunscreen. He had these visions, now. They were the tenets of his strange new religion.

2

The San Francisco Imperial's lobby bar was all but empty. Melody sat alone in a booth, over-alive to the place's details. Windowed afternoon sunlight and a deep-red carpet and a smell of forced cleanliness. A petite blond bargirl in a white shirt and black vest was slicing limes, the bottles behind her like hefty jewels: emerald, ruby, amber, diamond.

It had happened. Melody couldn't say precisely when, but for the first time in her life she wasn't alone. For the first time in her life the mystery that separated her from other people, like a thick layer of invisible fat, had dissolved. Her body had received a sly gift. Now she moved through her days rich with purpose.

She checked the time on her phone: 2:38 P.M. She'd barely touched her Diet Coke, and though her mouth was dry, she took only one more sip before getting to her feet

23

and crossing the lounge to the ladies' room. Adrenaline filled her with the familiar thrilling weakness. Her face was hot and her palms tingled, as if tiny stars were coming out in her skin.

The ladies' room was spotless, pale marble lit by Christmasy halogens. She went into a cubicle and tried to pee. Barely a trickle, but it helped her feel ready. She always wanted to be ready for him, clean, undistracted, the new, maximal version of herself. Pulling her underwear down excited her. She'd gotten a fresh bikini wax yesterday and now between her legs the skin was nude and sensitive.

Trembling, she washed and dried her hands, then carefully refreshed her makeup. She was a dark-haired woman with a round face and eyes the color of espresso. She had a look of both weight and suppleness. In the last few weeks she'd dropped twenty pounds, but she knew she still didn't turn heads in the street.

Except his.

He'd said to her: *I knew from the first moment I saw you. It's in your eyes. I can see these things. I'm never wrong.*

She hadn't liked the last bit. *I'm never wrong.* That meant there had been — or still were — others.

Melody shut the thought down. There was no end to the thoughts she could shut down. He'd said: *You've been waiting your whole life for this.* And he'd been right, of course. When he looked at her, he *saw* her. There was only one other person in the world who saw her like that.

She took the elevator, alone, to the eighth floor. The deserted corridor's spongy gold carpet made her wobble in her high heels. With any other guy she'd have needed a booze-buzz. Not with him. With him her sheer untouched self was a deafening excitement that kept taking her to a point from which she felt sure she would pass out, faint, die. But she didn't.

Room 809.

She swallowed. Raised her hand. Knocked.

He opened the door, and at the first sight of him all the dials of herself went up, though only moments before she'd felt her excitement couldn't possibly increase.

He had the curtains closed and the laptop open on the crisply made bed.

"We'll talk in a little while," he said. Then he kissed her. Soft heat encased her. It was as if every atom in the room were with them, a pliable intelligence holding them snugly close to each other. She'd never felt a perfect fit before. Now, with him, she recognized it like a memory from a previous life.

She was wet for his hand, her panties sodden. He led her to the bed and they lay down together. For Melody, everything was simultaneously a warm blur and fizzing with distinct detail. Kissing was a sweet, heavy blindness, a soft darkness filling her.

He rolled her onto her side and slid behind her. He pushed her skirt up and eased her underwear down to her shins. When she reached behind herself her hand met his, unzipping his pants. Her breathing quickened.

For a moment he held the tip of his cock against her cunt, making her wait. She wanted what she wanted. Everything she wanted was the one giant certainty that had taken control of her life so that there was no room — *no* room — for anything else. Sometimes the word "love" flashed in her, like an explosive drug, but she didn't say it.

"You want to see, don't you?" he said.

"Yes."

The familiar shock of that word. *Yes.* Everything between them derived from that word. *Yes.*

He eased into her, sliding one arm under her to pull her tight against him. With his other arm, he reached over her and turned the laptop to face them.

"We're going to have it all," he said. "You know that, don't you?"

Her throat was tight. Her cunt throbbed. She was desperate to make it last and desperate to begin.

His hand hovered over the laptop's keyboard as he moved inside her.

Then he clicked the PLAY button, and the footage began to run, and within seconds Melody entered the state she lived for now, when time dropped away and she forgot herself utterly and chaos and peace were the same and the disease of her past melted away and in the annihilating perfection of hunger and bliss she might as well have been God.

3

Valerie lay naked on her bed, limbs spread like a starfish, waiting for her history (and indeed the universe) to reassemble itself out of the sweet chaos of her most recent orgasm. Her third since waking. The window, with its curtains still closed, was an ingot of soft orange light.

"Holy fuck," Valerie said quietly.

Nick lay with his face sweat-stuck to her left thigh, his right hand doodling below her navel. He didn't answer, but after a moment moved his head and very gently kissed her between her legs.

It was the Saturday morning of their precious weekend off, which, since Valerie was Homicide, could be aborted at any moment. They were both in terror of her phone. Her phone was a sleeping ogre, a capricious god, a ticking bomb. The longer they stayed put the more they dared it to ring.

"We should get up," Valerie said.

"I know," Nick answered.

Neither of them moved. The plan was Napa Valley wineries in the afternoon, dinner in Calistoga, overnight at a luxury bed-and-breakfast, then Sunday to Gualala, the ocean, the big sky, the soft boom and salt smash of the surf, the quiet drive home at dusk with sun-chastened skin smelling of the beach, the good childhood feeling of spent energy. They grabbed pleasure whenever they could. A consequence of the job. The job of living daily with depravity and death.

"If you keep doing that," Valerie said to him, "you know what'll happen."

"Yes."

"It'll take longer this time. I'm only human."

"Good."

"You'll get bored."

He continued.

"And neck-ache."

He ignored her. She lifted her hips, delighted by her own languor and greed. The ghost of her ancestors' Catholicism said: this will all have to be paid for, you know. Especially second time around.

Second time around. After three years recovering from the first time around. The first time around had been breakage, betrayal, bloodshed. The first time around, Valerie had almost destroyed him. And herself.

But even walking away from the carnage the wiser parts of themselves had known they would come back. Which they had. With infallible gravity. They were *for* each other, without discussion. Literally without discussion: they didn't talk about their relationship. It wasn't a third entity or surrogate child to be nurtured with narrative. They were cops. There was action and reaction. Analysis was for regular people. They had the requisite dark matter: love. They were their own highest authority. Lawless, ironically. It was one of the things that helped them enforce the law.

They showered, quickly, while the coffee percolated. The Cole Valley apartment was new to them. *Home.* They were still getting used to calling it that. It had big windows and a narrow balcony and a lot of clean white surfaces. A bowl of tangerines on the breakfast counter looked like a still life waiting to be painted. Valerie's old place in the Mission echoed with too much of their history (it was where, for example, Nick had one day walked in — as she'd known he would — to find her fucking another guy) and Nick's own place in Chinatown might as well have been a cardboard box for all he cared. So without much talk they had pooled their resources and made the down payment. That they were going to live together hadn't been discussed at all. It was simply shared knowledge. For the first few weeks they'd felt like kids occupying a house abandoned by grown-ups. But gradually they'd eased into it, taken the upgraded appliances and zealous hot water for granted, found the signs of domestic life constellating humbly around them. "What do I think?" Will Fraser had said, when they'd invited him and his wife, Marion, over for a housewarming dinner. "I think it looks like cops live here. Cops from *Sparta*. Jesus. Put up some pictures. Get some *crap*." It had no effect. They couldn't get excited about these things.

"Bring the sex shoes," Nick said. Valerie was at the dressing table putting on makeup.

"Yes, sir."

"And the black lace demi-bra."

"You shouldn't even know what a demi-bra is. I'm not even sure *I* should. But you . . . If you're a guy it's like knowing what a duvet is."

"What's a duvet?"

"A comforter."

"A *French* comforter?"

"Why don't you get the stuff together instead of sitting on your ass?"

"I'm lying on my back."

Nick, dressed, was on the bed, ostensibly leafing through yesterday's *Chronicle.* In fact, as Valerie knew — as they *both* knew — he was watching her get ready. The first time she'd noticed him doing this (years ago, during their first time around), she'd said: Haven't you got anything better to do? And he'd said: Nothing better than this, no. It gave her pleasure. Because she knew he meant it. It was a revelation, his desire for her, because with him, for the first time in her life she knew it was desire for *her,* specifically. As opposed to the usual blind male desire for "a woman," or, if push came to shove, just for *sex,* in the abstract.

"My grandfather told me when I was a kid that swimming in the ocean rinsed your soul," Valerie said.

"Your grandfather was a dark genius."

"He was. My friends were terrified of him. He told Sarah Grady he was going to put her in his suitcase when she was asleep and take her with him to Alaska. We were about four years old. He wasn't even going to Alaska. He'd just been watching a wildlife show about it on TV. He said to Sarah, Oh sure, your mom knows all about it. It's all arranged. I'll put some sandwiches and a soda in there with you for when you get hungry. It's a long journey. Shall I show you the suitcase? It's a nice big one! She was practically hysterical."

In the mirror she could see Nick smiling.

"Okay," she said. "I'm ready."

He didn't respond for a moment. Then he said: "Yes."

"Yes what?"

"Yes, I still want to have a kid with you."

"I know."

"How about I knock you up in the four-poster tonight?"

"Okay."

"But you still wear the shoes and the demi-bra."

"Obviously."

He got up from the bed, crossed to stand close behind her, put his arms around her, kissed her neck. For a while, in the beginning of their second time around, she'd resisted full capitulation. A part of her was reserved for assuming the bliss was temporary, an unearned gift, an error the universe would soon correct. If you buy into this, the lone sentry in her heart warned her, you won't be able to bear losing it. So don't. Don't. Don't! — Too late. She hadn't even

33

felt herself letting go. It was just that at some point the lone sentry was gone and her heart was given over. Unearned or not, she wanted love, demanded it, took it and wrapped it around herself and let it be her element. If she thought about what it would be like to lose it a second time she came up against a feeling like a wall of raw earth. Burial alive. So she tried not to think about it.

Nick's hands slid to her hips. The bone cradle. For a second it was as if Valerie felt a flicker of nascent life in there. Which brought the miscarriage back. That, the first time around, had been a consequence of the breakage, the betrayal. That had been the blood. She'd scheduled an abortion but her body had taken matters into its own hands. Was it mine? Nick had asked her, when he'd eventually found out. She hadn't been able to answer because she hadn't known. He didn't say to her now: It's okay. It's all right. He didn't say anything, didn't need to. This second time around they enjoyed eloquent silence. She leaned back into him. *This is so much more than you deserve.* She wasn't sure where these judgments came from, whose voices they were.

"Let's go," Nick said.

It still took them another ten minutes.

Valerie had to hunt down her bathing suit. Nick packed prosciutto, Manchego, cherry tomatoes, and olives in a cooler.

"I need to stop at my old place on the way," Valerie said, slotting her sunglasses up onto her forehead. "My neighbor's holding a package for me."

"Oh yeah?"

"From Bed Bath & Beyond. Don't laugh. My mom. Who's so thrilled that I've moved in with you she's forgotten to change the delivery address."

"Maybe it's a duvet?"

"It's towels. *Luxury* towels, in fact."

They made it all the way down to Nick's car before Valerie's cell phone rang.

She tipped her head back for a second in a reflexive prayer to the random universe, then looked down at the iPhone's screen: LAURA FLYNN CALLING.

Detective Laura Flynn.

Please, no. *Please.*

She looked at Nick.

"Throw it out the window," he said. "I'll drive over it."

Valerie hit ACCEPT. "Hey, Laura."

"Sorry," Laura said. "No choice."

"Go ahead."

"We're in Noe Valley. Homicide victim is a fifty-four-year-old white female, Elizabeth

35

Lambert, found in her apartment. The ME needs time but the ballpark's thirty hours. Cause is strangulation. Wounds, but none fatal. Clear signs of sexual assault. We're looking at rape and mutilation."

The usual mix of feelings for Valerie. That she was trapped in this, the only gravity that was a match for love's. That the universe was a place in which, while one woman was enjoying the caresses of her lover another woman was being tortured and raped. That it was her obligation to catch the men who did these things. That it was too much. That the repetition of violence and death was killing her by degrees, like cancer. That she lived for it.

She didn't say anything. She was waiting (as was Nick, with his head resting against the driver's window) for the explanation: so far nothing Laura Flynn had said warranted calling her on her day off.

"So here's the thing," Laura said, reading Valerie's silence. "There was a note taped to the victim's body."

Valerie felt the weekend draining away as if a sluice had opened. Nick's deflation, resignation, understanding. He was a cop. He knew the cop situation, the cop contract, the fucking cop *deal*. A civilian would have gotten out of the car, slammed the door, stormed off.

"The note is addressed to you," Laura said.

4

Books. A reading life. Taste. According to her ground-floor apartment Elizabeth Lambert was — had been, rather — a woman who would occasionally spend more than she could afford if it was for something she truly believed to be beautiful. There were lithographs and woodcuts that didn't look mass-produced. There was a thin Persian rug in pale green and gold. There was a small abstract sculpture in the bay window that appeared to be made from solid lapis lazuli. The apartment, Valerie thought, was everything her and Nick's apartment wasn't.

"Sorry," Laura Flynn said to her when she arrived. "I couldn't not tell you."

"I know," Valerie said, already sweating in her scrubs. "Show me."

The place's odor was of clean domesticity but now with a new rotten nucleus exuding, unmistakably, death. They had to negotiate the CSI team, who went about their business with a silent intensity you might mistake for tenderness. Actually it *was* tenderness, but not for the victim. It was tenderness for the evidence. They were still taking photographs. Ricky Santayana, the medical examiner, was talking quietly on his cell phone in the bathroom doorway. He raised a hand to Valerie and turned away.

"She's as we found her," Laura said as they entered the bedroom. "Except the first on the scene removed the gag. He's over there when you want to talk to him." Valerie glanced at the young dark-haired uniform standing in the bay window with his hands on his hips, a posture of cocky indifference that did nothing to conceal his horror at having messed with the scene. He was good-looking and not used to being on his back foot. She imagined herself saying: Did you think she was going to tell you who did it if you took the gag out? Dismissed it. Love had done away with any need for small triumphs. Love had made her generous. Love had made her a laughable *soft touch.*

"Who discovered the body?" Valerie said.

"Cleaning lady." Laura flipped open her notebook. "Marley Hollander. Who has a key. She's in the car with Ed right now, trying to get her shit back together. Top floor we've got a Gianni Galliano, who'll be at work according to Marley, though she doesn't know *where* he works. Middle apartment's empty. No sign of forced entry. Back door's a deadbolt, front door dead bolt and mortise. Can't rule out a window being left open, but it's not likely. So either he had the means to get in, or she let him."

Elizabeth Lambert was on her back on the bed, naked, face turned to the left, arms up behind her head, legs spread wide. The sides of her mouth were bruised, presumably from the gag. One of the CSI team was sealing paper bags around the dead hands and feet. Valerie glimpsed manicured toenails painted the color of chocolate mousse, an awful effect with the skin's discoloration, as if she'd made herself up for a Halloween party. At least a dozen flesh wounds on her breasts and abdomen. A deeper one around her right nipple, where blood had congealed. It looked like a grotesque jewel. Valerie had an image of him doing that with the knife, slowly, whispering in her ear under her gagged screams: Does that hurt, cunt?

She shut it down. As you shut down all such imaginings, in the beginning. In the beginning you did the procedure, you did the work. In the beginning you dealt with the solid, the material, the evident. It was only later (much later, if you were unlucky) that you had to use your imagination. It was only later that you had to, as her grandfather had described it, *dance*. Elizabeth's bare underarms made Valerie remember Nick kissing hers only hours earlier. Shut that down, too, the wretched parallels, the dismal equalizations. It didn't mean anything. The world was just contingently crammed with opposites. The world wasn't, when you got down to it, meaningful.

"From the imprints it looks like he used plastic cable ties on the wrists," Laura continued. "Maybe curtain cord on the ankles, but he took them when he left. According to Ricky all the knife wounds are nonfatal. Clear ligature marks on the neck. It's a no-brainer strangulation."

Beyond the body Valerie was absorbing the room's details. A pair of white Nikes with orange laces under a cane chair. A hair dryer on the oak dresser. A *New Yorker* on the window seat. A cheval glass. With the exception of the bedclothes twisted on the floor, the place was tidy. So no big struggle. Could've coldcocked her then tied her down. Or held the knife to her. The plastic cuffs were designed so you only needed one hand to work them. Or maybe she had struggled but he'd straightened the place up when he was done? Chloroform? Get toxicology. Or maybe she'd let him tie her up? Consensual bondage turned homicide? (It wasn't that, she thought. Unless she'd lost all her instincts, she knew it wasn't that.) No forced entry. So he picked or tricked his way in. Or again, was *let* in. Because she knew him. Please let her have known him. Please shrink the pool of suspects.

Valerie looked again at the body on the bed. Reminded herself that she wasn't looking at a person. She was looking at a victim. Personhood had been removed and couldn't be reinstated unless they caught the individual who'd done this. When that happened the dead woman could be Elizabeth Lambert again. Until then she was just the work, the mystery object, the Case.

"Here you go," Laura said, handing Valerie a clear plastic evidence bag. In it was a slightly creased single sheet of white paper, bearing a few lines of printed text.

FAO: Detective Valerie Hart

Dear Valerie,
Katherine Glass stays in prison, more people die. You know who I am, but I've left you Danielle's ring by way of substantiation. They'll all get fair warning,

as Elizabeth did. (Look carefully, please.) No videos yet, but there will be. This one is just to open the channel. You've been waiting for this. More to follow.

That was all. Valerie stood still.
Katherine Glass. Six years. Now.
You know who I am.
Yes. She did. Instantly, at the cellular level.
"Jewelry?" Valerie said.
"One ring, left index," Laura said, handing Valerie a second evidence bag with the ring in it. "Rose gold with a red stone. A ruby, I think. Who's Danielle?"
"Danielle Freyer. One of their victims. His and Katherine's."
"There are a lot of rings like this, Val."
"It wasn't public. Only us and the family knew. She was still wearing it when they filmed her. But we're going to get a DNA match here anyway. He wants us to know it's him. Get the lab to rush it, will you? I'll call Deerholt and tell him to push."
"Well, at least we know he's crazy."
"How so?"
"If he thinks Katherine's getting out."
"That's smoke. He's not crazy. Katherine said he was the smartest man she ever met. And since she's the smartest woman I ever met . . . ."

"What about the 'fair warning' thing?"

"God knows."

"Shit. Your weekend."

"Yeah, my weekend." She pulled out her phone. "Give me a second. Tell these guys not to remove anything just yet."

She called Nick. "Do something for me, will you?" she said after she'd brought him up to speed.

"What?"

"Go to the winery. Go to dinner. Check into the B&B. It might be late, but I'll get there."

He didn't say anything for a moment.

"I know how lousy this is," she said.

"You going to talk to her?"

Ah. Of course. *That* was what the pause had been: him thinking about Katherine Glass. Or rather, him thinking about what Katherine Glass had meant to her.

"Not until I know more," Valerie said. Even as she said it she felt sick and thrilled. She wanted to see what the years inside had done to the most hated woman in America. A part of her wanted to see if she'd changed. But immediately she thought that she knew Katherine Glass would *not* have changed. It was a reflexive certainty, whether she liked it or not. The white skin and green eyes and pale blond hair and that tranquil, knowing

44

mouth. Katherine Glass was a question the universe had asked her. Valerie wasn't sure, six years later, that she'd ever really answered it.

"Will you go up and wait for me?" Valerie said.

Another pause. She pictured Nick's face, the dark features, the look of amused patience, the cop intelligence behind it, the knowing the world's ugly things, the willingness to take them on, without hysteria. She loved him. It still shocked her, that she had this love in her life, this certainty. Katherine had said to her: The Devil has a question for love. . . .

"Okay," he said. "But what if the chambermaid wants to have sex with me?"

"Fine. But not in my shoes or demi-bra."

"You say that, but I look good in them."

When they hung up Valerie looked at her watch. It was a quarter after noon. She had time.

"How do you want to do this?" Laura asked her.

"With OCD," Valerie said. "I'll come back here when these guys are done." She caught herself. "Sorry. You don't mind if I lead on this one, right?"

"When it's *literally* got your name written all over it?"

"Okay, so get everything you can from the cleaning lady and track down the upstairs neighbor. Do we know where the victim worked?"

"ID card in her purse says Environmental Protection Agency. Press officer."

"I'll talk to them. We need her movements for the last forty-eight hours minimum. Cell phone?"

"Bagged."

"Get it straight to tech. Let me know as soon as it's unlocked. Maybe she got her fair warning via voice mail. Let's get some uniforms down here and we can start door-to-door. Anyone with a view. What's out there?"

"Back garden."

"I'll take a look. Street cams?"

"Nope. We're blind on these blocks apart from possibly the coffee shop."

"Well, let's get that, at least. When the blues get here I'll get them to check private residences. Maybe a neighbor's got one that'll give us something. Next of kin?"

"Ed's on that."

"Will he handle it?"

"Yeah. He's got Sondra's parents staying this weekend. He'll take anything."

"It's an ill wind."

"What?"

"It's an ill wind that blows nobody good."

"What's that mean?"

"It means something has to be really fucking bad for it not to benefit *some*one. In this case, Ed. Thanks to this he gets time off from his in-laws."

Can't stop thinking about him. He's with me like an invisible person. No headaches for four days. He says don't write it down but I'm scared I'll lose it even though by the time I'm done I know it like a nursery rhyme. I've been waiting my whole life. Like I just now learned to breathe right. He told me stop eating crap and so I bought gourmet coffee and a fish called place. Some salad with that red stuff in it but it's bitter. There's nothing else except seeing him. Both of them. He just touches me and it all opens up like the sun coming out from behind a cloud.

The place fish tasted watery.

I'm going to do my exercises now.

5

Eight hours later Valerie stepped out onto Elizabeth Lambert's back porch, lowered her protective mask, and breathed deeply through her nose. California dusk, the sky soft silver-blue with a band of faint pink in its lower reaches. The garden smelled of its dry red soil and cooling concrete.

She'd spent the day doing the work, building the picture, *beginning the investigation* — but with a stronger-than-usual sense that the bulk of it was a waste of time. If the perp was who he claimed to be he'd have the routine angles covered. He'd have the obscure angles covered. He'd have angles covered that wouldn't even occur to them.

Nonetheless. Laura Flynn had called with the latest on the upstairs neighbor: Gianni Galliano had his last forty-eight hours accounted for. He'd either been verifiably at work (Realtors Corven & Mylett on Market Street) or at his girlfriend's apartment in

51

Pacific Heights. The girlfriend, a junior in a business law firm, confirmed his alibi, and Laura believed her. According to Galliano, he'd last seen Elizabeth *three* days ago, when they'd crossed in the downstairs hall. Nothing unusual to report, except that she seemed in a better mood than usual.

The unlocked cell phone said the last call Elizabeth had accepted was from the caller ID "Nancy Treece." (Dismally, of course, there were three subsequent missed calls from caller ID "Mom.") Door-to-door revealed Nancy as a neighbor from the next block, who, as far as Valerie could tell, might well have been the last person (killer excepted) to see Elizabeth alive.

Valerie had called her. She was out of the city, up in Deer Park collecting some of her belongings from a second home she co-owned with her estranged husband. She'd come by two days ago to make use of Elizabeth's scanner. The two women had spent an hour or so together, chatting. They'd finished the better part of a bottle of white wine, then Nancy had left. What was this about? Was Elizabeth okay? I'm sorry to have to tell you, Valerie had said, but the body of a woman we believe to be Elizabeth Lambert has been found in her apartment. As yet we have no official identification, so I must instruct you to keep this confidential until we've had confirmation from the next of kin. (In Elizabeth's passport the original next of kin details had been crossed out — obliterated, in fact: love gone wrong — and replaced with those of "Gillian Rose." Relationship: "Sister.") Ed Pérez, Laura's partner, was on his way out to Sausalito to give Gillian the bad news. Valerie waited out Nancy Treece's silence, the stammered disbelief, the tears stacking up, the fracture, the second wave of disbelief, the thrill in spite of everything (the amoral thrill that was nothing more than the human response to anything — *any*thing — that said the world was not predictable, that life could still surprise you, that all the information was not, in fact, *in*), then made an arrangement to meet with her tomorrow. Deer Park was — oh, sweet irony — practically next door to Calistoga; it would rationalize driving up there tonight for a few hours with Nick, even if she'd have to leave him again in the morning.

Elizabeth's colleagues at the Environmental Protection Agency hadn't — at first — had much to offer. Elizabeth was quiet, well-read, plain, ironic, took a conversational French class on Wednesdays, Pilates on Fridays, went to museums and galleries, had no enemies that they were aware of, and had, until recently, seemed resigned to life as a terminal single since her divorce a few years back. The hot rumor, however, was that a week ago, Elizabeth had spent the night with office heartthrob Luke Russell, a man fourteen years her junior. He'd invited some of them over for his fortieth birthday and Elizabeth had still been there when the last of the guests left. She'd been evasive when the girls quizzed her the next day, but there was a smile on her face as she dodged the questions.

Great. Could Valerie talk to Mr. Russell?

Not in person. He'd been away on vacation at his sister's place in L.A. since the party. Wasn't due back until Monday.

Valerie called him. Not surprisingly, he told her he'd been in L.A. since last weekend. Movements for the last two days? Accounted for. He'd been with his sister and her family all day yesterday.

Could they verify that?

Of course. Look, what is this about, Detective?

Motions, motions, motions. She'd spent the day going through the goddamned motions.

You know who I am. You've been waiting for this.

Rebecca Beitner, head of the attending CSI, joined Valerie on the back porch. Rebecca had a very thin, very pale face and bulbous blue-gray eyes that always looked short of sleep. Not unreasonably, since she *was* always short of sleep. Elizabeth's body had been removed and the team had just finished working through the area it had covered on the bed. The death space.

"Well, it's an embarrassment of riches," Rebecca said, lowering her mask. "We've got fingerprints all over the scene. I'm guessing there'll be good stuff from under her nails. If he didn't use a condom we've got that, too. She's going to be covered in him. If this is your guy, we'll know."

"I already know."

"You going to talk to Glass?"

"I imagine I'll have to. Oh joy."

"You know they moved her, right?"

"She's not at Chowchilla?"

"They've put her in the new place. There's no room at Chowchilla."

Valerie knew about the facility at Red Ridge built five years ago to cope with the expanding female population on death row, but she didn't know it now contained Katherine Glass.

"I've never been up there," Valerie said.

"Looks like a modernist bunker," Rebecca

said. "Apparently Katherine reads all day. *Literature.*"

Reading. Remembering Katherine's vast and casually accessible frame of reference, Valerie felt her scalp prickle. Katherine wasn't supposed to be like that, armed with understanding. Katherine wasn't supposed to have insight, depth, imagination, empathy. There were so many ways Katherine wasn't supposed to be, given the one significant way she was. But there she'd sat opposite Valerie in the interviews — in defiance of all the rules.

"You all done here?" she asked Rebecca.

"We're never done, but yeah."

"Tell the blues I'm going to be here awhile."

"Val, I know the note said to look carefully, but . . ."

"It's not that I don't think you got everything."

"It's not that I don't love you, but . . ."

"Shut up. You know I love you."

Rebecca shrugged: knock yourself out. "Tell me you didn't have any kind of Saturday night planned, at least?" she said.

Valerie looked at her watch: 8:20 P.M. Even with another hour here she could be in Calistoga by midnight.

"Oh," Rebecca said. "Poor Blasko."

"I'll make it up to him," Valerie said. "One of these days."

"If you want to pull an all-nighter here, I can go take care of him for you."

"I don't think he's ready for the whole Jewish —" Valerie stopped. She'd been looking down at the step. Next to Rebecca's foot was a thin deposit of white powder in the shape of a right angle. It looked as if it had been imprinted by the corner of a box. "Hey," she said. "What's that?"

Rebecca pulled a pen flashlight from her apron pocket. Both women got down on their haunches.

"Could be uncut coke or baking soda for all I know," Rebecca said. "I don't recommend tasting it." She pulled out an evidence packet and spatula. Scooped a little of the powder, deposited it, and sealed the bag.

"There's more," Valerie said. "Give me the light a second. Here. Look." A very fine trail of the powder led to the iron gate at the side of the building. As far as the flashlight told them it stopped a few feet beyond.

Look carefully, please.

Was this it? Was this what she was meant to find?

"Tell the lab to call me as soon as they know what it is," she said.

"Fine. I'll log this, then we're heading out. Have a good one. Let me know if you find any more . . ." — sarcastic wide eyes — "you know . . . *clues.*"

The CSI team were done for the day but everyone knew enough to assume the autopsy might prompt a second sweep. Therefore the scene would be held. Officers at the front and rear of the building. All the doorway evidence had been gathered, though Gianni Galliano had agreed to stay at his girlfriend's until the site was formally released.

All right, Valerie told herself, stepping back inside the kitchen, it's all yours. Now, what the fuck are we looking for?

6

If his note were to be believed, some form of advance warning to Elizabeth. There was nothing like that on the unlocked cell phone. The laptop, iPad, and desktop had been removed for analysis, but Valerie couldn't shake the feeling that it would be something old-school, physical. Another note? A letter?

She went through Elizabeth's wardrobes and drawers, checked all the pockets and purses. Nothing. She sorted through the mail, opened and stacked on the kitchen counter. Con Edison. AT&T. Chemical. Amex. A filing cabinet in the bedroom revealed Elizabeth as an organized keeper of records, with files labeled and alphabetized. All the usual stuff: medical insurance, DMV, paid bills, bank and credit card statements, lease contract for the apartment. There were old Christmas and birthday cards in a box under her bed. Handwritten letters from her college years. At a glance nothing unusual, but Valerie bagged them anyway, to look through later. Photograph albums. Elizabeth's life in snapshots, the family Polaroids, teen poses, endless prosaic group shots, barbecues, Thanksgiving dinners, college, graduation. What looked like a stint teaching nursery or kindergarten: a very young Elizabeth in a classroom with children barely up to her knee. Three, as far as Valerie could tell, boyfriends. Eventually *the* boyfriend, who became the Husband. *Our Wedding,* a separate album, silver inscribed and bound in olive-green velvet. Ornamental gardens. Elizabeth in a white tiered lace dress arm-linked to a tall, nondescript guy in a morning suit with a moppy head of dark hair and a weak chin. More life. An apartment. Skiing trips. Friends who didn't look like close friends. Then a drop-off. Ten years ago, Valerie estimated. The impact of digital, yes, but also the loss of will. Half an album in which the Husband — she remembered the crossed-out name in the "next of kin" section of Elizabeth's passport and her colleagues' mention of a divorce some years back — didn't feature at all. As soon as Ed called in the positive ID, they'd have to talk to him, wherever the hell he was.

On one of the bookshelves she found a pretty little pewter letter holder.

Look carefully, please.

An invitation to someone's art opening. A receipt for cookware. A couple of takeout menus. Ticket stubs from museum and gallery visits. Valerie wondered if *looking carefully* was just to amuse him. These were the times: he could have hidden cameras filming her right now. He could be gearing up to post her bewilderment on YouTube.

She dismissed it. The tone of his note implied a low tolerance for cartoon villainy or stock genre idiom. He wasn't fucking with her. Language was transparent that way. If you were being addressed respectfully, as an equal, you could tell.

She had started in the kitchen, gone through the living room and into the bedroom. There was only the bathroom left. CSI had cordoned off the footprints. The barefoot prints of Elizabeth and the grip-tread prints of whatever her killer had been wearing. Valerie had an image of Elizabeth, neck-deep in bath foam, hearing a noise in the bedroom, turning her head, seeing him. A peaceful evening for a civilized woman alone in her apartment blasted in a moment's horror, scented candles soft-lighting her nightmare. The familiar disgust surfaced. She forced it down. There was no place for disgust. Disgust didn't catch the men who did this. Only obsessive attention to detail. Only the Machine.

The medicine cabinet had nothing unusual to report. She trailed her gloved fingers along the window frame's upper rim. Dust. Nothing. The footprints were annoying her. The image of him pacing in here between assaults, glancing back at Elizabeth through the doorway, weighing what to do to her next. There was nothing in the note to suggest he wasn't working solo now. What was that like for him? A diminishment, surely? A cold space where the warmth of Katherine's collusion used to be. Maybe he would recruit someone new. Maybe he already had.

She went back out to the porch, removed her mask, and checked her phone. A text from Nick: "Managed to get B&B cancellation with no charge, so come home when you're done. I'll give you a massage. xN"

A couple of houses down the block, someone tossed an empty bottle into a recycling barrel.

I'll give you a massage. One of the worst things about the video footage was seeing the genuine intimacy between Katherine and the Man in the Mask, all the casual touches beyond the sex. You wanted it to be ritualized, robotic, a soulless dependence on fixed permutations. But it wasn't. There was visible ease and fit and trust. With a slight amoral contortion they were enviable. That, of course, was one of the reasons they'd stirred such profound public hatred. Whatever else was true of them, they were, literally, two against the world. They recognized no authority but their own. Once, when she was laughing particularly hard, Katherine had put her hand on his arm to keep her balance in the high heels. He said: "Easy there, tiger," and that made her laugh harder, as he'd known it would. Subtract the morality — subtract what they were laughing *at* — and they were the romantic ideal. An America of dead marriages was outraged, though they thought it was just the murders, the torture, the *pure fucking evil.*

Recycling. Bottles, cans, cardboard, paper. Paper.

Valerie walked to the trash cans at the end of Elizabeth's yard, removed the plastic bag from the recycling barrel and toted it back to the light of the porch.

A cop gift — one of the accepted Police Magics — was that you knew a thing just a split-second before you knew it.

In among the junk mail and menus, old *Chronicle*s and torn-up envelopes, was a bent postcard bearing, on its front, a reproduced painting of Adam and Eve standing under the tree of forbidden fruit, and on its back, in confident black felt-tip longhand the handwritten message:

You'll be the first. 072315.

For a moment, the numbers meant nothing. Then she saw. 07.23.15. Twenty-third of July, 2015. The day before yesterday. Almost certainly the day Elizabeth Lambert died.

Valerie looked again. No stamp. No postmark. Could he have delivered it by hand? Would he have taken that kind of risk? Since there was no street CCTV it wouldn't necessarily help if he had. But someone might have seen him. Seen him and assumed he was dropping junk mail or menus. Disguised? As a mailman? These neighborhoods, people *knew* their mailmen, or -women. Wouldn't he have risked running into someone from the building at the door, running into Elizabeth herself, for that matter? Surely?

She went back through the recycling. There were at least twenty empty envelopes, mostly junk or utilities, but three of them (all torn in half) didn't fall into either category. Two were handwritten, though the handwriting didn't appear to match the postcard. The third had been addressed using a printer. All were stamped and post-marked, though even with her phone's flashlight she couldn't make out the details of where and when. She couldn't, but tech could. They would know where and when it was mailed — though as soon as she thought that, she knew he would have anticipated it, would have driven to a red herring location to drop it in a box.

Run DNA and prints on all of them. Since he hadn't been shy of slinging biology around the scene, there was no reason to suppose his correspondence would be any different. She began to think to herself: It's better than nothing — but stopped. That needn't be true. If it was designed to point them in the wrong direction it would be worse than nothing.

Fair warning. More to follow.

7

Valerie dropped the evidence at the station, filed her report, and drove home. The darkness and the city lights were mildly palliative, as were the vague demands of steering the Taurus. Her face was sensitive and overfull, her hands throbbed.

You've been waiting for this.

Well? Hadn't she? Hadn't she wanted him to ignite the cold trail and give her the chance to finish the job? If that were true, what did it make her?

Years ago, her grandfather, a homicide cop himself, had said to her: Watch out for the Drift, Valerie. There are cases . . . there are cases that make it seem like it's not about doing the work. There are cases that wrangle your soul into the equation. That's the Drift. That's the undercurrent. Resist it. It won't help you. Crime is crime. It's never magic, it's never cosmic, it's never uncanny, it never *means* anything. It's just people breaking the law. Which means you do the work, that's all. Ignore your soul. You work homicide, your soul's no good to you. Homicide, your soul's a *false lead*.

Watch out for the Drift. She'd felt it six years ago and she could feel it now. Katherine Glass woke the Drift. To be in the same room with her co-opted you into a terrible unveiling. The covers came off everything and you were exposed to the raw elements of existence. She made you realize how everyone else you dealt with depended for their sanity on delusions, approximations, fantasies, compromises, denial, habits, lies, avoidance, displacement, postponement, an absolute refusal to look at themselves honestly. Katherine — morality aside — was sheer, present, resolved, unmysterious to herself. She was both her own unblinking scrutiny and its stripped object. Everything she'd done demanded you consign her to the scrap heap of dumb psychosis. Everything she'd done asked you to renew your subscription to the doctrine of the banality of evil. And every moment you spent with her made it impossible. You were in the Drift. Your soul was roped in. It mattered, beyond the practical. It *meant*.

Valerie changed lanes and lit a Marlboro. *I'll give you a massage.* She was nervous, suddenly, of her own domestic bliss. She had a fleeting televisual image of herself just now, a dark-haired woman, usefully scarred, live, dangerous, pragmatic, and more or less all right, driving home to love. It was nothing, a quirk of consciousness — and yet for a moment it was as if the universe shifted and revealed all her certainties from a damning new angle, showed the whole apparatus of her life — Nick, home, her family, her job, her self — as something piteously frail.

You going to talk to Glass?

I imagine I'll have to. Oh joy.

Understatement. Sarcasm. Always. Small utterances that were the tips of icebergs flaring thousands of feet below the surface.

You've been waiting for this.

Yes, she had. Six years. Yearning and dreading were not mutually exclusive. Again, the either/or world was gone. It was one of the first things you learned as a cop. Katherine had said: It's no accident police cars are black and white. America needs its morality simple. How many weeks did you spend on the force before you realized that all police cars, the world over, should be gray?

By the time Valerie was working homicide, academia and investigative journalism had

between them done away with the cinemati-
cally peddled vision of the serial killer —
charismatic genius apex predator who
hummed Bartók and quoted Shakespeare
— and replaced it with the unritzy truth:
that by and large the people who did these
things were dull and damaged, bereft of
insight and driven by dreary compulsions,
imaginatively and emotionally dead, cogni-
tively impaired, and not infrequently impo-
tent without the Viagra of psychotic violence. Even the ones who could string a
sentence together had nothing to express
beyond their own laughable megalomania.
If you didn't know they'd killed people you
could put them behind a mic onstage at the
Comedy Store and they'd be brilliant serial-
killer parodies. In short, hypothetical
stand-up aside, they were boring. More boring still once the psychopathic gene was
admitted to the party. Granted, it was
neither a necessary nor a sufficient condi-
tion for multiple murder, but still, there had
been palpable cultural disappointment
when killjoy Science reported that the great
monsters might reduce to nothing more
thrilling than lousy DNA.

Then, like a last hurrah for dark romance,
Katherine Glass and the Man in the Mask.

Over three years they abducted, raped,

tortured, and killed six young women, all between the ages of seventeen and twenty-five. They did it because they wanted to and because they could. They were articulate, good-looking, *extremely* intelligent, organized, calculating — and absolutely without remorse. It was as if the universe had had quite enough of all this uninspiring psychological reductivism, all this FBI *profiling,* and had decided to remind everyone that it could still go mythic old-school if it wanted to. Think you're over psychos? Get a load of *these* guys.

We knew, instantly, Katherine told Valerie, in one of the early interviews. From the moment we met. It was the simplest recognition. It always is. You see each other and you know. It's that moment of stepping from cold shade into warm sunlight. Every part of you says yes. I know that you know this. I know that you know love. I can see it. Love leaves an imprint in the tiny nebulae of the eyes. Yours have it. It's part of your beauty.

Children of their times, Katherine and the Man in the Mask had recorded the killings. Not just the killings, but a great deal of what preceded the killings. What preceded the killings were hours — days, in fact — of them doing whatever they wanted to their victims. Valerie had forced herself, courtesy of some bitter imperative to bear witness, to sit through all of it, a gesture of retroactive solidarity with the women who'd died, a futile attempt to stay with them through what they had endured. What they had endured was comprehensively thought-out torture, designed to make the suffering last. Katherine and her lover made the suffering last because their victims' suffering was what gave Katherine and her lover pleasure. The more suffering, the more pleasure, and the longer the suffering went on the longer their pleasure lasted. The simple equation. The Devil's math.

The images were in Valerie's head now, whether she liked it or not. The carefully administered cigarette burns, the broken flesh, the gagged screams, and the pleading. The Man in the Mask working up a sweat, Katherine blowing her blond hair off her forehead. Once you'd seen it there was no memory-wipe available, except the kind that might have come via a complete nervous breakdown. Watching the videos had been an education in the logic of extreme sadism, its brutality and nuance, the strange space it left its aficionados for black humor, a paradigm away from the playacting of consensual S&M, where the "victims" were willing participants, by definition not victims at all. Katherine and her man laughed, quietly and often, with what looked like exquisite, sophisticated delight. They shared a subtle ingenuity, a dedication to maximizing the contrast between their power and their victims' helplessness. The girls were always made to kiss and worship Katherine in exactly the places on her body she'd just burned or beaten on theirs: hands, feet, breasts, vagina, anus. Always with the promise that if they did that, if they degraded themselves sufficiently, the torture would stop and they would be released. Always, naturally, a lie. The Man in the Mask loved that, their repeated forced veneration, the complete inversion of their most basic value system. *You're an angel,* he said to Katherine, caressing her between her legs while Katherine dug her stiletto into a wound on Danielle Freyer's breast. *You're a sweet, perfect angel.* The girl's scream dulled behind her gag, her head flung from side to side. Nowhere for her to go and nothing for her to do except bear it. *Press harder, angel. I don't think she's feeling it.* Katherine had laughed, cozily, as if this were an indulgence in minor mischief. It went on. It went on, and on, and on. The repetition was integral. They wanted it to go on forever.

But it couldn't. Without exception, there came a point at which their pleasure turned to frustration, as if no matter what they did it was never sufficient, never wholly matched their imagination. Irritation crept in. Their contempt and desire became toxic, turned to rage. Or despair. They reached a point where nothing but the victim's death was enough, and though they knew death would end it, they couldn't draw back.

Valerie had been obliged to see one of the SFPD's psych counselors, Gayle Werner, a calm woman in her midforties with thick cropped curls of graying hair and pale-green eyes that suggested this was her umpteenth incarnation.

You watched all the footage?

Yes.

How did it make you feel?

Valerie had felt, at that moment, exhausted. She'd been impatient with the whole counseling process. It required the opposite of her usual verbal economy.

I didn't feel anything much. It's my job to stop the people who do that sort of thing. It's what I signed up for.

Did you feel guilty?

Why would I feel guilty?

A lot of the officers I see feel complicit. As if

knowing about — or in your case watching —
this kind of behavior makes them somehow a
party to it. It's not an uncommon response.

Valerie hadn't answered immediately. Then, after a few moments of something building up in her — a combination of annoyance and frustration and claustrophobia — she'd said:

I felt like I was watching people with rage
and despair inside them. Not even evil. Just
rage and despair.

She left out her other feelings. That seeing what she saw gave her a glimpse of the way the universe really was. That it was a completely indifferent machine. That whatever happened in it was just another thing that happened in it. That there was no cosmic moral order, no God, no meaning. The victims screamed and pleaded for help, and no help came. There was no help, no consolation, no justice. In their faces you could see the transition from hope (for rescue, for reversal) to the complete absence of hope. The complete absence of everything but the desire for death, the only kind of release left to them. Which, since by that point they had come to understand their torturers' needs, they knew would be a long, long time coming. By that point they had come to understand that their own death was literally the last thing their torturers wanted.

The responses to seeing this kind of behavior are unpredictable and frequently disturbing, Gayle had said. Valerie knew what she was getting at. It pushed her over whatever limit she'd been observing.

Look, I didn't get off on it. I know it's contagious. I know it works its way in. The police disease. I know that can happen, but it hasn't happened to me. I don't have it. That's what you're here to check, so let's not waste any more of our time.

And Gayle Werner, in the maddening way shrinks had collectively perfected, nodded calmly and made a long note on her yellow legal pad. Valerie had thought that would be the end of it, but Gayle said:

That's good to know. It's good that you understand. And I'm sorry if I seem patronizing. If everyone I talked to was as direct as you're being, my job would be a lot easier.

Interview clearly *not* over. Valerie regretted the outburst. She remembered a quote from high school Shakespeare: *The lady doth protest too much, methinks.* Could almost hear Gayle turning the same phrase over in her head.

Just out of curiosity, why do you think you feel so confident in your immunity?

Gayle's turn to be direct. Valerie thought:

Shrinks have to be like cops. Beyond surprise. Beyond shock. Beyond good and evil. It gave her a grudging respect for the woman sitting opposite her. It also made her consider the phrasing: Why do you think you *feel* so confident? As in, the feeling might be a delusion.

Good genes, she said.

Gayle didn't react. The nonreaction was her waiting for Valerie to give a proper answer.

Valerie didn't have a proper answer to give. All she said was:

I guess I'm not made that way.

Gayle had let it go. But the question had stuck in Valerie's head. Superficially, in the years that followed, she ignored it. Yet she knew some quiet mental apparatus was working away at it, revisiting it, probing it with the tense delicacy of a bomb-disposal expert. And gradually, over time, she had come to a tentative conclusion: She was immune because she had love in her life. The darkest part of herself understood the appeal of cruelty, of doing what Katherine Glass and her lover had done. She'd had the odd guilty fantasy herself, over the years. History testified that there was a dark part to all of us, cells of the human soul that could, given the right circumstances, mutate into a lethal cancer. What stopped that from happening, she came to believe (what stopped the fantasies becoming reality), was nothing more or less than the kind of life you'd lived by the time the right circumstances found you. The antibodies were love and warmth and imagination and humor. You could have cruelty *or* love. Not both. If you did what Katherine had done, you forfeited your ability to love. And if you had the kind of love she, Valerie, had in her life, the dark cells of the soul couldn't mutate.

But now, if she imagined offering that theory to Katherine, she pictured Katherine smiling, and the smile being an invitation to Valerie to know better, to see beyond what she needed to be true to what actually was true.

You going to talk to Glass?

I imagine I'll have to. Oh joy.

It was just after ten when she got home. She hadn't quite realized, until she closed the apartment door behind her, how deeply the day had exhausted her. The apartment's smell was still of new paint, clean laundry, and the polished oak parquet. Indian take-out Nick had brought home. He was asleep on the couch. The TV was on, sound low. AMC. Jimmy Stewart in *Harvey*. Comfort.

She didn't wake him. Instead she went to

the dark-tiled bathroom and turned on the shower. She shed her clothes and stood for a moment naked in front of the mirror. Love had made her friends with her body again, after a long period of numbness to it. Nick's desire had put her and her body back in quietly delighted cahoots. Katherine had said to her in one of the interviews: Don't you know exactly the sort of God who would give you a body that was your greatest source of pleasure, but only by dint of the same design that made it your greatest source of pain? Valerie thought of the footage. Danielle Freyer suspended by her cuffed wrists at a height that left her on awkward tiptoe. Naked, gagged, drenched in sweat, bleeding, crying, her face twisted with misery. The Man in the Mask said to her: I know you're looking for a way out of your body — but there isn't one. And you have miles to go before you sleep. On her knees in front of him, Katherine had laughed, softly, and taken his cock deep into her mouth.

Valerie turned away from her reflection and stepped into the shower.

Later, she lay in bed with Nick. She didn't need to say anything. He didn't need to ask. The day had left its aura around her. A big part of being Police was not needing to have the exchanges.

They were silent a long time. Valerie thought of a conversation she'd had with her colleague Sadie Hurst not long after Katherine had been arrested. Sadie had said: You know what the first thing every guy in the world asks himself when he sees Katherine's picture? He asks himself if he'd fuck her. The first question isn't: How could she have done those things, tortured and killed those people? The first question is whether he'd fuck her, given the chance. This is every guy, Sadie had said. Including the guys we're working with. And yeah, she'd added, seeing Valerie's look, including Nick. You don't believe me? Ask him. Valerie *had* asked him. Nick had said: That's the first question a guy asks himself about *any* woman. Why would Katherine Glass be an exception? They'd been having breakfast in a diner. Big windows and sunlight winking on the silverware. Valerie had conceded, inwardly, that none of this was really news to her. Nick had said, after thinking about it: That's not what bothers Sadie, anyway. What bothers Sadie is the question of whether knowing what Katherine did — what Katherine is like — makes guys want to fuck her *more*. Valerie had waited. No,

Nick said. Not for me. She'd known he wasn't lying. It had been their way from the start, not to bother lying to each other.

He was still awake. "Are you afraid?" he asked her.

"A little. I'm not as young as I used to be."

No jokes or platitudes. She felt him dismiss them. Instead he put his arm around her.

8

"Okay, everyone seems to be here," Captain Deerholt said, over the incident room's murmur. "Has anyone *not* yet seen last night's report?"

Everyone had. The atmosphere in the windowless room was a mix of excitement and dread. Ed Pérez, Sadie Hurst, Rayner Mendelsund, Will Fraser, Valerie Hart. With the exception of Laura Flynn, who'd joined Homicide in 2011, they'd all worked the original Katherine cases, under the unpredictable authority of the FBI, once it had become apparent they were dealing with a serial. Three of the Bureau's agents were here now, though Valerie recognized only Vic McLuhan, who'd been a special agent six years back and was now assistant special agent in charge. His colleagues were both around thirty, Agent Susanna Arden, a dark woman with a look of compact gymnastic flexibility, and Agent Christian Helin, a tall, lean guy with light-blue eyes and a trim blond beard.

The room hushed.

"Agent McLuhan?" Deerholt said.

"Morning, everyone. Déjà vu here for all of us, so I'll keep it brief. Technically we're waiting on the DNA results from the Elizabeth Lambert murder, but given the indicators — specifically, the gold-and-ruby ring belonging to Danielle Freyer — we're working on the assumption that this is in fact the man who partnered Katherine Glass in the serial case six years ago. As you all know, that individual has remained at large, but to our knowledge, and as far as database evidence can support, this is the first time he's been active in the United States since the arrest of Katherine Glass, thanks to your own Detective Hart here."

"Fluke," Ed Pérez said.

"Lucky break," Will Fraser said.

A little weary laughter. McLuhan allowed it, smiled himself. Valerie made a satirical bow.

"Obviously," McLuhan continued, "everyone needs to go back through the original files for anything we might have missed, but for now, Valerie, could you just nutshell what we ended up with from Katherine Glass's testimony?"

Valerie got to her feet and stepped to the front of the room. "As you know," she said, "Katherine played ball once she believed it would help weight her case in favor of diminished responsibility. She gave us a name — Lucien Chastain, which, assuming she was telling the truth, was the name by which she knew her lover. White male U.S. national, five eleven, fair-haired, blue eyes, thirty-four years old at the time, which would make him forty now. The composite artist rendering is in the files, for what it's worth, and there are the stills from the videos in which he's wearing the mask. According to Katherine he was highly intelligent, extremely wealthy, and could hack into any computer like its security was fresh air. His money was old Europe, apparently, though he left the details vague. Anyway, this is all in the files. The bottom line is that Katherine's 'Lucien Chastain' doesn't exist. We found plenty of candidates, none of them positively ID'd by Katherine and none with a fingerprint or DNA match. The Bureau's investigation has established that we're dealing with a professional ghost. Credit card transactions led to six different false identities, and following the cyber trail took us in an elegant circle. Katherine Glass wasn't lying when she described him as a prodigy. The cyber smarts could have come through the military, possibly even Intelligence, though we know the Bureau pursued that line as far as it's been possible to go and, so far, nada. In any case, we've got to assume the whole bag of tricks with this guy. Disguises, high mobility, resources, and a tech IQ off the chart. It's more than likely he's altered his appearance completely since the original killings."

"Did he communicate with us first time around?" Laura Flynn asked.

"No," Valerie said. "I don't doubt he still does what he does because he enjoys it, but this is a new development. He's savvy enough to know Katherine's not getting out, so I'm not sure what to make of the alleged agenda."

"The jury's still out on serials who communicate with the authorities," Susanna Arden said. "Statistically, there's no evidence that such communiqués increase the likelihood of catching the perp, but they massively increase the chances of securing a conviction if the perp *is* caught."

"In a lot of cases correspondence looks with hindsight like a killer's cry for help," McLuhan said. "Or at least the expression of a desire to be caught and stopped. I'm trying to keep an open mind, but in this case I'd say that's definitely not where the smart money is."

"The tone's all wrong for that," Valerie said. "We're dealing with ego, not self-sabotage. Either way —"

"Excuse me, Detective Hart?"

Everyone turned and looked to the door, where a young uniformed officer was standing with a manila envelope in her hands. She was wearing latex gloves.

"This just came in the mail for you. I think you'll want to see it right away. It's been handled, obviously, but . . . I brought more gloves."

The room went silent. Valerie put on the gloves and examined the envelope. It was addressed to her; as far as she could tell in the same handwriting as the Adam and Eve postcard. On the seal, another handwritten line: *You know who.*

"I need a . . . Anyone got a penknife? I don't want to tear the writing."

Ed Pérez produced a Swiss Army knife. Valerie worked the blade in and slit the envelope carefully along its edge.

Inside were six letter-size pages, held together with a paper clip. The first contained the following, which Valerie read aloud:

Dear Valerie

These pages contain the name and address of the next victim. Coded, obviously, in an interdisciplinary way. Hidden. Encrypted. There isn't enough mystery in the human lot, even for the police, so I hope you'll take this in the spirit in which it's intended. Let me not be disingenuous: you won't find it easy, since it's personal to me. Crossword and sudoku specialists will be of little use to you. In fact I doubt the entire department's pooled resources will yield a sufficiently broad frame of reference to see you through. You are very likely going to need outside help. Anyone spring to mind?

The victims won't be random. Elizabeth wasn't random. Think laterally. I won't tell you how long you've got, but the clock, to resort to cliché, is ticking. Good luck.

The team had gathered around her. Valerie was aware of their collective body heat and suddenly rich mental focus. The sounds of the rest of the station going about its business seemed far away.

"What does 'disingenuous' mean?" Ed Pérez said.

"Insincere," McLuhan said. "Pretending you know less than you really do."

Valerie went through the pages one by one. The first showed a printed grid, each square containing a letter of the alphabet, two or three hundred at least. Across the top of the grid a sequence of apparently random numbers. Along the left-hand axis what looked like Greek letters.

The next page was pictures, three color reproductions of old paintings, with their titles printed alongside them: Giorgione, *The Three Ages of Man.* Piero della Francesca, *The Resurrection.* Signorelli, *The Damned Consigned to Hell.*

The third page showed a poem, "Intimations of Immortality," by William Wordsworth.

"That's the daffodils guy," Laura Flynn said. " 'I wandered lonely as a cloud.' "

Three more images on the next page: a still of Sharon Stone from *Basic Instinct,* just before the famous leg-uncrossing scene; a photo of a pack of "luxury cigarettes," a brand called Nat Sherman, of which neither Valerie nor anyone else had ever heard; and a black-and-white reproduction of a head-and-shoulders portrait showing a slightly girlish big-eyed eighteenth-century gentleman in a dark jacket and white, large-collared shirt. An antique map of Italy on the next page. The last page contained a second grid, set out as the first, but with different letters of the alphabet in the squares.

"Fucking great," Will Fraser said.

"Let's write back and say we know it's all bullshit," Sadie Hurst said.

"It probably is," McLuhan said. "But he knows we can't afford to make that assumption."

Precisely, Valerie thought. She imagined him smiling at the prospect of the hours this would eat up. The team was still tense and intrigued around her. She couldn't help picturing them as a group of treasure hunters poring over the remains of a map. X marks the spot.

"Okay, first things first," McLuhan said. "Photograph these, then get the originals to Forensics. Everyone take a copy. Can't possibly *not* be our guy, but let's get it confirmed anyway. We've got people at the Bureau who can look at this for what he says it is, but frankly I *do* think it's fuck-with-the-cops nonsense. The paintings . . ."

"Katherine did two years of art history at Columbia before she dropped out," Valerie said. The words felt toxic coming out of her mouth. "She owned a gallery. Art's her

thing. One of her things. Literature, too."
Everyone looked at her as if she'd just said
something obscene.

"You're not suggesting . . ." Deerholt said.

"I'm not suggesting anything," Valerie
said. "But that's what the 'anyone spring to
mind?' line is about. He means Katherine.
We're going to have to find out if he's been
corresponding with her. Her mail's checked,
right?"

"She gets a *lot* of mail," Sadie Hurst said.
"Mostly guys who want to fuck her, or
marry her. Women, too, apparently. But
yeah, it's screened. Standard prison regs."

"All right," McLuhan said. "This is one
line of investigation, one of many, that's all.
Let's not let the fireworks beguile us. What
we're dealing with right now is the murder
of Elizabeth Lambert, so let's do the work.
We still have gaps in the forty-eight hours
prior to her death. I want those filled in,
and extended to at least a week. We're not
dealing with an opportunist, so he has to
have been watching her. We're still waiting
on the home computer analysis, but that
should come through by the end of today.
CCTV footage from the coffee shop like-
wise. Ed and Laura, talk to the family
members. Sadie and Rayner, neighborhood
and work. Elizabeth didn't have a steady

89

boyfriend, as far as we know, but I want a list of possible sexual partners, dates, whatever. We need to talk to this guy Elizabeth allegedly slept with, Luke Russell. Agent Arden will be going down to L.A. this morning to question him. Valerie, you and Will are going up to Deer Park to talk to the neighbor, right? Treece?"

"Yes."

"Red Ridge isn't far from there, so you might as well look into this correspondence thing en route. I know the warden there, so I'll call ahead."

A pause. Everyone in the room imagining Valerie and Katherine coming face-to-face, six years on. She didn't know it for a fact but forced herself to assume they'd all (guiltily) seen the grotesque little Internet fictions the case had spawned. At the time, the tabloid press had made her, Valerie, a sex symbol: "Hart*breaker.*" The online effects had been darker: fake porn images of other women's bodies with hers and Katherine's faces photoshopped in, sordid narratives of lesbian BDSM, invariably featuring her suffering at Katherine's hands. The sort of thing Valerie knew she was supposed to rise above in weary superiority. But it had hurt her. No matter how clean you were, the world had the power to make you feel dirty.

"You okay with that?" McLuhan said.

"Absolutely," Valerie said, though she could sense Will's eyes on her: Bad idea, Val. *Bad* idea.

"What about the postcard?" Ed Pérez said. "The fair warning?"

"We can't release that yet," McLuhan said. "Technically — but it's enough of a technicality — we don't yet have forensic confirmation that this is Katherine's guy."

"Yeah," Ed said, "but there could already be someone out there who's received one. If they end up dead and it turns out we had —"

"We release it now it's an open invitation to copycats for the price of a stamp. Let's get the confirmation."

9

Valerie drove. She could never bear being a passenger, whereas Will couldn't care less. Besides, he teased her, you know I get a kick out of having a white lady chauffeur.

"You talk to Treece," he said to her. "I'll deal with Katherine."

"Nope," Valerie said.

"Why give yourself the grief?"

"It's not grief, it's work."

"You don't know when to leave well enough alone."

"Who are you, my dad? Anyway, how're your balls doing?"

Will had had a testicular cyst removed a week ago.

"They're not happy. I'm supposed to be able to have sex, but every time I go near Marion it's like I can hear a drumroll."

"You know the longer you leave it the more nervous you'll get? Marion will have to start looking elsewhere."

"Thanks. She thinks it's hilarious, too, needless to say. Says I'm walking like the black John Wayne."

"I did notice you had a little delicacy in your gait."

"You've all got a castration fantasy. Marion was like that when we had the cat neutered. On the surface it was all, *oh, poor Jasper,* but you could see she was secretly delighted."

"You just have to ask her to be gentle with you."

"It's fucking bad design. Why your balls have to hang right there between your legs I don't know. Better off tucked inside the back of your skull or under your rib cage. Somewhere *sheltered,* for Christ's sake."

They fell silent. No levity was enough to dispel the waiting weather system that was Katherine Glass. Valerie was very conscious of the brightness of the morning, the sunlight flaring on the freeway traffic, the pale asphalt, a hard blue sky and the shivering green of the occasional trees. The world that was lost to Katherine. She wondered what incarceration had done to the sprawling intelligence that had to spend itself somehow within the confines of a prison. She had a brief image of Katherine lying on her bunk, staring at the close ceiling, every moment a grain of sand she must count, time the size of a desert.

"McDonald's in a quarter mile," Will said. "I didn't get breakfast."

"You can't eat your ball-anxiety away, you know."

"Yeah, but if I get fat enough Marion will leave me alone."

The interview with Nancy Treece had been straightforward, and unhelpful. Around six P.M. on Thursday evening Nancy had called over to Elizabeth's to use her scanner for documents pertaining to Nancy's divorce. The two women, who'd been friends for three years, ever since Nancy moved into the neighborhood, drank the better part of a bottle of white wine and chatted for an hour or so about Nancy's settlement, then Nancy left. As far as she knew Elizabeth was planning on spending the evening alone, catching up on her guilty pleasure, *House of Cards.* And no, Elizabeth had said nothing to her about a sexual encounter with Luke Russell, or anyone else. Elizabeth lived a life of diligent loneliness, apparently. I kept encouraging her to get on, you know, Match.com, Nancy told them. But Elizabeth got badly hurt by the first marriage. Scared her off men for good, it looked like. I can't believe she's gone. I just can't *believe* it.

The ex-husband lived in Boston now. He, obviously, would have to be talked to. Valerie made the notes, but she shared the same feeling of redundancy she could sense in Will. *We do the work,* McLuhan had said. Which meant starting at the center and working outward. The standard investigation model was the CSI's spiral-sweep pattern writ large. But to Valerie it already felt as if the standard model wouldn't be enough. Hunches and gambles, curveballs and wild cards, intuitions and risks — these were normally the last resort, the desperate resort, in fact, when *doing the work* had got you nothing but insomnia and a perpetual migraine. But Valerie had been trawling her sixth sense ever since her first sight of the note left with Elizabeth's body, ever since she'd understood that this was *him.* She knew what her grandfather would've said: Stop it. That's the Drift. That's your soul. Ignore it.

"Last chance," Will said when they pulled up at the Red Ridge Correctional Facility, current home to Katherine Glass. "You can sit here and chain-smoke."

"Give it a rest. Christ, Rebecca wasn't kidding about this place."

"What?"

"She said it was a modernist bunker."

The prison looked like the upturned hull of a brutally designed ship. A low-lying structure of dark concrete with tiny barred windows it was obvious did *not* form part of the cells. An angled wall of black brick surrounded it, festooned with razor wire. It sat in two acres of scrub: woodlands to the east, a soft golden haze of wheat fields to the west.

Valerie called the warden, Donna Clayton. "Come to reception," she said. "I'll meet you there."

Inside, the place smelled of cold surfaces and ammonia. In reception a big-boned Hispanic guard with short black-polished nails sat behind a blocky steel desk. "Have a seat," she said. "Warden Clayton will be out in a few minutes."

"This is why I became a cop," Will said, when they'd sat down.

"To put people in places like this?"

"To reduce my chances of ever ending up in one."

Warden Donna Clayton was a statuesque black woman with broad shoulders and a nifty boyish haircut. Well-cut taupe pantsuit and a cream silk blouse. Precise but understated makeup. Her aura was crisp confidence and the ability to see through bullshit.

Runs a tight ship, Valerie thought. *And doesn't suffer fools.* Will's sexual self livened, slightly, traumatized balls notwithstanding. *First question a guy asks himself about* any *woman,* Nick had said. Valerie felt a vague weariness at the thought.

They did the introductions and handshakes. "So," Donna Clayton said, "are we doing this with screen or without?"

Valerie and Will looked at each other.

"Katherine's a Grade B prisoner," Donna said. "Technically that means she gets no visits without a security glass between her and anyone else. We can waive that, obviously, if you prefer, since this is hardly a social call."

"No screen," Valerie said, before Will could speak.

"Okay." Then to the receptionist: "Renee, could you call C block and have them bring Glass down to Visiting? What've we got free there?"

Renee hit her keypad. "A-2, A-4, B-1 through 5 . . ."

"A-2's fine." She turned back to Valerie and Will. "If you'd like to follow me? McLuhan filled me in on the phone, so you'll have full cooperation, but I'd appreciate it if you kept me up to date on what goes down today. When you're done with the interview

I'll have one of our team bring you to my office. We can discuss Katherine's correspondence there, but I can tell you I've looked through it myself and there's nothing that shouts."

Three, four, five high-security doors with computer-coded entry and no-nonsense backup locks: the lingering mistrust of even twenty-first-century technology. Through the first set, Valerie and Will signed over their firearms.

"This might sound like a stupid question," Valerie said, "but does she know we're coming?"

"No," Donna said. "I figured you wouldn't want to give her time to prepare any nonsense."

"You're better at this than we are," Valerie said.

"Hey, you did the hard part catching her. I'm just keeping her."

Valerie liked the warden. She imagined the work that had gone into getting to where she was now, running a place like this. There was a vibe of not having come from money, a ghost of parental sacrifice for the Bright Black Daughter. Her composure hadn't come cheap. The easy smile and straight back testified to fierce application. Nor had she reached her limit. She couldn't be more than late thirties. According to Will, USP wardens could earn ninety thousand dollars annually, and the rate was higher in California. There was, Valerie intuited, a Donna Clayton game plan for the next twenty years. Red Ridge was a stepping stone.

"All right," Donna said after what seemed to Valerie an interminable series of left and right turns, doors, buzzers, locks, guards, "here we are."

The room was maybe fifteen by twenty feet, with a smell of stale coffee and raw disinfectant. Magnolia walls bare but for a laminated list of DOs and DON'Ts for visitors. A white Formica table and four orange plastic chairs. Down-lighting set too bright. All the joylessness of a bus station waiting room without the paltry cheer of windows or out-of-date magazines.

"Have a seat," Donna said, though she remained standing. "She'll be here in a minute."

"She give you any trouble?" Will asked.

Donna smiled. "She's in a single cell for all but two hours daily recreation, so there are limits. All death row inmates are supposed to take their rec in isolation, but the numbers don't allow it. She's kept as much away from the population as we can manage. She has charm. She's polite, and obviously her IQ's a blast. The staff hate themselves for liking her."

"Do *you* like her?" Will asked.

"If I think about what she did, no, of course not. You'd have to be Jesus on E. It's just that it's tough to square what she did with the person she appears to be. She's got language. Control. With the looks, it's quite a combination. She could've become anything she wanted. And it seems like a joke she shares with herself that she didn't." She looked at Valerie. "But I'm probably not telling you anything you don't already know."

"You have male guards here," Valerie said. "She have any contact with them?"

"Not without a female guard present, and then only for movement within the facility. Standing legal opinion for the last ten years has been that male custodial officers shouldn't be assigned to female housing units, and that's the line we follow. Pat-downs here are done by female staff only."

Valerie felt, suddenly, that she was coming out of a daze. All morning the idea of seeing Katherine again had been an intellectual admission, nothing more. Now, without warning, the reality of it rushed her. Her scalp tightened, as if in anticipation of a blow.

The door opened.

A guard entered, a stocky, big-breasted black woman with maroon hair in a tight bun. "Warden," she said, by way of acknowledgment. A moment later, Katherine Glass was there.

Prison-issue orange. Hands and legs in mobility cuffs and tether chain. The white heart-shaped face Valerie remembered, those green eyes peppered with black. The smiling look that said she knew your soul's story, negligibly amusing in comparison to her own. Her mouth, sans lipstick, was the color of raw pork. Regulations had stripped the cosmetics and reduced the long blond hair to a jaw-length bob, but it was still pulled back in a short ponytail. There was a very slight fullness to her cheeks, as if a silk-thin layer of fat had been laid beneath her skin. Her whole body had the same supple, dollish quality. Even at thirty-eight the little girl was still there. The clever little girl who kept secrets of which the grown-ups were afraid.

"Well, well, well," Katherine said, smiling. "Valerie Hart. And Detective Fraser."

A second guard entered behind Katherine. White, younger than the first, perhaps late twenties, dark hair in a French braid, big brown eyes with too much mascara and a large, full-lipped mouth. Narrow shoulders that made her look broad in the hips.

"I'm going to leave you to it," Donna said. Then to the first guard: "Warrell, take her straight back afterward. Lomax, you can bring the detectives along to my office when they're done."

"Actually, I'm sorry, but we're going to need to speak with her alone," Valerie said.

Authority clash. Donna lifted her chin an inch. A quick mental weighing of the protocols, slight irritation — then the visible concession that the cops would get their way sooner or later, if not today then the next time. No point wasting energy on a pissing contest. "The door stays open," she said. Then to Warrell and Lomax: "Okay, ladies, you can wait outside."

"It's appreciated, Warden," Will said.

"It better be," Donna sang, over her shoulder.

Katherine sat down opposite Valerie and Will. Rested her cuffed hands on the table. The former vamp nails were short and unpolished now, but the hands were still lovely. Matching veins the color of smoke showed in her pale wrists. For a few rich seconds the three of them sat simply absorbing the frisson. It was as if the room had filled with something nightmarishly festive.

Valerie felt sensitive in the bare parts of her skin: face, throat, hands.

"I take it he's back?" Katherine said.

"He might be," Valerie said. "We thought maybe you'd heard from him."

"I wish I had. It would be nice to have a literate pen pal. If I'd sold my panties to everyone who'd dyslexically offered to pay for them I'd be richer than Oprah by now. Who's he killed?"

She sexualizes every conversation. Valerie hadn't forgotten. Neither, palpably, had Will. Valerie took one of the ID photographs of Elizabeth from the file and slid it across to Katherine. "Elizabeth Lambert," she said. "Do you know her?"

"No. Should I?"

The victims won't be random. Elizabeth wasn't random. No need for her to know that yet.

"He left a note addressed to me," Valerie said. " 'Katherine Glass stays in prison, more people die.' "

"Oh God," Katherine said. "He's converted to melodrama. Like literature. Is nothing sacred?"

"That's what the note said," Valerie said.

"He's fucking with you," Katherine said. "I mean, don't get me wrong, I'm flattered. But please don't expect me to believe his

103

conscience is pricking him after six years. And you can't possibly think he's stupid enough to imagine I'm ever getting out of here, under any conditions short of a global zombie apocalypse. In which case I'd probably stay put voluntarily. Lock myself in the starved library and hope to make it through *Don Quixote* before they broke the door down. If it's him, he's fucking with you. If it's not him, it's an idiot. Don't you have a DNA or print match?"

"They're coming."

"What do you mean, his conscience can't be pricking him?" Will said.

Katherine looked at Valerie. As in: *You* know what I mean. Valerie did. The ease with which she understood Katherine was the worst aspect of dealing with her.

"Will," Katherine said, "you've got to get better at this. What are you reading? Do you read books worth reading?"

"I like pop-up books. Just answer the question."

Katherine smiled with what looked like genuine warmth. "I *mean,*" she said, with mock condescension, "that it's a tad late to come riding in on a white steed of murder after six years, don't you think? You're talking about a man who didn't even tell me his real name, a man who lied to me, compre-

104

hensively, for years, a man who left me, if you'll pardon the cliché, high and dry — and convicted." She smiled again. "I know you think a monster can't have her heart broken, but I promise you you're wrong. Oh, the nights I've cried myself to sleep!"

Valerie's phone rang. The screen said VIC MCLUHAN CALLING.

"Excuse me," she said, and stepped outside to answer it. Warrell and Lomax were standing with their backs to the wall opposite the door, hands in pockets, both with the worn look of daily exposure to extremity.

"We got a match," McLuhan said. "It's him. Prints and DNA from the scene, the postcard, the printed envelope, and the package. We're going to have to tell the fucking press."

"Okay. I'll call you back."

"You with Glass?"

"Yeah."

"She playing ball?"

"At the moment just playing. We just sat down. I have to go."

Valerie went back into the room. "Well, a tad late or not, it's your guy," she said to Katherine.

"Really?"

"Really."

"I'm amazed. I'm intrigued. Was she raped? Tortured?"

Neither Valerie nor Will answered.

"I'm not asking out of prurience," Katherine said. Then to Will: "That's dirty curiosity."

"Yes," Valerie said. "Both."

"And you think it's just him, alone?"

"No physical evidence to suggest otherwise, but we can't know for sure yet."

"It wouldn't be the same for him without a woman."

"Maybe they're not that easy to find," Will said.

"You're such a romantic, Will," Katherine said. "Sugar and spice and all things nice? You think I'm one of a kind?"

"We want you to walk us through his profile again," Valerie said, taking the mini-recorder from her pocket. "Anything you might have missed."

For a few moments Katherine didn't speak. She lowered her eyes, as if for self-consultation. Then looked back up at Valerie. "This would be the part where we have a little movie exchange," Katherine said. "I say something like: 'Assuming I might have anything that could be useful to you, what makes you think I'd want to help the people who put me in here?' "

106

Valerie didn't answer — and sent a mental imperative to Will to keep his mouth shut. She felt him almost ignore it. But they'd been partners long enough for him to know when to follow her lead.

"Except you've already thought of that," Katherine said. "And moved beyond it."

Still Valerie and Will remained silent. "Or," Katherine said, smiling, "am I missing something? Do you have something to offer me? Better books? Decent shampoo? A trip to the beach?"

"We don't have anything to offer you," Valerie said. "Apart from diversion. Unless of course you'd take some satisfaction in getting to the man who left you high and dry — and convicted."

"Diversion?" Katherine said. "Tell me more."

Valerie rested her hand on the file in front of her. "There are things here that might interest you. Boredom must be a problem."

"And with need of only a single arrow she hits the mark. What things?"

"Let's do the profile recap first," Valerie said. "Again: anything you might have missed."

"I didn't miss anything," Katherine said. "There wasn't that much to tell. It wasn't . . ." — pause for ironic weight —

"that kind of relationship."

"Nonetheless," Valerie said.

"Are you still with the gorgeous Nick?"

Fuck. This was what Katherine did. This was one of the things she did. During the original interviews six years ago it had become apparent that she knew Valerie and Nick were an item. The information had come to her, though Valerie had never been able to determine how. Her attorney, possibly, had let it slip, though he always denied it. Nick, working Homicide in those days, had been one of the investigators, and had testified at the trial, but that wouldn't have been enough for Katherine to know there was anything between them. At the time, Katherine had said to her: It's good between you two, isn't it? Good enough to make you afraid of how good it is. He even looks a bit like you, the dark features. You could be brother and sister. All the great love affairs have a whiff of incest about them, otherwise why do we feel such recognition? Otherwise why does your beloved become your family, your blood?

"You are still together, I can see it," Katherine said, leaning back in her seat. "Good for you. Doesn't look like it's gone stale, either. You have the quiet radiance. I can feel it. Did you get married?"

108

Valerie hadn't forgotten this, the weight of Katherine Glass's infallible instincts, the way she left you sickeningly visible, brought you up against no options but the truth. In the past Valerie had told herself it was just the effect of beauty and ugliness: the beauty of how Katherine appeared and the ugliness of what she'd done. But no matter how many times she'd rationalized it that way, the experience of being with Katherine hadn't changed. The woman had the gift of examining you not with hatred or fury, but with an expression of benign and very slight amusement, as if perpetually on the verge of giving in to her desire to smile at you, full of delighted understanding. Valerie had spent hours with her and it had always been the same. No matter what question you asked Katherine Glass, the question she asked you — just by sitting there, just by existing — was always bigger. It was exhausting.

And now?

Valerie paused the recorder.

"Yes," she said. "I'm still with the gorgeous Nick. No, it hasn't gone stale, but no, we're not married. This isn't *that* movie, either, where the psycho gets under the detective's skin and leverages her own life against her. There might have been a time when that would have mattered to me, but it doesn't now. The truth is I don't care what you know or think you know about me. We'll talk, and either it'll prove useful to this investigation or it won't. Whichever it is, it'll become apparent pretty quickly, and I don't intend to waste my time. You make me uneasy. You always have. Congratulations. I find I don't care much about my own unease these days. Shall we continue?"

Will didn't actually say *What the fuck?* but Valerie felt it coming off him. Her words had a curious effect on her. She hadn't quite known what she was going to say when she opened her mouth, but now she'd said it it was as if some of the tension in her muscles had gone. She almost laughed.

Katherine looked sweetly thrilled. "Holy moly," she said. "You've come a long way in six years. I love it. I'm almost lost for words — which is historic in its own right. I've missed talking to you, but obviously the precarious ingenue is no more. I have to recalibrate. All right. Good. And an ingenue is an innocent young woman, Will. As opposed to a French moose."

"I think we're already wasting our time," Will said.

"Turn it back on," Katherine said, leaning forward. "I'll tell you everything I can

110

remember. I don't get many interesting days in here. This is definitely one."

In the interview that followed, Katherine appeared to play it straight. There wasn't, as far as Valerie could tell, anything new. Physical description, old money, hyper-intelligent, cultured, well-traveled, tech genius. All as before. Two of the victims — Alicia Hooper and Julia Galvez — had been low-rent prostitutes he'd watched for a few days and picked up on the street. The remaining four — Leonora Ramsey, Hannah Weisz, Kate O'Donovan, and Danielle Freyer — had required full-strength surveillance prep, in which Katherine wasn't involved. "He never told me how he did it," she said. "But he knew where and when they were alone and off any kind of CCTV. It's rather incredible that I was still running the gallery when we started, although, obviously, that didn't last past the first one. Once we were sure of each other — or rather, once he was sure of me — all that changed. Then I was *on call.*" Katherine had, as Valerie knew from the original investigation, owned a small but successful gallery in Pacific Heights, inherited from her father when he died of a heart attack two days after her twenty-second birthday. "Lucien Chastain" had cash-financed her hiring a manager to take over most of the work, freeing Katherine to be there only when she wanted to be. In fact, according to Katherine, her lover had given her thousands of dollars over their time together, most of which she laundered through the gallery. "What can I tell you?" she'd asked Valerie, rhetorically. "I'm worth it."

"Any of this mean anything to you?" Valerie said. She passed Katherine the printed copies of the documents he'd sent, including the cover letter. The paintings, the poem, the photos, the cryptic letter grids. Katherine studied them in silence, carefully, page by page. For the first time in the interview her reflex archness dropped away. It was weirdly appalling, to see her for a moment undisguisedly engaged in something. It removed the barrier of difference, revealed her as a person. She might have been a prospective bride poring over a wedding dress catalog. Valerie could feel Will having the same reaction: Wait — *isn't* she a monster?

"Well, I know the paintings, obviously. And the poem," Katherine said. "Though I can tell you he hasn't included it because he shares its sentiment."

"What do you mean?" Valerie said.

"Wordsworth believed in the soul. Before

birth, we're part of God. Then we're born, and incarnation tears us away from Him. A bit of Him, a bit of this divine perfection, remains in us: our soul. In childhood, the soul has tantalizing memories of its former state of bliss:

> "Our birth is but a sleep and a forgetting:
> The Soul that rises with us, our life's Star,
> Hath had elsewhere its setting,
> And cometh from afar:
> Not in entire forgetfulness,
> And not in utter nakedness,
> But trailing clouds of glory do we come
> From God, who is our home:
> Heaven lies about us in our infancy!

"He didn't believe any of that nonsense," Katherine said. "He was an existentialist, for want of a better word."

Will shifted in his seat: *For God's sake, this is bullshit.*

Valerie was still adjusting to the strangeness of Katherine apparently with her guard down. "So why this poem?" she said.

"This is when I miss a cigarette," Katherine said, with a little cartoon grimace. "Honestly? I don't know. If you want my guess — and assuming he's not just messing with you — I'd say the thematic content's irrelevant. It's more likely part of the key to the letters in the boxes. Maybe a correspondence of letters with the paintings' titles . . . Could be the line numbers, but that seems too easy. He wouldn't make it that easy. You have to understand: this is a guy who could do the *Times* crossword in less than two minutes. Patterns tickle him, as they do me, because they suggest meaning in a universe which daily pistol-whips us with its absurdity. Lateral connections, as he says in the note."

"So 'anyone spring to mind?' is you — agreed?"

"Yes, it's me. Renaissance art is me, anyway. And probably the map of Italy, since I did my junior year abroad in Rome. He knew that. He also smoked Nat Shermans. Got me onto them, too. The portrait is of the Marquis de Sade, of whom even you must have heard, Will. And if you haven't, it's where the word 'sadism' comes from. As for Sharon Stone . . ." She smiled. "I have no clue. Except he said she should play me in the movie of my terrible life. I assume the hilarious FBI are marshaling their eggheads for this?"

"Yes."

"God, I'd love to be a fly on the wall for that."

"He says he's giving his victims fair warning. At Elizabeth Lambert's I found this." Valerie handed Katherine a photocopy, showing the postcard, front and back. Katherine smiled, a melancholy connoisseur among savages.

"This one's not Italian," she said. "It's by Lucas Cranach the Elder. German artist, 1472 to 1553. The image, obviously, is in the Catholic tradition, though Cranach was a Protestant, and in fact a close friend of Martin Luther."

"And?" Will said, impatience undisguised.

"And we had a seminal conversation about the Fall, Adam and Eve's expulsion from paradise. It was one of his favorite subjects. He thought of it as the first and greatest humanist narrative."

"What does that mean?" Valerie asked.

"It means Adam and Eve are heroes in spite of their superficial villainy. There are two trees in the Garden of Eden: the Tree of Life and the Tree of the Knowledge of Good and Evil. It's the second tree that causes the trouble. Genesis 2:17: 'But of the tree of the knowledge of good and evil, thou shalt not eat of it: for in the day that thou eatest thereof thou shalt surely die.' As soon as we read that we know where the story's going. More important, we *want* it to go there. The subtextual question is rhetorical: Who *wouldn't* do what our girl Eve did, sooner or later? We're on her side, because we know that the Fall, whatever the consequences, is a fall into knowledge — and we want to know. We always want to know."

Valerie could feel how much this was annoying Will. Not because he thought it was a waste of time, but because like everyone else he couldn't resist the Katherine fascination. When she talked, when she was in full flight, it was impossible not to listen. Throughout the trial Valerie had watched people's reaction to the woman on the stand: an incremental mesmerism. It wasn't what she'd done. It was her articulate serenity in spite of what she'd done. Superficially, people were appalled by her actions. Deep down they were curious about what her actions had given her.

Knowledge.

Valerie had been no exception. Even now, she realized, she regarded Katherine as a woman who had been out past the known frontiers. Even now she couldn't shake the feeling that Katherine knew something that she, Valerie, did not. It had always been part of the inequity between them. It was as if Katherine had gone out beyond the darkness to meet God and had returned carrying his inscrutable imprimatur.

God or the Devil.

In one of their interviews, Katherine had said to her: God and the Devil are one and the same. And they live in the same place. Which is where? Valerie had asked. Katherine had smiled and said: You know where, Valerie.

"He had a soft spot for this painting," Katherine said. "Because Adam and Eve are both holding the fruit, together. It's the collusion again, you see? Nothing binds us together like shared sin, the conspiracy of disobedience. It's the sweetest of all allegiances. Look at the end of the Genesis story: God kicks the lovers out of paradise. They're distraught, initially, but it doesn't last. They get over their guilt and start a farm and have kids and get on with it. The whole narrative is about God putting his money on fear and shame — and losing the bet. What does anyone think when they get to the end of the fable, apart from: Good. Serves the miserable old bastard right. Read Milton on the lovers' exit from Eden, the last lines of *Paradise Lost*:

"Some natural tears they dropped, but
    wiped them soon;

117

> The world was all before them, where to
>   choose
> Their place of rest, and Providence their
>   guide.
> They hand in hand with wandering steps
>   and slow,
> Through Eden took their solitary way.

"*Hand in hand.* It's beautiful. And inevitable."

"Do you run classes in here?" Will said, as much to shake himself out of his own seduction as anything else.

"You'd be surprised," Katherine said. "There are some lively minds among these ladies. Do you think Nick fantasized about me, Valerie?"

"We've got everything we're going to get here," Will said.

"I know *you* did, Will. Which is sweet. Be careful I don't creep in tonight, after you've turned your wife over."

Valerie forced herself to sit very still. Will switched the recorder off. Valerie could feel how badly he wanted to hit Katherine. But he sat back in his chair and appraised her. "You're too skinny," he said. "And it's obvious you're not getting enough vitamin D. Don't they exercise you in here?"

Katherine smiled languidly. "Good for

you, Will," she said. "I'm sorry. Old habits. Forgive me. It's the boredom."

"I'll be outside," Will said, getting to his feet.

As soon as he was out the door, Katherine said to Valerie: "You didn't answer."

Valerie resisted the desire to look away. Instead, she met Katherine's eyes. She wasn't sure why. Something drove her beyond her instincts. "I don't know if Nick fantasized about you," she said. "He's a guy, and you're a very beautiful woman. That's the only relevant part of the equation. But it wouldn't be the end of the world if he had. We're not responsible for our desires. Only our actions. It's only the actions that make a difference, in the end. But let me ask you something: Is that the only power you've ever had?"

She had astonished herself. The words had come out of her with a curious, gentle inevitability. It was as if she'd just casually brushed a cobweb from her consciousness.

Katherine didn't answer right away. A faint uncertainty in her face for a moment. She glanced down at her hands. To Valerie's mind, the first time Katherine had been the one to look away. But the green eyes came back to her.

"You really have grown," Katherine said.

119

"I've missed talking to you." There was a discernible shift in her voice. The musical playfulness had gone. "And yes, I think perhaps that is the only power I've ever had. We don't ask for our gifts."

Valerie was thinking of a conversation she'd had six years ago with Nick. It was during the time of the original interviews with Katherine. She'd come home exhausted. Nick had run her a bath and given her a huge glass of wine, then sat on the edge of the tub with a glass of his own. With everyone else I know, Valerie had said to him, I can imagine them lying down to go to sleep at night and thinking about things. What they did that day, their families, the random ordinary crap you sift through while you're lying there in the dark, drifting off. With Katherine, nothing. It's impossible. I can't imagine anything. I can't imagine her even thinking about the things she's done. I can't imagine what it's like for her to be alone with herself. I can't really imagine her sleeping.

It was still that way, Valerie thought now. She couldn't conceive of Katherine's inner life. If she tried, she got a vision of her lying with her eyes open in the dark, deafened by a continuous internal scream. It was easy to shift what Katherine had done to one side

120

and to be left with the knowledge that you were looking at the embodiment of absolute aloneness. Perhaps that was what evil was, when you got right down to it, an aloneness like no other. Unless you found someone in the darkness — as Katherine had. The Man in the Mask. It must have felt like love.

"Listen to me," Katherine said. "I can help you."

Valerie came back to herself. Time had stopped. She felt it flow again, as if a valve had been released.

"I don't think so," she said. She was exhausted. This was the way it had always been with Katherine: you spent minutes in her company and it was as if you'd been drained by an ordeal lasting years.

"You must have thought I might be some use to you or you wouldn't have come," Katherine said. "I can help with *this.*" She put her hands flat on the documents in front of her.

For the second time in their meeting it seemed to Valerie that Katherine's default artfulness dropped away, as if the force field had been lowered. She told herself she couldn't trust it. She told herself that the only thing about Katherine you could trust was that you couldn't, under any circumstances, trust her.

"You can't trust me," Katherine said. A nauseous telepathy had always flirted between them. "I know you can't trust me. I'm not asking you to. All I'm asking is that you leave this with me and let me see what sense I can make of it. Talk to Clayton and tell her that I can contact you if I come up with something. I know him. I know what he calls his 'frame of reference.' The FBI morons are going to be wasting their time. They'll run algorithms and code patterns and all the usual shit and they'll get nothing. Or rather, not nothing, but just enough to keep them going. He knows what he's doing. This isn't going to respond to the systematic, I guarantee you. This is going to require the lateral, the tangential, the personal. Again, that's assuming he's not fucking with you. Fucking with *me,* for that matter."

"But as you point out," Valerie said, "I can't trust you. You could feed us misinformation. You have every reason to."

"Of course," Katherine said. "Of course I could. There's nothing I can say to rule that out. Except to remind you of what he did to me. And to ask you to consult your intuition."

"My intuition?"

"We understand each other, Valerie. We've

always understood each other. We haven't wanted to, but we have. We know the differences between us. Don't you think?"

Valerie didn't answer.

Katherine let it go. "All right," she said. "But you do know one thing is true. This is the most interesting thing that's happened to me in six years. Can you imagine what being in here is like? For me, I mean?"

"Yes."

"I'm atrophying. It surprises me that I haven't killed myself."

"Why haven't you?"

Katherine smiled, again, genuinely. "Well, they don't make it easy, for one thing. But the truth is life is stubborn. The will to keep drawing breath. You know, like those stories of little kids they find alone in their houses after weeks, they've somehow kept themselves going on ketchup and sugar. It's astonishing. And weirdly obscene. I always wondered what happened to those kids afterward. Except of course for me that's where the analogy ends, since there isn't ever going to be an afterward. Just more ketchup and sugar, on and on, indefinitely. Or until someone in here puts me out of my misery."

"You seem established."

"No one's established in here. Established,

I *would* have killed myself. Danger does you the service of forcing you to act."

Valerie got to her feet. She'd had enough. The familiar claustrophobia.

"Let me find a way," Katherine said.

"A way?"

"Of convincing you. Let me see what I can figure out from this stuff. Face it: you're going to know soon enough if it's misinformation. In this video game I get one life. If I blow it, it's over."

The second guard, Lomax, put her head around the door. "Everything okay?" she said. Valerie wasn't sure if the question was addressed to her or to Katherine.

"We're fine," Katherine said, with a forced evenness, not looking up. Lomax glanced at Valerie, then withdrew.

"I'll talk to the warden," Valerie said. "If you come up with something . . ." She left it unfinished.

"I can't promise anything," Katherine said. "But give me a chance. You know this is water in the desert for me."

Valerie went to the door and called the guards.

"Valerie?" Katherine said.

"What?"

"There's something else I want to talk to you about."

"What?"

Katherine looked away from her. Looked, if anything, sheepish. "Maybe not this time. It's something you need to know. I think it's something you need to know."

"If it's about him, I need —"

"It's not about him. Will you . . . I mean, if I can make anything of this, will you come and see me again?"

"Let's see if you can make something of it."

"Will you ask Clayton if I can get access to a computer?"

"You know that's not going to happen."

"Supervised," Katherine said. "No e-mail. No chat rooms. No porn. Just for cracking this. You can send one of the FBI morons to make sure I'm not looking at anything pernicious or frisky."

"I've been with Clayton for five minutes and I know she's going to say no."

"Would you ask her? This is going to take forever with a pencil and paper. Not to mention a brain that's a shadow of its former luminous self."

"I'll take a temperature reading," Valerie said. "*I'm* not promising anything, either."

"It's been good seeing you. But you know that. I'm sorry about the childish remarks."

The Nick remarks. Valerie had an image

of Nick jerking off. Imagining Katherine, legs spread, smiling. *It wouldn't be the end of the world if he had.* Wouldn't it? Her head had room for it. Her heart was another matter.

"It won't happen again," Katherine said, getting to her feet. As Warrell ushered her toward the door, she passed close to Valerie. Perhaps only a foot separated them. Valerie found herself noticing that Katherine smelled of hard soap and the prison's nylon fatigues. When she'd arrested her, she'd smelled of complex perfume and cigarette smoke and cosmetics. Katherine stopped and turned to face her. They didn't speak, but for a moment Valerie felt again the terrible nakedness. It was as it had always been, as if she had known Katherine in a former life. The space between them livened, as with an electrical charge.

Then Warrell said: "Let's go, Katherine," and in a moment the two of them were out the door.

10

Six years, Nick thought, and Katherine Glass still had the power to fuck everything up.

He was in the Le Beau Market on his way home from work, ostensibly for Arborio rice, but in fact because the place exerted a calming influence on him. He supposed he was becoming eccentric. But after ten hours of staring at a desktop screen and trawling binary for the dirty secrets of criminal strangers, the raw colors and rich smells of a great deli were sensually therapeutic. Ditto cooking. Chopping yellow peppers or grating Parmesan or pouring out a slug of olive oil gave him back some of childhood's aesthetic innocence. Eccentric — or just middle-aged? He was only forty-one. But cops were like dogs: one of their years racked up seven on the soul. Either way, he was past caring. You were Police. You found things that helped — and did them. That was all. So among other things, he cooked. A waste, half the time, since Valerie's hours were still the inhuman mess Homicide demanded, not to mention that she ate like a fucking sparrow, but he didn't care. It gave him pleasure to hear her rummaging in the fridge at some random hour and discovering the wrapped leftovers of whatever he'd made. She ate, when she *did* eat, with the bulk of her consciousness elsewhere, on the work, but every now and then the deliciousness of something she put in her mouth brought her back to immediacy and she actually tasted it. A few months ago he'd woken at three in the morning and heard her in the kitchen. He'd lain in bed in the dark, following her via the sounds, knowing she was going to find the garlic chicken he'd made. After a moment, he heard her say to herself, softly, with delight: Fucking *hell.*

So let me get this straight, Eugene had said to him, between games not long ago. You do the shopping and the cooking? Yes. Eugene had shaken his head in pained disbelief. And what if you had a kid, and your woman wanted to keep running around chasing bad guys? Would you stay home and take care of it? Maybe. *Seriously?* Nick had shrugged. I don't know, he'd said. We'd work something out. Dude, Eugene had said, listen to me, that's a bad idea. Here's what'll happen: Initially — *initially,* mind you — your gal'll be all over it. Twenty-first-century enlightened man, so comfortable with his masculinity that he doesn't care if he's wearing the domestic dress. She'll talk you up to her friends. The friends will twinkle with envy. And then in about two years she'll wonder where all the butch went and end up having an affair with an asshole like me. I'm just saying: don't say I didn't warn you. Get an au pair at least. Eastern European, blond. You don't even have to fuck her. Just to keep your lady on her toes. Plus your kid can learn a foreign language.

Nick had brushed it off, as he did all Eugene's routines — but it had made him wonder. Not about a house-husband being a turnoff for Valerie (in comparison to the women Eugene claimed to know, Valerie was a different species), but about the ease with which he, Nick, could imagine his life as something *around* Valerie. It appalled him, slightly, that he had apparently found his sufficiency in her. He was forced to concede, with gentle bemusement, that work was no longer very important to him. It had been getting less important to him ever since he'd left Homicide and retrained in Computer Forensics. This truly astonished him. Working Homicide had felt like a necessary disease. It had defined him in the way it still defined Valerie. It wasn't just what they did; it was who they *were*. But he'd left it behind. It had taken so much of his life and soul that some part of him had rung an alarm bell: Get out now before there's nothing of you left. He hadn't thought about it that way at the time. In fact he'd gone through the motions of quitting Homicide as if he were watching himself from outside his body, as if he'd been shunted to one side of his life by a quiet demonic presence that had taken over and was making his decisions for him. It had felt inevitable, out of his hands.

And now?

He didn't regret it. He wanted other things. The moral core of him said it was just that he'd done his share: he'd devoted enough of his life to catching murderers and putting them away. He was entitled, now, to be a little more harmlessly selfish. Walk in the mountains. Cook. Have conversations that went beyond blood-splatter patterns and ropy alibis. Have a life that didn't, every fucking day, have *death* at its center. Be a father.

All of this, this strange, gradual metamorphosis, had led him to knowing that he was

130

going to ask Valerie to marry him, and knowing further that she *would* marry him. If she wanted to carry on working Homicide, fine. He would be part of the life that allowed her to do that. In fact — this was the crux of it — he would be part of the life that stopped her job from driving her completely fucking insane.

Was that it? Did he love her that much?

He was forced to admit that he did. It gave him a sense of surprised peace.

Except now Katherine Glass was back in their lives.

From the moment Valerie had told him about the killer's note Nick had known that his proposal would have to wait. Katherine stained what needed to be a blank canvas. It wasn't that Valerie would say no. It was that when she said yes it would be through the toxic haze of *Katherine.* If he asked her to marry him now, she'd say yes, but she'd wish he'd waited until all *this* shit was behind her.

He knew all of this without any of it needing to be said. He had to wait. Perversely, *not* working Homicide made it worse. If he'd been on the current case he would have at least been able to comfort himself with the thought that he was doing his share in closing it, progressing the investigation to its denouement and getting it off both their desks so they had a clear field ahead of them. He and Valerie would have been in it — as six years ago — together.

But was that true? Working the original murders with Valerie back then had been claustrophobic. Katherine and the Man in the Mask had been with them from the moment they woke to the moment they fell asleep, had been the dense air they breathed. That conversation they'd had, Valerie wanting to know if he found Katherine desirable. Superficially, in spite of what Katherine had done. In reality, *because* of what Katherine had done. Unlike Valerie, Nick hadn't watched all the hours of video footage. He hadn't needed to. An hour had been enough. More than enough. The material had gone in and stayed in. One of the victims, Julia Galvez . . . Katherine had watched while the Man in the Mask beat her with a cane, hard enough so that every resonant whack broke the skin in a bloody stripe. Katherine had told him to stop, then stood with her back to Julia Galvez and spread her ass: Kiss my asshole and you'll only get three more. Otherwise you get twenty. Your choice. And because Julia Glavez was long, *long* past anything other than the need for the pain to stop, because anything, *any*thing to minimize her suffering, she did as Katherine said. Nick remembered Katherine's calm, civilized voice. That's it . . . gently. . . . That's right. A little tongue now. . . . Katherine had laughed softly when she'd done it, turned and lifted Julia Galvez's face by the chin and looked into her wrecked eyes. Good girl. I said only three more, didn't I? Then to the Man in the Mask: Give her twenty. Actually, no, just keep going till I come. A little harder, I think. You must admit you've been strangely gentle so far. . . .

"Need any help?"

Nick started. A young guy in a store apron was standing in front of him.

"What? Oh, no — well, actually, yeah. Arborio rice?"

"Sure, let me show you. It's right over here."

Nick's face felt hot and overfull by the time he left the store. He got in his car and sat for a few minutes with the AC going full blast. He wasn't afraid. Just sad. He'd been Police long enough to know that the innocent days of either/or were long behind him, long behind everyone, if they were honest. Simplicity demanded that either you were fascinated by Katherine or you were repelled by her. He wasn't repelled by her, beyond knowing that what she was was wrong, had taken a fundamentally wrong turn somewhere in her past, or been compelled to take it by a combination of genetics and accident. Was he fascinated? He had asked himself at the time — and he asked himself, now that she was back in the scheme of things, again.

No, he wasn't fascinated. It was only her beauty that led your interest to what she did. If she'd been plain his interest simply wouldn't have engaged. Beauty was an amoral beguilement. It gave weight where there was none. It made what was ordinary and one-dimensional seem mysterious and complex. Beauty made you look. That was all it was. Beauty just made you fucking *look*.

Six years ago, he had said to Valerie: Katherine Glass is the smartest person I've ever met. But for all of that it's as if she's missed this huge, simple thing that so many of us less smart people take for granted.

What huge simple thing? Valerie had said.

It had put him on the spot. Because the truth was he couldn't explain it. He probably wouldn't be able to explain it now. It turned out this simple thing Katherine had failed to see wasn't so simple after all, or at least that it was beyond his powers of articulation. In the end, all he'd said was:

It's no good to be the way she is. It's just no good. I don't mean morally, none of that shit. I just mean you spend five minutes with her and you can see that everything she does, all the talk and the mischief and the razzle . . .

Yes . . . ? Valerie had said.

It's a massive distraction, he'd said. From herself. It's like she has to talk all the time because if she didn't she'd hear what she was in the silence. He'd groped for the analogy. She's like a shark. Has to keep swimming, or it dies. I think she's terrified.

Terrified or not, he thought now, she was back in their lives. And thanks to her he was going to have to wait to ask Valerie to marry him. It almost made him laugh. He had an image of himself confronting Katherine and saying, furiously: *Do you realize that you're getting in the way of a fucking marriage proposal?* In the chaos of her sins, what would that sound like?

He was excited today. But it was like he wasn't seeing me properly. I didn't say anything, but something must have told him because then he kind of dialed himself down and said Okay, okay, we don't need to do it all in five minutes, we can get to that later. Meanwhile come here. Something happens when he just tells me what to do, like my whole body goes deep calm and thrilled at the same time. The place he's got in the Caribbean he's got like servants. He showed me a picture. A skinny black boy in a bright-white jacket and past him a big glass window showing the beach, one of those where the sand looks white and the ocean that blue that says warm.

When I saw her that first time I told him I knew and he said it was the same for him. He told me the name of some philosopher guy I can't remember now, but anyways this guy said no one ever discovers anything, they just remember it. That's so true. That's what it's like with him. Both of them. Like I knew them in some past life. Like I forgot but now I remember. The feeling of homecoming, he said. God, he's so right. Like the first time I saw her picture in the paper I knew. And in the court it was like a line of warm light between us.

Bad food today. Cheeseburger at work and a packet of Doritos at home and a butterscotch cheesecake. I was mad at myself so I threw all the crap in the cupboards away. Headache. The bullfighter said serves you right. That was another thing. First time I saw that painting I knew it was something.

11

Valerie got in around nine that evening.

"So how was it?" Nick said. He was at the stove, stirring something.

"Ambiguous," Valerie said. "Surprise. She hasn't changed much. What's for dinner?"

"Risotto. In fact, come here for a second and keep stirring this. I need to pee."

"It smells like booze."

"Vodka."

"In risotto?"

"It's supposed to be white wine, but that's for sissies."

"If you've cleaned out my Smirnoff, you're in trouble."

"Just stir it, Skirt. All the liquid has to be absorbed."

"You know, your masculinity took a big hit when you left Homicide."

"Tell me that when you taste it. You know what look I get these days from women? It's the look that says: *I know you're not appreci-*

ated. One of these days . . ."

While Nick was in the bathroom Valerie checked messages on her phone. One from her mother, one from her sister. It gave her not just the usual vague feeling of guilt (her family had long since gotten used to her unavailability) but something more specific, though she didn't know what it was.

"Val, honey, it's just Mom calling. . . ." (Her mother was always "just Mom" or "only Mom," as if her existence was, by definition, insufficient; it drove Valerie and her sister nuts.) "I'm reminding you because you asked me to about Cassie's birthday. I've got something for her from you, a little bracelet from that store in Fremont you know she loves. . . ."

Guilt and more guilt. Guilt because she'd forgotten it was her sister's birthday — her fortieth, moreover — tomorrow, and they were having a barbecue party at her place in Union City. Guilt because she'd felt immediately annoyed at her mother for reminding her, despite having asked her to do just that. Guilt at having not picked up this message sooner (it was two days old), and guilt at having no fucking clue what store in Fremont it was that Cassie allegedly loved. Terrible daughter, terrible sister. Yeah, her father had said to her when he was still

140

alive, but a terrific cop. . . .

"In any case, I've got the gift receipt, so if she doesn't like it she can exchange it. . . ." Pause. Her mother trying and failing to disguise how much she wanted Valerie to make it to the party. "All right, that's all for now. Give me a call back to let me know you're okay. And don't feel bad if you can't make it. We just want you to do whatever you need to do, and we know . . . you know. The job. Love you, hon. Bye."

Redundantly, Valerie consulted her phone calendar. Of course the reminder had popped up, as it was technologically compelled to do, a week ago: *Event: Cassie's 40th. Time: 8:00 P.M. Notes: Mom get present.*

"Hey, Val, it's Cassie," the next message began. "Listen, you're probably going to get a call from Mom saying no sweat about Monday, but being Mom she'll make it sound like you really should come. So here's the thing: you absolutely do not have to come. This is me, speaking the truth, to you."

There was a short silence. The phrase — *This is me, speaking the truth, to you* — was one the sisters had begun using when they were young, for the delivery of sensitive or painful things without malice.

"Anyway, that's all. Regardless of this

141

dumbass party, I'd love to see you, just the two of us, anytime you're free. Call me when you can. Love you. Bye."

Nick emerged from the bathroom.

"I forgot Cassie's birthday party," Valerie said.

"She won't care."

"Her *fortieth* birthday party. It's tomorrow."

"So let's go."

"Yeah, I guess I'll try. My mom got her a gift from me."

"You're Police. You're absolved."

"Am I?"

"Yeah, but *I'm* Police, so you're not absolved from appreciating my risotto. Jesus, get out of the way. It's ready. You nearly ruined it."

They ate dinner at the breakfast bar, with Louis Armstrong on in the background. Valerie could sense Nick not asking any more about Katherine. She could sense him stopping himself.

Do you think Nick fantasized about me, Valerie?

It wouldn't be the end of the world if he had.

"I gave her the stuff he sent," Valerie said. "She wants in."

"For what? Revenge?"

"She implied as much, but I think it's just

that she's bored out of her skull."

Was she still supernaturally beautiful?

Stop it. He didn't ask that. Ask him if he fantasized about her. No. Don't.

"She recognized the paintings?" Nick said.

"Yeah. The paintings, the poem, the whole shebang. Says the Bureau's going to be wasting its time."

"Well, if he's got half her brains, they might be."

A pause. Nick was live to her, too. Could feel her not saying what she wanted to say.

"It still bothers you, doesn't it?" he said.

"What does?"

"That she's the way she is. The things she did."

"It'll bother me for the rest of my days. Doesn't it bother you?"

Nick didn't answer right away. Not because he was thinking about the question, but because he was thinking about what was underneath it.

"Seriously?" he said. "Of course it bothers me. But it bothers me like malaria bothers me. Or earthquakes. People like Katherine are a fact of the world. We know this. *We* know this."

Yes, we do know this, Valerie thought. We can't unknow the things we know.

"She asked if you and I were still to-gether."

"What did you say?"

"I told her we were."

"Why engage with that? You know what she's like."

"Because you don't gain anything by *not* engaging," Valerie said. "Not engaging shows her you care. I'd rather not give her that."

Nick opened his mouth to say, Well, just be careful — but thought better of it. Valerie, too, withdrew herself slightly.

"I'm wondering if she knew Elizabeth Lambert," she said.

"You asked her, presumably?"

"Yeah. She said not. But obviously we can't take anything at face value. He says the victims aren't random."

"People who pissed Katherine off?"

"It's possible."

"Not a bit obvious for him?"

"Maybe. But if he says they're not ran-dom, it's probably true."

"Or it's more smoke to eat up the hours."

There's something else I want to talk to you about.

"She looked surprisingly well," Valerie said.

"She's in solitary most of the time, right?"

144

"According to the warden. But the warden was half enamored."

Nick shrugged. "Must be like having one bright kid in a class of dummies," he said. "If she talks, it's hard not to listen."

"I thought Will was going to punch her at one point."

Be careful I don't creep in tonight, after you've turned your wife over.

"Why? What did she say?"

Now's your chance. Get it over with.

But she didn't. You don't want to know the things you want to know.

Instead, she shrugged. "She's always rubbed him the wrong way. Anyway, fuck it. Enough. This is delicious, by the way."

Valerie was annoyed at herself. This isn't *that* movie, either, she'd said. Wasn't it? Wasn't she, after minutes with Katherine, back in the Drift? When she was a kid in high school, her English teacher, Mrs. Hillyard, had given them a salutary little lesson in the power of language: Now do me a favor, she'd said. Think of anything you like except Napoleon's white horse. Naturally Valerie along with every other kid in the class had immediately had an image of Napoleon sitting astride a white horse. Language exerts control, Mrs. Hillyard had said. Poets know how to get images under your skin. Sometimes they do it without you even realizing it. It's one of the world's last forms of magic. So for all of you who think literature is a waste of time, just remember that. Control what's in a person's head, you control the person. In its lowest form it's advertising and propaganda. In its highest form it's art. Every time you open your mouth or write something down you have the potential to change the way someone thinks, and if you can change the way they think, you can change the way they behave.

And here Valerie was, *behaving.*

"You working?" Nick said, when they'd cleared away the dinner things.

"I have to," Valerie said. "Just a couple of hours." She had interview reports with Elizabeth's neighbors and family to go through. The postmark on the envelope had been identified and dated, too: Reno, mailed a week before Elizabeth's murder. For all the good that did them. The package of "clue" documents had been mailed from San Jose. Short of knowing they'd been put in a regular U.S. mailbox, that was as far as the information had gotten them. They knew which sorting offices the material had reached, and indeed the number of mailboxes in the offices' catchment area, but all that left them was looking at every box covered by street cameras. There were many. He could have had a third party make the drop, or made it himself, incognito. But most likely was that he chose a mailbox obscured from CCTV, if Katherine's claims for his tech omniscience were to be believed. The Bureau was looking through the footage, but it was needle/haystack labor. So far, despite the press release, they'd had only three probable hoaxes (no DNA or print match), two in San Francisco, one in L.A., but the "warned" victims were still under police watch, were still being investigated, were still gobbling up department resources and time.

"Okay," Nick said. "I've got some stuff to do as well. If I fall asleep, wake me up when you come to bed."

"All right."

"You always say all right, but you never do."

"You always look too peaceful. My kindness gets the better of me."

"Okay, but if I have a hard-on, wake me up."

"I'll think about it."

"I mean if it's *kindness* driving you."

It took longer than two hours, and Nick was asleep by the time she turned in. No hard-on, but he stirred and half woke when she slid in next to him.

"Doesn't seem like such a hot idea now, does it?" she said.

He put his arm around her and pulled her close. "Just give me five minutes," he slurred. "Then brace yourself." He kissed her neck and ran his hand down between her legs, cupped her there, snugly.

Within thirty seconds, he was deeply asleep again.

12

"Well, I think you're crazy," Valerie's sister said to her the following day.

"It's just work, Cass."

"For Christ's sake. Let Will talk to her."

"She's not going to say anything to Will."

"Right," Cassie said. "Because you and her have the special bond. Jesus."

It was a little after noon, and they were at the Volunteer Bureau drop-in center in Union City where Cassie, who worked there gratis twice a week, was just wrapping up her shift. Valerie had been in the neighborhood on a lead that had turned out to be nothing: Tech's trawl through Elizabeth's e-mail had revealed that she'd met up with an old college friend, Simon Garner, two weeks before she'd been murdered. According to her sister Gillian, a guy she hadn't seen in years. Valerie had questioned him, but even aside from him looking nothing like the Man in the Mask (he was five-seven, paunchy, and balding) he had a solid story and alibi. He'd run into Elizabeth more than a month ago at the Stonestown Galleria (where he'd been shopping with his wife of twenty years) and they'd swapped contact details. Two weeks later they'd met for coffee, caught up, and agreed to keep in touch. On the night of Elizabeth's murder, he'd been home with his family having a dinner party with two other couples, all of whom verified. He taught math at Mission Hills Middle School, and, with the exception of the occasional after-school club, was *always* home with his family. His narrative did nothing more than confirm her instincts, which had known, within the first few moments of speaking with Simon Garner, that he wasn't the man they were looking for.

Since she was driving right past the Volunteer Bureau, Valerie had stopped in to wish Cassie happy birthday, and to promise to do her best to get herself and Nick to the barbecue later that evening. The Bureau was half admin, half social club, a nonprofit coordination center that matched volunteers with organizations needing help; the "social club" was open to everyone from lonely retirees to adults with physical disabilities or nonviolent mental health troubles. Now that her kids were both in school, Cassie had gone back to ER nursing at St. Rose three days a week (the sisters shared a mutual I-don't-know-how-the-fuck-you-do-it attitude toward each other's profession) but still donated six hours a week serving coffees and lunches at the Bureau. See, you have this thing, Valerie had said to her, this *kindness* thing. You nabbed the whole genetic supply. There wasn't any left by the time I was in the womb. It was selfish of you, when you think about it. To which Cassie had replied, Yeah, you don't do anything for anyone except save their lives or catch their killers. You'll probably go straight to hell.

"You've done your time with that witch," Cassie said.

"Drop it," Valerie said. "It's not up for discussion."

There were a dozen or so visitors in the café. Three severe-looking old ladies were playing cards at a small table by the window. A woman in a floral-print housedress was at one of the two desktops, looking at wardrobes on the Home Depot Web site. An overweight guy with a shaved head and a lot of arm tattoos was sitting in a cracked vinyl armchair, having what looked like a furious whispered argument with an old blind guy seated in the wingback chair opposite him.

The blind guy's guide dog sat with his head in his owner's lap and a look of given-up hope that the argument would ever be settled. Glenn Miller's "Moonlight Serenade" was playing at a low volume.

"Don't tell me what's up for discussion," Cassie said. She was two years older than Valerie, a slim, energetic woman with their mother's high cheekbones and lively hazel eyes, who, kindness notwithstanding, was what their father had always called "a straight shooter."

"Fine," Valerie said. "It was up for discussion. We've had the discussion. She might be useful, so I'm using her. That's all."

"You're a moron," Cassie said. "And are you actually going to dry that cup or are you just going to stand there making love to it with your fingers?"

Valerie had absently picked up a towel for the dishes Cassie was washing, but she hadn't made much of an impact.

"Gentlemen?" Cassie said, looking past her.

Valerie turned. The tattooed guy and the old blind man were standing a few feet away.

"Are we doing this now?" the blind guy said.

"For Christ's sake," the tattooed guy said. "I just told you."

"Yeah, but have you got the —"

"Wait, will you? Jesus."

"What's wrong?" Cassie said.

"Could you turn the music down for a second?" the tattooed guy said.

"You don't like it, Tommy?"

"You should have asked Bree," the blind guy said.

"Will you just for the love of God let me handle this?" Tommy said.

"I like the music," the blind guy said. "Mainly because it actually sounds like music. As opposed to the goddamned car-crash crap some people —"

"Shut *up,* will you? I'm dealing with it."

"Tommy, John, easy, easy, calm down," Cassie said. Valerie concealed her amusement. She remembered these two from her last visit. They irritated the hell out of each other, though they always sat together, as if the irritation were a secret delight. You'd think Tommy was the problem, Cassie had confided to her. I mean, he looks the part. But that buzzard loves nothing more than jerking his chain. It's Tommy who gets John's coffee and sandwiches and helps him to the bathroom.

"We like it fine," Tommy said, taking a calming breath. "But could you just . . . just turn it down for a moment?"

153

Cassie shrugged, dried her hands, and turned down the volume.

"Okay, people," Tommy said, raising his voice. "One, two —"

"You said I was going to count us in," John said.

Tommy performed a sudden tension-relieving gesture by rolling his head on his neck. Another deep breath. "Fine," he said. "Go ahead. Jesus Christ."

John lifted his head and raised his voice. The guide dog looked up at him with forlorn loyalty. "One, two, three . . ."

Cassie's fellow volunteer, Bree, came in from a side door, carrying a chocolate cake with a solitary candle, as the room's group faltered their way into perhaps the least tuneful version of "Happy Birthday" Valerie had ever heard, and Cassie just stood there with her hands over her face.

The song ended with a round of applause as Bree set the cake down on the counter-top and Cassie bent and blew out the candle.

"Did she blow it out?" John said.

"Don't say 'she,' " Tommy said. " 'She' is right here in the room, for Christ's sake."

"Now, now, Tommy," Bree cautioned.

"I did blow it out, John, yes," Cassie said. "Thank you. You guys are totally evil. But I guess you all get a piece of this delicious-looking cake."

Bree handed her a knife.

"You know I'm only thirty-eight, right?" Cassie said.

Back at the station, Will had two updates.

"First, the white powder," he said. "It's flour. As in baking. Plain as opposed to self-rising. I went over there this morning: there's no plain *or* self-rising flour in Elizabeth's kitchen cupboards. Could be she had some that was old and she was throwing it out, but trash collection there is Tuesday mornings, and there was nothing like that *in* the trash that's still there now. If she threw it out before, it's not likely traces of it would still be there a week later — or at any rate not the amount you found. Second, we have the footage from the coffee shop CCTV. The only stuff available, but it's a block down from Elizabeth's, and shows only the interior, so unless he dropped in for a caffeine hit before doing his thing we're going to be sitting through hours of hipsters with laptops trying to look important and busy."

"Great," Valerie said. "I'll toss you for it."

"Screw that, it's your turn," Will said. "Plus, if I have to watch people who should be doing a real job instead of tweeting

155

pictures of their fucking croissants and nail polish *I'll* end up killing someone."

"Nothing from McLuhan?"

"They're doing a new streamline. They did it first time around, but they're redoing it so it doesn't feel like they're all just walking around in their suits pointlessly. Guys who fit the profile: educated California with old-money backgrounds with some connection to the tech smarts our guy has. So far it's the same list, but they're chasing it anyway, cross-referencing with cosmetic surgery, if you can believe that."

"And we still don't know how he got in?"

"Nope. Maybe he was an artisan flour salesman with samples."

"There probably is such a thing. It's Noe Hill."

"He either picked his way in or he knew her. Same story."

"All right, fine, I'll take the footage."

"It's on your desktop. I'm going to grab a sandwich. You want anything?"

"Vanilla latte," she said. "Since I'm going to be watching people drinking the stuff."

Valerie started on the coffee shop CCTV material. She'd gotten only five minutes in when she stopped it and smiled to herself. She hit REWIND, then PLAY again, and watched until Will got back with a meatball sub and her coffee.

"Look at this," she said. "Anything useful?"

Will came around to her side of the desk and observed, over her shoulder. As he had predicted, people talking on their cell phones, working on laptops, wiping cappuccino foam from their top lips. Occasionally a passing vehicle made the light in the café dim and flare. One of the baristas, a young Latina, took a moment to retie her thick dark hair, checking her reflection in the mirror behind the counter.

"Nothing?" Valerie said.

"What?"

"Seriously?"

"What?"

"For a man who looks in the mirror as often as you do . . ."

"Oh," Will said. "Ha-ha. Yeah. Fuck."

The coffee shop's mirror ran the length of the counter on the back wall of the café. The reflection, naturally, showed the *front* window, the outside tables beyond it — and a view of the opposite side of the street. The side on which Elizabeth Lambert's building stood. The building itself wasn't in view. It was too far up the block. But traffic, vehicular and pedestrian, was blurrily visible.

"Sherlock Hart," Will said. "Congratulations. There's sixteen hours of it. These guys are open seven till eleven."

"That's why we're splitting it. I'll go from here to five. You can start at five and go through till midnight."

"That's insane."

"It's the work."

"You can't see the license plates, Val."

"For all we know he was on foot. And I'll have a bit of that sandwich. It's too big for you. You know you made a Freudian choice with that, right?"

"What?"

"Meatballs. You're clearly still worried about your own."

It was irritating to have to keep waiting for — or fast-forwarding to — the CCTV's internal angle to switch back to the one showing the mirror's street view, and additionally maddening that the view itself was repeatedly impeded by the scuttling baristas. Plus, even when the view was clear, there really wasn't much to see. Traffic passed, but in profile. License plates weren't discernible and the light bouncing off the windows obscured the drivers anyway. There was a long, dispiriting stretch when two hipsters stood chatting to an old Ginsberg type at one of the outside tables, effectively blocking the view of the opposite sidewalk. She'd frozen the frame every time a lone male pedestrian appeared, logging the time codes for each (there were five), but no amount of scrutiny had yielded a face even vaguely resembling Katherine's guy. She would get the tech guys to do what they could with enhancement, but she wasn't holding her breath. Her sense of futility grew rather than diminished — until, three hours in, she found something.

A guy in a baseball cap, pale-blue overalls, and a backpack walked into the frame. Valerie had just time to notice he was carrying some odd-looking contraption before the Latina barista got up on a footstool to reach down for a mug and blocked her view. By the time she'd stepped down again, the guy in the overalls had passed out of the shot.

Her instinct twitched.

She rewound, slow-motioned, froze the frame. The pixelation was lousy. All she could really see of his face were sunglasses and a mustache and beard. Longish dark hair protruding from under the cap. She maxed out on the zoom option. Utilities? Maintenance? For the life of her she couldn't work out what he was carrying. It was a plastic gallon can filled with white liquid, with a hose attachment and a nozzle.

Spray paint? But why the backpack?

Even this slight speculation was enough to flirt a little more blatantly with her instinct.

She ran the footage again. Barely two seconds. But enough to see that the liquid in the container didn't move. So not liquid, obviously. Some sort of white powder.

Flour?

"Hey," she said to Will. "Have a look."

He looked up at her over his glasses. "It better be good," he said. "I've got a gal here with Lara Croft boobs. In a Lycra halter top."

"Just come and look."

He joined her. Watched.

"P. C. . . . S . . . ?" he read. The initials stenciled on the guy's overalls. "Looks about the right age and build. What's the gizmo?"

"Whatever it is, it's got white powder in it."

Valerie Googled "P.C.S. San Francisco." A first page of twenty hits. Personal Computer Services. Portable Cooler Supply. Pure Country Station. Pet Care Select. Primary Cosmetic Surgery. Pest Control Solutions.

"There," she said, clicking on the link. The uniform and logo didn't match, and the beaming controller lady in the picture looked considerably more high-tech tooled-up than the guy in the video.

"I don't like him," Will said.

"Me neither. And why's he on foot?"

"Keep the vehicle off camera."

"It's 4:12 P.M. on the coffee shop clock. Elizabeth got home around six."

"Enough time to get in and get ready."

"The backpack's wrong, too. Get on to P.C.S. Find out if they had anyone in the neighborhood. I'm going to get an enhancement and print of this and head back there. Jog some memories. Call me if anything else shows on the footage."

Thirty minutes later she was back in Noe Hill, doing door-to-door with the cleaned-up photo. Six queries in, she got a recognition.

"Yeah, I saw this guy. I talked to him."

The interviewee was Bernice Ashton, a spacey, big-eyed young mother with a toddler of indeterminate sex on her hip. The kid had longish dark corkscrew curls, but something made Valerie think it was a boy. Bernice and her husband lived three doors up from the coffee shop, on the opposite side, ground-floor apartment of a three-story just like Elizabeth's. She'd asked the guy if there were vermin in the neighborhood. Ants, he'd said. Farther up the block. "I was worried it was rats or something,"

Bernice said. "Ants I can deal with, but rats? Forget it. This is the murder — right? He a suspect?"

Beyond what the picture already told them, there wasn't anything by way of physical description Bernice could add. Dark hair and beard, shades, cap. Valerie asked about the accent. "Gosh, I don't know. I mean, he sounded well-spoken. I guess local. I mean, definitely not foreign or anything. We only exchanged like two sentences." The kid on her hip had his fingers wrapped up in her hair and was gently but insistently pulling. Bernice winced, reached up on maternal autopilot, and began untangling herself. It always amazed Valerie the way mothers seemed to accept the demotion of their bodies to the status of just another toy for their kids, a sort of experimental play station with things you could pull or push, pinch or squeeze or bite or suck on. It was no wonder so many of them looked like they were at the end of their rope. Would that happen to her if she and Nick had a child?

"Did you see him come back this way later?"

"No, but I was inside after that. I wouldn't have."

The rest of the footage would show that,

one way or another.

"All right," Valerie said. "Thanks for your help. Here's my card. If you remember anything else about him, give me a call. Any time, day or night."

She worked her way up the block, all the way back to Elizabeth's, with no further results. A uniformed officer was on guard duty at the secured scene — the same officer, Rockwell, who'd been first *on* the scene, and who'd removed Elizabeth's gag. She saw him tense slightly when he recognized her. She felt sorry for him but knew that if she referred to it directly it would probably embarrass him all over again. So instead she smiled and said: "You must be getting sick of the sight of this place by now."

He was relieved, and a little awkward in his relief. But visibly grateful. "I'm not complaining," he said. "Fresh air beats the squad car."

"You got keys?"

"Yes, ma'am."

She was at the side gate that separated the driveway from the backyard when her phone rang.

"What've you got?"

"Pest Control Services didn't have anyone scheduled to visit that area," Will said. "Our boy's not wearing their official gear, and that gizmo isn't theirs either. In fact they said it looked homemade. I've checked all the other companies offering the same service — ditto."

Valerie had the key halfway to the padlock on the gate. She stopped.

"Okay," she said. "We need to know if Elizabeth replaced any of her locks recently."

"Because?"

"Because the one I'm looking at is brand-new. So is the key."

Will's silence for a moment. Him working it out. "He bolt-cut his way in?"

"And put a fresh padlock on the side gate. Maybe. We need someone down here with magnification."

"I thought Sherlock always carried a magnifying glass?"

"Talk to the sister again. And the upstairs neighbor. Look at the rest of the footage and see if he shows up going back the same way."

Rebecca Beitner came down. Black light and magnifier. While she worked, Valerie went back into Elizabeth's apartment and retraced her original sweep. Nothing new.

"Val?" Rebecca called.

Valerie went out to join her.

"You're good," Rebecca said. She handed Valerie a Baggie and the magnifier. Without the magnifier the Baggie would have appeared empty. With it, Valerie could see two tiny metal fragments, perhaps a little wider than a human hair.

Later that night, at Cassie's after the party, Valerie and her sister lay sprawled in lounge chairs in the backyard, a big, lawned rectangle bordered by shrubs and jasmine, with a few small apple trees and the kids' swing set. It had been after ten when Valerie had shown up, and half the guests had already left. Nick, who had been there since seven, had drunk himself comatose on lethal margaritas mixed by Cassie's husband, Owen, and since Valerie and Cassie were now halfway through their third bottle of champagne, it was obvious no one was driving back to Cole Valley tonight. Their mother had made up the pull-out in the living room before she'd left. Owen was in the kitchen, washing the last of the wineglasses to the sound of Billie Holiday. Nick was asleep on the grass, lying on his back with one hand in his pocket. It was dark, but still warm. A few stars were out. The air was soft, edged with the scent of the trellised jasmine.

"I'm glad you came," Cassie said. "I know

it's not easy."

"Easier than turning forty," Valerie said.

"Rubbish," Cassie said, raising her bare leg, "I'm in hot shape for an old gal. Even Owen still wants to have sex with me. I love the bracelet, by the way. You must have spent hours choosing it."

"Very funny. Let me see it."

Cassie held out her wrist. It was a rose-gold chain with little green stones set between the links. It looked pretty against Cassie's tan.

"Green tourmaline," Cassie said. "I like the names of gemstones. Carnelian. Peridot. Chalcedony. I think I'm going to take up jewelry making when I turn fifty. I can see myself with a little workshop out back here. Don't you think?"

Valerie lit a Marlboro. Cassie topped up their glasses with the last of the champagne.

"How's it going with you two?" Cassie said.

"It's good."

Cassie observed the passed-out Nick. "A fine figure of a man," she said.

"He's not at his best at the moment, I admit."

A little pause.

"He's one of the good ones, Val," Cassie said.

"I know."

"I know you know. You know what I'm saying to you."

"Yeah: don't fuck it up."

"Exactly. Don't fuck it up. I know what you're like. The goddamned job."

"I did that already. I'm not doing it again."

"The worst mistakes are the ones that don't quit after one attempt."

"I'm not going to fuck it up."

A pause. "We might have a kid," Valerie said.

"What?"

"Assuming I'm physically capable."

"Jesus. When?"

Valerie didn't answer for a moment. "I don't know," she said. "Soon. Not another year. Well, definitely not another two years. However long it takes."

She felt Cassie working it out. "However long it takes you to catch this fucker."

Valerie didn't need to confirm the reasoning.

"Why do you do this?" Cassie said.

"Do what?"

"Why do you make everything depend on things like that? It's like some sort of dumb superstition. It's idiotic."

"It's just clearing the decks."

"You don't *need* to clear any decks. Just

walk off the deck. Let someone else clear it. Christ, I can see I'm wasting my breath."

"You're wasting your breath."

"And *this* deck. Fucking hell. Katherine Glass."

"We're not having this conversation again," Valerie said, closing her eyes.

Cassie was silent for a few moments. Then she said, with an almighty effort at reasonableness: "You know why you're back in this with her?"

"I'm back in this with her because he sent me the note. Naming her."

"That's superficial. You're back in this with her because you're afraid of her."

"I'm not afraid of her."

"You're afraid of her and it's not acceptable to you that there's anything you're afraid of."

Valerie didn't answer.

"You don't feel justified unless you defeat the things you're afraid of. I know that feels like some sort of fucking medieval nobility to you, but you're wrong. There's nothing shameful in walking away from what you're afraid of. Some things are worth being afraid of."

"Not this thing."

"You're insane."

"Fine, then give me my bracelet back."

They fell silent again. Valerie finished her cigarette, felt Cassie letting it go.

The door to the sunroom opened and Owen stepped out.

"Jesus," he said, "I wish you guys would stop working so hard. You're making me look bad."

13

Forty-two-year-old U.S. Postal Service mail carrier (and former assistant postmaster) Raylene Ashe was in the middle of feeding her late father's tropical fish when the doorbell rang. It was just coming up on eight fifteen in the evening.

"Balls," she said, more or less to the fish. "If that's Jessica back again I'm going to throttle her."

Jessica Bradley was one half of the retired couple who lived across the street. The Bradleys had been friends of her father's (her mother had died of liver cancer when Raylene was just seventeen) and Jessica had decided, when Raylene moved back to Portland two years ago to help her sister care for her dad, to take her under her wing. The husband, Karl, was undemanding: Raylene exchanged pleasantries with him if they happened to be out in their front yards at the same time, and that was as far as it went. But Jessica had taken to coming over to chat on an almost daily basis, frequently (as she had a couple of hours ago) pouncing on Raylene with baked goods the second she got home from work. Superficially, she was a sweet and well-intentioned old lady. Not so superficially, she was an indefatigable narcissist who saw in Raylene a captive audience for her endless narratives of self-congratulation. "Watch out for Jessica," Raylene's father had warned her. "The woman's a goddamned psychic vampire. You think Karl's quiet? Not by nature. He's been *drained.*" The Bradleys had been in a state of nervous excitement all day because their son Christopher was arriving to drive them up to their daughter Janine's in Seattle for their grandson's twelfth birthday party. Raylene had heard the details more times than she cared to remember.

She headed for the front door, mentally scrabbling for a reason not to invite Jessica in. She hadn't come up with one by the time she got there and opened it.

Turned out she didn't need one.

Just beyond the edge of her front porch a blond, bearded guy was kneeling over the prone body of a dog, a pale Labrador. There was blood on the animal's fur, and on the guy's hands and pale-green T-shirt. He looked up at her as she stepped out. Unnaturally blue eyes staring out from a face in shock. There was a canvas man-bag on the ground next to him.

"Ma'am," he said. "Could you . . . I'm sorry, but my dog's been hit and my phone battery's dead. I need to get him into a . . . I guess I need a taxi."

"Oh my gosh," Raylene said, coming down off the porch. "How did this —"

"He *never* runs into the road like that," the guy wailed. "I should've had the leash on. Oh, *God.*"

"Didn't the driver stop?"

"He didn't stop. I can't believe he didn't stop. Please, could you call a cab for me? I mean, maybe there's an animal ambulance service or something?"

Raylene wasn't given to panic. Her brain was already working. The *dog* was probably in shock. She would call. And bring a blanket. Should she offer to drive them herself?

"Where's the nearest vet?" she said. The guy was walking his dog, so he must be local.

"My regular's downtown but they're not twenty-four hours. Do you have . . . If you can get online . . . Just put in —"

"Okay," Raylene said. "I'm on it. Hold on."

She hurried back inside and went down the short hall into the kitchen, where her laptop was open on the breakfast bar. Before fish-feeding duties had interrupted her she'd been looking at microwave ovens on Amazon, since the one her father had had for years had gone kaput a week ago. She Googled "24 hour emergency vet Portland." The usual top five ads, with, underneath, a dozen full listings. The nearest looked like the VCA Southeast.

She carried the laptop into the living room and set it down next to the phone. She got halfway through dialing before something made her turn around.

The guy was standing a few feet behind her, with the canvas bag over his shoulder and a gun in his hand. Pointed at her.

"Don't make a sound," he said.

The impulse to scream tightened in her throat. Her mouth opened. But her brain stopped her. Her brain insisted the only thing preventing him from pulling the trigger was her *not* screaming. She did, in fact, make a small sound, the very beginning of what would have been her scream. Then the neural embargo fell. Very quietly, she said: "Please, don't."

"Lie down on your front," he said. His voice was calm, polite authority.

She just stood there. Her limbs were haywire. Heat filled her face. Her body was a warm mirage. A sound came from the hallway: the dog letting out a sigh.

"Please," she began again — but he took two quick steps toward her, raising the gun to the level of her face.

"Do exactly as I say," he said. "Get down on the floor. On your front. Hands behind your back." And then as if in afterthought: "Or I will shoot you in the head."

The words. Each one of them a nail driven in to force her to accept this was real. This was really happening to her. This was the *only* real thing. Her whole life up until this point had been a dream. Because none of it could help her. Not her father's laugh nor her mother's face with a smudge of icing sugar on her cheek. Not the idle hours with her sister, Allie, the two of them lying on their bellies in the yard in summer, flipping through music magazines and arguing over which celebrities were hot. Not all the days and weeks and years of going about her business, buried in work, occasionally noticing the beauty of a blue sky or leaf shadows on the sidewalk. Not dreams, not friendship, not love. It all rose up, precious and illusory and useless, because here was suffering, here was death, and nothing — *nothing* — had power against it.

It was barely a couple of seconds, but a dreary logic worked through her: if she lay down he would do something — tie her up, knock her out — to give his power leisure. He would rape her. At the very least he would rape her. But if she didn't lie down he would kill her. *He'll kill you anyway. You've seen his face.* Not all rapists are murderers. *This one is.* It had layers and conflicts and dead ends, this logic. Its strongest force insisted the only thing that mattered was the prevention of her death. And if she didn't lie down her death would come not in an hour or a day but now. *Now.*

She got down on the floor. It was almost impossible, to volunteer the action, to put herself further into his hands. But not dying — *now* — overrode everything. She told herself she would survive this. There would be time. Seconds, minutes. Time would furnish her with a way of surviving whatever happened. Whatever happened she would, when it was over, be alive.

Unless he kills you.

He knelt and put his knee on the back of her neck and pressed the gun's barrel to her skull.

"Hands behind your back, please," he said.

Her hands were heavy things. All the weight of her will was in them, saying: *don't . . . don't . . . don't . . .* Her arms moved slowly, bewildered, not understanding how they could be asked to do this impossible thing. She thought she was going to pass out. A part of her wanted it, to be sucked into unconsciousness, to be taken out of the equation, to be *gone.*

She heard the soft sound of his other hand going into the canvas bag. His silence was concentrated, a dense energy that filled the room. The room itself was in bright shock, all its details fierce with helplessness. Her father's brown suede Barcalounger. The rickety standard lamp she hadn't had the heart to throw out. Her own black knee-high boots standing by the kitchen doorway, one upright, the other half flopped over.

Something made of tough plastic snapped around her left wrist. A sound like a zipper, then another snap around her right.

The pressure came off her neck but was transferred almost immediately to her calves. He knelt on her with both knees now, a sensation so intimate and intense it triggered a wild reflex in her. A roar of misery pulled itself out of her throat and she began to struggle crazily against him.

Her body had this extraordinary capacity, it turned out, to take the law into its own hands, regardless of logic.

"Stop," he said. "If you struggle, it'll be worse for you. Please understand that."

His weight shifted again and she felt his fingers in her hair. Her head was yanked back and smashed down against the floor. Red pain exploded in her nose. The gun jammed hard against her ear. She was aware of the sound of herself, sobbing. It was as if she were hearing it from a long way away.

"Do you understand?"

The wild reflex was a single firework, spent in a second, her will the fading trail of sparks. Something in her that wasn't her body strained to get out. This part of her was desperate to leave her body behind. She thought of all the times she'd heard about rape. For the first time she felt it as a real thing. She knew now that, for every woman this happened to, none of the hearing about or thinking about or trying to imagine it would mean anything. There was only ever one real rape. The rape that happened to you.

He cuffed her legs.

Her voice was an automatic thing, a separate mechanism out of her control. She was saying: "Don't hurt me. Please don't hurt me. You don't have to do —"

He grabbed her and flipped her over onto her back, her tied wrists trapped under her. She felt a warm trickle from her nose. Blood. The sensation brought her childhood close. The surprise of it, the sudden little tenderness and sympathy for yourself. She was glad her parents were dead. They wouldn't have to know this had happened to her. At the same time she felt the dark openness of death and the unknown beyond rearing up on the edge of her awareness like a part of deep space where there were no stars. She wondered if she would cross over and see her mother and father again. If there was an afterlife, maybe they were watching this right now. Their little girl.

He ripped a length of duct tape and plastered it over her mouth. Her screams with nowhere to go dinned in her head. Hope rose in her that he was just going to rob the place. She couldn't believe she hadn't thought of this until now. She'd been so stupid. She should have said: There's money, credit cards in my purse. Right there on the couch. She tried to communicate it now, with her eyes, but he turned and walked away.

She heard him close the front door. When he came back in he was carrying the dog.

He laid the animal down on the floor and went past her into the kitchen. The dog blinked at her, groggily. It had an aura of sadness. She pictured him jabbing at it with a knife. She wondered how the creature could stand being handled by him. Some indestructible loyalty. She felt vomit rising. Fought it down. She would choke.

More sounds. He was in the utility room, which opened off the kitchen. From the utility you could get into the garage. He was stealing the car. He was stealing the car! Thank God. Thank *God.*

He came back into the living room and went straight to her purse on the couch. He was a thief. She couldn't believe he would kill her if he was just a thief. She was going to live. It was a great upwelling of relief to her. She was going to live. There were tears on her face. There was the warmth of the blood and the cutting pain of the ties on her wrists. There were all these sensations that testified to the life she still had and the life she would have beyond this moment. It was almost unbearable that she couldn't be certain of it.

He took her keys. For the car. And her wallet. Money. Good. *Good.* He was taking the car, cash, and credit cards. If she'd been able to speak she would have urged him on:

Yes, yes, take it all. It's yours. Take them, please, and go.

Just don't hurt me.

He didn't look at her. He carried himself as if he were alone in her home.

He left her again. Every atom of her being devoted itself to listening. To confirming that he was here to rob her, nothing else.

Sure enough, she heard the car start and the garage door open. It was hard to breathe through her smashed nose. The initial explosion there had receded. Now there was a deep rhythm of pain. Very bad pain. Getting worse. She imagined herself in the hospital. Nurses. The smell of antiseptic. Calm, routine capability, devoted to addressing her injuries. Just let me have that. Just let me have that and I'll never ask for anything else as long as I live.

She tracked the sounds, built the picture from listening. He pulled the Honda out of the garage and down the drive. The engine idled for a few moments, then died. The driver door opened and clunked shut.

Pause.

Drive away. Please, God, just drive away.

The car door opened and closed again. It sounded farther away. How was that possible? The engine started up. Wait. Not her Honda. A different car.

The same sequence of sounds in reverse. A vehicle coming *up* the drive and pulling into the garage. The garage door's mechanism cranking to life. The garage door closing.

He wasn't stealing her car.

Before she had time to think through what had just happened he was back in the living room. He was a little more aware of her now, as if he couldn't quite deny she was there. He still didn't look at her. Instead, he picked the dog up and went back into the kitchen.

He was putting the dog in the car?

What was this?

Her mind raced through a mess of possibilities. Got nothing. She couldn't make sense.

He came back to her. For a moment he stood over her. She shook her head: No, no, no. It was the only gesture of negation she had left. His face was wet with sweat, his mouth clamped shut. He breathed heavily through his nose. He looked remote and furious.

Then he bent down, grabbed her under her arms, and began hauling her toward the kitchen. She struggled. Adrenaline was frantic in her limbs. He ignored her. The bright furnishings of the clean kitchen and the bamboo shadows on the countertop. All the moments here, coffee and her father shaking his head at the latest political nonsense in the newspaper. Her and Allie sitting here after the wake, when everyone had left and the strange reality of both their parents dead had asserted itself like a new quality to the room's sunlight and silence. There had been love in the family. This house had been filled with taken-for-granted blessings. That time when her father, out of the blue, had put his hand over hers across the breakfast bar and said, with an awkward, quiet intensity: You're a good girl, Ray. What'd I do to deserve such good daughters?

They were through the utility room.

He turned her. Her knees scraped the edge of the doorway into the garage.

A silver car she didn't recognize backed in.

The trunk was open.

14

Valerie sat at her desk in the apartment, headphones on, listening to the tapes of the original interviews with Katherine Glass. It was late. Nick was in bed, asleep. But for the light from her screen the place was in darkness. It had been a hot, humid day, the city laboring under the weight of a storm that refused to break. Even indoors Valerie could feel it, as if the sky had piled up slabs of iron. It had given her a headache, though that hadn't stopped her getting halfway through a bottle of Smirnoff.

Ten days in, the investigation had made little progress since the discovery of the replaced padlock on Elizabeth's side gate. Or rather, only the cold comfort progress of routine elimination. McLuhan's people hadn't gotten anywhere with the paintings, poems, and letter grids. They'd conscripted a mathematician, an art historian, a linguist, and a professor of English literature, as well as their own code specialists. So far every attempt to find a coherent message in any form had failed. McLuhan, Valerie knew, was no longer convinced that there was a coherent message to be found. He'd managed to persuade Donna Clayton to grant Katherine access to a computer, under the strict supervision of Agent Arden, via whom Katherine had sent two communiqués back. The first was in response to the photo of the Noe Hill "pest controller."

Dear Valerie,
I've looked long and hard at the picture you sent. I can imagine how badly you want a positive ID from me. Believe me, I wish I could oblige. The truth is that while none of the superficial characteristics match — beyond skin color, height, and build — I can't definitively rule him out. However ludicrous this might sound, there's something about the cast of the shoulders (he always had enviable posture) that is pure "Lucien." In addition, the hands, which, for obvious reasons, I know very well. The image isn't sufficiently clear, but they look deeply familiar. If it is him, he's had work done. The nose, possibly even the jawline. (This over and above changing

his hair; or is it a wig? It looks suspiciously lustrous.) I'm assuming the Bureau is looking into cosmetic surgery patients to match whatever maddening short list they've drawn up? But I should warn you that if he went under the knife for this he won't have been dumb enough to have had it done locally, or even nationally. Again, I remind you: he has the resources. He could have gone to India for all we know. He's had six years.

I'm sorry to be inconclusive, but honesty (I know: a dirty word from my mouth) is better than either false elimination or false hope.

Thank you for working your magic with Warden Clayton. I am behaving myself scrupulously with the computer, as dear vigilant Agent Arden will aver, but even with cyberspace at my disposal, it's painfully slow going. Slow going, but not, I think, a waste of time.

K

The second came a few days later:

Dear Valerie,
The Bureau eggheads must all be committed skeptics by now, but there is

185

something here. The references he's sent are just markers. We've got to look between them. For example: Any idiot can find the relevant dates for the paintings and the poem, or birth and death dates for their creators — and though I believe the key to the letter grids has to be numerical, the numbers won't be in the surface information. They'll more likely derive from events the dates book-end. There's a great deal more I'm working on, but it would take time to explain, and since time — obviously — is what we don't have, I shan't waste any on hypotheses. The FBI will give up on this. I will not. Please don't let them pull the plug. I know what I'm doing.

K

For the rest of the investigation they had gone through the motions. They'd interviewed everyone identifiably connected with Elizabeth Lambert and had built a near complete picture of her movements in the days preceding her murder. Nothing out of the ordinary. On the assumption that the killer had watched her, they looked at all the available CCTV footage from places Elizabeth had been in recent weeks. Nothing suspicious and no one matching either

Katherine's description of the man who wasn't "Lucien Chastain," nor the pest controller. Elizabeth's surprising sexual encounter with Luke Russell yielded nothing except for the consensus that her getting laid was long overdue. For the period in question Russell had a rock-solid alibi: flight records verified that he'd left San Francisco the day after his birthday party and hadn't returned until two days after Elizabeth's death. On the Thursday Elizabeth was killed, he was on camera at his niece's school concert in Los Angeles, which took place between five and seven P.M. His sister's family confirmed (incredulous at being asked) that aside from when they were asleep, he was in the sight of at least one of them for the entire duration of his visit. He *volunteered* fingerprints and DNA. No match. Game over.

Not that Valerie had had the remotest belief it would be any other way. Katherine's lover wouldn't have fucked a target — let alone in such a socially visible way — a week before he killed her.

Everyone had been going through the six original case files, and everyone had been forced to concede that they yielded nothing new. After Katherine's arrest and apparent cooperation Valerie had asked her for places she'd been with "Lucien." Restaurants, gas stations, airports, hotels, in the hope that somewhere — *somewhere* — he would show up on CCTV. Katherine had said: You don't seem to be getting this, Valerie: it wasn't that kind of relationship, candlelit dinners and movies and walks on the beach. We knew what we wanted from each other, so we maximized that. That, and nothing else, aside from telepathically transparent conversation. All the things you do with Nick, all the ordinary things that knit you together with casual ease — we didn't do any of them. We didn't *need* any of them. The time we spent together wasn't measured in minutes and hours, it was measured by what we did with it.

Katherine hadn't seen him use the same vehicle more than twice, and of those she could remember only two: a silver Mitsubishi and a black Prius. She had no clue what years or license plates, but all the cars felt new. They ran traces on registered vehicles matching the descriptions going back five years. No dice. Several had been reported stolen — and never recovered. The ensuing probe into car-theft gangs and distributors turned up a single lead: in return for a blind eye to his trade, one of the fences they questioned admitted doing a deal on a silver

Mitsubishi a few weeks before the first murder. The customer description didn't match Katherine's — and the vehicle itself was never found.

A shiver of lightning lit the apartment. Thunder. A sound like a cosmic explosion that made it through the headphones. Valerie looked up from the screen. The first berry-sized droplets were striking the windows. Within seconds it was a furious downpour. She lit a Marlboro and increased the volume.

K: I've always liked it. For as long as I can remember. Even as a child it seemed the most natural thing. Though even as a child I knew it had to be hidden. None of this would even be worth mentioning if I were a man. But a woman? I do realize that as far as the world's concerned there's no excuse for any of this if you don't have a dick.

V: That's very interesting, but where did you meet Lucien Chastain?

K: In a cocktail bar in Manhattan. A place called Full Moon on Second Avenue, in the East Village, but I don't think it's there anymore.

V: What were you doing in New York?

K: I had some free time. I felt like going, so I went. There was a Mondrian show at MoMA. I stayed at the Empire Hotel on Broadway, where we spent the night. I don't know how long they keep their CCTV, but of course you'll check that. He told me he was staying at the Plaza, but that could have been a lie. He did have a cute opening line.

V: What did he say?

K: He sat down next to me and said: Only in Manhattan is a beautiful woman alone at a bar actually a beautiful woman alone at a bar.

V: What was he doing in New York?

K: He just said business. Finance. He wasn't specific. Don't you know what it's like when you know someone, instantly? Wasn't it like that for you and Nick?

V: And where did you meet after that, when you were back in San Francisco?

K: Monstrosity gives you the gift of being able to recognize other monsters when you meet them. I've wondered if it's actually pheromonal. And if it's peculiar to monsters. Surely when you and Nick laid eyes on each other —

V: Where did you meet in San Francisco?

K: Are you blushing?

V: Please just answer the question.

K: My apartment. Always and only my apartment. Always and only at night. If it had been a horror movie — a *different* kind of horror movie — I'm sure I'd have found myself wondering if I was sleeping with a vampire.

V: And in all that time you never knew where he lived, what he did for a living?

K: It was only later that he told me he was rich. He didn't do anything for a living. You're not understanding this, Valerie. Recognition on this scale, you don't bother with favorite colors and what music you like. After our first night together all the relevant information was in. We knew what we needed to know about each other. We knew *everything* we needed to know. Telepathy's not a rumor, it's a fact. There's a flicker of it between you and me, as you well know. I can see it in your face. You've got a little tumor of anxiety about what it might be like to have someone completely at your mercy. Or what it might be like for Nick. Only the very dull never wonder. It's the refined consciousness, the subtle soul, for whom the question never quite gets answered. And for better or worse, you *are* a refined consciousness, a subtle soul. Nick, too. It's why you became cops. You needed an antidote to your own latency. Stupider people become priests and nuns, but we've all seen where *that* leads. It fails as an antidote because it's a closed world. It encourages secrecy. Cops have to wear their morality in public. You've done the smart thing: you've made your own potential an unaffordable luxury. . . .

Valerie switched off the recording and removed her headphones. The rain was a deafening static. Six years ago she'd been less the cop than she was now, but even allowing for that she should never have given Katherine the room she had to talk. Nick had stopped sitting in on the interviews after the first two or three. It's not worth it, he'd said. She seems like a mystery, but she's not. She's just another person with the same old disease. We should leave it to the Feds. She's a dull contaminant, that's all. I don't need it and neither do you. But Valerie had carried on. She'd persisted. Why?

The lady doth protest too much, methinks.

"Hey," Nick said, startling her.

"Jesus Christ."

He put his hands on her shoulders, laughing. She had jumped, visibly, in her chair. "Sorry," he said. "I thought you heard me."

"You nearly gave me a fucking heart attack."

He bent and kissed her neck. "Come to bed," he said. "I just had a dream."

"About me?"

"No, sorry. Kylie Minogue."

"That midget?"

"She rescued me from hell and then insisted I go down on her."

"What was hell like?"

"A huge moldy basement with depressing

water pipes and air ducts."

"That doesn't sound so bad."

"Well, I wasn't happy there, I can tell you. There were people with huge axes for heads and their limbs on backwards. And all I had on were my socks."

Valerie looked at the desktop clock: 3:42. She'd have to be up in three hours. "Okay," she said, "but I'm disappointed with this Kylie business. If I come to bed I'm going straight to sleep."

She didn't go straight to sleep. After a few minutes of lying next to Nick and knowing he was awake, too, she said: "Something I never told you."

They had love enough to sense the moments.

"What?" he said. Quiet. Calm. Whatever it is it won't make any difference. He didn't need to say it. It was coming off him like radiant heat.

"When I was a kid, about I guess nine or ten. There was a girl in our neighborhood, Dalia Poole. I think she was a couple of years older, but she was mentally not all there. She couldn't resist us, you know, the little gang. She wanted to be part of it, even though we tormented her."

"Every neighborhood had one," Nick said. "Ours was a kid we called Mr. Ed. Because he looked like a horse."

"It wasn't just that we tormented her," Valerie continued. "We used to *trick* her. Into thinking that this time it was going to be different. Like whatever game we were playing, we'd let her join in. The thing was to lull her into a false sense of security. You could see the transition in her face. She'd approach us nervously because she remembered what happened last time, what happened every time. But we'd be friendly to her, and her face would go from suspicion to trust. That was the thing: we had to make sure she wasn't expecting anything bad to happen."

"And then you made bad things happen. It's nothing. It's kids. We did the same shit."

"One day there were four of us at this guy Joel Gaynor's house. Me, him, Dalia, and my friend Frieda Sumner. We had Dalia pinned down and we all took turns pinching her and scaring her and lifting her dress."

"Come on. Kids are cruel. You have to learn your way out of it. You did."

"Joel let his spit drip into her face. Frieda did it, too. When it was my turn, I couldn't do it."

Nick had the sense to wait. Valerie could feel him thinking it was nothing, making

195

room for it, easily, consigning it to the category of childhood peccadillos.

"I couldn't do it. I don't know why. I think it was because I imagined some weird mix of my mom and God watching. But I wanted to. Not just the usual shit of not wanting to be the odd one out, the sissy. I remember the fascination, that I could do this thing and nothing would happen. It was as if I would know something, something secret and momentous if I did it."

"So you did it."

"No, I didn't. But while I was sitting there, on Dalia's legs, and Frieda had her arms, Joel put his hand under my skirt, between my legs."

"And it felt good."

"Yes. I liked it. The two things were connected. Dalia's face wrecked with misery and the good feeling from Joel's hand. It was like the room's heat had been turned up. I felt rich."

Nick turned toward her and draped his arm across her. Pulled her toward him. "How many people do you think have something like that?" he said. "It's what we do. It's what we find our way out of. You can't seriously . . . I mean, it's just —"

"I know," Valerie said. "I know all that."

"So?"

"I know," she repeated. "But for a long time afterward, when I got myself off, I thought about it."

"These are small things," Nick said. "You know this. These are the small things. The common things."

"I know," Valerie said again. "I've done all that. Put it in perspective. I know it's a common thing. I know I'm not a monster." A pause. Then she added: "I know I'm not Katherine."

"So why are you telling me?"

"I've never told anyone. You say it's a small thing, but I still wanted you to know."

"Valerie, for God's sake. I assume something like that anyway. I assume something like that for *everyone*. It's nothing. It's not even worth remembering. We pulled Mr. Ed's pants down and Tony Cardillo put molasses and Cheerios all over his dick. You think I'm proud of that?"

They lay for a while without speaking. She didn't know whether she felt better or worse. Better, she supposed, both for having opened this small closet to the man she loved and for having him confirm it didn't matter. But Katherine's question wouldn't go away: Do you think Nick fantasized about me? It was Mrs. Hillyard and Napoleon's white horse all over again: if Valerie

197

asked Nick and he *hadn't* fantasized about Katherine it would be all but impossible for him not to now, just by having the idea in his head. And if he had fantasized about her, would he own up to it? Would he consider it in the same department of harmless peccadillos? Would she? That, of course, had been Katherine's entire motive in asking her in the first place: to put her in an impossible position.

"Just don't say anything," Valerie said.

"Okay."

"Let's go to sleep."

They lay still. The rain stopped. A block away, a truck downshifted with a gasp of hydraulics.

"Can I say one thing?" Nick asked.

"What?"

"You're the best person I know. You're the best person I've ever known. I know *you* don't think so, but there it is, for the record."

"You've got low standards, that's all."

"That's probably true, but they're my standards, regardless. Or it could just be you've got the prettiest ass in the Western world."

"Good. Don't go east."

To Valerie it seemed as if she'd slept for seconds when her phone rang, but when she opened her eyes it was gray daylight outside and Nick was already up, making coffee. She was annoyed at herself for getting sucked back into the useless recorded interviews with Katherine: all those hours she could have been getting the rest her body screamed it needed. Now here was the day again, with its demands — and the silent perpetual insistence that for someone, somewhere, time was running out.

She groped on the nightstand for her phone and checked the screen: VIC MCLU-HAN CALLING. The familiar cocktail of excitement and dread.

"Hey, Vic," she said.

"I just got off the phone with Portland Homicide," McLuhan said. "We've got another one."

Now Valerie felt sick that she'd slept at all.

"Our guy?"

McLuhan paused. She could sense him wishing he had something else to tell her.

" 'Fraid so," he said. "There's another note for you."

15

"He put her clothes back on when he was done with her," Carlton Reed told Valerie and McLuhan. "Presumably because he needed somewhere secure to put the note and the rest. Make sure you guys got it."

Reed was Portland Homicide, a tall guy in his late thirties, with long eyelashes and a calm, sensual mouth, skin the color of a strong latte. He'd met Valerie and McLuhan at the airport and driven them straight to the scene, an area of woodland some four miles northwest of the blink-and-you-miss-it town of Estacada, about thirty miles southeast of Portland and a couple of miles west of Mount Hood National Forest, where the body had been discovered by an insomniac dog-walker just before dawn. Portland CSI had found the note in the victim's pocket, and Reed — having actually *read* the Bureau bulletin that had gone out after the Elizabeth Lambert murder —

had called the local field office straightaway. As a result, word had reached McLuhan, and two of the FBI's Evidence Response Team had come in to assist. Valerie had read a scanned copy of the note on the flight.

Dear Valerie,
Manifestly, you have been too slow. Perhaps Raylene will help you toward the nonrandom nature of my selection? Do keep an eye on your inbox for the next special delivery — although since you couldn't solve the first puzzle, I fear for your chances with the second, which will be more demanding. You are getting the best possible minds on the job, aren't you?
    In the meantime, happy viewing. Apologies for the format, but I'm sure you understand.

"The format" was a DVD, sealed in waterproof packaging and shoved into the back of the victim's jeans. The Portland team had taken the prints and run the disc on a laptop. Because he hadn't been able to stop himself, Reed had watched the footage. Beyond telling them that it recorded the torture and murder of Raylene Ashe he'd said nothing, but Valerie knew he wasn't the same man he'd been a few hours ago. She was live to the admission of another person to the wretched club, the latest initiate into the sad freemasonry. She wanted to take him aside for a moment and say: I'm sorry. If I'd known, I would've told you not to watch.

"ME puts time of death at forty-eight hours plus," Reed said. They'd left the nearest road a few minutes ago and been on foot since then. It was warm and dry under the evergreens, with a soft layer of pine needles underfoot, that smell of an old wardrobe and the deadened acoustics of trees packed close, like a soundproofed room. "Her purse was right by the body. Driver's license, credit cards, even a few dollars cash. There's a second CSI at her address right now. Blood on the living room floor and, weirdly, on the front lawn. We've got a poor-quality tire dry-cast from near where we parked, but there's no way of knowing it's his. Make and specs are coming. Okay, here you go."

Reed lifted the tape and they ducked under. The scene was tented, and four CSI personnel were wrapping up their sweep. Valerie, McLuhan, and Reed donned protective gear and entered the tent. Inside were two Portland agents, Juliette Niles, a tall, slim woman in her early thirties, with copper-colored hair tied back in a ponytail, and Louis Frost, slightly shorter than his colleague, with a dark crew cut and fierce blue eyes. Reed did the introductions.

"The ME's gone," Niles said. "But he'd determined strangulation before we ran the disc. Multiple cuts and contusions. Her left ulna's broken. Cigarette burns. It's all as per the footage, obviously."

And here's another one, Valerie thought. Another two, in fact, since it was obvious from Frost's drained expression that he'd watched the DVD, too. Both agents were making an effort to remain crisp and professional, but there was no disguising that they'd paid the voyeur's price.

"She had this clipped into her hair," Niles said. "She's not wearing it in the footage, so he definitely put it there."

"This" was a small flower. Purple, half browned since it had been plucked, and about the size of a gumball, sealed and labeled in clear plastic.

"Mean anything to you?" McLuhan asked Valerie.

"No."

"I've sent an image of it to our forensic botanist," Niles said. "We're waiting for an ID."

Which won't help, Valerie's bitter inner

voice said. Aloud, she said: "Let's take a look at her."

The body of Raylene Ashe had been bagged, but at McLuhan's insistence not removed from the scene. Juliette undid the zipper. The sound of the little mechanism seemed loud and raw in the stillness of the tent.

No matter how many times Valerie went through this the moment of shock remained. Not the shock horror of her first months on Homicide, but the poignant shock to which it had given way, the sad jolt that testified to the victim's lost personhood, a living being brutally translated into a corpse. All that life, all the feelings and experiences, memories, thoughts, dreams, anxieties, desires, the perpetual prosaic symphony that Raylene Ashe would, just like everyone else, have taken for granted — gone. Some people, Valerie knew, were not so unthinking as to never consider their own death. Hardly anyone considered their own murder. Not until their murder was staring them in the face. In that moment it would seem to them that their entire life had been leading them, treacherously, to this. It would seem that their entire life had been an act of cruel distraction, a long joke designed to conceal its disgusting punch line.

There was nothing to say. Everyone in the tent stood in silence. The gendered responses flickered between them: Valerie and Niles excruciatingly sensitive to their own bodies, imagined in place of Raylene's (the burns in the V of her shirt were clear to see); McLuhan, Reed, and Frost conceding that a man had done this to a woman. A man, as they were men, a woman, as Valerie and Niles were women. The questions surged, unspoken and useless.

"I just wanted to see her face," Valerie said.

Niles closed the zipper with slightly ugly haste. "She's been swabbed," she said. "But we know what we're going to find. The DVD makes it clear, unfortunately."

"Run it," McLuhan said. Valerie was aware of him forcing procedure back in, after the moment of nauseous intimacy.

"I don't need to see it again," Frost said. "I'll step out, if no one minds."

"Go ahead," McLuhan said. "I want to see if it gives us anything by way of location."

"It doesn't," Niles said, but she took her laptop from her shoulder bag and flipped it open.

Back at Reed's car Valerie lit a Marlboro. The video hadn't, as Niles had predicted, helped them. It showed a windowless room, bare but for plastic sheets on the floor and the sad heap of Raylene's clothes and purse in a corner. Raylene cuffed, wrists hooked to the ceiling, ankles — a metal rod kept her legs apart — bolted to the floor. On almost tiptoe, as he obviously liked it. (The cold ironist in Valerie noted that Katherine spent a lot of her time these days wearing just such restraints.) The killer was in the mask familiar from the footage six years ago, a strange, eye-holed leather thing that covered his hair, nose and cheeks, a twist on Valerie's notion of a Viking helmet. No tattoos or scars, no distinguishing marks at all. Just a medium-build white guy in good, trim, muscular shape. Not a *Baywatch* lifeguard, but women would approve when he took his shirt off. Valerie remembered the earlier footage: Katherine running her gold-painted fingernails lightly over his abdomen, doodling in Danielle Freyer's blood.

McLuhan's phone pinged the arrival of a text: Niles had heard back from the forensic botanist on the flower clipped into Raylene's hair. McLuhan read the message aloud:

"Globe amaranth. *Gomphrena . . . globosa.* Clover-like flower heads. Papery flowers that last a long time. Depending on the variety, flowers are white, red, pink, lilac, or purple. 'Strawberry Fields,' with bright-red blossoms, and 'All Around Purple' are popular. Requires full sun to partial shade, moderate water. Grows as an annual in all zones."

"All zones," Reed said. "Fucking great. What's next?"

"Raylene's home," Valerie said. "We have to know how he's getting in. You've got door-to-door going on there, right?"

"My partner's been there since this morning. So far zippo."

"Let's go," McLuhan said.

Raylene's two-story was middle-class Portland suburbia, a whitewashed building with red roof tiles and a faux Spanish facade. Some developer's misguided idea of a hacienda villa.

Reed's partner, Burdeck, a gaunt guy with dirty-golden hair and greasy skin, was still on the scene.

"No one saw anything," he said, after Reed had introduced them. "There's blood on the lawn and inside, but not much. No street cams here, obviously. Would your guy have known that?"

"Yep," Valerie said. "I'm sure he would."

One of the CSI team appeared in Raylene's doorway, one hand in a thumbs-up, the other raised, holding a sealed Baggie. "I guess they found what you said they'd find," Burdeck said. "Here. Gloves."

The Baggie contained another painting on a postcard, sans stamp and postmark. This time the picture's title was printed on the back: *Landscape with the Fall of Icarus — Pieter Bruegel the Elder c. 1525–1569*. Of the image itself, Valerie noted a guy in period dress with a horse-drawn plow in a field on a cliff by the sea. Galleon-type ships on the water. More cliffs, clouds. Beyond remembering from high school that Icarus was the mythological guy who flew too close to the sun, so that the wax on his homemade wings melted, and he fell, Valerie knew nothing of what it might mean. The handwriting was the same as on the postcard she'd found at Elizabeth's, and the message was, to her, unambiguous:

Number Two: 073115

"July 31, 2015," McLuhan said. "Fuck."

"You're looking for an envelope, too," Valerie told the CSI guy, beyond whose scrub mask she could see only a tan face and gentle hazel eyes. "McLuhan? You got the image? The last one was printed, but just bag every envelope you find. Trash,

208

recycling, the house, everything."

They were interrupted by the arrival of a large SUV, which was halted by the two uniforms at the taped barrier. A worried-looking elderly couple and a guy in his late thirties got out. After a few moments' tense confab, one of the officers came over.

"Karl and Jessica Bradley," he said. "And their son, Christopher. They live right there." He indicated the bungalow opposite Raylene's. "They just got back from their daughter's in Seattle."

"Let them through," Valerie said. "Stick to the perimeter. I want to talk to them."

It took a while. Following the Bradleys into their house, Valerie could feel their quivering mix of excitement and fear. *The police.* The dizzying discrepancy between TV cop shows and the actual arrival of *crime,* in your life. Jessica Bradley, a small hawkish woman in her seventies with large, neurotic eyes and pinned-up gray curls, couldn't get the key in the door, her hands were shaking so badly. Her husband, tall, headmasterly, with a shock of white hair and a tough, thinned-down masculinity, had to take over. The son, Christopher, had his father's height, but he looked like his mother. He was carrying at least thirty pounds more than was good for him.

"We were with our daughter," Jessica kept repeating, as if it were the credential that would resolve everything — whatever everything was. "I mean, we're never away. We're *always* here. Normally she comes to us. But it was Matty's birthday. That's Janine's middle boy, just turned twelve. What's happened? I mean what *is* this?"

The Bradleys' home was scrupulously tidy and unassumingly furnished, with a smell of carpet cleaner and, faintly, medicine. The living room was a photo gallery of children and grandchildren: thin fair hair and Jessica's slightly unhinged eyes had been inherited here and there. You shouldn't notice that a family was plain — not under these circumstances — but Valerie couldn't help it. She came from a good-looking clan. Nick was good-looking. Unjust life was unjustly kinder to you if you were. She thought of Katherine again, for whom "good-looking" was a ludicrous understatement. Maybe if you looked the way she did, your life went too far past kindness, into the wide-open territory beyond, where anything was possible.

Valerie knew from experience with people like the Bradleys that the best way to get the information through was by way of a dispassionate report of the facts. The body of a woman we believe to be Raylene Ashe has been found. This is a murder investigation. When did you last see Raylene? Did you notice anything unusual or suspicious in the neighborhood?

It took a while before her questions were actually landing. Jessica's tears came after the first phase of disbelief and denial. Even then, as the old lady plucked a handkerchief from her sleeve and dabbed at her nose (her long nostrils had turned raw with the first sob) she couldn't quite accept it. Valerie could see her going down mental avenues in search of a way back into a reality where this couldn't have happened. Every one of them, naturally, a dead end. Karl Bradley, meanwhile, sat next to his wife and rubbed her back, speechless. He hadn't said a word since Valerie had broken the news. Partly the shock, but partly a paralysis with which Valerie suspected he was struck when anything came into his life with a huge emotional demand. Born in the forties, grown up in the fifties, he was of a generation of American men who Did Not Cry — for fear that if they did the entire apparatus of manliness would unravel.

"Oh my God," Jessica said, suddenly arrested by a thought. "Was it the man with the dog?"

"What man would that be?" Valerie asked.

"Oh my *God,*" Jessica repeated.

"Easy, Ma," Christopher said.

"Just take your time and tell me," Valerie said.

"Just before we were leaving," Jessica said. "I was on the phone to Janine saying we were expecting Christopher any minute . . . and I was saying that I wish he hadn't left it so late because I don't like for anyone to be driving in the dark. We were all packed and ready to go, and I'd just gone into the little room at the front to look and see if Christopher was coming."

"You didn't tell me this," Karl said, breaking his silence. "How come you didn't tell me this?"

"You were in the *yard,*" Jessica said.

"Please go on," Valerie said.

"I was looking out," Jessica said, "and I saw Raylene in her doorway just there, and there was a guy kind of kneeling on the lawn. He had a dog. . . . It was lying down, so I didn't see it at first, but Raylene was talking with this fella about something. I mean, it was weird that he was on her lawn with the dog, but I thought maybe he was someone visiting. But right then Christopher drove up and I . . . You know, it took my mind off it. And then you" — to Christopher — "said you were starving and could I fix you a quick sandwich and then Karl couldn't find his reading glasses and by the time we got going . . . I mean I was planning to pop over to Ray's and say good-bye, but it was getting late and Karl said leave her in peace. I was going to go over there!" This last was with compressed anguish. Another nail of the fact of Raylene's death had gone in. They would keep going in, Valerie knew, over the days and weeks ahead.

"Don't blame yourself," Valerie said. "Believe me, it's better for you you didn't go over there."

"I don't get why you didn't tell me that," Karl said.

"It went out of my mind!" Jessica wailed.

"Mom, take it easy," Christopher said.

"What time was it, roughly, Christopher, when you arrived?" Valerie asked, notebook and pencil poised.

"Oh, gosh, I don't know," Christopher said. "Maybe around seven?"

"No, no, it was past eight," Jessica said. "Because I remember thinking it was going to be so late when we got to Janine's, and she said she was going to let the kids stay up. You know, they still get excited to see us."

"Could you tell me what this man looked like?" Valerie asked.

Jessica shook her head. "I just saw him from the back," she said. "I didn't see his face at all. Do you think . . . I mean, could it have been *him*?"

"You saw the back of his head?" Valerie said. "What about his hair color?"

Jessica went through a visible effort of recollection. "I guess kind of a dark blond," she said.

"Long? Short?"

"Over the collar, I think. Oh, God, I *wish* I'd gone over there!"

"What was he wearing?" Valerie asked.

"I can't remember. Wait — maybe a khaki jacket . . . Or light green. I really couldn't see properly."

"What about the dog?" Valerie said. "Could you see what kind?"

"No. Light-colored, though. I could barely make it out."

"Did it seem to you that Raylene knew him? Did she seem at ease when she was talking with him?"

Jessica shook her head, pressed the handkerchief to her nose, had another moment of teary disbelief. "It's no good," she said. "I don't know. It was just a couple of seconds. Just a few seconds and Christopher's car pulled up. Oh, dear God, I can't believe poor Ray's gone. How can this happen? I mean, what kind of person . . . ?" She trailed off, shaking her head. Then a little viciousness took her. "You're going to get him, aren't you? You're going to get the man who did this?"

"We'll get him," Valerie lied.

"If someone did that to . . . If someone . . ." Fresh tears. "She was such a good girl!"

Valerie wondered how long she, Valerie, could keep doing this. Facing the demand for justice knowing justice was never enough. Knowing justice couldn't bring back the dead. Death had been part of her life for so long she couldn't remember who she'd been before. She knew she had been innocent, a child, a girl, but the recollection was intellectual. Now death felt like part of her DNA. When she and Nick talked about having a kid, neither of them could really face the question of whether Valerie would carry on working Homicide. It *was* unimaginable. To go home from a day like today carrying the images of Raylene's torture, Raylene's rape, Raylene's corpse — to read *The Hobbit* to a wide-eyed daughter. She always thought she would have a daughter rather than a son — and even that, she knew, was driven, perversely, by the knowledge that the world was less safe for girls. She couldn't think of having a baby without thinking of it as female, with all the wretched possibilities that entailed. For a moment, just then, it seemed absolutely clear to her that she *shouldn't* have a child, that she would never be able to bear the fear of what might happen to it. Her. What might happen to her.

"One last thing," she said to the Bradleys. "Did either of you notice any car or vehicle you didn't recognize parked on the street? Not just on Friday. I mean anytime recently?"

The Bradleys looked at one another, sadly. No.

It was after midnight when Valerie drove back from San Francisco International alone. McLuhan was staying in Portland to force a rush on the evidence found at the scene.

Perhaps Raylene will help you toward the nonrandom nature of my selection?

Assume that was true. (While simultaneously suffering the knowledge that it might well be false.) Nonrandom how? He knew them. They knew each other. They knew Katherine. They had something in common.

Nothing, on the face of it, indicated that they had anything in common, except that they were both more or less single, both over forty, both childless divorcées, and both either lived or had lived in San Francisco. Elizabeth had been a lifelong local, born in Sausalito, where her parents and her sister, Gillian, still resided. Raylene had been born in Portland, but moved to San Francisco when she was twenty-two, whereafter she'd worked in the postal service for seventeen years (married for four) until she moved back to Portland to take care of her father. They were physically dissimilar. Elizabeth, fifty-four, was thin and angular, with dyed auburn hair, pale green eyes, and a complexion that had been kept out of the sun. Raylene, forty-two, had long, dark, thick wavy hair and eyes the color of prunes. She was fuller-figured, with a tan body that was manifestly no stranger to the gym. At the USPS she'd gone from processing clerk to city carrier, then through a confusing three or four job title changes until she'd made assistant postmaster at the San Francisco office. Transferring back to Portland had forced her to take a salary cut and step back down a couple of rungs, but according to her sister, Allie, Raylene had been determined to come home for what they both

217

knew was going to be their father's last few months.

Sexual and romantic background so far (with Raylene's investigation barely begun) was unspectacular. Certainly nothing in Elizabeth's case that yielded a suspect. Portland PD was interviewing, but not, as yet, with results. On the surface Elizabeth Lambert and Raylene Ashe were two women with quiet, ordinary American lives.

Postal Service. His penchant for letters and packages? It sounded ridiculous. And Elizabeth had nothing to do with the U.S. mail, as far as they knew.

She'd have to show Katherine the picture of Raylene Ashe. Do you know her?

The answer would be no. Which in any case couldn't be trusted. No matter what contortions Valerie went through, they left her at the same impasse: Katherine could neither be trusted nor ignored.

It was as if, in the cosmic scheme of things, that was the fucking *point* of Katherine.

16

Everyone was in early the following morning.

"Okay," Valerie said. "We've got fake Pest Controller out to all the agencies. Katherine's description and composites plus CCTV still are going to the national press today. It's probably only going to make life harder, but right now we don't have a choice."

She was standing in front of the board, the Murder Map, which, around the pinned-up photos of Elizabeth and Raylene, looked ominously ready for more. Next to Elizabeth's picture was a blow-up of the postcard she'd received, Lucas Cranach's *Adam and Eve*. Next to Raylene's, another enlargement of Bruegel's *The Fall of Icarus*. Valerie's online research had turned up the painting's little joke, a detail of the canvas she hadn't noticed at first: the small splash in the ocean and Icarus's legs disappearing beneath the water, while the farmer went on with his plowing, oblivious.

"We've got three women, all of whom — since the press release — have received warning postcards, now under surveillance and investigation. There's no physical evidence from *their* postcards and envelopes to tie them to our guy, but we have to take them seriously. What we do have is metal fibers from the driveway at the Elizabeth Lambert scene to suggest that he used bolt cutters to get in through the side gate, then replaced the padlock and key. As far as we know Elizabeth didn't have the padlock changed herself. If he got in through the kitchen door we have to assume he picked the lock, because there was no sign of forced entry there. It's a mixed MO, but that might well be for our entertainment."

The team bristled, slightly. At this stage, Valerie knew, they were still sharp. This was the mental crispness you got at the start of a serial investigation. Which would be eroded by each additional victim. You had to maximize the window, get as much done while the energy and belief were still there. Soon — another dead woman, two, three — the shoulders would drop and resignation would fill up the room like a stale smell.

"The Raylene Ashe MO looks *completely*

different," she continued. "Neighbors saw Raylene talking to a guy with a dog on her front lawn on the evening she was most likely abducted, a guy for whom what little description we have clearly doesn't match Pest Controller, though it's closer to Katherine's original. Unfortunately we're dealing with someone who both (a) has most likely changed his appearance physically since the original murders and (b) is capable of inhabiting convincing disguises on top of that. The fact that Raylene was talking to him doesn't mean she knew him, but we have to go down that road too, especially if we're attaching credence to the idea that the victims are, in his words, 'nonrandom.' Portland PD and the Bureau field office there are dealing with that line of investigation. Elizabeth was killed in her own home. Raylene was taken somewhere, then dumped. I doubt any others will be killed at home. Elizabeth was just the initial calling card. A rush job to get our attention. We know he likes time, privacy, leisure. The damage Raylene suffered testifies."

"What's the deal with this Icarus painting?" Sadie Hurst said.

"You know the story of Icarus, right?" Valerie said.

"Yeah: he made some wings out of feathers and wax, and flew too close to the sun, and the wax melted and he fell."

"So the painting is about how when big things happen, no matter how big they are, to someone they're just a missed detail. The ordinary world goes on, no matter what. Something like that. Icarus falls, the farmer doesn't notice, just carries on with his plowing."

"You think it's a coincidence that Raylene worked for the postal service?" Laura Flynn asked. "I mean, this letter fetish . . . ?"

"Unknown," Valerie said. "I've got a call in to Raylene's former employers at the service here in San Francisco and in Portland. We'll be getting a list of her colleagues from her time there, as well as the routes she worked when she was on the beat. It's possible she delivered our guy's mail. Or maybe even Elizabeth's."

"Or Katherine's," Will said.

A palpable negative charge at the mention of the name.

"Yes," Valerie said. "Or Katherine's."

"Anything from her?" Ed Pérez asked, with visible skepticism.

"No."

"She must be loving this."

Valerie didn't answer.

"I mean, for Christ's sake," Ed said. "He

could have planned all this ages ago. I know her mail's checked, but they could have one of his fancy codes going between them. He could have been corresponding with her from day one. And if he's so loaded, what's to say he hasn't bought every screw in Red Ridge, including the warden?"

"Of course that's a possibility, however unlikely. But what do you want us to do, Ed? Ignore the package he sent?"

"No, just leave it with the Bureau. If they can't crack it and someone dies, tough shit. We did our best through legitimate means. That's assuming there's genuinely anything to crack, which I doubt. It's a waste of time."

A murmur of assent went through the room. And underneath it something worse: the unspoken suggestion that Katherine's involvement was down to Valerie's fascination with her, regardless of its relevance to the case. In spite of herself Valerie felt her face warming.

"It's costing us one federal agent," she said.

"Until she starts feeding us bullshit," Ed said. "Then it's going to start costing us a whole lot more."

"Look, Ed, it's noted. At the moment it's a risk I'm willing to take. I don't think she's going to give us disinformation, but if she does, it's on me. As she said herself: she gets one life in this game. She blows it, she's out."

Two hours later, McLuhan called from Portland. Valerie was at her desk, drinking the morning's third cup of wretched station coffee.

"The blood at Raylene's place isn't blood."

"What is it?"

"Corn syrup and food coloring. Fake. Most of it, anyway. Couple of drops inside are real blood. Hers. DNA and prints all match."

Valerie downloaded. " 'Help me, I've been in an accident'?" she said. "No — wait. 'Help me, my *dog*'s been in an accident'?"

"Maybe. Sympathy hook. Like Bundy with the arm in a cast. Was there any at Elizabeth's?"

"Not found. But if it's his entry MO it would've been by one of the doors and there's nothing like that in the report. Plus we've got the replaced lock that says he got in that way. The scene's been released, anyway. Is the blood commercial or home-made?"

"Impossible to tell. According to forensics it's missing something called methylpara-

224

ben, which would have increased the likelihood of it being commercial, since it acts as a preservative, but really, there's no way of knowing. It's more likely homemade. A purchase would leave a trail."

"Okay," Valerie said. "But we know what he can do with dummy credit cards."

"There's one other thing. From the door-to-door. One of the other neighbors — a teenager — says he saw a guy sitting in a silver car he didn't recognize as one of the regulars on the block. On the evening Raylene was snatched."

"You got a description?"

"Nothing beyond blond hair and beard. Usual average-everything-else. The kid was on a skateboard, so, a glance, he says."

Blond hair and beard. The blond hair fit the Bradleys' sketch — and Katherine's description — but again, not Pest Controller.

"We might've heard about this earlier," McLuhan said. "But the kid's an apprentice stoner, barely thirteen. Needed to work up to it and get rid of his stash."

This was the way it happened, Valerie knew, as if Crime were an intelligence that used its minor aspects to conceal its major ones.

"Obviously this doesn't help with Pest

225

Controller," McLuhan said. "But we're just going to have to stick with running them as separate suspects."

"Yeah, well, if he can do fake blood he can do wigs and beards."

"I'm e-mailing you the report right now. We're looking at traffic cams on the exits and approaches to Raylene's neighborhood, but it's going to take a while. I'll let you know if we get anything."

"Got it. Thanks."

Will looked over his desktop. "I think the postal fixation's just a joke," he said.

"Because?"

"He knows his own CV: high-tech smarts. So he goes old-school. Paper. Stamps. Post-cards."

"And?"

"And nothing. I'm just telling you because you don't think I go in for psychological speculation."

"I never said any such thing."

"You don't have to say it. You're subtextual."

"I wish I'd never taught you that word. In fact now that I think of it I'm pretty sure I said sub*sexual.* Anyway, heads-up: fake dog-blood at Raylene's. I'm e-mailing you the latest. Make sure everyone —" Her cell phone rang again.

"Valerie Hart."

"Detective?"

"Yes?"

"It's Connie Lopez calling from USPS. You spoke to my colleague, Jason Darnell? About the routes for one of our former employees? Raylene Ashe?"

"Right. What've you got?"

"I'm sorry it's taken this long, but you might know we're in the middle of an industrial dispute at the moment and it's been . . . Well, anyway, we have some of the information you requested."

"You've got all the addresses?"

"Not all of them, no. Problem is a lot of carriers work pivot and we don't have all the records for that."

"What's 'pivot'?"

"That would be when a carrier's route doesn't necessarily take the full eight hours, so they get shifted — that's the 'pivot' — onto a secondary route to make up the time. I mean it can happen on a daily basis."

"At this stage I'm interested in the primary routes. Addresses you know she hit with some regularity."

"Right. I can send you a pdf for everything we've got. I'm sorry it's not . . . I'm sorry it doesn't cover everything. We're still waiting on the office in Portland for over there, but

227

they've promised it before five this afternoon."

"Great. Send through what you have, and the Portland list as soon as you get it. You have my e-mail address?"

"Yes ma'am, Jason passed it on."

"Okay, I'll be waiting. Thanks for your help."

"Make sure everyone what?" Will said, when Valerie had hung up.

"Make sure everyone gets the dog and fake blood update. Okay. Here's the list of Raylene's San Francisco routes. Jesus, this is a lot of addresses."

"It's not worth it, Val. It's *remote.*"

"Tell me what else we've got?"

"Yeah. I know. But *fuck.*"

"Why are you in such a bad mood?"

"Where do you want me to start?"

"Anywhere other than your balls."

"Listen. You're a woman. You don't know. When your balls are wrong, everything's wrong. Plus, if your boyfriend beats me one more time at racquetball you're going to have another fucking homicide on your hands."

"He beat whatsisname a couple of weeks back."

"Squash Boy? Eugene?"

"Yeah. I'm name-blind with that guy.

Who's called 'Eugene' in the twenty-first century?"

"You haven't met him?"

"I met him once for about five seconds."

"Nick's so gay for him."

"I'll tell him you said that. And that it's got nothing to do with how much the squash has killed your racquetball."

"You should be worried. Eugene's a bad influence. Tales of sexual liberty. I'm just saying: these things rub off. The grass is greener, et cetera."

"Greener than *my* grass? I think not. Now stop talking to me, please."

Valerie started on the list. It established that neither Katherine's last address nor Elizabeth's had ever been on any of Raylene's regular routes — but nothing else. She cross-checked the Bureau's revamped short list of profile possibles: none of their addresses either. More joyless elimination.

When Will went to get lunch an hour later she went with him. Not for food, but to smoke three cigarettes and pick up a coffee that was actually drinkable. She was in a phase of eating virtually nothing during the day. Not vanity. Sometimes the work just took you that way. The coffee and cigarettes flew by and before you knew it it was dark out and you hadn't had a bite for twenty hours. Lately, Nick had been forcing her to eat some sort of breakfast, even if it was just toast, and he gave her a hard time if she didn't eat when she got home. It had occurred to her that he was (subconsciously, probably) trying to keep her healthy so that she could Carry His Child. About which she couldn't resolve herself. She wanted it, yes — but every time she conceded she did her inner voice said: Not yet. Not *yet*. It wasn't that she couldn't see a future in which she and Nick had a child. She could. (In fact, the ferocity of her latent mother-hood terrified her; she knew she would be a lost cause, dangerous, precarious, crazy with love.) It was just that she couldn't imagine that future starting right now. But every now was right now, every time she tried to imagine it. Soon, she would run out of right nows. The countdown to infertility went on, no matter how many murderers you caught. And now, dear God, the return of Katherine Glass and the Man in the Mask. Neither she nor Nick had needed to say that *this* right now was absolutely the wrong right now. In the moment of thinking this clearly for the first time (as Will supervised the building of his enormous sandwich amid the deli's cheery colors and reassuring products), she knew, in a humble but lucid epiphany, that if she caught the Man in the Mask, if she put him away, if she took that *particular* ugliness out of the world, she would be ready. She would say to Nick: Now. Let's do it. It was arbitrary and dangerous and irrational. But she knew the equation was set. Standing there in the sunlight, in that moment of realization, Valerie felt the street, the city, the world, suddenly scintillate, as if with delight that she'd worked it out at long last. The certainty and the risk of it dizzied her. But it was fixed in her now beyond argument. She imagined telling Cassie. You're fucking insane, her sister would say. When she imagined telling Nick it was immediately apparent that she didn't need to. He already knew. After this one. After we get him. (After *Katherine.*)

"Here," Will said, handing her the to-go cup. "You got a free cookie the size of your head. I think Ashan's got a crush on you."

"No, he's just a feeder," Valerie said. "You should be ashamed of that sandwich."

Her phone rang. She didn't recognize the number. A little awkward negotiation with coffee cup and cigarette to get it to her ear. "Valerie Hart."

"Detective, it's Susanna Arden. I have

something. Katherine thinks she has a name."

Valerie stumbled mentally. Hadn't McLuhan told his agent the next victim had already been found? It was, she supposed, possible that he hadn't, occupied with rushing things up in Portland, and in any case convinced that the Katherine Glass line was a waste of time.

"She cracked the documents? What's the name?"

"She's not a hundred percent," Arden said. "The sequence of the letters is uncertain because she can't pin down the number order for the second grid. But what she's got is 'Helena Ayres.' " Arden spelled the surname. "Or possibly 'Helena Sayer,' although that doesn't sound a likely surname to either of us."

Valerie tossed the cigarette butt and stubbed it out with her toe. *To either of us.* She wondered what it was like for Arden to be spending so much time with Katherine Glass. She wondered if they felt like a team, two schoolkids working on an intriguing assignment. "Well, tell her thanks for playing," she said, "but we already have a second victim. Not that name. She get anything else?"

A slight pause, in which Valerie could

sense Arden's irritation that this news hadn't reached her. It wasn't Valerie's responsibility, but she still felt guilty. "I thought McLuhan would have told you. Sorry. The body was found this morning. Portland. Your boss has had his hands full. He's probably on his way back here now."

"Right," Arden said. "I see. Well, no, there's nothing else."

"You should get out of there," Valerie said. "I know it can't have been any kind of fun."

"It's weird. She was so convinced. So was I." Arden sounded genuinely deflated. "I'll call McLuhan. I've had just about enough of this place."

Back at her desk (woozy from too many smokes crammed into too short a time; if she was going to have a kid, all *that* would have to stop) Valerie wrote the name "Helena Ayres/Sayer" on the yellow legal pad next to her keyboard and picked up where she left off with the list of addresses.

She'd only been at it a couple of minutes when she stopped. The legal pad kept insinuating itself in her peripheral vision. She picked up her pencil. Her hands were sensitive, suddenly. The room noise around her receded.

Crossword and sudoku specialists will be of little use to you.

It was as if she could feel his body heat right next to her.

H E L E N A A Y R E S, she wrote, in capitals.

Oh.

Her brain had gone on ahead of her, but she forced herself through the confirmation.

Underneath, she wrote R A Y L E N E A S H E.

Then she began striking through the corresponding letters, one by one. She did it twice, just to be absolutely sure.

She sat back in her chair.

The sequence of letters is uncertain because she can't pin down the numbers in the second grid.

"Will," Valerie said. "Take a look at this."

17

Valerie met Katherine in the same visitor room as before. Warden Clayton wasn't available but sent one of the guards to show her in. Valerie recognized her from the previous visit: the narrow-shouldered woman with too much mascara. Her hair was in the same French braid. LOMAX, the name tag said. Small talk en route to A-2 was labored.

"She been any use to you?" Lomax said.

"Hard to say just yet," Valerie replied. "We'll know more after today."

"You did her a big favor. Got her out of her cell."

"Well, not for nothing, I hope."

After that, they walked in silence. There was a little energy coming off Lomax, as if she were pissed about something. Not a very bright person, Valerie thought. She could imagine how many of Katherine's velvet-wrapped put-downs had landed here, or

passed just over Lomax's head, leaving her
with the knowledge that she'd been mocked
without any comprehensible proof of it.

Two more guards, one male, one female,
were on duty outside the open door to A-2.
Katherine, in the same fatigues and restraints as before, sat at the Formica table,
facing the door, laptop open, surrounded
by papers filled with notes and numbers.
Other sheets with printouts from Web pages.
Agent Susanna Arden sat just out of arm's
reach but with a clear view of the screen.
Again, there had been no forewarning to
Katherine of Valerie's visit.

"Valerie," Katherine said. Then a smile. "I
don't know if I'm right with the name."

"Well, you're either very close, or it's an
almighty coincidence."

Valerie crossed to where Katherine sat and
picked up what Katherine had been writing
with: a half-blunt wax crayon. Of course: no
sharps. She wrote the name "Raylene Ashe"
in the margin of one of the printouts (an
extract from something called *Lives of the
Artists,* by Giorgio Vasari). She turned it to
face Katherine.

For a couple of seconds Katherine studied
it. The same curious psychological nudity of
her face, stripped for a moment of its usual
look of strategy. Valerie observed her unfold-

ing the anagram.

"Fuck," she said. "Right letters, wrong order." Then, as the realization dawned, she looked up at Valerie. "Wait. You have this name because . . . Oh. I'm sorry."

"Yeah."

"She's dead, obviously."

"Found yesterday. Filmed, this time."

"What did he leave you?"

Valerie showed her the note, the postcard. "You know this?"

"*The Fall of Icarus.* Yes, I know it. It's a very famous painting. But it's not about the painting. It's for me. It's a reference. 'Musée des Beaux Arts.' A poem by W. H. Auden."

"Want to clarify that for me?"

"It doesn't matter, does it? I mean, this woman's already dead. The poem's about suffering, and the universe's indifference to it."

"Another of your landmark conversations?"

"Well, we did have them. Instead of the movies and the walks on the beach, as I said."

"I'm going to need you to detail the process," Valerie said. "How you arrived at the right letters, albeit in the wrong order."

"Why would I do that?" Katherine said.

"Because I don't doubt we're going to get more of this shit."

"I don't doubt it either," Katherine said. "But you're asking me to render myself redundant."

"What?"

"If I tell you how I did it, you won't need me when the next shit, as you tellingly put it, comes in, and I'm back to spending all but two hours a day staring at the ceiling and masturbating. Even for me there's a limit to the diversion value in that. My mental material gets worn, as will a brass doorknob, with enough handling, enough time."

They looked at each other. Valerie was aware of Agent Arden's tiredness. Naturally. She'd spent hours, days with Katherine. The cost was visible. Not just in the dark eyes' deepened orbits, but in the slightly unraveled composure, an effect similar to a shirt done up with one button in the wrong hole. McLuhan should've sent someone older, with circuits already burned out.

"I hope you're not trying to dictate terms," Valerie said, though she couldn't quite hold Katherine's eye as she spoke.

"Don't look away," Katherine said. "Looking away betrays weakened resolve. You know I only need an inch for my miles."

Valerie's skin warmed. There was a heat to Katherine that reminded her of an operating room lamp. She forced herself to look back at her, eye to eye.

"Did you ask Nick?" Katherine said.

Don't look at Arden. Don't say anything. No. Say something.

"Sure," Valerie said. "We had an interesting conversation about it. Probably not as erudite as yours with your boyfriend about Adam and Eve or poetry or whatever, but still, definitely worth having."

The latent smile that was always on Katherine's lips burgeoned fully. Years ago, Valerie and Cassie had visited Europe. In the Louvre, the line to see the *Mona Lisa* had crawled. It had taken them an hour to get themselves in front of the canvas. Behind them were two stoned British girls with loudly dyed hair: electric pink, electric blue. One of them had said to the other: Well, at least now we know what she was smiling about. She had a premonition of all the millions of morons who were going to wait forever in a line to get five seconds to wonder what the fuck she was smiling about.

"That was a lie, Valerie," Katherine said. "Good people are terrible at lying. I know. It's one of the perks of being a bad person.

Don't go down that road. You don't have what it takes."

For the first time in a long time, Valerie wanted to hit her. Not just hit her. Rip her to pieces. She felt both the impulse — and the futility that followed it, immediately.

"Think what you like," she said, and via some miracle managed not to look away. But Katherine's eyes were unbearable. They were full of recognition. For a moment, neither of them spoke. Valerie could sense Agent Arden observing, actually with relief — because it wasn't just her Katherine managed to mess with. Yeah, Valerie felt like saying, welcome to the fucking Katherine club.

"I don't think what I like," Katherine said. "I think what I can't *not* think. As do you. Clarity of consciousness is the curse of the wicked as well as the good."

For no reason other than to break what was between them, Valerie moved back around to the other side of the table. There was no chair there, so she leaned against the wall. It was, regrettably, good to take some of the weight off her feet. She felt as if she'd *walked* all the way up here.

"The novelty of you wears off, Katherine," Valerie said. It surprised her. Not just because it had come out unpremeditatedly, but because she couldn't remember ever addressing Katherine by name before. Was that possible? In all the hours they'd spent in conversation? It was almost obscene, an unwanted feeling of intimacy that spread from her mouth (having spoken the word) through every part of her body. The operating room lamp warming her limbs. With a subtle, true, horrible adjustment, Valerie knew it could be slightly arousing. *Katherine.* Such an ordinary name. Such an extraordinary person.

"I keep forgetting how much you've changed," Katherine said. "How much more room you have, how many layers have been stripped away. You wouldn't have been capable of saying that six years ago. Not convincingly, anyway. And yet here you are, saying it. And, courtesy of the same wretched and infallible talent, I know you're *not* lying. Or that you're only half lying. Either way, it's impressive. We could have been something, you and I. Imagine if we'd been sisters. We are sisters, in a way. Tied by blood. *Shed* blood, but still, blood."

Sisters. It ruffled Valerie that only moments ago she'd been thinking of her and Cassie in the Louvre. It was, she told herself, just paranoia that made her wonder if Katherine hadn't somehow picked that up. She imagined her own thoughts coming off her like invisible flames. Invisible to anyone but Katherine. With Katherine you were handicapped as much by what you didn't say as by what you said.

"Well, it's up to you," Valerie said. "Tell the Feds how you did it — or your involvement's over and you can go back to staring at the ceiling and masturbating."

"Can you afford that?" Katherine asked.

"What?"

"Can you afford for it to get out that you had the means — or at least the chance — to prevent the next murder, but didn't use it?"

"Yes," Valerie said. "We can. It's the same logic as not giving in to terrorists' demands. The public will understand. In any case, it wouldn't get out."

"There's directness," Katherine said, "which you've clearly acquired — and then there's brittle bravado, which doesn't suit you at all. First, don't be so sure it wouldn't get out. I'm in prison, not on Mars. Second, I'm not talking about the public. I'm talking about the loved ones of the woman who ends up dead. Don't answer that 'we' can afford it. I'm not addressing the collective psyche of law enforcement. I'm addressing *you,* personally. I'm asking if you want it on *your* conscience."

Katherine never raised her voice, and she didn't now. But the operating room lamp heat went up a little. Valerie was aware of Arden wondering which of the two women in the room with her was crazier.

"I'm not worried about my conscience," Valerie said.

For a moment Katherine didn't reply. Arden shifted in her seat.

"Yes you are," Katherine said. "It's your one weakness. Well, that and love."

"Fine," Valerie said, straightening, taking her weight back onto her feet. "You're making the decision for me."

Katherine, who had been leaning forward on the desk, now eased back in her chair. Her white hands were like two rare and lovely flowers in her lap. She sighed, then looked at Valerie as if with an invitation to stop teasing each other. All right. Come on. I know we've been playing. Let's be friends now. Valerie forced herself to give nothing in return, neither resistance nor concession. She just held herself still. A little backroom or subdepartment of her consciousness was, however, enjoying the discovery of a new working maxim: if in doubt, say nothing.

"Sorry," Katherine said. "It's my fault. It's me. I can't resist baiting you." She leaned forward again and put her cuffed hands on the mess of papers. "Seeing you makes me realize afresh how much less of myself there is than when I came in here. Makes me ramp up the paltry little bit of me that's left. Which isn't much, is it? Just a spiteful cat with blunt claws. I know I can still irritate you, but that's nothing in comparison to what you can do to me. Which is to make me ashamed of the narrowness of my mean little scope. Whereas if you ask Agent Arden here, she'll tell you: with her I've been absolutely angelic, the model of diligent cooperation."

Because she couldn't help herself, Valerie glanced at Arden. All three of them understood — Arden with a slight delay — that Katherine's last remark had been an insult to the agent. As in, she's not *worth* baiting. Again Valerie thought: Bad choice, McLuhan. She's too young for this.

"The truth is it's all here anyway," Katherine said, indicating the papers under her hands. "I'm a good college girl. I have *shown my work*. Even the FBI should be able to follow it. I suppose I should have eaten every page, destroyed the evidence as I discovered it. That would have left me something to bargain with. But I'm sure Susanna would have prevented it, or had my poor guts opened up to retrieve it, like that awful nanny goat in *The Wolf and the Seven Little Kids.*"

Outside the door, the two guards were talking quietly. Valerie thought she recognized Lomax's depressed monotone in the murmur. Elsewhere in the building a buzzer sounded. She imagined the reduced aural life in here: doors slamming, a mop clanking in a bucket, keys jangling, screams. It made her grateful — deeply, simply grateful — for all the sounds freedom allowed her to take for granted: traffic, car radios, the wind, the ocean, birdsong. You couldn't enter a prison without wondering how long you'd last if they locked you up in one. No time at all, she thought. Katherine had managed six years. It seemed impossible.

"That said," Katherine said, "we're both winners here."

"Are we?"

"Yes. Please believe me, Valerie, I'm not boasting when I say that there is no way on earth any third party would have understood the way this information works. It's personal to him, as he said. You have to know him. More important, you have to know what *I* know about him. In fact, you have to know *us,* the bizarre little history we had. Take the Marquis de Sade, for example."

"What about him?"

"You could research every last detail of the man, his life, his work, *everything*. But it still wouldn't tell you what you needed to know. What you needed to know was that one night we were having a conversation about personal ads. Neither of us had ever placed one in our lives, but we were discussing the most economical way of finding what we needed, had we not been fortunate enough to find each other organically. I don't have to spell that out, obviously, what we needed?"

"You don't have to spell it out, no."

"He said he would have placed an ad containing only the following: *Dolmance seeks Saint-Ange.* That phrase and just that. The right woman, he said, would know exactly what that meant. Dolmance and Saint-Ange are male and female characters, respectively, in a little drama Sade wrote called *Philosophy in the Bedroom.* It's hilarious and vicious in equal measure, but you wouldn't like it, trust me. Or you wouldn't like yourself for liking it if you did. But I digress. The point is no one would know that the portrait of Sade he included in the package referred to that specific phrase, a phrase which isn't contained in anything the dear Marquis wrote. And even if, by some miracle or cosmic accident you came up with the phrase, it still wouldn't help you. Because you wouldn't know that when we had that conversation, I realized — in one of those wonderful sweet, trivial epiphanies — that 'bedroom' is an anagram of 'boredom.' It became a joke between us, calling the bedroom the boredom. Ironically, obviously, since whatever else might have been wrong with us, we were rarely bored in the bedroom. Without knowing that play on the word I wouldn't have gotten anywhere near cracking the letter grids. And even with it I wasn't completely right. Each of the clues provides a word or a series of numbers. The word is a cipher. The numbers take you to the letter grids. But I had the numbers wrong. The Greek alphabet symbols don't mean anything. They're just to throw you off. You know how I know that?"

"How?"

"Because we both derived a snobbish little satisfaction from knowing the origins of phrases people use every day in ignorance of where they come from. One of them — one of many — was 'It's all Greek to me.' Meaning, of course, something is incomprehensible. Do you know where *that* came from?"

"No."

"No. You don't. I do. The consensus is it's a direct translation from Latin, *Graecum est; non legitur,* or *Graecum est; non potest legi,* which means: 'It is Greek; it cannot be read.' Monastic scribes in the Middle Ages used it, because *by* the Middle Ages knowledge of the Greek alphabet and language was dwindling. A major headache for scholars copying Classical manuscripts."

Valerie thought of the look of careful delight on Katherine's face, applying the cigarette burns to Danielle Freyer. In one of the videos, she'd said: Hold her still. I want these two exactly symmetrical. So she'll look like she has four nipples.

"Anyone can Google that information in seconds," Katherine said. "I'm sure Agent Arden's elves did. But it wouldn't have helped them. They probably wasted days trying to integrate the Greek symbols into whatever systems they were working."

She paused to let it all settle in. Valerie was thirsty. Once again the minutes weighed like hours.

"The fact is," Katherine continued, "that for whatever reason, these things are addressed to me. I have no more idea why than you do. But we both know you need me. And in any case, you've got nothing to lose and everything to gain."

Valerie remained silent.

Katherine rolled her head on her neck, as if to ease tension — and indeed Valerie heard a little tick in her muscles, as startling in its way as if a firecracker had gone off. It occurred to her that among the many things she couldn't imagine Katherine feeling, tiredness and physical discomfort were two of them.

"He's probably getting off on the idea of you and me spending time together," Katherine said. "In close proximity. When we saw you in the papers we both agreed you were sexy as hell."

Ignore it.

Except of course she couldn't. Katherine had said in the past that she'd had female lovers, and when she'd first told Valerie had followed it a few moments later with: Are you wondering if I'd go to bed with you? I mean, obviously my monstrosity ought to rule out you wondering if you'd go to bed with me, but all of us want to be desired, even by monsters. If you met the Devil you'd be a *teeny* bit disappointed if he didn't want to fuck you, regardless of your not wanting to fuck him. Valerie had said: No, I wasn't wondering that. But it had been Napoleon's white horse again. Katherine — a more brutal version of herself in those days — had stared at her and said: Well, I would go to bed with you, for the record. You've got reluctant knowledge and you're not afraid of yourself. Plus the short upper body men love. You must drive Nick fucking *crazy.*

Arden swallowed, audibly, and looked down at her hands.

"Perhaps you're right," Valerie said. "But it's irrelevant. What we're going to do is give all this to the Bureau. You can talk Agent Arden through the process if there's anything missing from your notes."

"I've made you uncomfortable," Katherine said. "And just this once I didn't mean to. I'm sorry. I'm my own worst enemy. And Susanna, please don't fret. You're not my type. I haven't thought of doing wicked things with you once the entire time we've been together. Oh gosh, now *you're* blushing. I'm like the proverbial bull in the china shop. Valerie, help me out."

Valerie had an image, naturally, of Katherine masturbating, thinking about her. She let it all in, assumed the fantasies would be sadistic, murderous, as ugly as anything she'd seen on the videos. It ran through her head like a high-speed horror film. She found she didn't care. For herself, she

250

didn't care.

And for Nick?

"You're beyond any help I could give you," she said. "We both know *that.*"

"What a lot we both know," Katherine said. "I told you we were sisters."

"Agent, could I talk to you outside for a moment?"

Arden got to her feet. With visible relief.

"Wait," Katherine said. "Am I still on the team? Tell me you're not cutting me off. Please."

Valerie turned to her. She felt curiously light of being. "Has it ever occurred to you that we might catch this guy without your help?" she said. "Not to be old-fashioned or anything, but, you know, via police procedure?"

"Of course," Katherine said. "You caught *me,* didn't you?"

"It seems I did."

"But look how long it took you. Time is blood. Listen: you have the address for your latest, don't you? This, whatshername . . . Raylene Ashe?"

"Yes."

"Don't tell me what it is. Give me half an hour more with this."

"For what?"

"Because now that I know where I went

251

awry with the letter grids, I'll be able to work it out. If I get it wrong you can abandon me. I was too slow with this one. If I'd got there sooner she might still be alive. Next time I'll be faster."

In the corridor, Valerie said to Arden, quietly: "Fine, give her her thirty minutes. Let me know if she delivers. Either way, get yourself out of here when she's done. You don't need to tell me this hasn't been any kind of fun for you."

"Well, I've had better assignments."

"I'll talk to McLuhan," Valerie said. "It's his call, obviously, but —"

"No, don't do that. I can handle it."

Valerie looked at her. Looked at her properly, human to human, woman to woman. *Can* you handle it? Really?

"I know," Arden said. "Don't worry. She's not getting in."

To my head, she didn't need to add.

"Besides," Arden said, "I can't afford it. *Some jobs too tough for girls,* etc. The Bureau's still a fucking boys' club, whatever *The X-Files* says."

Katherine didn't need thirty minutes. Valerie had just got into her car and lit a cigarette when her phone rang. It was Arden.

"Sorry," she said. "She nailed it."

Nutty dreams again. I was with him. We were in a mall and everyone for some reason was in pajamas. We got separated and it was like being a kid lost. Then I realized I was carrying a baby in my arms and it was his. But when I looked properly it wasn't a baby at all, it was a cat that looked like it had been in a fire. It was looking at me with big green eyes.

He called me like he said he would to go over the stuff. I got it perfect. I wanted to see him but he said no, you know how it has to be for now. I do know but it's hard sometimes. He said trust me and of course I do. I know it's going to be worth it when we get to the island. I can't believe I've got a passport!!!

18

On her way in to work the following morning Valerie got a call from her former neighbor in the Mission, Rita Sorenson.

"Honey, I'm sorry to bother you, but I've still got this package for you from your mom. You said you were going to come by for it a couple of weeks back, so I'm thinking she's probably had a handful of aneurisms by now."

"Oh, shit, sorry, Rita, yes, you're right. I got sidetracked."

The luxury towels from Bed Bath & Beyond. She'd been going to collect them on the morning she and Nick were supposed to have their precious weekend in Calistoga. Her mother would have thought she'd received them and said nothing. It was dreary to Valerie that she knew how her mother functioned — a maddening combination of thoughtfulness and need. The generous impulses were genuine, but so was the insatiable appetite for having them recognized. In her most perverse self, Valerie believed, her mother *preferred* it if something kind she'd done went unthanked. Not because she exemplified virtue being its own reward, but because she loved the idea of herself as a wounded saint. You couldn't win: If you were grateful it stroked her ego. If you weren't grateful it stroked her *martyr*'s ego. She was a kind woman who ruined it by so nakedly needing to be thought kind.

"I wouldn't pester you, hon, but I'm going to Carlotta's in L.A. for a week of debauchery, and I didn't want it to be just sitting here, and then if you came by and I wasn't home, that would be, you know: valuable police time wasted. . . ."

"Very funny. It's my fault. And thanks for holding on to it for me. Listen, I'm not far. How about I swing by and pick it up in ten?"

"Sure, but don't mess up your day."

"It's on my way. I'll see you soon. And thanks again."

"Okay, hotshot. See you in ten."

A guilty detour, she knew. She wasn't looking forward to work. Her surface mantra told her that she was dealing with Katherine, that she'd built up an immunity, that she was, for fuck's sake, *fine.* But around her colleagues she had a queasy sense that she was being watched. For signs that she was succumbing to the woman's gravity, that she was losing the plot, that she was once again in the goddamned Drift. McLuhan had been swayed by Katherine's near miss with the name. Helena Ayres. Raylene Ashe. He agreed that if another package came she should be given the chance to take a look at it (as before, with the Bureau's team running parallel), but Valerie knew he didn't like it. His decision was based more on the fear of Katherine somehow making good on her threat that the story would get out. Even on death row she was entitled to see her attorney. Or to hire one friendly to the idea of making the authorities squirm. There were two nightmare tabloid headlines. One would be something like: DESPERATE COPS RECRUIT SATAN'S DAUGHTER. The other (worse) would hold them to blame for leaving Katherine out: THIRD VICTIM NEEDN'T HAVE DIED: ANGEL OF DEATH HAD VITAL INFORMATION. This is like fucking Christmas and Easter and her birthday have all come at once for her, McLuhan had said. The simplest thing would be if we just had her killed. At least then she wouldn't be an option. When he'd said this, everyone in the room (Valerie, Will, Laura Flynn, Ed Pérez) had the same thought: Well, *can't* we have her killed? Mc-Luhan had read it, though no one had said a word. What he'd said in response was: Yeah. I know. Maybe. But not quite yet. Ed had said: Just so you know: If you need a volunteer . . .

Valerie pulled up outside her old building on Capp Street. It was a beautiful morning, clean sunlight and a pale turquoise sky. Even the asphalt looked innocent. A gourmet grocery had opened up on her block since she'd left. From its doorway the smells of fresh oregano, cured meats, strawberries. She was naturally receptive to these things, but the recent visits to Red Ridge had sharpened her sensual appreciation. All the things Katherine Glass couldn't have. Good.

Rita was leaning on the sill of her open third-story window.

"Hey, stranger," she said.

"Hi, Rita."

"You coming in — or are you on a hot lead?"

Valerie looked at her watch. "I'm on my way to work," she said. "But I can —"

"Stay where you are, hon. I'll bring it right down. Burn some of these bastard carbs."

Rita Sorenson, a very attractive divorcée in her early sixties, lived in the apartment across the hall from the one Valerie had oc-

258

cupied and was aggressively active. Con-
certs, movies, art classes — a *poker* group.
She'd left her husband fifteen years ago for
a man ten years younger. It hadn't lasted,
but she had no regrets. The marriage had
been stale for more than a decade, she said.
The affair was, in her words, just the kick in
the ass she'd needed. You know how it is,
she'd confided to Valerie over homemade
margaritas one evening. You stay in these
things because you're just plain terrified of
Being On Your Own. But the fact was, my
soul spoke. I told myself I was in love with
Peter (the affair) but really I just used him
as the dynamite to put under the whole
static mess of the marriage. Sometimes you
need to make your own apocalypse, then
come out, blinking in the new light. I was
dying, and I wanted to live. Thank God.
Now look at me: I'm a walking bohemian
renaissance! Valerie liked her very much.
Granted, it didn't *completely* fly — there
were fractures of loneliness a keen neighborly eye could see — but Rita was recon-
ciled to them. I might never be in love again,
she said, but at my age there's more to life
than love. The world's still farcical and ugly
and beautiful and fascinating. I went to the
beach at Santa Cruz the other week with
my friend Juliette. You know that dusk light,

when the sky's dark peach and the ocean looks like mercury? I was just sitting there with my toes in the sand and there was such a feeling of tenderness. I'm aware that I sound like a fucking rambling hippie, by the way. . . ."

"What exactly *is* a luxury towel?" she said, when she greeted Valerie at the door.

"I have no idea."

"Does it sense when you're in need and turn into a man? Because if it does I'm hanging on to at least one of these. Jesus. How many are in here?"

"Four, I think. Do you want a couple? I don't need them."

"Are you insane? Your mother would have me killed. Speaking of killing . . ."

"Yeah."

"How's it going? I mean, I know you can't talk about it, but you doing okay?"

"I'm good. We're doing the work."

"That heroic man still treating you right?"

"More than I deserve."

"Well, it's not the same without you here, you know. I can't believe you *betrayed* me for Cole Valley. All those goddamned yoga-Nazis."

"*You* do yoga."

"Yeah, but I don't want to have people shot for *not* doing it."

They chatted for a few minutes, hugged good-bye.

"Listen," Valerie said, "when this business is over, come for dinner, will you? It's been too long."

"All right, hotshot. Gimme a call. Meantime, stay alive, okay?"

Valerie loaded the package into the trunk. She got in the driver's seat, checked her phone, started the engine.

Then she saw the flowers.

Several of the ground-floor occupants on this block had cheered up their stoops and window ledges with potted plants, shrubs, hanging baskets. Next door to Valerie's building on her left, the young couple had installed two hefty concrete tubs with silvery-green olive trees in them.

But that wasn't what had caught her eye. What had caught her eye was the window box on the ground-floor apartment two doors down, on the right. The window ledge was a foot wide, and the box ran the full length of it, four or five feet.

Flowers, to Valerie, were "flowers." Beyond daffodils, roses, and tulips she would have been hard pressed to identify anything.

Except, now, globe amaranth. The flower Raylene Ashe had had pinned in her hair. The flower her killer had put there.

Perhaps Raylene will help you toward the nonrandom nature of my selection?

She got out of the car and went up the stoop. The flowers in the window box nodded, as in gentle confirmation. She pulled the image up on her iPhone.

"Depending on the variety, flowers are white, red, pink, lilac, or purple. 'Strawberry Fields,' with bright-red blossoms, and 'All Around Purple' are popular . . ."

All Around Purple.

The back of Valerie's neck livened. As if he were standing right behind her, whispering. It took an effort not to spin around, and even then she couldn't help herself from turning, slowly, and taking a visual sweep of the block. Nothing unusual. Or all the nothing unusual that could just as easily be concealing something extraordinary. Him. A young couple across the street were walking their brown-and-white Jack Russell. Its tongue protruded like a little pink scroll. At the gourmet grocery a pretty white-aproned girl was adjusting the striped awning. Sunlight glinted on her nose ring. A bus passed, faces in the windows, people deep in their details and schemes.

She closed the image on her phone and opened the pdf of Raylene's delivery addresses. There were too many. She called Will.

"Hey."

"Raylene's postal route addresses. You got them handy?"

"I'm not at my desk."

"How long?"

"Two minutes."

"Call me back when you're there."

Less than two minutes. Will knew her tones.

"Okay."

"Document search the list for my name and Capp Street address."

"What?"

"There's a window box two doors down from my old building with globe amaranth growing in it."

"Globe . . . ?"

"The flower in Raylene's hair."

"Jesus. Hold on."

First, concede that it might be a co-incidence. Concede that the flower head could have come from anywhere. "Grows year round in all zones." Put that on one side.

Now, assume it wasn't a coincidence.

The too-dumb-to-be-true scenario was that he lived right here, two doors down from her. They would do the interviews, of course (no matter how unlikely, it had to be eliminated), but it would be a waste of time. One of their very few certainties was that he *wasn't* too dumb to be true. He wouldn't have made it that easy. Nor would he have been reckless enough to pick it from this particular window box.

Rather, he was telling her three things. First, that he'd watched Raylene on her route. Second, that he'd selected Raylene because she'd delivered her, Valerie's, mail. Third, that he knew where she, Valerie, had lived, and most likely where she lived now. He was telling her she was an object under his scrutiny. He was telling her he was watching her.

All conjecture. But the Machine said otherwise.

"Will?"

"I'm doing it. Wait. Fuck."

"Am I on the list?"

"Yeah." Will exhaled. "Yeah, you're on it."

"How soon can you get here?"

"Twenty minutes."

"Is McLuhan in?"

"Yeah. I'll let him know."

A face appeared at the ground-floor apartment window. A plump, gray-haired woman in her fifties, olive skin and Middle Eastern features. Valerie recognized her. They'd crossed each other on the block in the past, though it had never gone beyond exchanging a neighborly "hi." They didn't know each other by name.

"Hang on, Will."

Valerie waved and held her badge up for the woman to see. The woman raised the window and stuck her head out.

"Hey," Valerie said. "Hi. Could I come in and talk to you for a second?"

"Wow, you're a cop?"

"Yeah."

"What's going on?"

"Could we talk inside?"

A little excitement (and, naturally, anxiety) crept into the woman's face. "Yeah, sure, I guess. Let me get the door."

Valerie switched back to her phone. "We're going to need a list of occupants, management company, you know the drill. I'm going in to talk to one of the residents right now."

The neighbor, Mrs. Zarbib, had nothing useful to tell her. She had globe amaranth every year. No one suspicious hanging around. No idiot plucking a flower.

"Elizabeth Lambert's stuff," Valerie said to Will, when he turned up with Agent Helin and two uniforms, just as she was exiting the building. "Who's got it now?"

"The sister, I think," Will said. He flipped open his notebook. "Gillian Rose. She's out in Sausalito. What are you thinking?"

"If he selected Raylene because she delivered my mail, then maybe there's a connection between me and Elizabeth, too. *Non-random,* right? I need to go through it. I need all the background."

"Well, you're better off with the sister than the parents. The father's having a fucking nervous breakdown."

Valerie called Gillian Rose. She sounded as if she'd just woken up. But she was home, and willing to talk. Valerie told her she'd be there within the hour.

19

Elizabeth Lambert's fifty-six-year-old sister, Gillian Rose, lived with her husband, Paul, two Persian cats, and a Dalmatian, in a two-million-dollar home on Santa Rosa Avenue, part of the Glen Grove Estates enclave. The white concrete house looked to Valerie like several boxes stacked to give the impression they might topple over in a strong gust of wind. Paul Rose ran a high-end architectural firm. Gillian was an artist, currently specializing in collage. She wasn't famous, but you couldn't buy one of her pieces for less than six thousand dollars.

The morning was heating up by the time Valerie got there. Broad sunlight with just enough of a breeze coming off the water to ruffle the tips of the evergreens that dotted the hill below. Gillian was home alone, but for the pets. She was a tawny, high-cheekboned woman with honey-brown hair in a thick braid. Faded jeans and a white silk blouse. Tan bare feet with unpainted pedicured nails. An intelligent face, but exhausted. There was, within seconds, an ease between the two women. A mutual recognition that patience wasn't a virtue either of them possessed.

"Do you want one of these?" Gillian said, having led Valerie up onto the top-floor terrace, an oak-decked space with wrought-iron furniture and a spectacular view of the bridge and the bay. The glass-fronted room it led back into served as Gillian's studio. "One of these" was a large, heavily iced gin and tonic.

"No, thanks," Valerie lied. "I'm fine."

"Of course," Gillian said. "Not while you're on duty. Something like this happens and you find yourself speaking TV lines. Coffee? Juice? Water?"

"Really, nothing, thank you."

"Some of the jewelry's gone back to my parents," Gillian said. "And some of the clothes have gone to thrift. I don't know . . . I'm not sure what you're looking for."

"Neither am I," Valerie said. "But before we get to that, what I'd really like is for you to tell me as much about Elizabeth's life as you can. Some of the facts, obviously, we have, but I want to make sure we're not overlooking something. I know it's painful for you right now, but I'm only asking to give us the best chance of catching the person responsible for her death."

"Her rapist and murderer," Gillian said. She was the sort of woman who would always force herself to say what needed to be said.

"Yes," Valerie answered.

"Will you kill him?"

"I'll do everything I can to catch him."

"I want him dead."

"So would I, in your shoes. When we get him, he'll go to trial. And if we get the conviction a judge will sentence him. California, as you probably know, has the death penalty."

"And the law is an ass. If they don't execute him I'll find a way myself."

Valerie didn't respond. There was no point. Gillian Rose, it was plain to her after even these few minutes, had the psychology and the resolve to do just that, once she'd decided on it. She wondered what the relationship between the sisters had been like. Everything she'd learned about Elizabeth suggested a quiet life. Gillian's life, she imagined, had had its share of fruitful noise. There was, among the other complex energies surrounding this formidable woman, a current of guilt. For having overshadowed

Elizabeth. For having gotten the glamour and the talent. And of course, simply, now, for being alive when her sister was dead.

"Excuse me for a second," Gillian said.

She went through the open glass doors into the studio and down the stairs. When she returned she was carrying a tray. Coffee and iced water for Valerie, and what looked suspiciously like another large gin and tonic for herself. Plus an onyx ashtray and a pack of American Spirits.

"I know you said no, but it's there anyway."

"Oh, that's kind of you. Thanks. Coffee, I guess."

Gillian didn't offer her a cigarette when she lit one for herself, and Valerie left her own where they were in her purse. It was working policy for her: you didn't smoke when dealing with civilians because even the smokers among them saw it as a weakness. You didn't do anything that would make them think of you as less than maximally competent, maximally strong. Instead she took out her notepad and pen and set the cup of coffee on the table next to her.

For the next hour or so, Gillian talked Valerie through Elizabeth's life: family, school, college, boyfriends, jobs, the marriage that ended. Valerie took notes, but nothing jumped out at her. Elizabeth hadn't had a passion. She'd started off studying history and literature at college, but had been academically mediocre. Switched to journalism, took a year out, halfheartedly started teacher training but abandoned it after a few months, worked as a temp, went back to school, eventually graduated as a journalism major, but all without a driving focus or single ambition. Since then she'd worked in publicity for a small publishing house, the San Francisco tourism bureau, a local radio station and, eventually, the Environmental Protection Agency.

"She was an Expander," Gillian said. The Dalmatian had loped upstairs and joined them on the deck. It lay on its side half under Gillian's chair. Occasionally, Gillian stroked its flank with her bare foot. Each time she did it the dog closed its eyes in ecstasy.

"A what?" Valerie asked.

Gillian smiled. All the Elizabeth-related smiles now were smiles of loss. "An Expander," she said. "My label. I told her there were two types of people in the world, Seekers and Expanders. Seekers are people who are forever chasing some elusive thing that would, you know, make them once and for all happy. Whereas Expanders just identify

271

whatever it is that already makes them happy, then try to get more of it. Sorry, that's of no use to you, I realize."

"And you're a Seeker," Valerie said. She was thinking she and Nick were Expanders. No elusive mystery for either of them. Just the two certainties: love and the job. Beyond that they were uncomplicated animals: food, sex, weather, friends. All the times they simply lay together enjoying the sunlight on their skin, the need for language gone.

Gillian closed her eyes, rolled her head on her neck, opened her eyes again. "Yeah," she said. But her face said: None of that matters anymore. None of anything matters anymore.

"Okay," Valerie said, flipping her notepad closed. "I guess, if you don't mind, I'd like to take another look at Elizabeth's stuff."

The boxed remnants of Elizabeth Lambert's life were in an ivory-carpeted dressing room on the floor below Gillian's studio. There were rooms and rooms in this house. This one had floor-to-ceiling walk-in wardrobes and a striped futon and the faint odor of patchouli. Having been left to herself, Valerie opened the walk-in and found ten percent clothes and shoes, ninety percent random crap, albeit neatly stored in plastic clip-lock crates. Elizabeth's leftovers were in cardboard boxes occupying the area under a big window that looked out from the back of the house, up the hill into the shade of the plump, dark-green conifers.

Valerie went through it, box by box, but found nothing that made a connection. The stuff was the stuff she remembered from her first trawl though Elizabeth's apartment. If she, Valerie, was the link, there was nothing in the remainders of Elizabeth's life to confirm it.

"Anything?" Gillian asked, appearing in the doorway.

Valerie was holding Elizabeth's ring-bindered First Republic Bank statements in her hands. She shook her head. "Nothing," she said.

Gillian stood in the doorway, arms wrapped around herself, examining her. "Why don't you just tell me what you're looking for?" she said.

The room was filled with light. A passing seagull cawed. Valerie imagined saying to Gillian: I'm looking for anything to link me to Elizabeth. There's been another victim, a U.S. postal carrier who delivered my mail. *My* mail. Me. I think it might be me. The victims are connected to each other because both of them were connected to me. But I can't find the connection with Elizabeth.

She knew what the consequences of telling Gillian would be. Among other things, Gillian would be disgusted that her sister's death wasn't even really about her sister. She'd be disgusted that her sister could have been merely instrumental. And she would hold Valerie, however partially, to blame.

That she could see all this so clearly was wearying to Valerie, the thought of having to contend with Gillian's feelings, her likely hatred. She didn't want it. Not out of tenderness for herself, but because it would get in the way. It would be an encumbrance.

"I'm really not sure," she said. "But there were some photograph albums in Elizabeth's apartment. They don't seem to be here. Do you have those?"

Gillian eyed her, visibly sensing if not a lie then a concealed truth. Valerie was on borrowed time with this, she knew. Any moment, Gillian would be out of patience and demand a full explanation.

"They're in the studio," Gillian said.

The two women went back upstairs to the top floor. Gillian took three albums from a bookcase shelf and set them on one of the room's two big work tables. The large dark-colored collage canvases hanging on the white walls were like quiet, self-involved intelligences. The smell of turpentine and paint took Valerie back to her junior high art room, the lessons no one took seriously apart from Andrea Lipschitz, who was a prodigy, and who later went on to make a fortune set-designing for TV commercials.

Gillian left Valerie and stepped out onto the deck. She stood at the terrace rail with her back to her, one arm still wrapped around her waist, the other hanging by her side, fingertips holding a freshly lit American Spirit, the smoke from which went straight up for a few inches, then rippled madly. The breeze had died.

Valerie had been through all three albums and was flicking back through the last one when she stopped. It was the photograph of Elizabeth, aged perhaps twenty, in what looked like a preschool classroom. Elizabeth was in half-body close-up, occupying the left third of the shot. She was sitting at a desk, molding a piece of Play-Doh, her hair tucked behind her ears, her mouth caught mid-sentence. Two small girls stood next to her, both with blond hair in pigtails, both absolutely absorbed in what Elizabeth was making (from their faces, they might have been watching sorcery), while next to them stood a dark-haired boy of similar age in red denim dungarees and a white T-shirt, holding a multicolored ball of Play-Doh and looking away to his left at something that had distracted him. Behind Elizabeth you could see half the blackboard and the Mickey Mouse wall clock that hung next to it. To the right of the wall clock a pine store cupboard, and alongside it a window that looked out onto a hedged yard. Out of focus, but flecked with the blurred bright colors of playground equipment. A paint-spattered work bench ran the length of the window, and a group of children stood there, under the eye of the room's second grown-up, a woman with short-chopped black and gold hair, wearing a knotted plaid shirt and jeans. She was drawing something on a large sheet of paper. The kids were on tiptoe to watch. At the very edge of the shot, on its right-hand side, you could see another little girl walking out of frame. Only half her figure was visible, her face turned away. Dark hair. A thin yellow cardigan with an orange flame design around the cuffs. A tiny gray pleated skirt. White kneesocks. Red sandals.

Valerie wouldn't have been able to identify the details.

If it hadn't been for the fact that the little girl in the yellow cardigan was her.

20

"It's me," she said to Will, via cell phone, from her car.

"I know. What's up?"

"No, I mean it's *me*. I'm what Raylene and Elizabeth had in common."

Elizabeth Lambert — Elizabeth *Turner* in those premarital days — had spent a month as a classroom assistant at Happy Learners Preschool during her year out from finishing her degree. Valerie didn't quite remember it. She had only a generic memory of preschool: the smells of chalk and ammonia and clay; the strange privacy of the cloth playhouse; the general noise and the occasional boom or bark from the adults; the alarming otherness of other kids. There were a very few specific memories. A small freckled boy gouging a lump of earwax out and wiping it on his shorts. A girl with a large, porcelainish head tripping over in the yard and biting her own tongue, the astonishing amount of blood and the panicked teachers grabbing more and more paper towels. A dark-skinned boy with liquid black eyes and very white teeth putting his hand down the back of Valerie's shorts, her turning and slapping him. She didn't remember Elizabeth, but the photographic evidence was incontrovertible.

"Raylene delivered my mail," she said. "Elizabeth worked at my preschool. It's people connected to me."

"How the fuck did he know Elizabeth worked at your preschool?"

"There'll be a record, somewhere. There's a record, you dig it up. These are the times."

"You think you *know* this guy?"

"I don't have to know him. He knows me. And he wants me to know he knows me."

"Okay. You coming back now?"

"Not yet. I've got to go to Union City."

"How come?"

"I need to tell my mom and Cassie. Call my brother, too, I guess."

Will processed. Worked out the logic. "Even if you're right about Elizabeth and Raylene," he said, "the connections are remote."

"They're remote so far. The next one could be closer. I'm not taking any chances. They need a heads-up. My mom lives on her own. Go down to Nick's department and fill him in, will you?"

"Got it."

"I'm going to talk to Deerholt, get a couple of uniforms out there."

"Fair enough." Pause. "Shit. Now you've got *me* worried. Marion, the kids. I mean, *I'm* connected to you. Christ, we're going to have to draw up a list."

Valerie drove out to her mother's house, called Cassie en route to meet her there.

Deerholt, all but audibly biting back the suggestion that she was being paranoid, promised her two uniforms.

"What are we supposed to do?" Cassie said. "Lock ourselves in until you catch this guy?"

Valerie just looked at her. Don't make this harder than it is.

"No, you don't have to lock yourselves in. There'll always be at least one officer here at Mom's and at your place and when you need to go out he'll go with you. You can do all your normal stuff, but you're going to have a little police company for a while. I'm sorry, but I'm not taking any chances."

"I'm not going around with a police officer the whole time, Val," Cassie said. "Owen can take me to and from work, for God's sake." Owen was a graphic designer who worked from home. They'd converted the loft into a studio ten years ago.

"If it's Owen, then fine," Valerie said. "But there might be times when he's not available. There'll be a uniform here just in case. Owen's not going away anytime soon, is he?" she asked her sister.

"No."

"Fine. Just be aware. That's all I'm saying. You take the kids to school and pick them up — right?"

"It's summer break."

"Okay, but they don't go anywhere without you or Owen. Don't go out alone at night, and during the day stay public, stay where there are people."

"Val, we live in a city. There are always people, everywhere."

Valerie thought: Elizabeth Lambert lived in a city. So did Raylene Ashe. And now both of them are dead.

Cassie walked her to her car. "This is fucked," she said.

"Yeah, I know," Valerie said. "But be careful, will you?"

"You know, just once in a while I'd like to be the one looking out for you."

"You've done your share."

"Holding your hair out of the toilet while

you puked up tequila is hardly the same thing."

"It felt like it to me at the time. *Times,* I should say. Let the officers open your mail."

"What?"

"The postcards. The fair warning."

"He's not going to send *me* fair warning, is he?"

"We don't know what he's going to do."

"And Katherine Glass?"

"Don't worry about Katherine Glass. I'm dealing with her."

"That's what worries me."

Valerie's phone rang. McLuhan.

"Where are you?"

"Union City. Heading back. What's happened?" Jesus Christ, not another one. Please, not yet, not so soon.

"You've got another package," McLuhan said.

21

Dear Valerie

How close did you get? Are you seeing the connection yet? I confess, I find myself wondering if I've overestimated you. But then I remind myself that you're the woman who put Katherine Glass away — so how can that be?

Regardless, we have no choice but to proceed. Here is everything you — and your specialist(s) — need to save the life of Number Three. It's a little more cunningly gift-wrapped than last time, but the rewards are potentially greater: not only the victim's name, but the intended scene of the crime.

You'll be wondering how long you've got. (I'm in danger here, of allowing my misgivings to increase my handicap.) Tradition dictates that these things start slowly, then speed up, but you'll know

by now that I have no respect for tradition.

Let's say days rather than weeks.

Good luck.

The material had gone, electronically, via
Susanna Arden, up to Katherine at Red
Ridge yesterday, as well as to the FBI team
working the clues. The contents this time
were six pages, each with a single image:

1. A map of Iraq, with the east point
   of the compass icon circled in red
2. An early edition of George Orwell's
   Nineteen Eighty-Four
3. A still of Scarlett Johansson from
   Lost in Translation
4. A letter grid, numbered as before,
   but twice the size of the first ones
5. A highly magnified photograph of
   what looked like the tip of a needle
6. A line of apparently random digits

So far they'd had nothing back.

"What are you doing?" Valerie asked Will.
They were both at their desks. She'd just
taken the headphones off: the Katherine
interviews. Again.

"You won't like it."

"What?"

Will sat back in his chair. "It's a profile list of prison personnel," he said. "Mc-Luhan's not convinced there isn't a snitch to Katherine. And frankly neither am I. The Bureau's still chasing two of the people known to have visited her while she's been inside. One potential biographer, who apparently didn't last, one Catholic priest bent on saving her soul. That's plus three attorneys and her financial adviser, but none of them seems dumb enough to get into anything like this."

"Why wouldn't I like it?"

"Because you think it's a waste of time."

"I don't think it's a waste of time. It's elimination. In fact I'll help you. I've got one more of these to go through, then I'm never listening to them again."

"Still think she gave something away we missed?"

"It was six years ago," Valerie said. "My memory's not what it used to be."

"I've noticed a lot of alcoholics say that."

"Hey, I'm practically teetotal these days."

This was a gross exaggeration, but it was true that Valerie had cut down on the booze. The weekly glass recycling bag now looked more like forgivable hedonism than a shameful addiction. She'd told herself it was good physical accounting in preparation for

Having a Child with Nick. But the truth was that she just didn't need it anything like she used to. Love was generous like that, casually relieved you of your other dependencies — so that you depended solely, perilously, on love. Love's generosity was purely self-serving.

"I was looking at some of the trial footage last night," Will said.

"And?"

"I was wondering how come you've got skinnier and I've got fatter."

"Try asking Ashan for a smaller sandwich now and again. Why were you looking?"

"I had the weirdest feeling that he might have been *at* the trial. In disguise. I think he'd have gotten a kick out of it."

"Katherine would have recognized him," Valerie said. "Disguise or no disguise. She could have cut herself a deal and pointed him out."

"Maybe. Maybe not. Anyway, you're skinnier, but I'm aging better. I've got understated gravitas."

"What?" Valerie said.

Will laughed. "We had a parents' evening at Logan's school. When he came home next day he said he'd overheard two of his teachers discussing me and Marion. According to Ms. Vickery — who looks younger than *Logan,* by the way — I've got *understated gravitas.* I like it."

Valerie put the headphones back on, picked up where she'd left off.

K: I know what you want to know.

V: What's that?

K: You want to know why.

V: Actually I'm not really interested in why. That's not my department.

K: It's everyone's department. You're Police, yes, but you're human first. Worse than that, you're a woman. I'm letting the team down egregiously.

Pause.

K: *Very badly.*

V: I see. Well, as I said, I'm not really interested in —

K: Has it occurred to you that Nick hates you?

Longer pause.

V: What I can't figure out is why you think asking me things like that could possibly help you.

K: Oh, I know they're of no practical use, but they help me enormously, psychologically. I'm compelled to unwrap things. My mother had very well-kept fingernails, and she had this slow, methodical way of peeling an orange. As a little girl, I used to watch her, mesmerized. Life offers us these objective correlatives, but so often we can only see them with adulthood's hindsight. Do you want me to rein in the vocabulary?

V: What I want is an answer to the question I asked: You never, after that first time in New York, stayed in a hotel?

K: No, not to my memory. An objective correlative is an outer world representation of an inner state.

V: Thank you very much for explaining that. You said his money was European. Which part of Europe?

K: No idea. If his name had really been

"Lucien Chastain" you could have gotten a genealogist to look into it. Since it was an alias, you'll be better off with a Freudian literary critic. The conventional wisdom is that all such noms de guerre reveal something about their subject. Not that it takes a genius. "Lucien" evokes "Lucifer" and "Chastain" suggests "chaste," "stain," "chain," and "chastise." It's not just me, by the way. Read Germaine Greer: "Women have very little idea of how much men hate them." Don't you feel the subtle accents of contempt when he's fucking you in a certain way? A certain position? Does he fuck you in the ass? On his birthday?

V: Did *you* ever use a false name?

K: Oh, I wish I had! It amazes me that I didn't. Not for practical reasons. I've just always liked the idea of disguise. And this is the perverse universe: when I actually *needed* to be in disguise, when I had the perfect rationale, I let it pass me by. What a consummate moron! The only thing more astonishing to me than the stupidity of other people is the stupidity of myself. And to the eventual transcriber of these tapes I can only apologize for the gracelessness of that last sentence. Have you read *Wuthering Heights*?

V: No. If you —

K: You don't know what you're missing. The heroine — or I suppose one must say *antiheroine* — is another Katherine, albeit Catherine with a "C." A gorgeous little sadist, as it happens, but that's not the point. That's not *my* point. *My* point is that the author, Emily Brontë, and all her siblings — goody-two-shoes Charlotte, drippy Anne, and hopeless, talentless asshole Branwell — were all, as children, forced by their father to wear masks from time to time. Actual physical masks. Because he, the father, a parson, naturally, believed that having their faces hidden would encourage them to reveal their true characters, to act without lies or dissemblance. Obviously — witness "Lucien" — a false assumption. An ironic assumption, too, since all three girls went on to publish their novels under androgynous pseudonyms. Branwell just went on to be an annoying waste of time. What do you think Nick would do if he were an interrogator given carte blanche with a hot nineteen-year-old girl suspect?

Long pause.

V: You do understand that these interviews are being conducted on the basis that you're willing to talk to us in a meaningful way? They can be terminated at any time.

Pause.

K: I'm sorry. It's possible I have ADHD. In the nicest possible way, obviously. Ask me anything, and I'll tell you the truth.

V: Where did he live?

K: I asked him. Now wait, Valerie, this is the truth: I asked him and he just said: "Lots of places." A deliberate imitation of that simian Christopher Lambert in *Highlander.* He told me he had a house in Pasadena, but I never went there. And he made it very clear that I never *would* go there. He was much more foresighted than me. For the first few months I assumed he was secretly married. But he had places — if his testimony is to be taken at face value — *everywhere.* Zurich. London. São Paulo. He was either the most strategic budgeter in history or he really was fabulously rich.

V: What do you mean?

K: You've searched my apartment, right? You've seen the jewels?

V: Yes.

K: They're all kosher. That diamond necklace is worth three years' salary for you. Do you want to borrow it? Maybe I'll leave it to you in my will. Can you imagine the fun the newspapers would have with that? If you saw what was in my safe-deposit box . . .

V: We're getting a warrant for that, so I guess I will.

K: Oh, you *minx.* I knew I should have inventoried it. Now half the SFPD's ladies are going to be walking around in gold. There's a garnet bracelet that would suit you. Red stones look so much better on brunettes. And you've got pretty hands. I mean, they're not in *my* league, let's be honest, but —

V: Did he ever visit the gallery?

K: Never.

V: Did he ever mention family? Ex-wives, girlfriends?

K: Only one. The legendary Selene. Although who knows if that was *her* real name?

V: An ex?

K: My failed predecessor. He thought she had what it takes. It turned out she didn't. They were all set to go in Rio, if you can believe that, but Selene got cold feet at the last minute.

V: When was this?

K: God knows. A couple of years before he met me. At least a couple of years, I should say. Maybe more.

V: Had he done this before?

K: Apart from the abortive adventure with Selene, no, I don't believe he had. We lost our you-know-what virginity together. Afterward it was as if for the first time in my life all my muscles and joints had come into their proper alignment. Now come on, admit it: you *do* want to know why, really. I know you do.

Another pause.

Listening back now, Valerie remembered the effort she'd had to make *not* to ask why. In the silence of the pause between them on the recording she felt the same claustrophobic curiosity she'd suffered at the time. And yes, Katherine had been right: the curiosity was gendered. Even back then Valerie had been Police long enough to be dead to the mystery of why men did these things. With men there *was* no mystery. The world — especially her world — was a daily reminder that she'd accepted male violence as a fact of the universe, like the hardness of stone or the coldness of ice. She would have been incapable of doing her job if she hadn't. The job made mystification an unaffordable luxury. If a stone hit you in the face it would hurt, and if you lay on a frozen lake long enough you'd freeze to death. Those were the only relevant facts. Rapists and murderers had always done what they did and always would. Or perhaps in some remote future version of the world there would be no rapists or murderers. She doubted it. Regardless, it wasn't her world — and never had been. Her world was the one where men did what they did. But Katherine was a woman. It had shocked Valerie that in spite of herself this made a difference. Intellectually she knew there were cruel women, violent women, homicidal women. But she was forced to admit, faced with Katherine Glass, that she, Valerie, had always taken it vaguely for granted that the behavior of such women derived from something that had happened to them. Look hard enough into their pasts and you'd find the damage, the spoilage, the derailment, the pain. You'd find *something* that went a way to explaining the extremities at which they'd ended up. Women, she'd assumed, were *driven* to it. Yet the whole time with Katherine she'd felt that assumption short-circuiting. Before the trial the psychologists had, one by one, effectively given up. Not because they doubted that Katherine's "supernatural evil" had very natural antecedents, but because she, Katherine, seemed determined to deny them. All the shrinks had concluded (shrugging, throwing up their hands, or calmly drawing a line under their pages of notes) that Katherine was a psychopath. She met, in one doctor's words, "enough of the standard criteria." For all its controversy, the twenty-point Hare PCL-R Checklist from the mid-seventies still informed a lot of evaluation. Katherine was (mockingly) familiar with it. Let's save some time, she'd told one psychiatrist. Superficial charm? Check — and *more* than "superficial," I think we can agree. Grandiose sense of self-worth? Perhaps, but leavened by a sense of irony and a taste for the absurd. Need for stimulation/proneness to boredom? Oh, *check.* Pathological lying? No. (But then of course what pathological liar would say otherwise?) Cunning/manipulative? Check. Lack of remorse or guilt? Let's leave that one for now. I'm not sure I can answer it without poetry. Shallow affect? No. Callous/lack of empathy? Well, actions speak louder than words, you'll say, but you'd be missing the point. Parasitic lifestyle? No, but not for want of trying! Poor behavioral controls? No. Promiscuous sexual behavior? No. Early behavior problems? They're only problems if you get caught, and I never was. Lack of realistic long-term goals? No. Impulsivity? No. Irresponsibility? No. Failure to accept responsibility for own actions? No. Many short-term marital relationships? Hilarious. No. Juvenile delinquency? No. Revocation of conditional release? Not applicable, nor imaginable, since I doubt I'll ever be released, conditionally or otherwise. Criminal versatility? Probably. I'm smart and resourceful. There you are, doctor. I'd score myself about eleven or twelve out of the maximum forty. And I don't need to remind you that that dreadful *potato* of a woman, Karla Homolka, only scored five. Where will you go next? Hybristophilia? Malignant narcissism? The first doesn't quite cover it, does it? Obviously I'm attracted to sadistic men, but we can put that as much in the category of practical necessity as we can pathology. The second is a good contender, but I don't have a hair-trigger, nor do I dehumanize the people with whom I associate. Including the victims. Quite the contrary, in fact. Their humanity is essential.

K: Have you read *Sophie's Choice*? Seen the movie?

Valerie started, slightly, at the sound of

Katherine's voice after the tape's long pause.

V: I saw the movie, yes.

K: The Nazi officer tells Sophie she must choose one of her children to die, and that if she doesn't make the choice *both* children will die.

V: Yes, I know.

K: Do you think the Nazi lacked empathy?

V: What?

K: Empathy is the ability to understand and share in another person's feelings. Do you think the Nazi understood and shared in Sophie's feelings?

V: Of course not.

K: Oh, Valerie, it would be so comforting if that were true. But it isn't. Of *course* he had empathy. Empathy was essential.

V: Okay. We're drifting a little here.

K: Listen, Valerie, this is important. I'm telling you something that will deepen your understanding. It's what you're afraid of in me, but it's a fear you're ashamed of, so I'm going to help you past it. Empathy is supposed to be the antidote to cruelty. But it's just the opposite. Cruelty *depends* on empathy. You have to empathize with the victim in order to know — to *really* know — that their suffering is guaranteed. The fairy tale says that if you really knew how much something would hurt someone, you wouldn't do it. But the fairy tale underestimates cruelty. It has to; otherwise it wouldn't be a fairy tale. Inflicting suffering on someone without understanding isn't cruelty, it's mere brutality. It's *only* the understanding that makes it cruel. Cruelty is a passenger on the train that slows down for the empathy stop, waves, then goes on past it. Empathy simply isn't the last stop, however much you'd like it to be. Don't you see? The Nazi probably had children of his own.

V: You might be right, but let's move on. Let's go back to the first victim, Alicia Hooper —

K: Is that enough for you? Do you think I've answered the question?

V: You said in your earlier statement that you picked her up in a car on Folsom Street —

K: No, I said that he'd watched her on Folsom Street. He didn't pick her up there. He made contact with her somewhere else.

V: Where?

K: I don't know. The answer, by the way, is because it's the most natural thing about me. The discovery was immediate and intuitive. I couldn't have been more than four or five years old. At that stage when kids have always got their hands down their pants. Abstractedly, most of the time. I wasn't often abstracted. I can't remember a time when I didn't masturbate. I thought of it to myself as "the good feeling." Getting the *good* feeling. Irony's there from the start, like the Devil. Anyway, one day I heard my father shouting at my mother in their bathroom. He shouted at her a lot. I knew she was afraid of him. There was that energy that came off him sometimes. I crept to the door and looked through the gap. He had her by the hair and was twisting her neck and forcing her to her knees. She was crying. I never knew her to fight back in any way. I just knew the vague sound of her pleading. It was the depressing little weather system in the lovely home, absorbed by the white countertops and state-of-the-art gadgets. I wasn't close to her. I wasn't close to either of them, particularly, but my father never did anything to me. There was a strange pause between them. Her on her knees, him standing with his fist wrapped in her hair, breathing through his nose. She was just saying, please, please. I was curious. My father held her hair and stared down at her. Then he looked away, as if he were concentrating on something on the floor. He stayed like that for what seemed a long time. Then he unzipped his pants and his cock sprang out. It was the first time I'd ever seen it. It looked huge. It looked the size of my *arm*. He pushed it toward her face, and her face seemed to crumple. When I remember her face now it's like the Tragedy mask, that perfect inversion of a smile. It was extraordinary. But I knew what was going to happen. She opened her mouth and in it went. I watched. It went on for a long time. It was so odd to hear her gagging and watch his hand moving her head. She banged her head, actually, on the side of the bathtub, but he just kept going. I heard him say, very quietly, but focused, like a carefully held scalpel, You swallow it. *Swallow* it. He shuddered. It was strange and ugly seeing his hairy legs because his pants had slipped down. Afterward my mother wiped her mouth and he just stood there, looking ill. His face was different, swollen. I crept away. And later that night, when I masturbated, there it was. The good feeling, but better than ever before. You see, I knew she didn't like it. I knew she liked it less than if he'd just hit her. But I liked that she didn't like it, and that was that. So do you think I'm a different species? Do you think I had the wrong reaction because I have the wrong wiring? Or because the Devil had marked my card from the moment of conception?

Another long pause.

V: You know what? It's not my job to answer that question. That's why I'm not interested. My job is to stop you from doing what you do. *Why* you do it is for other people to decide. I can see that it's important to you that I care, but I'm sorry, I really don't. Believe me, there are plenty of people who do care. But the fact is I'm not one of them.

K: And yet you listened. Not entirely strategically, I think. Why do you think Nick's stopped sitting in on our conversations? I miss him.

V: Interview terminated at 7:18 P.M.

22

Four days later Valerie got an e-mail from Susanna Arden.

Detective Hart, please see below from Katherine Glass:

Dear Valerie,
I haven't cracked all of it yet, but I'm close. I'm sorry it's going so slowly. Ironically, so far I've spent more time on the map of Mesopotamia than on anything else. Ironically because the cipher it reveals is a version of my annoyingly common name. I could kick myself for being so dim. The map shows the whole of the ancient territory now covered by modern Iraq, but the relevant area is in the south, where the Tigris and Euphrates run into the sea. Relevant because since St. Augustine that's been one of the most popular choices among

the demented and the credulous for the original geographical location of — don't laugh — the Garden of Eden. I doubt I would have worked that out, but the "East" point on the map's compass is circled. With risible belatedness it clicked: *East of Eden,* which is, of course, a novel by Steinbeck. The novel's anti-heroine (and gal after my own heart) is named Cathy Ames. According to our friend, one of my many fictional avatars. Well, let me be truthful: according to our friend *and* me. Cathy is, after all, blond and beautiful, with small but manifestly seductive breasts, and, in Steinbeck's own words, a "pearly light" which makes her irresistible to men. Naturally, she's also a monster (a common criticism of the novel is that in its biblical schema "Cathy" is Satan, a being of pure evil with a psychological narrative insufficient to support or explain it), and equally naturally she doesn't end well, crippled with arthritis, a "sick ghost" in a brothel, eventually a murderer and ultimately a suicide. Charming. But there you are: Cathy Ames it is, whether I like it or not.

Nineteen Eighty-Four was much easier, since we talked once (memorably) about the concept of Room 101, where poor Winston, like all the room's unfortunate visitors, is forced to confront his greatest fear. In his case it's rats. Our friend's was drowning. Mine (ha-ha) is burial alive, which I'm all but living through even as I write this, courtesy of God's insatiable and perverse sense of humor. I'm working through permutations using both "drowning" and "burial/burial alive" as ciphers, since it could be either, but as you can imagine, that doubles the work.

Scarlett Johansson mystifies me, as yet, and I'm racking my brains for the significance of the magnified picture of the needle (I don't know if I'm looking for numbers or words), but please bear with me. I am *devoted* to this. Not, obviously, out of some lately developed conscience, but because it remains the most fun I've had in six years.

I would ask how the "police procedure" is going, but since I assume you're in the thick of it I know you'll have better things to do with your time than hammer out an update e-mail to me. But don't let me forget the other thing I want to discuss with you, next time we meet.

You will come and see me again, won't you?

Okay. Enough. Back to the coal face for poor, exhausted — but diligent — Ms. Glass!

K

23

"Natalie Dormer," Eugene said.

"Who's Natalie Dormer?" Nick asked.

"The girl from *Game of Thrones* with the turned-up nose. Margaery Tyrell. She has the thing."

They were back in the locker room at the Bay Club. Nick, naked but for his underwear, was sitting on the bench massaging his left knee. He'd crashed into the side wall chasing down one of Eugene's drop shots. Nothing broken, but pain enough to draw a slight wince with his weight on it. He wondered if the bone was chipped. They'd had to abort their third game, having won one each. Eugene, naturally, had claimed the tide was turning back in his favor.

"Cersei ought to have the thing," Eugene said. "And Melisandre *half* has it. Daenerys Targaryen has got that fabulous body wasted because she absolutely does *not* have it. But Margaery's got it. She's got *all* of it."

Nick picked up his jeans and began easing them on. "I realize you're speaking English," he said. "But I don't have a fucking clue what you're talking about."

"You don't know *Game of Thrones*? The TV show?"

"I've heard of it, I think."

"You've *heard* of it? Jesus. Do you own a television?"

"Yeah, but I don't watch it much."

"Holy mother of God. What do you watch?"

"We don't get the time to watch much of anything," Nick said. "The news. The occasional ball game. I was following the English Premier League for a while, but I've lost touch. We start watching a movie, but I fall asleep."

"Well, you need to watch this show. It's like X-rated Tolkien. Genius."

"That's the *Lord of the Rings* guy, right?"

"For God's sake," Eugene said. "Never mind do you have a television. Do you live on *Earth*?"

"I don't care for fairies and wizards and whatnot."

"Okay. *Mad Men? Breaking Bad?* Jesus, *The Wire?*"

"Yeah, I saw *The Wire* once. I don't need it. I might as well stay at work."

Eugene made a gesture of impatience with his hands. "Look, never mind any of that. Just give me your top five."

"My top five what?"

"Breakfast cereals," Eugene said. *"Women, you dolt. Your top five members of the female species."*

"What, *any* women?"

Eugene closed his eyes. Sighed. Opened them. A theatrical performance of patience. "The five women — *famous* women, you understand, not your *girlfriend* — that you'd have sex with if you could. No strings, no consequences, no pregnancies or STDs — and you have your lady's full and complete permission. Are you following this? It's a thought experiment. It's a hypothetical."

"I haven't really thought about it," Nick said.

"What do you mean you haven't thought about it? *Everyone* thinks about it."

"Well, you're going to have to give me a minute. Actresses, right?"

Eugene pulled his T-shirt over his head. "Look, you don't know anything. You're in bad shape. What you're aiming for is top fives in every category. 'Actresses' is way too broad. You want movie actresses, yes, but that's a separate category from TV actresses. And we've got to divide U.S. and non-U.S.

talent. *Porn* actresses, obviously, are a whole different animal. Then you've got pop stars, athletes, news anchors, weather girls, politicians, writers. . . . Actually, even I struggle with writers. But I've got most of my categories divided into *decades.* I mean, you want Brigitte Bardot, right, but not the way she looks *now.*"

"Do you actually do anything for a living?" Nick said. Eugene worked as a freelance business consultant (for which read: the guy who goes in and tells them who to fire, he'd said) off the back of a Harvard MBA and was, in spite of all evidence of congenital idleness, doing pretty well. The car in the Bay Club lot was a Mercedes AMG GT S. Not much change from a hundred and fifty grand. The Rolex *was* a Rolex. The women, when Eugene wasn't grappling with them, were dined at Saison, Jardinière, Gary Danko. No one wants the responsibility for making some poor schmuck unemployed, Eugene had explained. They feel so shitty about it they'd rather recruit someone to shoulder the blame. I'm a white-collar prostitute. No — I'm a white-collar *hit* man. That should be the name of a band. White-Collar Hit Man. See how many ideas I have? I'm like a goddamned idea factory. I usually have ten ideas before breakfast. I just don't have the energy to follow them through. My suntan suits, for example. These are like weightless microfiber cooling bodysuits with cut-outs, like a body stocking. You put it on when you're getting a tan, and thanks to the cut-out bits you end up with tiger stripes or leopard spots or whatever. You could tan your lover's name on your ass. And unlike tattoos, if you break up, it's no big deal. It fades. Tell me there's not a market for that.

"I don't think about this stuff when I'm working," Eugene said. "I think about it on the squash court. Because I have so much time, while you're floundering around and crashing into the walls, courtesy of my satanic drop shots."

They went to the bar and settled in for their ritual two beers. Nick's knee was throbbing rhythmically, but he felt, as always after the blur of combat, usefully purged. Eugene was, as per usual, slightly flushed. He had a gym-worked body and an alert face, lively blue eyes, and dark-gold hair in a buzz cut. I'm going for Celtic Arthurian meets soulful marine, he said. Not many people can get away with this cut without looking like a thug. But I've got my supermodel cheekbones and a very nicely shaped head. The whole effect is one of an

311

elegant jewel. Masculine, yes, but with a little sensitive mystery. I carry myself as if I know I'm worth knowing, but I'm trying to hide it.

"Debbie Harry," Nick said. "In the 'Heart of Glass' video."

"You're combining categories there," Eugene said. "She's a pop star *and* an actress. But you're a novice, so I'll let it go. What number?"

"What do you mean?"

"Where in the top five?"

"I don't know. Give me a chance."

"Debbie doesn't have the thing," Eugene said. "There's too much kindness and self-mockery there. The vamping was always ironic. What you're after is cynical filth. That's the thing."

"There's something truly wrong with you."

"That's what you have to tell yourself because you're in denial. Whereas I . . . I am standing, looking fearlessly into the heart of the light."

"You need to cut down on your porn."

"Don't get me started on porn. Do you know who Chanel Preston is?"

"No."

"Google her. If I were going to marry anyone, I'd marry her. Porn models come and go for me, but Chanel is constant as the Northern Star. We were made for each other. We'd get along. It hurts my heart that I'm never going to meet her. That's how I feel about Chanel. How's the knee?"

"Painful."

"You want Tylenol? I've got some in my bag."

"It's fine. I've had worse."

"You say that, but I'm wondering how long you're going to string this out as an excuse."

"So, Chanel whatsername's not on the horizon. Any other business to report?"

Eugene exhaled, smiling. "Michelle," he said. "Thirty-five, brunette. Still with the hyperditziness she should've outgrown ten years ago. Cute rather than sexy, and truth be told a little thick in the wrists and ankles. Certainly not my usual racehorse. Third date last week. We had sex. I think I only had sex with her because she'd made it so obvious that she was a two-dates-before-sex kind of girl."

"I'm already sorry I asked."

"Well, surprisingly, it was quite nice. Kind of a gentle jackpot. She had some skills, albeit you could tell she'd acquired them with a sort of sadness. She had a resigned, docile enthusiasm. If it hadn't been for what

313

she said I might have seen her again."

"What did she say?"

"It was when we were lying there in bed together afterward. You know, standard postcoital arrangement: my arm around her, her head on my chest, the scene in the movie where the girl trails her fingertips over him and asks how he got the little scar or whatever. . . . Anyway, we're lying there, just chatting, and eventually the pauses get longer and I can feel myself drifting off to sleep. Just as I'm about to, she squeezes me with her leg and says, in my ear: 'I like it here with you.' "

Eugene shuddered theatrically.

"Christ," Nick said. "What a monster."

"You don't get it, do you? She might as well have stabbed me."

Nick shook his head in resignation. Eugene smiled — then stopped smiling suddenly. "Oh shit," he said quietly. He was looking past Nick toward the bar. Nick turned. A heavily built guy in Adidas whites and a red bandanna was approaching their table. He was deeply tanned, with a bright-white smile and glittery blue eyes: an overall look of deep physical indulgence, of calmly slaked appetites.

"Mr. Eugene *Trent,*" he said, beaming.

Eugene had gotten to his feet. "Mr. Don

Lewis." The two men did the handshake that morphs into a butch handclasp, with a little mutual tugging as if to confirm shared testosterone.

"Who knew you played here?" Lewis said.

Eugene had reconstructed his smile, but Nick could see it masked discomfort. He was expecting Eugene to introduce him. Eugene didn't. Lewis didn't acknowledge Nick's existence. Just kept his delighted eyes fixed on Eugene.

"Yeah, I'm a regular, dude. I didn't know you —"

"I don't. It's a one-off. We're still good for Friday, right?"

"Right," Eugene said.

"The numbers are working," Lewis said.

"Yeah, but not in my favor, I'm guessing," Eugene replied, at which *both* men's smiles broadened.

For a peculiar, silent moment, they just stood there, grinning at each other. Then Lewis pulled off his bandanna to reveal a head of lustrous dark hair. "Alrighty," he said. "I gotta bounce. I'll see you Friday."

"See you Friday," Eugene said.

As Lewis walked away Eugene resumed his seat with a visible slump. Nick raised his eyebrows.

"Fucking Facebook," Eugene said. "I went

to college with him. We do the catch-up bullshit, then it turns out he's looking for investors in a goddamned nightclub. I shouldn't have gotten drunk. That's my trouble. I get drunk, I fill up with love. Friday I'm going to have to break the bad news."

"Really?" Nick said. "I can see you as a nightclub owner."

"So can I," Eugene said. "But not with that nut. He's a total fucking loose cannon."

"He doesn't look like the type to take bad news well."

Eugene made a dismissive gesture. "He'll get over it. I just have to remember not to drink."

They walked out to the parking lot together, Nick limping slightly. Beyond all the nonsense, he felt vaguely sorry for Eugene. (Although less sorry for him than for the unfortunate Michelle.) He was lonely, Nick thought. Transparently lonely. The philandering cynicism revealed precisely what it was meant to conceal: an increasing sense that either he would never find someone real, or that if he did, he was too far gone in his character to be able to keep her.

"You know who really had the thing?" Eugene said.

"Who?"

"Katherine Glass."

Eugene, like everyone else in the country, had never forgotten the trial, and when he had learned that Nick had been one of the investigators had naturally wanted to hear all about it. As far as the facts of the case went, there wasn't anything Nick told him that wasn't already a matter of public record. But of course that wasn't what Eugene (or anyone else) was really interested in. Eugene (and everyone else) wanted to know what Katherine Glass was really like. Nick had said nothing to him of the current case. No one outside law enforcement knew Katherine was involved. It made him uncomfortable to have her brought up again between them.

"You wouldn't say that if you'd met her," he said.

"I know I shouldn't joke about it, but come on. You said yourself she was a piece of work."

"Sure," Nick said. "If you like sadistic homicidal psychopaths."

"It is possible I might not have been able to handle her."

"Trust me, you wouldn't."

"She was so *hot,* though."

"Well, she's up at Red Ridge prison for the foreseeable future. You could go visit her. I wouldn't recommend it."

"Are you kidding? I'd be scared shitless. But she's definitely number one in my psycho top five."

"Stick with Chanel," Nick said. "Or quit deluding yourself and admit you're ready for love."

"Well, if it was Chanel . . ."

"I'll check in with you when this stops hurting," Nick said.

"Yeah, I don't want you blaming your next crushing defeat on a weak knee."

Nick drove home with his head full of Valerie and Katherine. There had been a point — right at the beginning, when Valerie called him and told him about the note — when he'd missed his opportunity. He should have said: Don't see her. Get off the case right now. Let the Feds do it on their own. He'd had it right there on the tip of his tongue. But he'd known, even in the moment of almost saying it, that it would have been a waste of time. It would have meant patient, painful argument. And in the end the result would have been exactly the same.

For the umpteenth time he wished Katherine's death sentence had been just what it was supposed to be: the end of her.

But she lived. And thanks to Valerie's intractable sense of responsibility, thanks to the job only half done, Katherine Glass was back in their lives. She might as well be living with them.

Nick didn't believe in God, but it didn't stop him from mentally uttering the occasional forlorn prayer.

Please, God, let it be over soon.

24

Cassie Hart had a headache. It had been building in sympathy with the morning's gathering thunderstorm since waking. Now she was at the drop-in center, hunting for Advil in the kitchen. The rain hadn't come yet. The air was massed and electric. She was sensitive to the weather, unlike her sister, whose relationship to the physical world these days was determined, it seemed to Cassie, exclusively by how it affected her ability to do her job. These days Valerie's relationship to *everything* was determined that way. Except, of course, Nick. One night, a couple of months after Valerie had started seeing him again, the two sisters had been out to dinner at their favorite Italian restaurant. They'd been going there since their early twenties, a small place with lots of soft red drapes and tea lights in little blue shot glasses. Valerie had said: I know this is my second chance. And even thinking that makes me feel like I'm daring the gods to take it away. Cassie had let it go, but even at the time she'd thought of her sister as living proof that understanding what was wrong with you was no guarantee that you'd ever be able to change it.

The painkillers were not under the sink. "Goddamnit," Cassie said, half to herself, half to Bree, who was loading the dishwasher. "I thought we had Advil in here?"

"In the third drawer down," Bree said. "We moved that stuff when the sink leaked — remember?"

Bree was a floaty woman in her early forties with heavy-lidded eyes and a lot of thick, dyed red hair, invariably held back from her face by a psychedelic head scarf. Twenty-five years ago she'd moved west from Texas to study art history at USC, from which she'd just about graduated (she was a vague student who daydreamed and dawdled through her degree with a gentle resignation to the fact that it wasn't ever going to amount to more than a hobby for her) and married a young doctor (now a big-bucks cardiologist) not long after leaving college. She'd been a stay-at-home mother until her one son had turned sixteen and now spent her time mildly enjoying museums and galleries, gardening, and having endless cappuccinos with idle friends, salving her not-very-robust social conscience by supporting a few charities and volunteering at the drop-in two days a week. Lately, Cassie had noticed an aesthetic stepping-up in Bree, a little weight loss, fitted clothes, makeup more precisely applied. She assumed Bree had begun having an affair, but they weren't sufficiently close for her to ask.

"It's this goddamned weather," Bree said, as Cassie found the painkillers and popped a couple. "Even these guys seem strangely subdued."

"These guys" were the drop-in's patrons. Most of the regulars were there, but there was a pent-up atmosphere in the lounge café. The three card-playing ladies (the "poker posse") were in their usual spot by the window. Moya, an eccentric fifty-two-year-old who wrote poetry no one could understand (or indeed *stand*) was at one of the desktop computers looking at — God only knew why — archive footage of whales being flensed. Tommy, the tattooed guy, was at a table alone, going through a file of old telephone and utility bills. He had these occasional fierce fixations, part of his ongoing belief that the world was a conspiracy dedicated to ripping him off. Today his mood was worse than usual because blind John hadn't shown up. Tommy looked as if he'd been deprived of a curious but desperately needed fix.

"Honey, why don't you take off if you're feeling lousy?" Bree said. "I can handle things here."

"Oh, no, it's fine," Cassie said. "These babies should kick in soon. I'm just being a wuss." This was Cassie's reflex mode, her share in the family trait of not feeling sorry for yourself, overdeveloped in her case thanks to years of nursing, of dealing with people who were *really* suffering.

"Well, I wish you'd go see Denise," Bree said. "I'm telling you: You go once, you'll want to go every day." Denise was Bree's massage therapist. "I haven't had a headache in ten years," Bree continued. "It all starts with what's going on in your trapezoids. Or wait, maybe it's your mastoids. . . ."

Cassie's shift passed uneventfully, but she was glad when it was over. For all her dismissal of Valerie's warnings as paranoia, she didn't feel properly at ease until she was at home with Owen and the kids safely tucked up in bed. Her feelings were the basic you-don't-give-in-to-terrorism model, but they were hard to sustain if you had kids. There might be first principles worth dying for, but there were *no* principles — first or otherwise — she was willing to let her sons die for. Since Valerie's alert, she and Owen had tightened up. There were new security locks at home. The kids were confined to their own backyard. For the last week of school, drop-offs and pick-ups, either she or Owen went *inside* the building, much to the boys' mortification.

"Vincent's only six," Jack had protested, "so I get that. But Mom, I am *eight and a half.*"

It had delighted her, secretly, that she'd brought them up with a sense of independence and responsibility. She'd wanted to *hug* Jack when he'd come out with this. But any pride in her sons' autonomy took a distant second place to keeping them safe. She'd invoked the rarely used maternal right of veto without appeal. "This is one of those times, Jack, where, hard though it might be, you are just going to have to do exactly as I say, with zero argument. Now how often do I say that?"

"All the time," Jack had said, without much conviction.

"Tell the truth. Come on, look me in the eye."

Much eight-year-old shifting from foot to

foot. "But *Mom . . .*"

"How often, Jack?"

"Yeah, but —"

"Look me in the eye and tell me I'm not the most reasonable mother on the planet. I should get some sort of *award* for how reasonable I am."

"You're not *that* reasonable."

"Spell 'reasonable.' "

"What?"

"Come on."

She'd watched him sketching it out in his head. She'd watched him recognize a lost cause. She'd watched him let it go. He didn't really mind, deep down. Of course his little burgeoning masculinity was affronted, but his wiser child self knew, inarticulately, that the proscription came out of love. She'd watched all this going on in him and been filled for a moment with the richness of her life, its fabulous gifts and priceless treasures, all wrapped up in the plain paper of ordinariness. All that wealth you took completely for granted — until someone exploded it.

Valerie had wanted her to get a gun, but she'd resisted. There's no point, unless I'm going to carry the goddamned thing around with me the whole time, and I'm not doing that. One gun-toting woman in the family is enough. I'd probably end up shooting myself in the foot. Besides, the kids already spend half their lives firing Xbox guns at robots. I'm not having them anywhere near the real thing.

The sky was heavy, and a few thin drops were falling by the time she stepped out of the center into the parking lot, just after two thirty in the afternoon, but the main event still wouldn't break. The short walk to her car was a wade through molasses. She needed to stop at the supermarket on her way home to pick up stuff for dinner (salmon steaks, she thought, maybe some kale and fixings for a bean salad, though Jack and Vincent would groan; what the hell, she'd make some french fries, too, by way of compensation) and to collect a suede jacket she'd had dry-cleaned. Drop those at home, take a quick shower, then it would be time to go and get the boys from her mom's, where the presence of one of Valerie's delegated police officers (there were three of these guys on rotation) had been at first a source of amazement to them, then, in the way that kids had, assimilated, courtesy of Cassie's explanation that they were Neighborhood Watch officers "in training," sent there by crazy Aunt Valerie.

Cassie was looking in her purse for her

keys when she heard a strange sound — a sob? — a few feet behind her, and turned.

"John?" she said.

"Who's there?"

"John, it's Cassie from the drop-in. What . . . what's the matter? Hey . . ."

He was leaning against the flank of a brand new pick-up truck parked a couple of spots away. He had his white stick in his hand, but he was shaking, obviously in distress. There was no sign of his Seeing Eye dog.

"Oh, Cassie," he said, straightening and putting out his hand. "Thank God it's you. They took Frankie!"

"What?"

"I don't know . . . I was . . . They must've taken him."

"Someone took your *dog*?"

For a moment, John just stood there, trying to get himself under control. What she could see of his face (aside from the half-gray beard and dark glasses) was moist. He looked overheated, in fact, in a combat jacket and sweatshirt.

"I need a . . . Can you give me a ride to the police station? I mean, do I even go to the police? I don't know what to do! Frankie's my *eyes,* he's my *eyes.*"

Cassie stepped over to him and took his

outstretched hand. He was fever hot.

"Okay," she said, "take it easy. Take it easy now. Tell me what happened. Just calm down and tell me what happened."

"What am I going to do?" John said. "I mean, how am I supposed to get *home* even?"

"John, seriously, calm down. Don't upset yourself. We'll get you home, don't worry. Just tell me what happened."

"He's microchipped," John said. "But that's only any good if someone hands him in. What if they hurt him? What if they *kill* him?"

"John, listen to me. Come with me into the center. Let's get you —"

"No, no, I need to sit down for a second. I'm . . . I need to sit down."

"Okay. Listen, my car is right here. Just a few steps. You can sit down and tell me what happened. Come on. Take my arm."

Cassie helped him to the Mazda and got him settled in the passenger seat. The first thing she wanted to do was cool him down. It would take a few minutes for the air-conditioning to work its magic, but she had faith in its restorative effects. She started the engine and turned the dial up to max. A sheet of lightning shivered. Followed a few seconds later by loud, brittle thunder. Big droplets began to fall, an urgent calypso on the car's body.

"Here," she said. "I've got a brand-new bottle of water in my purse. Have some. You're a little overheated. Do you want to take your jacket off? It would help."

"No, no, I'll be okay in a minute. Thank you. You're kind. I'm sorry I'm so upset."

"Don't be silly. Here, drink some water."

He was still shaking, but his breathing was easier. He took a couple of swallows from the bottle.

"I waited and waited," he said. "When the bus came, I thought, you know, if I could get here someone would . . . someone . . ."

"It's okay, hon," Cassie said. "We'll figure it out. I promise we'll figure it out."

"But when I got here I got lost in the parking lot. I'm so used to Frankie knowing the way, you know?"

"I know. Of course. Of *course.*"

"Who would do that?" he said. "I mean, goddamnit, who would *do* that?"

She got the story out of him, in bits and pieces. As far as he could tell a girl had spoken to him at the bus stop. She'd made a big fuss of the dog. "I *knew* she was with someone," John said. "But when I asked her, she said it was just her. Now I think there might have been a few of them. She sounded young, like a teenager. She said she'd wait with me till the bus came."

But she hadn't. At some point John had felt Frankie's harness snatched out of his hand.

"There was a car idling the whole time," he said. "They must've just bundled him in there. You know Frankie. He's good with people. He probably thought I was going to get in there with him."

Cassie was furious. Or rather, depressed because she *wasn't* furious. She wasn't furious because she wasn't surprised. Kids did cruel things. Small things to them, it seemed, ephemeral transgressions that added a little capital to the idea they needed to have of themselves as heartless. She imagined some of the gang who'd done this would've had mixed feelings. But they would've been outweighed by the one or two strong, contemptuous personalities in the group, the kind of kids who were moving through the last phase of willed hardness from which it might still be possible to escape. These kids would have a year, maybe months, maybe days before their commitment to killing compassion in themselves would be set in stone. Somewhere in her calculations she understood *her* kids would never be that way, not terminally. She knew she and Owen had already done enough. Then she thought: maybe *these* kids' parents thought the same thing? Could you ever know for sure?

"Okay," she said, when it was obvious that John was just going to keep repeating the same handful of facts, "tell me what you'd like to do. My guess is we should report it. I mean, it's a theft. The station's down on Alvarado. I can come with you, if you like, if that would help?" Screw the shopping: they could order in pizza. At least the boys would *eat* it. The rain was coming down hard now.

"You're very kind, Cassie," John said. "I don't want to put you to all this trouble. I just don't know what the hell I'm going to do."

"Well, let's start with the report," she said. "After that, I can drive you home, if you like. Where do you live?"

"Faber Street," John said. "But I'm messing up your day. I'm sorry."

"John, it's nothing," she said. "Is there someone else we should call? A relative? I mean, will you be able to manage?"

"I'll call GDB when I get home," he said. "They'll figure something out."

"GDB?"

"Guide Dogs for the Blind."

"But I mean, what about this evening? Is

there someone . . ."

"My neighbor upstairs will help," John said. "He's a good friend of mine." Then he added: "I live alone."

Jesus Christ, Cassie thought. Alone and *blind*. We don't know how lucky we are. How did he cook? Was it a life of deliveries? Were there braille microwaves?

"Just give me one sec," she said. She called her mother and explained she might be a little late for the boys.

"I'm so sorry this has happened, John," she said. "Here, let me get your seat belt for you."

"Thank you, Cassie. I don't know what I would've done if you hadn't come along. I really don't."

"Just relax," Cassie said, shifting the car into drive and easing toward the exit. "You just sit back and relax, and I promise we'll get this straightened out."

They had driven five or six blocks when he pulled the knife from his inside jacket pocket and pressed it against the soft flesh of her waist.

"Do exactly as I say," he said, "or this goes into you and you'll never see your family again."

25

Valerie was alone in the incident room when her phone rang.

"Owen, what is it?"

"It's Cassie," Owen said. "Something's wrong. She's late and her phone's switched off. Something's happened. Jesus fucking Christ —"

"Slow down. Tell me."

"She called your mom this afternoon and said she was going to be late picking the kids up because she was helping one of the guys from the drop-in. Some old blind guy who'd lost his dog. Said she was taking him to the police to file a report and then maybe drive him home. Since then we haven't heard. And she doesn't switch her phone off, ever. She just *doesn't*."

"Let me call the precincts —"

"I already called the one near the drop-in. No one came in and made a fucking missing dog report. Val, it's wrong. You said this guy was going after people connected to you."

"Where are you now?"

"I'm home with the kids and your mom."

"Is the officer there with you?"

"Yeah."

"Put him on."

"Val, for Christ's sake —"

"Just let me talk to him for a second."

Owen passed the phone over.

"Officer Wilson, Detective."

She went through the drill — hospitals and precincts — in case there'd been an accident, but even while she was doing it a cold sickness filled her body. The officer sounded first calm, then, as Valerie's tone tightened, scared shitless. She told him to put Owen back on the line.

"We need a list of names for people who attend the drop-in," she said. "Is there someone you can call for that?"

"Jesus, I don't know. I don't know who's in charge there, and they'll be closed now anyway."

"Who's the woman who works with Cass?"

"Bree? Your mom called her already. She said Cassie left at two thirty."

Valerie looked at her watch. It was 6:40 P.M.

"Call her again and get the names. Get the *blind* guy's name. I'm coming over there right now. Was Cassie in her own car?"

"Yes."

"Do you know the license plate?"

"It's 62R . . . J243."

"Okay, listen to me. Stay where you are. All of you. I'm going to get an APB out on Cassie and the car. Do you know what she was wearing today?"

"What she . . . No, she was in her pajamas when I left this morning. But your mom —"

"Put her on."

Valerie's mother was in tears.

"Mom, calm down. We're going to deal with this."

"Why wouldn't she have the officer with her? I just keep thinking if she'd only listened to you —"

"Just tell me what she was wearing when she dropped the boys off. Think clearly, Mom. Just think clearly and tell me what she was wearing. It's going to be okay."

"Jeans," her mother said, sobbing. "Blue jeans and a pink blouse and sneakers, her white sneakers."

"Okay. Tell Officer Wilson that, too. I'm on my way. Try to stay calm. She's probably fine."

Lies, lies, lies.

On her way to her car she raced through the photos on her phone for one of her sister. The clearest was from her birthday party only a few days ago, e-mailed to her by her mother: Cassie standing over a pile of wrapped gifts and flowers at the garden table, smiling into the camera. All that happiness.

She called Will.

"Cassie's AWOL. I'm going out to Union City."

"Jesus, Val —"

"I'm e-mailing a picture to you right now," she said. "Get an APB out on Cassie's vehicle: metallic blue 2011 Mazda 3, license Six Two Romeo Juliet Two Four Three. Cassie was wearing blue jeans, pink shirt, white sneakers. Call McLuhan and tell him. I want them to drop everything else."

"Done," Will said. "Fuck. I'll meet you at Cassie's."

"No. Stay on it this end. I'll call you when I get there."

The drive to Union City was a warped dream, wrapped around with the siren's keening and the traffic's sluggish parting like the Red Sea resisting the miracle. Valerie's civilian self flailed around all the harmless explanations — a confusion of lost phones and dead chargers and she ran into an old friend and lost track of the time and the car broke down and — but her cop self was already set in dead certainty. Images of the victims' bodies and he uses the knife on them while he fucks them and this can't happen this *can't* happen except it happens all the time and all of Cassie's beauty and strength and love would count for nothing, nothing, nothing, because there's no God and the universe is innocent, press a knife against someone's flesh and it cuts, it goes in, it doesn't matter who they are because no one is watching and no one comes and you could see in all the videos of Katherine and the Man in the Mask that their victims kept going in that same wretched loop of thinking this couldn't be happening to them but it was and all that was left to them was the desire for it to be over.

Stop it. That pulls you into madness. You don't get him that way. You don't save Cassie that way. Cold. Think. Machine.

One of the guys from the drop-in. Some old blind guy who'd lost his dog. Valerie remembered him — the graying beard and dark glasses and white cane, the gentle dog in the Seeing Eye harness — but not his name. Two possibilities: one was that he was genuine and had nothing to do with it. Something could have happened after Cassie called in to say she'd be late. Maybe the guy changed his mind, or they found the dog, or there *was* an accident. The other was . . . the other was obvious. He was a fake. Neither blind nor whoever he said he was. Her own words came back to her: *In any case, we've got to assume the whole bag of tricks with this guy. Disguises, high mobility, resources, and a tech IQ off the chart. It's more than likely he's altered his appearance completely since the original killings.*

Some old guy. How old had he looked, really? Dark glasses. The beard. Fake blood at Raylene's house.

Raylene's. The man on her front lawn had a dog.

Fuck.

She could see how sweet that would be to him. His "blindness," which stopped them from seeing what was right under their noses. She'd been in the same room with him. And Cassie, all these months, serving him coffee, chatting. He'd been right there. He'd been *right there.*

At Cassie's house, Owen had to be virtually physically restrained from getting in his own car and going out to look for his wife.

"I need you to stay put and take care of the kids," Valerie told him. "What have you said to them so far?"

"Just that their mom got a call from the hospital to cover a shift."

"Good. She didn't, right? I mean, you called there?"

"Yeah, I called."

"Everyone who can look for her is looking for her. This is a federal case, so we've got extra eyes from the Bureau. We'll find her, Owen."

"You can't know that. How can you know that? You know what this sick fuck does. You *know* what he does."

"Oh God, don't say that, Owen," her mom wailed. "Don't *say* that!"

"Keep your voices down," Valerie said. The kids were in the den, watching TV. "Both of you, listen to me. The way to do this is by letting us do what we do. That's how you maximize the odds. Did you get the names and addresses from Bree?"

"She doesn't *have* names and addresses. It's not that kind of place, for Christ's sake. It's a drop-in center. It's first names. All she knows about the blind guy is that his name is John and he lives here in the city. Faber Street. She says his surname *might* be Hendricks, but she's not sure."

"What about the Volunteer Bureau? Who runs it?"

"It's a city-funded nonprofit. I got the cell phone number for the manager but she's not answering. The place closed at five thirty."

Valerie called McLuhan. She needed access to the Volunteer Bureau's CCTV. If the FBI couldn't get hold of someone who could let her into the building, she'd break a fucking window.

"I'm going out there now," she told McLuhan. "We know she left the building on her own, but there's half a dozen stores there that share the parking lot. They might have externals that picked her up. You need to run a full check on residents of Faber Street, Union City. Possible suspect, first name John, surname possibly Hendricks."

"On it," McLuhan said. "Valerie, listen, all the resources are dedicated. We'll find her."

Or maybe you'll just find her body. Tortured, raped —

Stop. *Stop.*

She called Susanna Arden. "What has she got?" she said.

"Part of a first name only so far. Andra."

Andra. Sandra. Cassandra. Cassie. Valerie's center of gravity fell away.

"Listen to me. Forget the name. Tell her to focus exclusively on the location."

"The location?"

"His last note to me said he was including the scene of the crime. Tell her to deal with that and only with that."

"You have the name already?" Arden said, lowering her voice. Valerie assumed she had stepped out into the corridor once she saw who was calling.

"Is she within earshot?"

"No."

"Yes, we have the name. We need the location."

"What's the —"

"It doesn't matter. Just get her to work on the location."

She'll know you've got a live case on your hands. What will she do with that?

"Okay," Arden said.

"And no restriction on computer access, time, whatever. She works, that's all. If you have to, call McLuhan and tell him to make it right with the warden. Whatever the existing parameters are, they're gone. I don't care what he has to do. Understood? McLuhan can send someone to relieve you."

Pause.

"Understood. We're live, I'm assuming?"

"Yes, we're live. I'd say don't tell Glass,

but it doesn't make any difference. She'll know. Any resistance, any trouble with Warden Clayton, you call me immediately."

"Okay."

"Tell her right now."

At the doorway, Owen said: "If she's . . . If anything happens to her . . ." He couldn't finish. A vestigial part of Valerie knew in her old life she would have put her arms around him and given him a hug. But she was oddly removed. There was an outer blaze of terror and desperation, but inside, a cold, dead swooning surrender to something, as if she'd known all along that this was what her life of the last weeks had been leading toward. Ever since the first note. *Katherine Glass stays in prison, more people die.* Katherine Glass. Every step forward was a step into darkness. There was nothing beyond it. Only the force of it, drawing her on, like the current of a pitch-black river.

26

Cassie came up from darkness into pain.

Pain was the first thing. Her head's warm throb and the stone ache of her arms. Thirst. Her mouth was stuffed with something sour. There was a smell of raw earth and kerosene.

For a moment, she knew nothing but these sensations.

Then her mind found its gear — and she knew everything.

Everything that had happened. Her situation. The worst situation.

The sourness in her mouth was a cloth gag.

The understanding was like death. It was impossible that she was living through this. But she was.

The room was the room she'd seen through the blur of tears. Small, dilapidated, gracefully cobwebbed in its corners. Old floorboards. A dead fireplace. The bare brick wall at her back. The wooden stool. Two windows with curtains shut, twin squares of orange light. The front door was closed. Frayed red and green bungee cords hung on its coat hook. To her left, a doorway into a room she couldn't see. She had supposed hunters, climbers, no-frills hikers, a rough place to hole up in overnight. But years ago. Decades, it felt like. The place had a ghost of generic masculinity.

How long had she been unconscious? Hours? Days? It was light outside. The air was different. The storm must have passed. Or he'd driven far away from it. Yesterday?

Dad, how come Mom's not home?

The sense of her children rushed her. Their faces somehow seeing this, what seeing this would do to them, what it was doing to them. The countless times they said, for countless reasons: *Mom?* Her boys. The horror wasn't her own death but Jack and Vincent having this forced into their lives. And Owen alone in the wreckage, a man in a bomb crater. All the love. Her life. Now this. You'll never see your family again. Valerie. She had an image of her sister searching for her. That focus Valerie had. Somehow forcing concentration through the sickness and panic. She'll find you. Stay alive, because she'll find you.

Pain forced her to move. Her knees straightened and she took her weight back onto her bound legs. Her arms, tied with twine above her head to a vertical iron pipe, reported their relief immediately. Blood began unpacking itself in her limbs.

Her shirt was open. Which brought the memory of him undoing the buttons, pulling the center of her bra away from her chest and going through the elastic with one movement of the knife. The tip of its blade had nicked her flesh, and the intimacy of that had registered in a distinct, mean detail. The terrible exposure of her breasts. The yearning to cover them tightened now in her throat. She'd pleaded in her head. Please. Stop. Please. Don't. He hadn't said a word. Just sat on the stool and stared at her like a serene animal.

He.

Him.

I'm not going around with a police officer the whole time.

Him. She knew who he was now, what he'd done. Valerie had spared her the specifics, but the whole world knew about the videos. Cassie knew what he'd done, which meant she knew what he was going to do. The certainty of it hit, suddenly, like the heat from an explosion.

Scream for help. Someone passing —

But when he'd dragged her from the Mazda's trunk she'd seen trees in the twilight, in all directions. Screaming might bring him. He could be right outside the door.

She didn't scream.

Where was he?

Her ankles were bound with the same fibrous twine, but they weren't attached to the pipe. She twisted her neck and looked up. Her wrists were fastened above a small bracket holding the pipe to the wall. To prevent her from lowering herself, from sitting, from finding any comfort. She'd seen it in his eyes, a calm relish in the maximized awkwardness of her position.

She had to get her hands free. Without that there was nothing. She remembered Valerie telling her the drill instructor's mantra during hand-to-hand training. You will survive. You *will* survive.

Oh God, please. Please.

Could she reach the stool?

Maybe. With her feet.

Which would mean more pressure on her wrists. The pain there was already searing. It felt as if any tightening of the twine would cut through to the bone. Some devious knot that increased the constriction the more you struggled.

But there was no alternative. The last time she'd seen her boys was at breakfast in the bright kitchen. Fresh sunlight on the surfaces. The gentle morning chaos. Scrambled eggs and the smell of coffee. She'd said: One of these days someone is going to say, Thanks, Mom — and I'll die of shock. *Then* what are you ungrateful creatures going to do?

Cassie arched her back and forced her feet in tiny slaloming movements forward. It was another obscenity that the adjusted angle opened her shirt wider. The room's warm air on her breasts and belly was a sly assault, brought a feeling of childhood shame. The way he'd just looked at her, as if he were watching from another universe.

The ties sawed at her wrists. She couldn't stretch any farther. She had to. The tips of her toes were inches from the nearest leg of the stool. The muscles in her back were at their tearing point. She heard herself moaning, sobbing. Forced herself to stop that. She had a history of being tough on herself.

Two inches she had to find out of impossibility.

One inch.

She couldn't. Her arms would dislocate.

But she reached it.

She knew she wouldn't be able to hold

the position for long. The labor now was carefully separating her feet to make a pincer for the stool's nearest leg. Get it wrong and you knock it farther away. Millimeters would put it absolutely beyond her. But for the open shirt and severed bra her clothes were intact. Jeans and sneakers. Sneakers, you can run. Adidas. In high school she'd run the fifteen hundred, made the track team for a couple of years. The good smell of mowed grass and the lime-marked lanes and the sweetness of going past someone, knowing you had enough in the tank. Then parties, drinking, boys. Her and Valerie and all the ordinary deviance they hid from their parents. Too long ago. Beneath the adrenaline her body was filled with honest warnings of its exhaustion. How fast could she run? How far?

Fuck that, Cass, Valerie said. You can run forever.

She trapped the stool's leg between her feet. Dragging it toward her was worse: her legs could take less of her weight than on the outward stretch. She had to do it in short jerks, every one of which risked her losing her grip and being forced to watch the stool topple and roll away from her. She was making too much noise. If he was right outside, he'd hear.

Her concentration silenced her. Then she thought the silence would draw him more surely than sound. He would have the requisite sixth sense. Valerie's face when she'd talked about Katherine and her lover always went the same way: a sort of remote fascination with how smart they were.

Do exactly as I say, or this goes into you and you'll never see your family again.

She got the stool close to her. Closer. She twisted a second time and used her thighs to wedge it up against the pipe. Odd thoughts flickered: she'd bought these jeans on last year's vacation in Mexico. Owen saying, in the neutral tone he used for compliments: Your ass is beautiful. That's not right, at your age. The kids like sunlit sprites on the beach, going about their kid business with great intent and obliviousness to everything else. She'd only ever imagined dying in a bed, with her family near her and the impersonal comfort of medicine. All those times you heard on the news: *The body of an unidentified woman was found . . .* Please, God. Please, God, let me see my children again. Let the last time not be the last time. I'll do anything.

It wasn't easy, but she got her knees up onto the stool. It wobbled under her. She slid her hands a little way up the pipe.

349

Gripped. Hauled herself to her feet. Balance. Her legs were cramped, the jammed blood dragging back into circulation, like someone being forced to get out of bed after not enough sleep. Every second she expected the door to open. His face — the face she'd thought she'd known — changed. He would see her. He would take stock. He would move toward her. He would put his hands on her.

Hurry.

Hurry and do *what*?

Oh God, please. *Please.*

She had had, she supposed, some wild idea that the bracket would be loose, that with an unholy effort she could work it free.

But the screws holding it to its backplate were big, rusted, immovable. There was nothing she could do. Her whole body was trembling. Her hair was sweat-stuck to her face. There was nothing.

There was one thing. Her hands were now at the level of her head. She worked her fingers toward herself around the pipe and wrenched the gag from her mouth, nearly tearing her bottom lip off in the process. The relief was instant and disproportionate. An illusion of liberty. But still, it was a relief. Even if he walked in she would have a brief space for language, for an appeal, for something. A purely practical part of her had wondered if she could seduce him, somehow convince him that she could make it better for him if he untied her.

But this was the Man in the Mask. Compliance wasn't what he wanted. It would only be good for him if it was bad for her. And the worse it was for her, the better it would be for him. The thought sickened her. The plainness of it. The simplicity.

She grabbed the pipe and brought her knees up and set her feet against the bare brick and pulled with all the strength she had. For five seconds, ten, twenty. You will survive. You *will* survive.

Nothing. The pipe didn't budge. She imagined him watching her. Smiling.

She stood back down on the stool. The effort had nearly made her pass out again.

She rested her head against the pipe. Fresh tears welled and fell. For a few moments she had nothing, just a complete surrender to her own powerlessness.

But she thought of her children again. The times she'd caught herself telling them what her own mother had told her: You don't have to *be* the best, honey, you just have to *do* your best. The memory broke the feeling of surrender, and the breakage hurt, the not being allowed to give up. It measured her

351

weakness and hopelessness all over again.

In something close to rage she lifted her head. A scream — of despair, of fury — was coming whether it brought him or not.

She stopped.

Not by choice.

By what she'd seen.

27

About two feet above her head there was a small, rusted crack in the side of the pipe. Perhaps a couple of inches long, with a gap of only a few millimeters between each of its eaten-into edges. Not, she could see immediately, big enough to threaten the metal's integrity, but if she could get her hands up to it . . .

She examined the ties on her wrists. Knots. A confusion of knots. She didn't know. It would be blind luck if she could break through the right one.

If.

It was hopeless. The time it would take. The twine was the rough sort her mom used to tie parcels with in the old days. But there was nothing else. She felt Valerie seeing this, urging her on: You can do this, Cass. You *have* to do this.

She slid her hands up the pipe. It took several attempts, but eventually she got one of the stands wedged into the crack. Her calves burned. She wouldn't be able to do this.

The physics were appalling. *Saw through.* After the first three or four strokes the twine drew blood. She made a curious decision to keep going into the pain until it made her pass out. She made a deal with the pain, dragging her wrists back and forth, every movement insisting it would have to be the last, that the fire in her skin had a weight of blackness to draw down on her, that surely it was unbearable, unbearable, unbearable. But she made the deal: If you want me to stop, then make me unconscious.

The twine broke.

One of the strands broke.

Her hands were still fastened.

Her face was wet with tears and sweat.

The unbearable made bearable because the one broken strand said yes, it works. Do it again. Don't stop.

But for a few seconds she had to stop. Get off her tiptoes and rest her calves. Breathe through the agony in her wrists. She remembered giving birth to Jack, the sixteen-hour labor, the pain so bad that everything dropped away. Owen had meant nothing to her in those moments. If anything, she wanted him to stop trying to make his love for her somehow help. He'd kept saying, you're doing great, angel, breathe, just breathe. . . . To her he might as well have been a complete stranger speaking a foreign language. Afterward, when it was all over, she'd felt sorry for him, that she'd been to a place where even their love meant nothing. She felt bigger than him, owner of an experience that had, whether she liked it or not, given something of her self's privacy back to her —

Something snapped outside.

She froze.

Footsteps coming nearer.

Oh God oh God oh God . . .

The footsteps stopped.

She didn't breathe.

Please . . . Please . . . Please . . .

The footsteps receded.

Cassie knew nothing after that, only the endless sawing against the pipe and the pain in her wrists growing to a white light and time being an eternal *Now,* no future and no past, nothing but the silent scream of going on, anything anything anything as long as she got free and could run, with the whole world to run into away from here, away from him.

When the ties broke, she almost fell. The abrupt return of her body pitched her into precarious balance. The stool wobbled, tipped — she flailed and just — *just* — grabbed the pipe in time. The stool settled back on its legs.

Her hands were free.

Vaguely, as from a long way off, she was aware of her mind working, telling her to be quiet, that any sound now could ruin everything. But she couldn't listen to it. Her body or soul or supreme animal instinct overrode it. She dropped from the stool and twisted to get her feet in front of her. The knots were tight and many. Her hands had fevers of their own and within seconds her fingernails ached.

Valerie, behind the wheel of the Taurus, driving, searching. The information would come to her. She would make the information come to her. Stay alive, Cass, I'm coming.

One knot undone. Her jaws were clamped. Ferocious pins and needles filled her arms now, all the unlocked blood shocked back into its flow. Three knots picked. Time boiling away like water in a forgotten pan. Now more than before she was convinced the door would open. She would look up. She would understand in a split second that everything she'd done had been for nothing. His weight and strength would fall on her.

When the last knot went, all the constriction disappeared with a kind of intimate magic. Agonizing seconds of frantically untangling the slack twine — then she was free. She had her arms and legs and voice back. In the midst of the nightmare the bare fact of being able to move through space was a blissful drug.

The impulse to bolt through the front door all but threw her toward it, but the image of him standing only a few feet away outside — the image of *running straight into him* — checked her as if God had reached down and grabbed her by the scruff of the neck. Her legs were weak with the need to run. But she had to know where he was. Valerie, watching this, speeding toward her. Don't panic, Cass. Cold. You have to be *cold.*

She crept to the window. Very slowly, in tiny increments, eased the curtain an inch open.

A bright hot day in a forest clearing. She saw a shallow wooden porch. One step down onto bare ground. Fifteen feet away, at the edge of a dirt track that cut through the trees, the silver car. Somewhere they'd switched vehicles. In the trunk she'd been

357

continually jolted. Hit her head on the jack.

Did he take the keys when they'd stopped? He must have. He *must* have.

But she didn't know. If you get to the car and the keys are in it, you're free. You drive. You put miles and miles between you and him. The vision of this was almost a physical sense, her hands on the wheel, the vehicle's obedient acceleration, the trees racing backward, him darting out, seeing her getting away, joy filling her limbs and the sweet knowledge that she would hold her children in her arms again.

And if the keys aren't there? You're out in the open, and he sees you. You start to run and the space behind you fills with his speed, his determination. His hands on you again, the strength and the wind knocked out of you when you hit the ground.

It was too much. Whatever the risk, she couldn't wait. If the keys weren't in the car she would run as fast and as far as she could. Nothing else mattered.

She went to the cabin's front door and tried the handle.

It was locked.

28

Of course it was locked. What had she expected? She went back to the windows. Newly fitted security bolts. For which keys were required. Could she break the glass? Aside from the noise that would make, the windows themselves were small, divided into four panes each by wooden cross-frames. Even if she demolished them, getting herself through would be a tight, broken-glass-edged squeeze. All that time for him to hear the crash, and for her to wriggle through, gashing herself. All that time for him to get to her.

She went quickly to the door that led off into the other room. Empty but for a sleeping bag and a backpack.

The back door, identical to the one at the front, was locked.

One window. Slightly bigger than the others, a sliding sash. It looked out onto a small space of roughly cleared ground, blazing in the sun, before the dense trees began again. Opened by releasing a screw clamp where the upper frame met the lower.

No visible security locks.

She began unscrewing the clamp. It was rusted tight. A grinding squeak with every turn. She glanced behind her. Nothing.

She put the heels of her hands under the horizontal length of the sash. Pushed. The wood ticked, but it didn't move. She pushed harder. Was it locked from the outside? Oh God.

She was about to give up when the sash shot upward with a screech. It startled her, this sudden tear in the silence. The shock of it weakened her legs again, discharged fresh adrenaline: if he was anywhere near he would have heard that. Move. Now. No time.

Shoving herself over the sill, something in the bottom of the frame gouged her belly, snagged her navel, briefly. She bit back the scream. Twisted and lifted herself, felt the weathered wood of the narrow back porch and the sunlight's brash heat on her flesh. Her hips crossed the sill and she toppled forward awkwardly. More noise. Run. Forget the car. Just get into the trees. *Hide.*

Reflexively, she pulled her shirt together and fastened it. It was a minute relief, a precious portion of integrity reclaimed.

The trees climbed uphill, with no sign of a trail. Knotted undergrowth and a few small blue flowers, nodding. It went against her instincts to go that way. She imagined the road — a road, *any* road, traffic, people, civilization — lower down.

A few paralyzed seconds of her weighing it up.

Then he stepped out from behind a tree, twenty yards away, up to her left.

They looked at each other.

Everything imploded.

She moved without thinking. The world blurred as she went, stumbling, around the cabin's flank. Birdsong and the trees like arrested giants, precise black shadows and the bristling light. In the nausea, she knew he'd lost a moment computing his surprise. She'd seen it in his face: *How the fuck . . . ?* But even as she'd registered it she'd known that the face would change, that his look of ambush would morph into one of focus.

She rounded the cabin's front. The car. It would lose her seconds, but if the keys were in it she was home. It glowed in the sun like a symbol of happiness.

Dust kicked up around her as she skidded to a halt at the driver's door and yanked it open. The familiar smell of warm vinyl, the dash instruments ready to light up into life. Please, please —

The keys weren't there.

She could hear him crashing down the slope behind the cabin.

She ran.

29

Every step jolted her blood. Within twenty strides her lungs were burning. The forest was full of dense heat, the dirt track strewn with brambles. Through the fear a weird strand of joy to be running, to be unraveling space between them. Her body was coming back to her, her body was working. Sun-shafts through the trees, the bright leaves shivering. Home was a remote gravity, pulling her on. Jack and Vincent, the taken-for-granted miracles of negotiated bedtimes and the feel of them leaning against her hip and the crazy things they said. There's this kid at school whose head's pointy like a wasp's butt. Their young voices and limitless energy and her own guilty bliss when they were asleep and she could think about the disordered vague desires for things she hadn't yet done in her life.

Run, Mom. *Run.*

She glanced over her shoulder.

He was close. Maybe thirty or forty feet.

How could he be so close?

Even in the glance she saw the dead resolve in his face, the dark eyes focused, the mouth open in the gray beard. His combat jacket flapped behind him. For a split second the sunlight made a gold nimbus around his hair. It was as if she saw every individual strand.

Cassie screamed. Half reflex, half because her brain told her there might be someone — anyone — within earshot. Her imagination willed it: a couple walking their dog; a family picnicking by a fallen log; a dedicated jogger in top-of-the-line gear and a sports watch. She saw all of these in a vivid rush. But the forest's softly abrasive sound track went on, undisturbed.

He was faster than her. She was dehydrated and aching and her body wouldn't lie: in a straight line he would run her down. He would get to her. She could feel the reality of it in her own legs. The trees and the ground and the distant sky confirmed it, with a smiling neutrality.

Lose him, Cass, Valerie said, as if in her ear. *Hide.*

She cut to her right, off the trail. The forest was thick enough. A branch whipped her face. Ferns and bracken grasped at her ankles. There were loose stones underfoot. Twice, she nearly fell. But she kept going, zigzagging between the trees, left, right, always downhill. Her quads and calves trembled with the effort of keeping her on her feet.

She didn't want to look back — it would take her further off-balance and cost her breath — but she had to know where he was. She looked over her shoulder. She couldn't see him. Her breathing was loud in her own head. She had the sick feeling that he had somehow gotten behind her, that she would turn to find him right there at her shoulder, close enough to touch.

Then a twig snapped uphill over to her right and she picked him out. He had the knife in his hand now and his drawn face was moist. But he wasn't looking at her. He was looking in the wrong direction, thirty degrees off. He'd left the trail too early. It thrilled her, that he'd gotten that calculation wrong.

Despite which she had to move. She was visible. If he turned his head he'd see her. The undergrowth had given way to moss here, knuckled through by ancient roots and, in places, dark stone. She backed toward the nearest tree, five feet behind her, treading softly. She kept her eyes on him. At any moment he would look to his left. She could feel Valerie's attention on her, the Taurus windshield bouncing sunlight. She was aware, too, of the brightness and heat of the day, that regardless of everything the natural world went on. As a child she'd believed in God, the benign old man with an incalculable beard and hurtable feelings. Adolescence and education had done away with that, but there had remained a sense that beauty was somehow on our side, the human side. Sunsets poured out grand love. Bluebells dipped their heads in shy affection. Adulthood hadn't quite erased the idea. But now she saw with absolute clarity that beauty was either oblivious or self-involved. It was nothing to do with us. Our sufferings meant nothing to it.

A wood pigeon exploded from the branches above her and went rattling away.

"I know where you are," he called, in the tone of a kid playing hide-and-seek. "I know where you are."

Cassie could hear the new calm purpose in him as he waded through the undergrowth. He hadn't seen her, but he was coming the right way. He was coming straight toward her. The choice: stay where she was and pray that he missed her, or run again while he was still far enough away.

Run, Cass. You can run. It's all still there in your legs.

She wasn't aware of making the choice. Just found herself moving, her legs propelling her downhill, bearing right to where the trees looked closer packed. She'd gone no more than thirty paces before the ground got suddenly steep. She couldn't slow herself. Her own momentum had become her enemy. She flung out a hand to grab at the trunk of a tree, but she was moving too fast. Her weight carried her, stumbling and flailing, through a deeper bank of ferns, and she saw the drop-off too late. An outcrop of mossy rock with a fall of maybe fifteen feet. The whole hillside, she realized, was a series of giant steps. There was the sound of running water somewhere far below. She crashed onto her side, but she was still slithering toward the drop-off. She grabbed at the ferns, felt them slip through her wet grasp. A moment of seeing, like a pretty snapshot above her, lime-green leaves against the blue sky.

Then something hit her hard in the small of her back and pitched her, winded, over the edge.

30

Valerie watched her sister help the old blind man, who was neither old nor blind, into her car, pull out of the lot, and drive away.

Rite Aid and Met Foods had external cameras that covered half the lot, and since she knew the time Cassie had left the drop-in it took her less than an hour to find what she needed. Another hour for Mc-Luhan's FBI elves to catch the last sight of the blue Mazda on street surveillance, turning east off Mission Boulevard at 2:49 P.M. And that was all there was. In the hours that had elapsed since then they could be more than two hundred miles away.

What's she going to look like the next time you see her — if there is a next time?

Valerie was a numb blaze. The central certainty said she was doing everything she could do and that it wasn't enough and that Cassie would suffer and die if she wasn't dead already and if she was that would be just another thing that happened in the world because at the back of it all was nothing, or if not nothing, then a God with a smile like the Katherine Glass smile — which might as well be nothing. This certainty was a quiet, looped statement in Valerie's head or soul, a nucleus of cold understanding. But around it the human habits swarmed. There had to be something else she could do. There wasn't. There *had* to be. There wasn't. The desperation just expanded, indefinitely, demanding that she find a way — *any* way — to translate the screaming need for action into action itself. Do something. *Do* something.

She'd seen it countless times in the families of the missing. How much could you pace the floor, wring your hands, stare at the phone, stay awake, drive around searching until your eyes started playing tricks on you? How long could you exist at the extreme edge of yourself, in the torment of knowing that every passing moment might be a moment of agony for the person you loved? It was worse than sitting by a hospital bed watching someone being taken from you by sickness. At least in that case you were with them, you were *there*, to bear witness if nothing else. At least in that case the sufferer wasn't alone, and the proof that you could do no more than you were doing was in front of your own eyes, beyond argument or doubt. This was worse. The not knowing was worse. The not knowing gave your imagination and guilt infinite material to work with. There was, literally, no end to the horrors you could conjure.

There was no "John Hendricks" on Faber Street. Of course, although McLuhan insisted on checking out the two dozen listed individuals of that name in San Francisco who at least fit the age range. (Half of them were over sixty-five.) Valerie had brought Bree in to work with a police artist on a representation of "John Hendricks" (Valerie's own memory of the guy was vague, beyond the beard and glasses and cap) and the resulting image had gone out to agencies and press.

She didn't sleep and she didn't eat and she didn't go home. For the twenty-four hours that followed Cassie's disappearance neither (with the exception of Sadie Hurst, whose husband was off work with a broken leg) did anyone else. There was nothing to do but keep going over the material and willing it to lead them somewhere new. She was aware of her colleagues not saying anything to her. They knew that anything they said would be the wrong thing. You didn't try to offer comfort because some things defied comfort. Instead the station's volume went down around her. Death was with her, wherever she went. The living knew their weakness in the face of it.

Nick stayed close to her, took a laptop and set it up next to her desk and began working his way through the case files. No one said anything about that, either. Deerholt stuck his head around the door, noted it, withdrew. There were the protocols and there were the brutal exceptions. Valerie's mother stayed at Cassie's house with Owen and the kids.

The kids.

Owen had told them Cassie was visiting with Aunt Valerie. Something had come up, he told them — a grown-up thing — and their mom had gone to help her sister. What grown-up thing? Jack had wanted to know. Something you wouldn't understand, you're too young. It's no big deal. It'll just be for a day or two. Vincent, six, had swallowed it, but Jack, eight, was sharper. When is she coming back? Is she *sleeping* there? Owen had watched his son refiguring the presence of the uniformed officers. The dots weren't connected yet but there was a lot of thinking going on behind the dark eyes. How long before they'd have to tell the kids the truth? Two days? Three? A week? Valerie's mother was a liability. She was holding it together for the sake of her grandchildren but she could go at any moment. On the other hand, taking care of the kids gave her something to do. She'd already laundered and ironed every item of clothing and linen in the place. Cooked and filled the freezer. And what was the alternative? Home alone, but for one of the officers? It was too much to ask.

By a supreme effort of will Valerie had stopped calling Agent Arden to check on Katherine's progress with the ciphers. Arden had sounded ragged on the last call. Valerie knew she hadn't asked McLuhan for another agent to share the babysitting. According to her, Katherine hadn't slept, either. *We could be sisters, you and I.* Arden knew now who the live case was, but the information was kept from Katherine. Don't give her that. The meal she could make of it. Valerie could imagine her face, the smile. But the facts wouldn't go away: Katherine had been close with Raylene Ashe. Like it or not, they had to use her. In the absence of anything else, they had to. *You've done your time with that witch,* Cassie had said. No, Cass, I haven't.

Nick's phone rang. He looked at the

screen. Ignored it.

"Who?" Valerie said.

"Nothing. Eugene."

Very faintly, a charge of despair detonated in Valerie. Not because of Eugene, personally, but because in this moment Nick's squash partner was the representative of the rest of the world going about its business, carrying on in either ignorance of or indifference to the fact that what had happened to Cassie had happened. Was happening right now. As if the theater lamp's heat was on her, she thought of Katherine saying: The poem's about suffering, and the universe's indifference to it. *The Fall of Icarus.* The plowman going on with his work as the hero plunged, unnoticed, into the sea. Wherever Cassie was and whatever she was going through, elsewhere people were hailing cabs or weighing up dinner options or swapping inanities or watching TV.

She was aware, in the wake of the little exchange, of Nick forcing himself not to touch her. They had a gesture between them, had had it for as long as they'd been intimate: the hand in a grip on the hair at the back of the head, a squeeze, a gentle shake. It meant, I'm here. It meant, however rough your day's been, however tired and fucked-off and worn-out you feel, you're

373

not alone. You're *not alone.* It was instead of words. The body was honorably dumb that way. It stepped in when words weren't enough.

But there were times when nothing was enough. There were times when you *were* alone, no matter who was with you or what they did. Right now even Nick's desire to comfort her felt like an obscenity, an endorsement of her own helplessness. Which was precisely why he stopped himself, she knew. Knowing it ought to have helped. But it didn't.

Valerie got to her feet. She couldn't bear it, the stillness, the waiting, the nothing to be done. In spite of knowing the futility of getting in her car and driving back out to Union City, she couldn't stop herself. The hours of blocked action simply pushed her out of her chair, as if her body were no longer hers to control. She saw Nick was about to say: Where are you going?

Her phone rang. It was McLuhan.

"We found Cassie's car," he said.

31

When Cassie came to, she thought it had been a dream. She thought she had passed out tied to the iron pipe and her broken brain had concocted a fantasy of escape.

Because she still *was* tied to the iron pipe.

But something was different.

Her shirt was fastened. Her bra still hung loose inside it. There was duct tape over her mouth.

And it was dark outside.

Not a dream.

Oh God.

She looked down. Duct tape at her ankles. Her sneakers and socks were gone. She looked up: the same tape at her wrists. No possibility for movement there either.

She'd had all the time in the world, as she'd fallen, to register what was below her: knolly turf, more boney roots, and two flat, lichened slabs of black rock, one with a pale-green fern pressed against it like a brilliant fossil. She'd had all the time in the world to make the relevant calculations: that no amount of midair twisting was going to avoid the rock; that she would dash her brains out and that would be the end; that that would be a better end, that she could cheat him of what he'd thought he'd have from her; that she had people in her life — Valerie, whose strength and courage astonished her — who would make sure he didn't get away with it, that it would give their love a new purpose, though it would deform them; that as he had threatened, she would never see her family again.

Yet here she was, with the all-but-lost future receding beyond her reach. Her head had a weight of wrongness in it, as if someone had forced a lump of iron under her skull. Every time she blinked, blackness loomed, an almost eclipse.

Concussion.

Sickness came up in her. She fought it. Vomit with your mouth blocked like this and you choke to death, like all those rock stars. Concentrate. For now just concentrate on not throwing up.

What for?

Why *not* choke to death?

Better than the alternative. Death — *any*

death, now — was better than the alternative.

But she couldn't. Life persisted, tormented her with the possibility — however remote — that she could survive this. As long as you were alive anything was possible. The memory of having moved freely through space was too close, the goodness of it, the promise. The drug of hope still had a hold. Hope or desperation. There was nothing between them now. It was impossible to tell them apart. Whichever it was, it kept her breathing, thinking, wanting.

"That was amazing," his voice said. "That you got out like that."

She turned her head to see him standing in the doorway of the other room, looking at her. He was holding a plastic bottle of Evian with a drinking straw in it. His hair was damp. She could smell the sweat cooling on him. "You've got your sister's determination. What fabulous genes."

She screamed behind the tape.

He didn't move.

The loss of her shoes was a distinct subtraction. Ludicrous that she could feel it, but she could.

He turned and disappeared into the other room. Came back a few seconds later with the knife. Her heart quickened. He stood in front of her and set the water bottle down on the stool. Then he pressed the blade's tip against her abdomen, through her shirt. With his other hand he reached up and carefully peeled the tape from her mouth, left it attached, hanging from her cheek. He lowered the knife.

"Scream," he said.

She didn't move or make a sound.

He withdrew the knife and stepped away from her. "Seriously," he said. "I won't do anything to you. If you want to scream, go ahead. It'll help things, in the long run."

She thought she wasn't going to. She was half aware of beginning to work out whether she should do as he said, but the scream ambushed her anyway. Everything she'd been through rose up and roared out of her open mouth. It was, for the two seconds it lasted, a relief. It gave her, for these two seconds, pure blankness.

But of course the two seconds passed. Of course they returned her to herself. Her head fell forward on her chest. She was, at a stroke, completely exhausted. There was an aching emptiness inside her where the ability to cry had been. It saddened her, that the part of herself that could cry had gone, had been burned away, though at the same time she knew she had no more use for it.

Her being was jettisoning the things it no longer needed, since the trip to death was one-way, since there was no point keeping provisions for the return journey.

"There's no one to hear," he said. "No one for miles. No one heard you scream in the woods, and no one heard you scream just now. I want you to know that."

"Why the tape then?" she said.

The first words she'd spoken since he'd gagged her and bundled her into the trunk, a lifetime ago. Her mouth was dry and alien. How long since she'd had water? The acute dehydration was new: she had literally never been this thirsty before. It was a deep, rhythmic thud in her cells.

He came back to her, picked up the Evian, and lifted it to the level of her mouth. "You must be very thirsty," he said. "Here. Have some."

No matter what, there was no *not* drinking. If he'd laced it with arsenic, fine. She took the straw between her lips.

"They always say in movies when someone comes out of the desert: 'Just a little, not too fast,' but I never bought that. What earthly difference is it going to make?"

It was irrelevant to her. She drank until the bottle was empty. Her body, regardless of her soul, sang its relief. She wanted more.

Didn't dare ask.

"To answer your question, the tape is because I decide when you talk and when you don't," he said.

"How long have I been here?" she said. Keep him talking. The longer he talks the longer he doesn't do something else.

"Since this afternoon," he said. Then chuckled. "You should've seen your face."

This afternoon? How many hours? She had a clear image of Owen on the phone to Valerie. Listen, something's wrong. . . . The kids in their rooms not knowing yet, not knowing that they would never see their mother again, their lives still the lives that were swirled through by superheroes and Little League and candy bars and school, their lives that still took her touch for granted. The word "mom" still waiting to have its meaning changed.

"My sister is going to kill you," Cassie said.

He smiled and rested his hand on her hip, gave it a little shake. "I don't doubt she's going to try," he said. "But in the mean-time . . ."

He pulled a syringe out of his pocket.

32

Cassie's Mazda was in the grounds of a decommissioned electrical substation three miles outside of Daly City. The driver's window had been smashed and the panel around the ignition switch removed. By the time Valerie got there the Bureau's emergency response team had just finished their sweep of the building. A plump, yellowish moon was low in the sky. There was a motorcycle cop waiting for her by the car. A tall, well-built guy with sandy hair almost exactly the color of his deep tan. He had the kind of Clooney jaw some people liked but that always made Valerie think of Buzz Lightyear. TORVAL, his badge said.

"Did you touch anything?" she asked as soon as she was out of her own car. The five FBI vests were regrouping outside the substation's entrance. Two local officers were with them.

"No, ma'am," he said. "I mean, I stepped

up close just to make sure there was no one *in* it. I picked up the APB this morning."

"Did they check the trunk?"

"The trunk?"

Valerie fetched gloves from her car and pulled them on. The trunk was locked. You needed the key fob even if the doors were open.

"Hand me your flashlight."

She got in the back of the Mazda and found the mechanism for dropping the rear seats. She wasn't expecting to find her sister — dead *or* alive — but she found herself moving like a frantic automaton.

The trunk was empty.

Her mind raced. Cassie's car. Okay. Broken into? What the fuck?

"Whoever it was," Torval said, "they couldn't get it started. From what I can see it's a wiring problem in the ignition. Wear and tear, you get that, even with these Japanese babies. I mean unless the battery's dead. They knew enough to take the panel off, not enough to fix it."

Valerie got out. "How'd you find it?" she asked.

"Precinct got an anonymous call on your suspect," Torval said. "I was the nearest officer."

"Which version of the suspect? We've got

three out at the moment."

"The most recent," Torval said. "Apparently he was parked at the substation entrance talking on a cell phone."

"Move away," Valerie said. "There's more than one set of tracks here."

She hadn't been careful. In her haste to look in the trunk she hadn't examined the ground. Now she moved the flashlight around the Mazda's perimeter.

Different tracks. He'd switched cars. Get a dry cast. Time all the while hemorrhaging.

"Detective Hart?"

Valerie looked up. A short, compact Latina in Bureau fatigues and bulletproof vest approached her, hand extended. "Nina Moreno," she said. "If anything happened here, we missed it. The building's clean. There's a local CSI team on its way."

"I'm going to take a look."

Moreno opened her mouth — then remembered who they were looking for. Adjusted her tone. "I've just taken the guys through there, Detective," she said gently. "I promise you it's empty."

Valerie didn't answer. Just headed toward the building. It wasn't because she thought the team had missed anything. It was because she couldn't stop herself. The demand for action was indiscriminate. Sheer irrational instinct told her that if Cassie had even *been* in the building, somehow she would know.

And if she died in there . . .

What? Her raw ghost in the ether? A palpable rent in the air where her beautiful life had been ripped from the world? Valerie was lightheaded, almost weightless. It was as if only fear were keeping her alive. Fear and desperation. Her imagination was running its own footage: the Mazda's dropped seats and exposed trunk revealing Cassie's body, limbs twisted, clothes torn, a puddle of blood long congealed, long cold. The moment of discovery insisted, as if it were a predetermined point in her future trying to force its way into the present. If she tried to think beyond it there was nothing. That moment, when she arrived at it, would be the end of her own life. She wouldn't, she knew, have what it would take to move beyond it.

Something glinted in the flashlight's beam. She hadn't gone more than ten paces from the car. She could feel Moreno's eyes on her back. She got down on her haunches and steadied the light.

"You got something?" Moreno said, coming up behind her.

"Yes," Valerie said. "Get me some tweezers

and a packet."

"What is it?"

A rose-gold chain with green tourmaline stones set between the links. Broken.

"My sister's bracelet," Valerie said.

Moreno wrapped up a call on her cell. She looked guilty. "We've got to go," she said. "You okay to hold the scene here? CSI should be here any minute."

"You're not going anywhere," Valerie said. She'd been through the substation. Moreno hadn't lied: of course it was empty. Every detail of its emptiness testified. *She's not here. You're too late.* "We need a three-sixty search of the surrounding area," Valerie said. "Starting here, starting now." She took out her phone.

"You'll get it," Moreno said. "They're pulling local blues and search specialists right now. Dog team, the whole nine yards. I don't have a choice, Detective."

Valerie had more footage running. Cassie struggling, his arms wrapped around her, the bracelet snapping and falling to the ground. *You must have spent hours choosing it.* Adrenaline pounded, as if it were a trapped prisoner in her body, desperate to escape. It seemed she must fracture, tear, break. *He uses the knife on them while he fucks them.* Her own words, her own thoughts. With Elizabeth and Raylene her analysis had been pure, cold cop. Now Cassie. Now her heart eclipsed everything else. Now there was *only* her heart.

"Who's your superior?" Valerie said.

"Look, Detective, I know. But we're five people. You need fifty. Hell, you need a *hundred* and fifty. The officers will stay and join the search team when it gets here. I promise you this is moving fast."

Not fast enough. Never, by definition, fast enough. She had an image of the five FBI agents heading off each in a separate direction, with hundreds of square miles to cover. She knew it was ludicrous, but the knowledge made no difference.

She got on the phone with first Deerholt, then McLuhan, who was on his way. Same story. The search team was being assembled. Sit tight.

Dusk had slipped into full darkness now, but for the low moon's creamy light. The land around the deserted substation was soft and empty. The first stars were out in a sky that had no memory of yesterday's thunderstorms. Cassie was sensitive to gathering storms. Valerie thought of the arguments they'd had down the years, occasionally vicious, never fatal. As an adolescent, she'd been occasionally jealous of her sister's two-year lead on her, watching Cassie edge into the female mysteries, breaking the new ground before her: cosmetics, confidences, parties, dating, sex. Cassie, as far as Valerie was concerned, was *glamorous.* She had a bigger public personality and a sharper tongue. Valerie sometimes watched her getting ready to go out and felt the agony of the age difference between them, as if, thanks to being older and prettier, Cassie was already grabbing all the treasure and excitement, so that there wouldn't be any left for her by the time she was old enough to claim it. But for all that, they were close. They laughed at the same things in the same way (they were merciless, loving observers of their parents) with a shared delight in each other's collusion. They were deeply and intuitively in cahoots. They had the rare gift, both of them, of knowing that they were loved. They had been loved and *they* had loved. But what did love do except raise the power of loss?

She took her phone out again, torn between knowing she should update Owen and knowing she shouldn't. How could she possibly tell him *this*? What would it mean to him except that Cassie was already dead? And at the same time she knew that every second he was going through an agony just like her own, that he was standing with his phone in his hand, willing it to ring. She tried to imagine *him* beyond Cassie's death, beyond the kind of death Cassie would experience. He would have to stay alive for the kids. He would have to, somehow, survive it. What would she say to him? A version of herself might have said: Owen, she's gone. But I promise you I'm going to kill the man who did this. Wherever he goes, I'll find him. I'll find him and *end* him. A version of herself might have said that. But where was that version of herself? If Cassie died like this, she couldn't imagine *any* versions of herself. She could see nothing but final blackness.

Her phone rang, startling her.

Arden calling.

"Go," Valerie said.

"We have a location," Arden said.

"I wanted to tell you myself!" Katherine's voice called, cheerily, in the background.

"I'm e-mailing you the relevant map," Arden said, "but you want to write this down just in case?"

Five seconds. Ten. Valerie heard her e-mail in-box ping.

"Buchanan Creek Woods," Valerie said to Torval when she'd hung up. "It's near here.

Do you know it?"

The other two officers had come back to their squad car, nearby. Both of them were texting.

"Yeah, sure," Torval said. "It's just —"

"Here." She held up her phone. "Look at this map. This *X* marks a set of latitude longitude coordinates to six decimal places. That's an exact spot. Can you find it? Don't waste time. Just look at the map."

To his credit, Torval looked. "I don't think there's anything up there," he said. "It's just woods. That right there is Winnet Lane, and there's a track runs off it up the hill after the creek. But I mean, it doesn't go —"

"Okay," Valerie said. "You're coming with me. Let's go. You guys" — to the two officers — "stay put."

"What're we —"

"Go ahead of me on the bike. Fast. No siren. Stop when we get to the creek. Don't talk. Just do it."

33

They stopped about fifty feet past the bridge at Buchanan Creek.

"Where are you going?" Torval said as Valerie took the bulletproof vest from the Taurus's trunk and slipped a flashlight into her pocket.

"Where do you think?"

"I called for backup," Torval said. "It's ten minutes, tops."

"My sister doesn't have ten minutes. Stay here. Get back on the horn and tell them no sirens. They come on foot from here. You understand?"

"Ma'am, you know the drill. We should —"

"Save it," Valerie said. "This isn't a discussion. Wait for them here and come ahead on foot. No flashlights. You got it?"

She checked her Glock. Full clip and two more in her purse, which she removed and stuffed into her vest pockets. "Here," she said, handing the purse to Torval. "Hold on to it for me."

Torval wasn't happy, but he took the purse and put it into the bike's left storage compartment. "I'll come with you," he said.

"No. You're my guarantee the cavalry doesn't fuck it up when they get here."

"Wait," he said when she turned to go. "Take this." He pulled a headset from the storage compartment. "Talk to me, okay? Channel's open. I'm on your side."

Valerie put the headset around her neck.

"You're not going to be able to see shit," he said — but she was already moving away up the track.

The flashlight was a risk. She'd have to switch it off when she got close, but without it she'd be moving at a crawl. Aside from the little ellipse of illumination at her feet, the darkness was dense. The trees embraced over her head. The moon wasn't high enough yet to be any help. The wheel ruts in the track were overgrown, but discernible, and in any case, the two or three times she veered too far left or right, brambles scratched at her. She switched her phone to silent. Her body was sharp and present and fully in her control, despite the swarming adrenaline. Shreds of her professional self were, she knew, busy with the predictable fears and calculations, but it was peripheral, a necessary automation, negligible next to her personal self, which was wholly given over to willing Cassie to still be alive. Should she be willing that? Wouldn't that depend on what Cassie had already suffered? Weren't there things you'd rather not survive? Weren't there things that someone could do to you that would leave you so changed, so unrecognizable, and so immune to love that you'd wish you *hadn't* survived? Until now she'd asked herself only how Owen and the kids (and her mom, and herself) would be able to carry on if Cassie were killed. Now she asked what they would do if Cassie remained alive, broken and alien to all of them, transformed, beyond reach. You could have things done to you that forced you to become an entirely different person in order to carry on living. You could have things done to you that would make any continuation of who you used to be before they happened impossible. When torture victims spoke of their ordeals they left themselves out of it. They talked through the list of what was done to them, but not what it did to them. They talked about it as if it had happened to another person. Of course they did. It had. It was only by becoming another person that they could carry on. The person to whom such things were done had to die, otherwise the self's grief was unbearable.

She quickened her pace. The vest was heavy. She couldn't remember the last time she'd worn one. Her face and armpits were hot. How much farther? She was going fast, despite the darkness. There was no getting lost: the track didn't fork and the woods on either side were unbroken.

She had just unholstered the Glock when Torval came through on the headset.

"You okay?"

"I'm okay."

"ETA twelve minutes."

What the fuck happened to ten minutes, tops?

"Roger that," she whispered. "Stay off the air. I'll shout if I need to."

"Got it."

Twenty more paces. A bat whirred past her head. The smell in the moist air was rich and old, wood and damp earth. It gave her a brief feeling of the planet's age and grand indifference. Human lives came and went, tiny lights, winking for a split second in the void. Cassie had been through a phase of reading odd things when she was a teenager. One night, she had come into Valerie's room and said: Imagine a dark winter landscape with a firelit feasting hall in the middle of it. Valerie, who had been half asleep, had said: Imagine being allowed to lie in your bed without someone coming in and bugging you. Cassie, in her calm, delighted way, had gone on: Inside this feasting hall, everything is happening. People are eating and drinking and singing and arguing and screwing and laughing and having conversations. There's an open window at either end of the hall. (In spite of her superficial objection, Valerie had seen it quite clearly. Something like a scene from the days of knights and damsels.) A little bird, Cassie said, flying through the night, flies in one window, through the bright hall, and out the window at the other end. It takes no time at all, just a second. That's your life. You're the bird and the world is the feasting hall. You have to *make sure you see everything.* All of it, as much as you can. You've got a moment, that's all. Valerie had lain on her bed thinking about it. Eventually she asked Cassie: Who said that? And Cassie had said: the Venerable Bede. He was a monk in England in the eighth century. Neither of them had forgotten it. "Bede" had become part of their private shorthand, as in: Why are you dating Justin Trask? He's an asshole. Yeah, but, you know: *Bede.*

Valerie stopped. She'd heard something.

She held her breath.

Silence.

A twig snapped. Then silence again.

She killed the flashlight and switched the Glock's safety off.

Still silence. Her eyes strained to adjust. Seconds. The moon had just begun to clear the tree line. It gave a very faint avenue of light between the embracing branches above her, but the darkness around her still swam. It was like looking up to the surface from deep underwater.

The soft swish of the undergrowth.

Someone was moving up ahead and to her right.

She didn't have to go anywhere. He was coming toward her.

Because he'd finished?

Finished.

With Cassie.

Valerie eased herself silently into the edge of the thorny darkness on her side of the track. He wouldn't see her. He'd get level. She'd hit the flashlight and train the gun. Police. Don't. Fucking. Move.

Five seconds. Ten.

He was moving erratically, stopping, coming on. Caution. Why? Had he heard her? Glimpsed the flashlight before she'd switched it off? Fuck. She should have found her way without it.

Tiny sounds now, across the track. As if he were tiptoeing. But he was almost level. The last steps had been less than ten feet away.

Valerie raised the flashlight and Glock. Made her arms stone.

When the sound came, it startled her.

A single wet exhalation. Like a horse snorting.

She steadied herself. Leveled the light and the gun again. Swallowed.

The undergrowth sighed, and a full-grown stag stepped daintily onto the track.

For a few moments it stood still, a solid mass of deeper darkness. It was aware of her. She didn't move. In spite of everything, her urban self livened to it, the strangeness of a wild animal suddenly close. The antlers were like candelabra.

It bent its neck, briefly, sniffed, then stepped with the same delicate movement across the track and disappeared into the trees.

34

Valerie moved faster. The moon had cleared the trees now, and in its light the track was faintly discernible. Streaks of chalk showed through, an occasional white stone. She didn't dare risk the flashlight. She stumbled, went down on one knee, got up again. Her lungs ached. Beneath the surging adrenaline her body was reporting that she hadn't eaten or drunk for a long time. She ignored it, the threat of weakness when the finite supply of energy was burned through. She would have enough. She would make enough out of nothing.

The clearing surprised her.

The air thinned and the trees fanned out from her, suddenly, curving away left and right in twin crescents.

She didn't see the cabin at first. The hill climbed in a wall of blackness — but the woods' quiet sentience was focused here. The trees were like a circle of observers, bearing witness, holding their breath.

She crept left, skirting the edge of the open ground.

Five paces. Ten.

She smelled the place — mold and weathered wood, something like kerosene — before her eyes picked it out, another fifteen paces ahead of her. Gradually the hard edge of its angled roof resolved itself in a thin line of reflected moonlight.

No lights, no sound. Two windows at the front. A short porch. One door, facing her, shut. *He likes time, privacy, leisure.*

Silence and speed. The terrible conflict between the need for both.

Keeping low, she ran to the door.

It was, naturally, locked.

The Machine insisted on the protocols: Circle. Check access points. Get the layout.

But if Cassie was hemorrhaging to death the extra seconds could cost her her life. No point not using the flashlight now. Valerie took it from her pocket, steadied it alongside the gun, aimed at the lock — and fired.

Fine. You know I'm here now, fucker.

She kicked the door in, Glock and light raised.

"Cassie?"

A muffled moan.

Valerie swung the light left.

The first things she saw were her sister's bare feet, bound with duct tape. She flicked the light upward.

Cassie.

Squinting. Taped. Arms above her head, face wet with tears and dried blood, hair matted.

But alive.

Alive.

In spite of the danger (where was he?) there was room for the flood of relief, of joy. All their shared life was there between them, a miracle, a vivid, glorious bouquet — *still here, still* — darkened only for Valerie by the immediate question of what her sister had suffered, what had been done to her, what her survival would cost her. But postponement flung itself up. *Alive,* for now, was all that mattered. Valerie realized she was thanking not God but Death. Death had come close and whisked away. Nothing but a glimpse of its black rags, moving on, letting this one be. For now. Thank you. Thank you.

"What the fuck is going on?" Torval's voice said in the earpiece.

"Quiet," Valerie said.

Valerie raced the flashlight around the room. Just the one door, another room beyond it. She hugged the wall to the doorway. Her hands on the gun and flashlight were wet. She could hear Cassie breathing hard through her nose. Nothing else for it. She eased her head around the doorframe and shone the light.

The wretched seconds as the beam swung, clearing the darkness section by section. Any moment a shot. Any moment . . .

But the room was empty. A rumpled sleeping bag. A couple of empty water bottles. A door and a window that looked out into the clearing. She went to it and peered out.

Nothing. Just the hill's empty incline for thirty feet, then the soft mass of the ascending trees.

Had there been time for him to get out after the gunshot? He could still be close.

But wherever he was he wasn't right here right now.

She ran back to Cassie. Eased the tape from her mouth.

"Be calm, Cass," she said. "It's okay. I've got you. Are you hurt?"

"I'm okay. Where is he?" Cassie gasped.

"I don't know. Backup's coming. We're getting the fuck out of here."

Time, like Death, was indifferent to human concerns. It took precious, aching seconds to get the tape from Cassie's wrists. Time, Valerie knew — *plenty* of time, surely — for him to have heard the shot and located the shivering light, for him to make his way back from wherever he was hiding, for him to be standing in the doorway when she turned. Plenty of time, in fact, for her to realize that Death *hadn't* moved on, but was merely waiting for a more cruel denouement.

Her fingers worked, frantically, screaming against the all but overwhelming imperative to go for brute force. Valerie had a pocketknife in her purse. She saw herself handing the purse over to Torval. A pocketknife would have . . . More haste, less . . .

"Torval, where the fuck is my backup?"

"They should be here by now. Any second."

Cassie's hands were free.

"Keep watching the door, Cass," Valerie said.

"The knife," Cassie said. "There's a knife. Quick."

"Where?"

Valerie swung the flashlight. Seconds, seconds, seconds . . .

She saw it. It was on the floor by the window, lying among a scatter of empty water bottles. She ran and grabbed it. Two strokes, and Cassie's legs were free. She collapsed into Valerie's arms. Not all her weight, but most of it. *I'm okay,* she'd said. In the distension of the moment part of Valerie had wondered what that might or might not mean. Her soul searched even now, looking for the scarred aura, the fracture, the indelible stamp, the *rape.* Her intuitions weren't infallible, but Cassie seemed free of that. The unbroken strength was still there. Please let it be. Please.

"The kids," Cassie said. She was unsteady. Valerie had to take some of her weight.

"They're safe. They're home with Owen."

"It was John," she said. "The fucking blind guy from —"

"I know. Shh shh shh. It's okay. Come on. It's over. Can you walk?"

"My shoes. There."

"Okay, quick."

It was another risk. But outside there was the good darkness. Valerie switched the flashlight off. Unless he was right outside the door he wouldn't see them.

"No noise, Cass."

"Give me the knife," Cassie said.

"Here. Wait. Put this on."

Valerie got out of the vest.

"Don't be stupid," Cassie said.

"No argument. Put it on."

402

Her sister's authority. Her own ragged weakness. The blocked blood's sudden release in her arms and legs. Cassie put the vest on. Valerie fastened it around her. A moment for their eyes to adjust to the darkness. Then the open door's faint light coalesced. They kept close to the wall. Valerie held her around the waist, one of Cassie's arms around her neck.

"We're going to the right along the porch," she whispered. "Down the step and across into the trees. Okay?"

"Okay."

"But quiet."

Was he here? Watching? Gratitude to the universe was still pounding out of Valerie, but in spite of it her stubborn cop self was outraged. He could be twenty feet away. She might never get this close to him again. And for all she knew he could have them in the crosshairs right now. He could be waiting until they thought they'd made it. Bittersweet. The bitterer, the sweeter. She knew how he worked.

Awkwardly, they crept quickly along the porch. The night was warm and heavy around them. A forlorn fragment of Valerie's physical system reported that she was weak from thirst. The report came without hope. It knew the bigger reality didn't care.

"They're here," Torval said.

Valerie didn't answer at first. She and Cassie staggered across the last twenty feet of open ground and made it into the cover of the trees. No disguising the sound, but it hardly mattered now. If he was here he would have seen them.

"How many?"

"A dozen officers and the FBI guys from earlier. An ambulance. There's a chopper coming in right now."

Valerie could hear it. Half a mile maybe.

"They're going to need more," she said. "I think he's loose in the woods. For now get the chopper up here. Half a mile up the track there's a cabin in a clearing. Room enough to land."

"Roger that," Torval said.

Cassie was standing bent with her arms wrapped around her middle, sobbing quietly. Valerie put her arm back around her. "Hey," she whispered. "It's okay. It's okay."

"I knew you'd come," Cassie said. "The whole time . . . I knew . . ." She couldn't get the words out.

Valerie held her, though she felt as if she needed holding herself.

It was a long minute.

35

Valerie stayed with Cassie in the hospital. Redundant to wait around for CSI at the cabin: she knew what they were going to find — and in any case she couldn't stand to let Cassie out of her sight for now. Owen and their mother were on their way with the boys. *Mom had a car accident, but she's fine.* No point telling them anything else. (It had been difficult for Owen to carry the lie off, since he was so visibly happy.) Blood tests revealed the remnants of a hefty dose of diazepam in Cassie's system. Nothing else. Aside from that she had a lump the size of a small egg on the back of her head. She'd chipped the edge of her sacrum when she fell. Lacerations on the wrists from the twine. Dehydration, cuts, bruises. The trauma that was greater than the sum of its parts. She was in pain, but she was whole.

He hadn't done anything else to her.

It was a source of endlessly renewable joy

to Valerie to see her sister, bandaged, cleaned up, attached to an IV, and surrounded by the serene whites and reliable technology of medical care. Even the plastic name tag on her wrist — CASSANDRA LOUISE HART (no adoption of Owen's surname; she wasn't that kind of woman, nor Owen that kind of man) — gave Valerie a feeling of deep satisfaction, testified to Cassie's survival with prosaic innocence.

"I don't know if it looked fake," Cassie said. Her voice was still hoarse. "I just know that his eyes weren't the eyes of an old person."

"It's fake," Valerie said. "The beard, probably the hair, too. He's not an amateur with this stuff."

"He broke the Mazda's window," Cassie said. "I guess to make anyone think it was joyriders or whatever."

"Well, we've got Officer Torval to thank for listening to his APBs like a good boy."

"And Katherine Glass to thank for everything else. Jesus, of all the people I don't want to be indebted to."

"Yeah, I know. Me too. Shall we send her some flowers?"

"How's she doing it?"

Valerie exhaled, shook her head. "It's a bitch," she said. "The key information —

406

the cipher to the letter codes — is always derived from something only she would know. I won't bore you with it, but he's clearly designed it for her. It's driving the Bureau nuts. I still don't know how she got the longitude and latitude coordinates. I mean, that's numerical. But you know, she's not exactly a dummy."

Cassie's eyes filled up. A tear hurried down her cheek. She brushed it away. "For God's sake," she said. "Enough with this blubbering."

Valerie smiled. Cassie had been ambushed by tears a few times since they'd brought her in. Aftershocks. Delayed relief.

"Yeah, what's wrong with you? Anyone would think you'd had a rough couple of days. I thought you were supposed to be tough?"

The searchers' sweep of the woods had been fruitless. For whatever reason, he had driven away some time between giving Cassie the shot and Valerie turning up. (Why?) Cassie remembered that the vehicle was a new-looking silver Camry, but nothing else. She'd been berating herself for not noting the plates. Stop it, Valerie had said. No one in your situation would have noted the plates. To which Cassie had simply said: *You* would.

"Why wasn't he there?" Cassie said.

"I don't know. Everything so far says he's well-organized. Maybe he's eavesdropping on police radio. Maybe he heard Torval call it in."

"I don't think there was anything like that in the car. I didn't hear anything in the cabin. But then I was out of it half the time."

"It might have just been luck," Valerie said. "Maybe whatever called him away played into his hands, accidentally."

"Do you really think that?"

"I don't know. Luck's not interested in who the good guys are."

"And what about this 'fair warning' shit? I didn't get a postcard."

"He might assume I'd warned you if he knew I'd worked out the victims were all connected to me. But we don't know that he did know that. And if he did know it, that's a worse prospect, because how the fuck *could* he know?"

A silence while Cassie worked it out.

"He's watching you," she said.

"Seems that way. And not just me. We need to get all our phones checked. Maybe time for new laptops and online IDs. For all of us."

"What happens now?"

"I go back to work. You go home. The officers stay until we get him. There's absolutely nothing to say he won't try again. You don't go anywhere alone, no argument."

"You're not getting any," Cassie said.

"And you stop Mom from having a nervous breakdown."

"She can stay with us for a few days. I don't like her being in that house, even *with* the uniforms there. I'm assuming Owen won't divorce me for it. Not after this."

For a moment the two women were silent. Then Cassie took Valerie's hand.

"I did know you'd come," she said. "I could see you. Driving. I tried to think what you would do."

Valerie felt close to tears herself. Not just of relief, nor of closeness to her sister — but of her own guilt and frailty, the nearness of this miss. Cassie had been taken because of her. If it weren't for her being who she was, what she was, doing what she did, none of this would have happened. *But then I remind myself that you're the woman who put Katherine Glass away . . .* He had made her, via the cunning and irresistible contortions, responsible. Morally, Valerie knew, it was uncomplicated: the families of Police were always potentially at risk. You signed up for that when you *became* Police. If people like her stopped being Police the

409

bad guys had won. No one in her family — certainly not Cassie — would blame her for any of this. (Actually, her mother might, in the honest privacy of her soul. But her mother's currency was weak; she was incapable of seeing beyond the personal, the particular. She was wholly — and sometimes aggressively — deaf to abstract argument. In the sweetest possible way, she simply had no principles, beyond the well-being of her family.) Still, it hurt. It had never come this close before. No one had ever made it about her, Valerie, personally. Sitting there with Cassie's hand in hers she wondered if she should quit. If she had a child she'd be signing *her* up for the same risk. If she had a child, would she be able to carry on doing what she did? And if she could, would that be fair to her child?

"Don't *you* start," Cassie said, sensing the state Valerie was in. "I'm allowed. I was *abducted*. You've got no excuse."

Valerie left after Owen, the kids, and her mother had arrived, with two officers who would make sure no one other than medical staff had access to Cassie, and even they would be double-checked. Her phone rang as she was getting into the Taurus. Susanna Arden.

410

"McLuhan just called me," she said. "Well done."

"I didn't do anything," Valerie said. "Just followed directions."

"Do I tell her? She's been asking ever since we sent the coordinates."

Valerie hesitated. It was impossible not to think that any information you gave Katherine was potential ammunition. But the fact was she'd saved Cassie's life. If they got another package, they'd need to have her invested. If they withheld and she found out, she could fuck them over with the next one — or simply refuse to help at all.

"She didn't get the rest of the name, right? She doesn't know it's my sister?"

"No," Arden said. "We switched focus to the location when you told us."

"She's not still looking at the material?"

"No, she's back in her cell. I have it all with me."

"Keep it that way. You can tell her we made it in time, but I don't want her knowing who it was."

"Understood. I'll give her the news, then I'm heading back to the city — unless I hear otherwise from McLuhan."

"If I were you I'd get out now. I'm sure our boy's not done, but take the breather while you can. If something else comes in from him I'll go up to Red Ridge myself. You've earned some R and R, agent."

"You can say that again," Arden said. "I feel like I need a week in a fucking *spa.*"

"Well, when we get this guy, let's you and me go out and get bombed." Valerie surprised herself, somewhat, saying this. She barely knew Arden, but she was so high on relief from Cassie's survival that she had an indiscriminate love for everyone. Besides, she had liked the woman's quiet dedication. There was the strange sorority between them now, of having Katherine Glass in their lives.

"Count me in," Arden said, not quite masking her own surprise at Valerie's invitation. "By the way, she asked me to tell you she wants to see you. She was very polite about it. She said: 'I do realize this is entirely at Detective Hart's discretion.' But obviously she feels like she's earned it."

"Well, maybe she has," Valerie said, although she sank at the prospect. *There's something else I want to discuss with you.* She hadn't forgotten that. She didn't like it. On the other hand, she didn't like it hanging over her, either. "Maybe I'll come up there tomorrow."

Late that night, Valerie and Nick lay on their

bed together, more or less top to tail. They'd both just taken showers and were too warm to get under the sheets. Between them they'd gotten through a couple of bottles of Bordeaux. Valerie was shifting, gradually, to wine. It had at least the superficial identity of a civilized indulgence. "Fine wines," as the phrase was, connoted legitimate aesthetics, like poetry or going to the opera. It sounded so much less brutal than "vodka," which according to Nick just sounded like a Russian hit man with a contract on your liver.

The hospital was keeping Cassie in overnight. Tomorrow Valerie would go over and talk to the officers, make sure they were properly primed. She didn't seriously think he would try for her sister a second time, but there were her mom, the kids, Owen. She wasn't taking any chances.

It had been a sweet evening. Valerie's endorphins were still waltzing from the fact of Cassie's survival. Nick had cooked some delicious thing with chicken and white wine and cream and wild mushrooms, and for once Valerie had had an appetite. They'd eaten and drunk and had music on and Valerie had lain on the couch with her feet in his lap and given in to the feeling of relief. Not without a struggle. She was under no illusions: it wasn't *over.* Katherine's lover was still out there. He'd failed this time, but it wouldn't be long before he tried again. Still, with Nick's unspoken encouragement, she'd allowed herself the satisfaction of having won (with Katherine's help, unfortunately) a battle in the ongoing war. It had given her a sense of respite, and no matter how fleeting it might turn out to be, she had, eventually, surrendered to enjoying it.

They lay together now like weary teenagers, Valerie on her back with her head on the pillows, Nick up on one elbow, looking up at her across the flatness of her belly and the swell of her breasts, his other hand moving idly over her, alternating between the sexual and the therapeutic. It was delicious to her to be languidly in possession of both options, heat between her legs when he touched her there, but also the less complicated pleasure of muscular bliss when he squeezed her aching calves and thighs. He knew her calibrations. Sex was available, but so was comfort. It came to her that she'd been far from him these last couple of weeks. He gave her room, let her go into the Work. He knew her and, unlike any other man she'd ever been with, had no interest in trying to change her. Most of the time she took it for granted. But there were these moments of renewed revelation when she realized the wealth she had in him, her own outrageous good fortune. Thinking this, now, she felt such an access of love for him that she smiled involuntarily. Nick, having bent to kiss the top of her right thigh, didn't see it.

"Hey," she said.

"What?"

She touched his cock, very lightly with her fingertips. Felt it stir. Slid down the bed so that it was level with her mouth. Close enough for the warmth of her breath to register. She took it between her lips, softly, felt it thicken as she made the first slow, deep pass.

It had been a while since they'd made love like this, dreamily, as if they had all the time in the world, as if nothing else mattered. Two years on, the greedy desire was still there for both of them. Even when it was just a case of getting each other off it was rarely perfunctory or merely serviceable. Or rather, on occasions when it started that way it often morphed into something more intense. Valerie was in possession of a rare certainty: she knew sex with her was the best Nick had ever had, and knew, too, the feeling was reciprocal. It ought to have made her complacent. Instead it inspired and liberated her. It didn't feel to her like something she had to maintain. It felt to her like a wholesome power she wanted to enjoy, to push beyond its known limits into every nuance and subtlety. She had surprised herself, more than once. *I'm going to give you the best loving up you've ever had.* Part of it was sexual generosity: she loved him. Part of it was that she simply wanted to give him as much pleasure as was hers to give. But part of it was delight in herself, in *knowing* she could do this for him, that it nourished his idea of her, and hers of herself. It was a self-affirmation so sweet and rich it sometimes made her happily appalled at herself.

But the mind was treacherous. In the hour that followed, Valerie wasn't free. Her body wanted what it wanted — and it was good — but the intensity responsible for her pleasure was lawless: images rose and drifted and dissolved. More than once Katherine's smiling face bloomed, like the image of a golden demon or angel. She saw her watching from the bedroom chair, one hand between her spread legs. The wiser Valerie knew it was nothing, just more of Napoleon's white horse. But still, she felt herself shutting it down, working to let pleasure's drug pull her into the salving thoughtlessness of her body. And so she went, alternating between delicious oblivion and mild fracture as she and Nick, sometimes urgently and sometimes languidly, changed positions, until her third orgasm, when Nick, having held back for as long as he could, joined her. The last image in her head was of Katherine bent over them as they had ended up (in a sixty-nine, as they had begun), her white hand wrapped around Nick's cock, guiding it as Valerie sucked him, the blond hair and green eyes (Will's phrase, *bitch eyes,* was in the mental mix) very close to her, filled with understanding, with intimacy, with something like triumphal joy.

He said everyone wants what we want but most people are too chickenshit to get it. Scared of getting caught. I said SHE got caught and he said she got careless.

I can't sleep so well for thinking of how it's going to be. Leave all this shit behind. The last ten pounds are the hardest. Everyone knows that.

No time tonight. Have to memorize. We're close, he says.

36

The following day McLuhan took Valerie aside after the morning briefing. He looked tired.

"Listen," he said. "We've got a problem."

"What is it?"

"There are gaps in Glass's work. Our guys are telling me that in what she's showing you can get close to the information she's come up with. Close, but not all the way. Especially with the numericals. There are only two explanations. Either she's leaving out crucial steps on purpose, or she's getting the information from somewhere else."

"Leaving them out on purpose fits her," Valerie said. "It's her involvement insurance."

"I know. But we're putting more energy into the alternative. It's not just her correspondence, nor the handful of people who've been granted visiting access over the course of her incarceration. It's potentially anyone who's been into either Chowchilla or Red Ridge during her time there. That's hundreds of visitors to the entire prison population over six years. Not to mention staff. We've looked at the correctional officers, but so far no one flags."

"It doesn't help us, though, does it? I mean, are you suggesting we stop using her? My sister would be dead."

"I'm aware of that. But here's what doesn't go away: Why the fuck would she be helping us? You really buy the boredom story? The revenge story?"

"More the boredom than the revenge," Valerie said. "Have you met her?"

"No."

"You have to understand what she's like. Her mind's a computer on coke. It's bad enough in prison if you're a moron. For someone like her . . . I don't think she has any interest in helping us beyond the fact that it's a lifeline to everything she's lost. It's a reengagement."

"With you."

"With the world. She hasn't asked for anything."

"She hasn't asked for anything *yet.*"

"*Are* you saying we stop using her?"

"I'm saying I know how difficult it would be for you if we did stop using her. I'm saying there's a dependence. A dangerous dependence."

Valerie felt her face warming. She hadn't seen this coming, that it was about *her* credentials. She took a moment before answering. "With respect, the Bureau's got nothing. I know the resources are going in, but so far we're no closer to this guy than we were six years ago. The only reason my sister's alive right now is because Katherine Glass gave us her location. I'm not stupid, Vic: I know she's not doing this out of the goodness of her heart. She might well have an agenda beyond her own boredom or a need for revenge, but until we know what it is, she's pretty much the only thing standing between the next potential victim and death. *That* doesn't go away, either. If you had any grounds to show she's misinforming us — any grounds beyond the gaps she's left in her work — fine. But you don't. I mean, you're *telling* me you don't. If there's an alternative to using her at this stage, tell me what it is."

"I'm not saying there's an alternative. I'm saying I don't like it."

"I don't like it either."

"You sure?"

"What the fuck is that supposed to mean?"

"There's a fascination there, right?"

"I can't believe I'm hearing this. I *put her away,* in case you've forgotten." Valerie's voice was even, but the images from last night's sex with Nick flashed. "Don't make me say you're just pissed because she's doing our job for us," she said.

"And don't make me say that while you're jazzing on your supernatural connection with Miss Glass we're putting in thousands of hours on the donkey work of elimination."

For a moment they looked at each other in deadlock. Valerie had an image of him as the sort of father who would scare a daughter's boyfriend shitless: the heavy eyebrows and dark bushels of hair up each nostril.

Then the tension went out of him. He put his hands in his pockets. "Okay," he said. "Jesus, forget it. I was just trying to say be careful."

Valerie softened. He was obviously exhausted. There were pressures coming down on him from the directors. How old was he now? Fifty? It occurred to her that he wasn't going any higher in the Bureau. She wondered what he would do when he retired. The things that men like him did, she supposed: bought a small boat, watched the ball games, kept up with current affairs. But all with the sadness of having lost the life of urgency, the life of knowing what you did made a difference.

"I am being careful," she said, not without a pang of guilt. "And I appreciate the concern. Let's just catch this fucker."

"Yeah," McLuhan said, without conviction. "Let's do that."

She put it off as long as she could. She told herself, in fact, that she would drive up to Red Ridge tomorrow. She went over to Union City to check on Cassie, who was discharged from the hospital around three in the afternoon. The house's atmosphere was renewed. When Owen hugged her, she could feel the new, shocked tenderness in him. Death had come close and ripped the layers off everything. Now, because Cassie had *not* died, the preciousness of the world with her in it dazzled him like fireworks dazzled the innocence of children. Suddenly there was beauty everywhere. Suddenly life — from the sunlight on the lawn to the fibers in the hall carpet — was denuded and exalted. The humblest details were sources of joy — because his wife was alive, right there, in freshly laundered Levis and a white T-shirt, her hair tucked behind her ears, her eyes holding all their history and her voice, which he'd thought he'd never hear again.

There couldn't be a clearer demonstration that humans only ever truly valued life when they'd narrowly missed losing it. It should happen to everyone, Valerie thought. Everyone, just once, should get this reminder.

Cassie, too, moved with a new awareness. When she put her hand on Jack's shoulder; when she tilted her face up to catch the window's sun; when she cut a slice of the lemon meringue pie her mother had made and bullied Valerie into tasting it. The horror was still there, Valerie could tell, but Cassie's survival of it had given the ordinary goods of her life back to her revealed for what they were, fabulous treasures beyond price.

Vincent, the youngest, was manifestly untouched by his mother's brief absence from home. He went about the important business of his life of toy cars and cookies and Nickelodeon in contented obliviousness. But Jack stayed closer to Cassie than usual. The curious ruck in the fabric of the home hadn't gone unnoticed. He didn't, of course, know what had happened, beyond the "car accident," but Valerie could see in his face there were silent questions being asked. There was a hint of suspicion, as if something huge and dark had passed in his peripheral vision, and though it *had* passed, and he'd more or less missed it, it had left him with a confused sense that the world might not be the way it had always seemed.

Valerie spent an hour with them, and before she left spoke to the two assigned officers in a way that made it clear that if anything happened to this family on their watch their lives wouldn't be worth living. To their credit, the officers looked like they believed her.

She was getting in her car when her mother came out and stopped her.

"Valerie?"

She turned.

Her mother put her arms around her. She'd been in tears, continually, over the last seventy-two hours, and her face was wet with them now.

"Come on, Ma, it's okay."

Mrs. Hart clung to her daughter. Struggled to get the words out.

"We don't appreciate you," she said.

"I've been telling you that for years," Valerie said, giving her a squeeze.

"When I think . . . When I think that if you hadn't . . ."

"Ma, come on. It's over."

"You're always so strong," her mother said. "Even when you were a little girl . . ."

But the words "little girl" fractured her again.

"You're embarrassing Officer Wilson," Valerie said. "You don't want him to see you like this, do you?" But she held her mother, thinking, as she did so, that she felt newly small and frail in her arms. She smelled, as always, of Shalimar and coconut oil shampoo. She was sixty-eight, but the little flames of sensuousness and female vanity were still there. Valerie liked that they were. She dyed her gray hair a rich auburn and referred to women of her own age (and younger) as "elderly," as if she didn't belong to that category. Valerie and Cassie teased her about it, but really, they loved her for it.

"I give you such a goddamned hard time," her mother said, snuffling. "About the job. But I know that if you didn't do what you do . . ."

"I'm no good for anything else, Mom. You know that."

Mrs. Hart held on for a moment, then said: "I just wanted to say thank you."

It hurt Valerie. All the love she took for granted. She thought of her mother dying. Being gone. Surprised herself with the sudden bleakness it brought up, as if with that loss there would be nothing between herself and the keener air, the cold wind that found everyone, eventually.

"Thank you," her mother said. "I love you, hon."

Five minutes later, heading back to the station, she thought: It's not me you should be thanking, Ma. It's the woman up in Red Ridge. Sadist. Murderer. Monster. Katherine fucking Glass.

She took a right.

37

"This puts us in a peculiar position, doesn't it?" Katherine said. "I can imagine the mixed feelings for you. But they're mixed for me, too. This morning I woke up not quite knowing where I was. *Who* I was, even. Like those first mornings in foreign hotels. I had to lie there for a while, letting my dismal history find me in the confusion. If they hadn't come to shake down my cell I don't know how long it would have lasted."

Valerie sat opposite her in the now familiar visiting room. Katherine looked slightly different. There was a wide-awakeness and luminescence to her, as if she'd caught up on much-needed sleep. All the details of her — teeth, fingernails, eyelashes — looked as if they'd just that minute arrived in the world.

"Arden said you were asking to see me," Valerie said.

"Yes."

"Well?"

"Well, of course I want to know all about it. What happened? Wasn't he there?"

"Apparently not," Valerie said. "Guess he got lucky."

"Incredible," Katherine said. "That's God with the coin."

"What?"

"It doesn't matter. Who was the woman?"

"Just a woman. Like they're all just women."

"Did you get to her before any damage was done?"

"Before any lasting damage was done, yes."

Katherine looked at her and smiled. "Don't fret," she said. "It's not as if I expect you to thank me. I do realize my balance in the moral account will be forever negative, no matter how many damsels I save from distress. Perhaps if my heart were in the right place it would count for something, but unfortunately I am what I am. I did toy with it, mind you."

"With what?"

"Repentance," Katherine said. "All extremes end up very close to their opposites. Morality's like that. The worst kind of sinner is only a hairsbreadth away from the best kind of saint. They travel far enough, they bump into each other, eventually, back to back. What follows depends on whether they turn and face each other. It depends on what sort of conversation they have, like Jesus and the Devil in the desert."

In spite of herself, Valerie understood. Katherine had this knack for making the worst kind of sense. It gave you something, a wretched insight, but it was exhausting.

"Where was it, by the way?" Katherine said.

"Where was what?"

"The scene of the crime. He cheated, incidentally, with that. There was an extra cipher. *Eratosthenes.* Not terribly cleverly hidden, but still, I wasn't expecting it. I was looking for the *name* of a location."

Valerie didn't say anything for a moment. Then she said: "It's okay with me that you enjoy this. You have all this extraordinary intelligence, knowledge, and yet you're in here and I'm out there. If I were in your shoes I'd probably feel exactly the same."

"It's not that," Katherine said. "It's not that at all. It's just the habit of talking to myself. I'm sorry. Without Agent Arden there's no one else in here worth talking to, except Warden Clayton, and she doesn't like to do more than dip a toe in the water with me. She knows there are sharks down there.

She's a morally middle class thrill-seeker. For a while I thought of seducing her. You know, as a *project.* If you don't have a project in a place like this it's not long before they find you dead by your own fingernails. Plus she's got those Amazonian boobs. She's open to it, but only as a fantasy. She wouldn't risk anything that interfered with her game plan, which is some trivial little adventure in contributing to *black advancement.* She's too terrified of making her mommy and daddy feel like they made all those sacrifices for *nuthin.* She wants achievement — but she wants it for herself. She wants to sit on her achievement like a smug bear on its stash of honey. Luckily for her, she has the advantage of a political rationale. She's a greedy little soul blessed by the injustices of history. If she were white everyone would know she's a monster-cunt of ego. But she's black, so no one sees it. Or rather, they feel guilty if they do. They start wondering if they're *racists.* Smart black people get away with murder. At least I've got the decency to be in *jail.*"

Listening to Katherine, Valerie thought, was like being stuck on a sickening ride you couldn't jump off. But again she was struck by her uncanny choice of words. Hadn't she, Valerie, mentally used the phrase "game plan" when speculating about Warden Clayton?

"I have digressed," Katherine said. "I'm sorry. I worry about my mind. Eratosthenes, for the record, is credited with the idea of longitude and latitude, you see? If the Bureau monkeys had spotted the cipher they would have gotten the location themselves. The coordinates weren't even scrambled. They were just *there,* in the correct sequence. I wasted some time, initially, because I thought it was just 'Erato,' in Greek mythology the Muse of lyric poetry. It's sometimes thought her name derives from the same root as 'Eros,' which would yield an approximate translation of 'lovely' or 'desired.' Which is where my own monster-cunt ego got rather in the way, as you can imagine. Anyway, I got there in the end. The photograph of the needle gave me a migraine, too. But it's 'angels.' The cipher. How many angels can dance on the head of a pin? A question wrongly attributed to Saint Thomas Aquinas. You'll ask me if he studied medieval philosophy. Answer is I don't know. He was, by his own account, an autodidact. You look different, by the way. Have you had some sort of uplifting trauma?"

"Not that I'm aware of," Valerie said. "Just

work. What's an autodidact?"

"Self-taught," Katherine said. "I'm not kidding, you look radiant. You're a woman of such wealth. A job you love and a man you love. What more could you wish for? You can see how your presence here throws my own risibly stark life into such brutal relief. I ought to want to pluck out your eyes."

"Don't you?"

Katherine smiled. *The* smile. "No. I don't. Superficially, because they're lovely eyes — you've got those un*justly* long lashes, too, like a deer, but without quite the innocence — and I'm hopeless in the face of beauty. But really because I'm fascinated by you. Having a genuine nemesis is psychologically compelling. We're like the saint and sinner I mentioned before, so close to each other by having traveled to almost the same point from opposite directions."

"We're not anywhere near the same point," Valerie said.

"Come on," Katherine said. "Think about it."

Her voice was so calm and reasonable. She might have been a patient professor coaxing a favored student to a truth. Valerie imagined Nick watching this exchange, shaking his head. Get out. Get *out.* She told herself she could do just that, get up and walk away whenever she chose. She kept telling herself that, kept going to it for re-assurance, as if it were a talisman in her pocket. But she didn't move.

"Believe it or not I have thought about it," she said. "Since you keep insisting it's true."

"And still?"

"Yes, still."

Katherine sat back in her chair and raised her cuffed hands to brush her bangs from her eyes. Valerie remembered that in one of the videos strands of her hair had been floaty with static. Worked up by the heat of her actions. It was details like that that confirmed what you were watching was real. A real man and a real woman, doing what they were doing. She remembered wondering if their victim — it was Leonora Ramsey — had noticed it, too, if in the gaps between the extremities of her suffering the world's humble details still fell on her like soft sparks. The madness of all of it still there, going about its business of physics, of prosaic cause and effect, of *normality*.

"We see the world in the same way," Katherine said.

"Do we?"

"You're Police. You see that there's no

natural justice in the universe. The evil do not get punished nor the virtuous rewarded. Obviously it so *happens* that I'm in here and you're out there, but you know very well that's entirely contingent. It turns out you caught me, but the world is full of those who don't get caught, who do just the kinds of thing I've done and get away with it and go on to live pleasurable lives of cold beer and television and sex. How many times haven't you looked into the eyes of those who suffer and seen it, the hunger for justice, the call for help, the desperation for redress? And how many times haven't you understood that justice is illusory, that the help didn't come, that nothing — absolutely *nothing* — can undo or balance what has been done to them? We've both seen it, albeit for very different reasons."

"So what?" Valerie said. "That doesn't make us —"

"I'm not saying we're the same," Katherine said. "I'm saying we're close. You see the world for what it is and do everything you can to make it otherwise. I see the same world and do everything I can to make it work for me. We're both looking at the same blank canvas. It's just what we paint on it that's different."

"Well, call me ignorant, but that's what

makes the difference."

"Yes," Katherine said, with a slightly tired version of the Smile. "That's what makes the difference. Do you still have God hanging around?"

"I don't need God to know the difference between us."

"There's a theory that the amount of good and evil in the world is equal. So you get genocide and rape and monsters like me, but meanwhile there's great art and giant acts of compassion and doctors saving lives. The idea is that it evens out in the end, always in secret equilibrium. God tossing the coin."

"You keep saying that," Valerie said.

"That's the sort of God I could believe in," Katherine replied, leaning forward again. "Listen. Have you heard of dark matter?"

Valerie opened her mouth to say that she hadn't — but then, courtesy of the lawlessness of consciousness, recalled that she had, in fact, heard of it. Some barely attended-to PBS science documentary. Eggheads talking, whiteboards filled with impenetrable equations like colorful barbed wire, flashy graphics of swirling nebulae. It sounded like something that ought to be science fiction.

"I've heard of it," she said. "But I don't

know what it is. Or care."

"Come on," Katherine said. "Don't posture. Don't talk as if you're playing a cop in a TV show. Dark matter is this stuff in the universe they can't even detect, but they have to assume is there because they can see the gravitational effects it has on regular matter. That and the radiation. It's purely hypothetical, but if the hypothesis is right it means that eighty percent of the universe is made up of it. Can you imagine? Eighty percent of everything is this stuff that can't be detected." Katherine gave a little laugh. "I love that," she said. "Everything's just the tip of the iceberg. When I picture God I picture him living in a nest of dark matter, tossing a coin over and over to determine the horrors and the beautiful poems. Heads a Hitler, tails a Mandela. The coin tosses would even out eventually, you see. The world *is* a reflection of God's nature. It's just that God's nature is a pure and infinite form of schizophrenia, and his love is nothing more than the tossing of a coin. If there were a church for that sort of God, I'd probably go."

Involuntarily, Valerie went to switch off the recorder — then remembered there *was* no recorder. She hadn't brought it. This wasn't an interview. It should have been, if

439

only to rationalize the time. Instead all she had was an insane social call. The time. She was — again — wasting it. A warmth of guilt went through her.

"You said there was something else you wanted to discuss with me," she said. "I'm assuming it's not Philosophy 101?"

"There's no end to the things I want to discuss with you," Katherine said. "But right now I'm wondering what you'll do when the next package finds you. Is my currency still good?"

"You don't think he's been burned by this?"

"Of course, but that's not going to make him stop. If anything, you've made it more interesting for him. You know that. It's probably what he wanted. Or at least, it's probably what a part of him wanted. He prides himself on his ability to pull your strings. All you've done is remind him your strings are worth pulling. Like his mythic forebear, pride is his defining characteristic."

Pride. Mythic forebear? Lucifer. Lucien, Lucifer.

"*Is* my currency still good?" Katherine said. "You know how much I've come to depend on this."

"Presumably that's why you're leaving gaps for the FBI," Valerie said.

Katherine gave her a mock look of sheepishness. "Well, you can hardly blame me," she said. "I'm sorry, Valerie, but I need this too much. Anyway, what do you care? All that matters to you is finding them in time. The end justifies the means. Unfortunately the favored maxim of too many Police without your integrity."

"If we get another package, I imagine you'll get to take a look at it," Valerie said.

"But it's not your call? I suppose Arden's people think it's a scam."

"It's crossed their minds."

"And yours?"

"Yes, of course."

Katherine's shoulders dropped, as if she'd been holding tension. She looked away for a moment, at nothing. To Valerie it was another jolting glimpse of the artless version of the woman. Katherine was so wrapped up by the performance of herself, her apparent compulsion to advertise mercurial artifice, that its sudden disappearance was always a shock, as if she'd torn off a wig you'd thought was her hair. There was a brutal poignancy to it. When she looked back at Valerie the nakedness was disconcerting. *Valerie* wanted to look away.

"I exhaust myself," Katherine said. It was the other version of the voice, too, stripped of its musical play. "Look at me. It's pathetic, and yet I can't stop myself. I'm sorry."

Valerie could neither answer nor look away. Katherine's eyes held hers. She felt exposed.

"Do you know what the most vicious absurdity is here?" Katherine said.

"What?"

Katherine's smile this time was one of resigned incredulity — at herself. "It's that I still expect sympathy. I was going to say I still expect sympathy, *even from you,* but that's not right. What I really should have said is that I still expect sympathy, *especially* from you."

Valerie was very aware of her physical self, the weight of her hands in her lap, the heat of her scalp. It was incredible to her that she could have been anywhere else in the world — at work, buying coffee from the deli, down in computer forensics talking to Nick — but she was here, in the pale windowless room, with Katherine Glass.

"I do know — of course I know — that what I've done ought to have burned the rest of the circuits out," Katherine said. "Or that there oughtn't to have been any other circuits *to* burn out. I understand. It's supposed to be an either/or situation. But here

442

I am. I still care for myself. Intellectually I know I've forfeited the right to expect anyone else to care for me. But the emotional . . ." She looked down at her hands, then back up at Valerie. "I see you and I know that you think of me as a person. And my pathetic, wretched little scrap of personhood can't help responding. I can't be any other way with you, any more than a person freezing can help moving toward the warmth of a fire. I know you understand me, and it makes me want things I know I have no right to want."

When Valerie spoke, her mouth seemed to ache. "But I don't understand you," she said quietly.

"You do," Katherine said. "You understand that all the things that are not supposed to be part of me still are. I think you understand why I've done the things I've done."

"How can I?" Valerie said. She hadn't meant to say anything.

For a moment Katherine didn't reply. Their eyes were locked. For Valerie the silence of this pause was like Katherine's body weight on her.

"You understand that I couldn't stop myself. There are things you can't stop."

"You chose it. Everyone chooses."

443

"Do you choose to love Nick? Could you *stop* yourself from loving him, by an act of will?"

"It's not the same."

"It's not the same superficially. But it's the same in principle. Either you accept there are forces to which you're compelled to submit, or you believe everything's resistible. The moral status of the force is irrelevant. *That*'s why you understand me."

Valerie wanted to move. Get up, at least take a couple of paces. But she couldn't. She could feel the neural signals failing in her limbs.

"What did we look like to you in the videos?" Katherine asked.

"What do you mean?"

"Did we look happy?"

"Yes."

"Yes. At first. But not at the end. What did we look like when they were dead?"

Valerie couldn't help it: she remembered her words to Gayle Werner. *I felt like I was watching people with rage and despair inside them. Not even evil. Just rage and despair.*

"You looked like you knew you'd failed," she said. It seemed she had lost the ability to speak to Katherine any way but honestly.

Katherine smiled again. A self-recognizing sadness. "See?" she said. "You do under-

444

stand me." She leaned forward. Her cuffed hands on the table. Strange, the white skin, the fingernails, the small lines in the knuckles: a person, as she had said. Flesh and blood. Valerie smelled hand cream. Faint vanilla. She wanted it to stop. Whatever it was. But she remained silent, pinned.

"We never got what the Devil promised," Katherine said. "They don't call him the Father of Lies for nothing. He promises you something extraordinary. He promises you everything, in fact. But all you get is the sordid details."

"You're talking about the Devil?"

"It's a way of talking. You've got the Catholicism, so you know what I mean. I know neither of us believes in the Devil."

Valerie thought of her grandfather, the last member of her family for whom the Devil was a real entity. What had he said? *First the Devil lets you know there are terrible things. Then he tells you which room they're in. Then he invites you in to look. And before you know it you can't find the door to get out. Before you know it you're one of the terrible things.*

Katherine Glass was a terrible thing.

"I'm made this way," Katherine said. "When I saw the things I saw . . . My father . . . I liked it. I liked it from the first. I didn't, as far as I know, have a say in it. It

445

wasn't a discovery. It was a recognition, as if it were something I remembered from a former life. Where was the choice in that? How do we choose what we recognize? You recognized Nick, didn't you? Isn't that what love is? This almighty, transcendent recognition?"

Valerie looked away. Then back at Katherine. She didn't want the intimacy, but it had an irresistible gravity.

"But so what?" Katherine said. "It's faulty wiring. A genetic predisposition with exactly the right conditions of experience to trigger it. That's the thinking these days, I know. The psychopathic gene. It doesn't make any difference to what has to be *done* with me. Until the neuroscientists come up with something wonderful, people like me have to be put in places like this. Given the way the world is I am exactly where I belong. Out of the equation. That's your job: to remove people like me from the equation."

"Yes," Valerie said. "That's my job."

"And here I am, no argument. But all the other aspects of me come alive the minute you walk in the room. Yes, all the other aspects. There oughtn't to *be* any other aspects, but there are. And you know there are, and that's what flows between us like a perverse little electric current."

Yes, all the other aspects. It occurred to Valerie that Katherine was trying to seduce *her.* The madness of the idea went through her system like a contained explosion. It was both incredible and weirdly inevitable. In spite of herself she had an image of Katherine leaning toward her, green eyes glimmering, lips parted for the first, sacrilegious kiss. The image was so clear she found herself thinking beyond it to the simple fact that she'd never kissed a woman in her life, not sexually. She'd simply never wanted to. She didn't want to now, either, but that didn't stop her filling up with something like sensual panic.

"No," Katherine said quietly. "I'm not coming on to you." The usual version of her would have smiled as she said this, Valerie knew. But this time she didn't. The unsettling, calm, lucid sadness was still there. It would've been better if she *had* smiled. Valerie's defenses against Katherine's default mode of vicious mischief were well-fortified. It was what she brought to every one of their encounters. But the artless Katherine wrong-footed her. The artless Katherine was, in so many ways, worse.

"I know that's what you're thinking," Katherine said. "And I'd be lying if I said the thought hadn't occurred to me. To the lesser me, I should say, the me that inclines to baroque deviousness. But even I need time off from that now and again. Besides" — and here she did smile, but simply, with apparent spontaneity — "where exactly would we go on a date? My cell?"

Valerie imagined telling Nick about this conversation. Knew immediately that she wouldn't.

"I just mean you're rain in the desert," Katherine said. "No one wants me to be anything other than Satan's daughter, except you. I'm not supposed to *be* anything other than that. But you know that I am. For me that's like being able to *breathe.* Naturally it's atrocious logic: I want him to go on with what he's doing so I can go on with what *I'm* doing, namely exercising my starved brain and getting the benefit of contact with real human beings. And of course the same logic leads me into trouble, because if *that*'s true, then my real goal will be to string it out as long as possible."

"Yes," Valerie said. "That is the logic, unfortunately. It doesn't help you."

"I know," Katherine said. "But please listen to me. I'm doing this honorably. I *am* working as fast as I can. Fast enough, it turned out last time." She paused. Looked down, as if gathering herself for a risk —

448

then her eyes flashed back up at Valerie. "I want to ask you something," she said.

"Is this what we've been waiting to discuss?"

"Yes. One of the things."

"So ask me."

"I want you to promise me that if I help you catch him, if the work I'm doing leads to you stopping him, really stopping him, you won't abandon me. Promise me that when it's over you'll still come and see me, once a month, until they kill me."

Valerie's circuits jammed. On the surface, incredulity, ridicule, annoyance, futility. But underneath there was something else. A version of déjà vu. As the words had come out of Katherine's mouth Valerie had been overtaken by the feeling that she'd known all along that was what Katherine was going to say. It was ludicrous — and yet it eased the ground away from under her. Her regular self was already offering the obvious calculation: promise her whatever the fuck she wants. It doesn't count. By no sane standard can it possibly count. But her other self, wherever it was located, was appalled by a dreamy feeling of inevitability.

"Sure," she said, looking away.

"No," Katherine said, very quietly. "Look at me."

449

And as if invisible hands were guiding her, Valerie turned her head and looked at Katherine. Katherine's younger self was there in her face. It showed through despite the glamour of the peppery green eyes and the knowing mouth. Valerie had an intimate sense of the girl in the woman, a complex creature still uncertain of herself.

"Please," Katherine said. "I'm calm. I'm in full command of my faculties. I know exactly what I'm doing. If you look at me, and say the words 'I promise,' I know it'll mean something to you. I trust you."

Valerie was thinking of childhood, the crossed fingers whipped out from behind the back to invalidate whatever promise had been extorted. That she was even thinking this meant something. Again, she imagined Nick watching. Don't do it. Because either way, you won't have peace. You not having peace is what she wants. It's what she wants.

Right up until the words came she was unsure of what she was going to say. Then, with the feeling of falling away from herself, she found herself speaking. "Okay," she said. "I promise that if your information leads to his arrest, I'll visit you once a month until they kill you."

Her hands were on the table, though she hadn't been aware until now that they were only inches from Katherine's. She wasn't surprised when Katherine moved hers closer, so that the tips of her fingers covered hers. As far as Valerie remembered it was the first time there had been any physical contact between them.

"Thank you," Katherine said.

38

There was, of course, a next package. It arrived for Valerie two days later. UPS overnight, with a sender name and address, both of which, naturally, proved bogus. They barely even bothered to check. It was sent from a San Diego office, paid for with — again, zero surprise — cash. The note was as follows:

Dear Valerie,
I must offer you my congratulations. Cassandra is, I trust, well? We had very little conversation, but it was more than enough for me to understand how much faith she has in your resolve. I quote: "My sister is going to kill you." Quite an utterance from a woman facing death. I was impressed — but not surprised. Your credentials are already established. In any case, I salute you, and, implicitly of course, your code-breaking specialist(s).

You must have been very disappointed to miss me at the cabin. If we ever meet, remind me to tell you how that happened. (I see us sharing a bottle of Thorevilos — 2006 was a good year — by a log fire with snow falling outside. And no, don't bother to add "wine specialist" to the Bureau's floundering profile; it won't help.)

Cassandra's two uniformed minders made it clear you'd alerted her, thus obviating my preferred method of fair warning by good old U.S. mail, and naturally this makes plain to me that the nonrandom nature of my selection is no longer a mystery to you. Again, my congratulations. Was it the globe amaranth? I was of two minds about that, but a flower in the hair is irresistible to an old Led Zeppelin fan like me. Like all monsters I am occasionally at the mercy of both whim and sentimentality. And please, have no fear for dear Mrs. Sorenson. I promise you she is entirely safe.

So much for the story so far. We must, as the British say, crack on. (An interesting idiom, since despite etymologists' best efforts no clear derivation is available. Naturally, my own preference is for the theory that it refers to the "crack" of a whip, used to drive work forward ever since its invention.) To that end, I enclose your next set of teasers. No name this time, since you've upped your game. Location only.

As you know by now, I don't move at a leisurely pace. Once again I say: days rather than weeks.

Good luck.

The enclosed five pages displayed the following:

1. A photograph of a crocodile basking on a rock
2. A reproduction of *Venus and Mars,* by Botticelli
3. A drawing of a woman's face, her hands covering it
4. A picture of a postcard showing the Italian beach town of Terracina
5. Two more letter and number grids

"I have an idea," Nick said to Valerie that night. It was after two A.M., and despite her best efforts he'd stirred and woken when she slipped into bed next to him.

"What's that?" she said.

"We emigrate."

"Okay. Where?"

"Polynesia."

"Why Polynesia?"

"I think you'd suit a grass skirt. And the beaches are quiet."

"We could set up a detective agency."

"No. No work. That's the whole point. I restore a boat incredibly slowly and you lie in a hammock slung between two palm trees."

"And spear fish. I'd be good with a spear."

"I can see that very clearly. Your passport in order?"

"I think so. When were you thinking of going?"

"Tomorrow?"

"Suits me."

She was thinking of Katherine. Audibly, it seemed to her. You spent time with her and brought something of her away with you, as if she'd marked you with her scent.

Polynesia, Valerie thought. If only.

"We got another package," she said.

"Same shit?"

"Same shit."

Nick was silent for a few moments. He had turned on his side, his hand resting flat on Valerie's midriff. "More work for Glass then," he said. "She'll miss all this when you get him."

Promise me that when it's over you'll still come and see me, once a month, until they kill me.

"Yes," Valerie said. "She will."

No sleep again and a headache but it's gone and now I feel GOOD.

He made me go over it too many times. He didn't even kiss me when I walked in.

39

Nick had just arrived at the Bay Club for his Saturday squash match when his phone rang. Eugene calling.

"You better have a good excuse," Nick said.

"Nick, Jesus, listen. I'm in deep shit."

The tone startled Nick. Eugene wasn't joking. "What's up?" he said.

Eugene lowered his voice. "I can't talk on the phone," Eugene said. "There's . . . Fuck. Can you meet me?"

"What the hell is the matter?"

"Please, Nick, I can't discuss it over the phone. I only have a second. I just need you to . . . I just need your advice. I'm sorry, man, but there's no one else I'd trust with this. They're . . . I'm in a fucking tight spot here."

Nick's initial thought was that Eugene had fucked the wrong woman. Been rumbled by a jealous husband with old-fashioned reactions. But he now found himself thinking it wasn't that. Money? It occurred to him that Eugene had just the personality to live beyond his means. Even *his* means. The car, the gear, the fancy restaurants. Nick had the sudden conviction that Eugene had been spending *someone else's* money. He remembered the Don Lewis encounter at the club. *He doesn't seem the type to take bad news well.*

"Are we talking nightclubs here?" he said.

"No, no, personal. *Personal.*"

Nick relaxed a little — though he wasn't entirely convinced. Maybe it was domestic after all. Some crazy fuck who needed frightening off by the badge. It wouldn't be the first time someone had asked him to apply the threat of the Law.

"Okay," he said. "Where are you?"

"Pacific Heights. I'm staying at a friend's. I'll text you the address."

Staying at a friend's. Presumably because it wasn't safe for him in his own home. As far as Nick knew, Eugene had an apartment over by Golden Gate Park, though Nick had never been there, nor had Eugene visited him at home. It wasn't that kind of friendship. They met at the Bay Club, occasionally for a drink in the Haight, and that was it.

"I'm not going to get beaten up, am I?"

"Christ, no. It's nothing like that. How soon can you get here?"

"Well, I guess thirty minutes," Nick said. "I won't be able to hang around. I'm due at my sister's in a couple of hours."

"I really appreciate this, Nick. I'll explain everything — shit, I have to go. Texting the address now."

The address on Washington Street turned out to be a white detached house with a faux colonial front and a black wrought-iron balcony that would have looked at home in the New Orleans French Quarter. It was midafternoon by the time Nick pulled up. Aquamarine summer sky with a few faint stratus clouds. Heat came up from the winking asphalt. The white building and short green lawn looked pristine. A large maple at its edge shaded the sidewalk. A driveway to the left led around to the back of the house.

Eugene appeared in the front doorway.

"Hey," Nick said. "What the fuck, dude?"

"Come in," Eugene said. "Christ, am I glad to see you."

"You don't look in imminent danger to me."

"It's complicated. Come on inside. I need a drink to get through this."

Nick followed Eugene into a large hallway of red floor tiles and white walls hung with a few abstract canvases. Several doors led off, two open, the first showing a luxuriously furnished living room — carpet the color of Bahamian sand and an ivory leather couch, more paintings, wafer-thin TV — the second revealing an open-plan kitchen — high-gloss white everywhere, a state-of-the-art range, burnished copper pans hanging from a rack, and beyond the central island at least twenty feet to the huge French doors that opened onto a travertined pool patio and more lawn beyond. The sunlit room smelled of lemony cleanliness.

"This place belong to a lady friend?" Nick asked.

"No, no, a colleague," Eugene said, going to the fridge and taking out two bottles of Corona. He opened them and handed one to Nick.

"You carry a gun?" Eugene said.

"What?"

"I might need one."

Nick rolled his eyes, exasperated. "Eugene," he said. "Will you for God's sake tell me what kind of trouble you're in?"

"You don't carry a gun? You're a cop."

"Christ, look, I *own* a gun — but I don't take it to leave in a locker at the goddamned

Bay Club. I just came from there. And believe me, if I had it with me right now, I wouldn't let a lunatic like you anywhere near it."

Eugene let out a deep breath. Nick could see he'd been holding tension. It occurred to him that he'd never seen Eugene looking anything other than upbeat. It was his standard mode, a kind of bouncy, bright, mischievous energy. Now he looked depressed. It was startling to see.

"Okay," Eugene said. "Fuck. Wait here."

"What?"

"There's something I need to show you. I'll just be a second."

Nick sat down on one of the central island's high stools. He was convinced, now, that Eugene was in money trouble. Loans. The mob. A debt to someone against whom you'd need a gun. Eugene's life suddenly looked like a thin disguise over recklessness. Nick could so easily imagine him simply ignoring the cost of his excesses, hemorrhaging cash, borrowing more, digging himself deeper with every restaurant check or luxury dirty weekend, all the time with gaze averted from the silently escalating crisis of debt. And now it had reached critical mass. Now there was no ignoring it because *it* was refusing to ignore *him*.

You're not going to believe this, Nick imagined telling Valerie later. Turns out Eugene's bankrupt. Up to his eyeballs and contemplating a getaway to Mexico.

He took a sip of the Corona.

Then the Taser hit him in the back.

There was no thinking. Fifty thousand volts shut him down. Consciousness, yes, but with time sloughed away, the details of the white kitchen and the pool's reflected sunlight frozen in a moment of infinite stillness, as if the barrier between him and his experience had gone. Pain fused everything.

He was on the floor, though he had no awareness of pitching forward. He could hear the Taser, a sound like a rattlesnake. In his peripheral vision the Corona bottle, smashed, in an expanding puddle of beer.

The pain stopped. Through the white light of its withdrawal he felt himself being flipped over. His brain began unscrambling itself. Eugene's enemies had found him. The copper pans were vivid above him. His limbs were haywire. Eugene's enemies had found him and now he, Nick, was just collateral damage. They wouldn't even know he was a cop. Would it make a difference if they did? He wondered if Eugene was about to be executed. How many guys? Guns? Valerie had given him a hard time for *not*

carrying a weapon. You're Police, she'd said.
You put people away. They get out. They
don't forget. It's stupid to walk around
without a gun. And here she was, being
proved right. It occurred to Nick that this
might be his death. He had nothing to bring
to that except a rush of longing for Valerie,
to see her, feel her, smell her, hear her voice
just one more time before the plunge into
darkness. There was this rush of longing,
yes, but in some vague higher part of
himself a feeling of gladness for having
known and loved her, for having been given
that gift. He surprised himself with this clarity. All of this and the strange sense that
today — *this* day, from waking with her,
showering, making breakfast, sorting
through admin crap at home, then driving
out to the Bay Club — had turned out to
be the day that carried him to his death.
Ordinary details stacked up to reach an
extraordinary conclusion.

His vision cleared.

Eugene was standing over him, holding
the Taser in one hand, something small and
black in the other. It didn't make sense.
Nick opened his mouth to begin to frame
some sort of question (though he was
unsure what it was), but Eugene hit the trigger.

Again Nick went out of time. His eyes were open. Through the pain he watched Eugene raise the other thing he had in his hand. He recognized it, but in this newly unhinged world the word for it wouldn't come. He just knew he had to close his eyes. But he couldn't.

Then Eugene pressed the trigger on the Mace, and fire blotted out Nick's vision.

The moments that followed were a maddening confusion. Pain came through his blindness in blows from something hard and cold and heavy, giant detonations in his shoulder, his wrists, the side of his knee — but with the pain the labored flashes of understanding: Eugene was doing this. Eugene was —

The air went out of him. Aside from this new agony the outraged admission that Eugene had kicked him, hard, in the balls. In training, the female officers had been told: kick a fucker in the balls — get it *right* — and that fucker isn't going anywhere anytime soon, no matter what you've seen in the movies. Nick was aware of his own neural failures. He had (hadn't he?) been trying to get to his knees, to grab Eugene, to throw his weight against him. But the reflexes, the intentions, the *will* — it all went nowhere. He was choking and blind and unstrung, swimming in useless adrenaline. It had happened so fast. How had it happened so fast?

He didn't feel the final blow.

Just the briefest sensation of deafness — then all his lights went out.

40

"You still messing with that?" Valerie said to Will. He was looking at the trial footage again.

"I wasn't," he said. "I left it alone. But something's niggling. Either that or I'm just running out of ways to kid myself we're doing something useful. In fact, fuck it." He shut down the video. "It's probably just Alzheimer's. Nothing from Bitch Eyes?"

The last package had been copied and sent to Katherine three days ago. Poor Agent Arden was back on babysitting duty at Red Ridge.

"Nope," Valerie said. "Although according to Arden she's putting in the hours."

"I thought you were supposed to be off today?"

"There's no off anymore."

"By my reckoning you've done three weeks straight. You look like shit."

"Thanks."

"I'm just saying —"

"He works, I work."

Valerie's phone rang. It was Nick's sister, Serena.

"Hey, Serena."

"Val, hi. Sorry to bother you, but have you talked to Nick today?"

Alert. Calm down. Alert.

"No," Valerie said. "Wasn't he coming out to see you guys?"

"Yeah, but he didn't show. I've tried calling him, but it's just voice mail. I wondered if he had to go in to work unexpectedly?"

"Let me call down there and check. Maybe he came in and I didn't see him. Hold on a second." Valerie switched to the internal phone and called Nick's department. No. He wasn't there, nor, as far as his colleagues were aware, had he been in all day. Valerie looked at her watch. It was almost six P.M. Nick had said he was playing squash with Eugene around noon and that he was planning on driving out to Danville to see Serena and the kids straight afterward. Say two hours total for squash. That's two P.M. Forty-five minutes would be more than enough to get from the city to Serena's. Two forty-five P.M. That's more than three hours off radar.

But be calm. He doesn't take men. Only

women. And in any case it's Nick. He can handle himself. It's nothing. Could be anything. It's nothing. It's people connected to me. Doesn't get closer than Nick.

"He's probably just left his phone somewhere," Valerie said.

Serena was quiet for a moment. The silence between them said all the things they weren't saying.

"It's just . . . You know . . . ?" Serena said. "With what's going on."

Serena, naturally, was on the list of people to whom they'd had to give a heads-up. One of the reasons Nick had planned to go and see her was because he couldn't resist checking on her.

"Yeah, I know," Valerie said. She could feel Serena trying to stop her mind working down the dark ways. "But our guy's not targeting men."

"Well, let me know if you get hold of him, would you?" Serena said.

"Absolutely," Valerie said. "I'll be going by the apartment in a while. I'll stop in and see if he's left his phone. I'll check back with you either way. Call me if he shows up."

Will had overheard. He and Valerie looked at each other when she'd hung up the phone.

470

"We being paranoid?" he said.

Valerie didn't answer right away. It was, on the one hand, obviously paranoia. Katherine and the Man in the Mask had never taken a male victim. It was impossible to think of Nick *as* a victim. It was *Nick,* for fuck's sake. But on the other hand . . . On the other hand, everything.

"Probably," Valerie said. "You got a number for whatsisname? Eugene?"

Will called it. Waited. Voice mail. "Hey, Eugene, it's Will. Trying to track down Nick. Did you guys play today? Call me back as soon as you pick this up, will you?"

Valerie called the Bay Club. Nick had signed in just after noon. The receptionist working during the day had already left, but her replacement told Valerie that as far as the record showed Eugene Trent had *not* signed in. In fact Nick had let them know at the desk that he and Eugene wouldn't be needing their two-hour slot after all.

Valerie was slightly reassured. If Eugene hadn't shown up for their game that meant Nick's planned day had changed. Some logistics had fouled up. Innocently.

Not so innocently, Nick could have been in an accident. Guiltily, Valerie thought of the standard Police response to someone off the grid for three hours. Three hours, you weren't missing. You were just doing something no one knew about. But this wasn't the standard context. Her entire life wasn't the standard context.

"I'm going to the apartment," Valerie said, getting to her feet. "If his phone's not there, we start checking the hospitals."

All the way to the apartment and throughout the fruitless search there for Nick's phone, Valerie oscillated between the mechanics of rationalization and the fall into nightmare. But as the minutes and hours passed the nightmare's gravity grew, until the rationalizations were frail, distant things. The ordinary world persisted — the evening lowering into Californian dusk, the weight of her phone in her hand, the city's sluggish traffic, the station's mix of fluorescent light and muttering keyboards — but all of it with a surreal energy and mass, and she moved through it as if wading the invisible weight of a dream.

Nick, in a crisp white shirt and Levi's, toting his sports bag, was on the Bay Club CCTV, exiting at 12:16 P.M. It hurt Valerie to see him not knowing whatever it was he didn't, at that moment, know. McLuhan's guys had tracked his Chrysler via street cams heading east on Pine toward Pacific Heights, but lost it just south of Lafayette

472

Park at 12:43 P.M. Valerie had been out there herself to scour the streets, and door-to-door inquiries were still going on. So far no sign. No reports at the hospitals. Nothing back from Eugene. There was now an APB out on him as well as Nick. Valerie had called everyone she could think of who Nick knew. No joy. Serena, naturally, was freaking out.

Valerie's phone rang. McLuhan.

"I'm sending over DMV pictures of California registered owners named 'Eugene' or 'Gene Trent,' " he said. "You know what he looks like, right?"

Valerie felt her throat constrict. She had only the vaguest memory of having met Eugene, one bright afternoon maybe a year ago, when Nick's car was in the shop and she'd driven him to the Bay Club for his game. They'd run into Eugene in the parking lot. She remembered a toned, athletic guy with a fruitily alive face and a buzz cut. She'd felt, in his first glance, sexual appraisal, but there was nothing unusual about that. Nick had already entertained her with tales of Eugene's alleged satyriasis. The entire encounter had lasted less than two minutes. Still, she thought she'd recognize him if she saw him again. In any case, Will knew what he looked like, and Will was still

473

here, fifteen hours into the working day.

"Yeah," she said. "If he's there we can ID him."

It took Will maybe three minutes to scan the thirty-four images and confirm what Valerie already knew.

"None of these guys is him," he said.

Valerie's desk phone rang. She had an immediate surge of certainty that it was Nick. She could hear his voice as she reached for the receiver. She could feel the weight of relief waiting for its release.

"Valerie Hart," she said. Her own voice felt intimately deafening, as if all other sounds had been silenced.

"Check your in-box, Valerie," the male speaker said — then hung up.

The newest e-mail in Valerie's inbox was from the address notbuilttolast_1@gmail.com.

The single attachment was a five-second video clip.

It showed Nicholas Blaskovitch in a bare brick room, hands cuffed above his head, shirt open, duct tape over his mouth, face swollen, eyes open, blinking.

On a small table in front of him was the leather helmet-mask worn by Katherine Glass's lover.

41

McLuhan's crew worked fast. The call had been made from a place called Headspace, a collection of purpose-built artists' and designers' studios in the Haight, though no one expected to find the caller sitting by the phone. They didn't. What they found in one of the units was a landline and laptop rigged for remote operation. "The space is registered to John Hendricks," McLuhan said. "One of our boy's ghosts, obviously, albeit this time presumably without the blindness and the dog. We'll get tech down here, but it looks like he can run this setup from a goddamned cell phone. He could be anywhere. There's one security camera out front that might give us a license plate, but we know he's already thought of that. Have to go through it anyway. We're pulling a list of the other occupants, but he'll have fed them horseshit."

"He knew we'd find this place," Will said.

"He wants us to *know* he could be anywhere."

Valerie was simultaneously numb and sickeningly alive. The world around her was an unwanted intimacy. The image of Nick from the video was a continuous loop in her head. Nick. Alive. The killer wanted her to know the man she loved was still alive — and completely at his mercy. He wanted her to feel the preciousness of the time between now and Nick's death like sand slipping through the hourglass's midriff. He wanted her hope. Just as he and Katherine had wanted their victims' hope, renewed, repeatedly, for as long as their own desire could bear it. Hope, renewed and betrayed, was their aphrodisiacal drug of choice. Her body ached with sensitivity. It was as if she could feel her own hands cuffed above her head, her torso stretched, warmed by the nearness of all the damage waiting to be done. There was no shutting out the images. They flashed and bloomed. Nick screaming, his face wrecked with pain. The calibrated subtraction of all resistance, dignity, personhood, the full, indifferent ugliness of suffering, the body with no choice but to report its sensations, until there was nothing of the person left to receive them. In those moments all her and Nick's love and shared life would count for nothing. In the faces of the victims on the tapes there was always a final stage in which even the reflex to feel pity for themselves was worn away, as if the soul had nothing left — not even the appeal to mercy nor the rage at its absence. Just the resignation to waiting for its release. Her mind refused. Not Nick. Not my love. But the refusal wouldn't hold. Yes, Nick. Yes, your love. It was unbearable and she could do nothing but bear it. There was no escape.

"Tech is on its way," McLuhan said. "We may be able to get a fix on the remote. Unless he's doing some shit with the IP addresses. Christ, he could have a dozen of these setups, like fucking Russian dolls."

Valerie had her phone in her hand. When it rang, it tore through her tension as if she'd been slashed with a blade.

SUSANNA ARDEN CALLING.

Even hitting ACCEPT was a challenge. Her hands were haywire.

"Go ahead," Valerie said.

"We've got a location," Arden said. She sounded different. Precariously balanced. In spite of which Valerie's hope surged.

"Name it."

"I can't. Glass says she'll only talk to you. In person."

"What?"

"She knows the location. She won't release it, except to you, I repeat: face-to-face."

Valerie burned through the rage in a second. The flamed feeling of having walked into an idiot trap — but it would have to wait. Just get the information. Even knowing there might not *be* information made no difference. There was no choice. No choice.

"I'm on my way," she said. Then, when she'd hung up, to McLuhan: "We need a chopper to Red Ridge, right now. I'll explain en route."

Will was visibly hurt when Valerie told him she didn't want him with her.

"It's just me and her," she said. "I don't want any other element for her to fuck with. I don't want McLuhan in there with me, either, though I know he's not going to like that." They were driving flat out to the helipad, sirens carving them clean through the night traffic. The city rushed by in planes of black and scrolls of neon. Valerie's system had shed its numbness. She flowed into the relief of action, of *doing something,* like water through a burst dam. Nothing had changed except that there was no longer nothing she could do. "And besides," she added, "for all we know Nick could be half a mile from the station. I need you here to move fast and make sure no one fucks *that* up."

"Okay," Will said. "I'm not going anywhere. But for Christ's sake be careful."

McLuhan *didn't* like it. It took Valerie the entire short flight up to Red Ridge to talk him into letting her speak with Katherine alone — at least initially.

"As you sow, so shall you reap," he said. "This is where we find out what she wants. We should have killed her instead of just talking about it. Fuck."

In a state visibly combining misery and rage, he waited outside the visiting room, in the silent company of two guards, neither of whom Valerie recognized. Inside the room, Susanna Arden was on her feet, leaning against the wall and staring at the back of Katherine Glass's head. The agent looked raw-eyed and pale, drained not just by the hours she'd put in but by the continual exposure to Katherine's wretched psychic vampirism. The room itself contained too much energy, as if Katherine had turned the dial of her aura up to max, an effect like the heat and density of a tropical greenhouse.

"Valerie," Katherine said. "You came. Thank you."

The smile was there, but for once it didn't look arch. The laptop on the desk in front of her was switched off. The usual mess of papers was in a neat stack, topped by a paperback road atlas of California. She wanted it to be as plain as possible that her work was done.

"McLuhan's outside," Valerie said to Susanna Arden. "I need to speak with her alone."

When the agent had exited, Katherine said: "I take it the pronoun is to let me know I'm not in your good books?"

"What?"

" 'I need to speak to *her* alone.' Not 'Katherine' or 'Ms. Glass.' 'Her.' I am here, you know. I am *present.*"

Valerie felt sick with the need to get the information without letting Katherine know how much it mattered. Contained frenzy. She might as well have had her mouth full of vomit.

"I got your message," she said. "I'm here, we're face-to-face. What's the location?"

Katherine raised her eyebrows. "You *are* angry. I haven't seen you this agitated, though I can see you're trying to control it. You're quite terrifying when you control your anger. Nick must have to tread very carefully. I can picture him, tiptoeing,

480

psychically. You're one of those people for whom the phrase 'seeing red' was invented. I must mind myself."

Nick. Don't give her that. Could she know? Maybe there was more to the ciphers than just the location. It was a private language. A private language of two speakers.

"Do you have the location or not?"

"Yes. But who is she?"

She. She didn't know. Or was making it seem she didn't. For every possibility its opposite. That was Katherine. That *was* Katherine. The image from the video clip bloomed, died, bloomed again. The wrongness of seeing Nick like that. The inversion of everything. The end of everything. Unless.

"We don't know," Valerie said. "Tell me the location."

"I see," Katherine said. "The clock must be ticking *awfully* loudly to make you this way. What an opportunity for wicked old me! I suppose that's what you're expecting, to be tantalized, to be made to jump through my ringmistress hoops."

Valerie was sick with what it was costing her not to do violence. Her jaws ached. She thought of the killer's e-mail address: notbuilttolast. *Not built to last.* It meant both

481

things: that the address itself would evaporate from cyberspace — and, of course, that Nick was on borrowed time. She was very close to some sort of madness.

"All right," Katherine said. "You're obviously in extremis. I don't want to make you hate me. I'll play against type and give it to you straight."

Again, as if she could switch it on and off at will, Katherine dropped the cruel-cat demeanor. It fell away like a veil and there she was, apparently without strategy — though to Valerie the room still felt crammed, as if a small storm had gathered and was pressing on her head. For a moment she thought she was going to pass out.

"You got close last time," Katherine said. "You might have caught him. And if you had, you wouldn't need me anymore. I know you've promised to come and see me, but . . ."

"I'll come," Valerie said. "Just give me the location."

Katherine shook her head. "I'm sorry," she said. "No, I won't give it to you."

Valerie had a very clear image of herself holding the gun she didn't have to Katherine's head. Give me the fucking location, you cunt, or I'm going to shoot you in the skull right now.

"I won't give it to you," Katherine re-peated, as if she'd seen precisely what was in Valerie's mind. "I won't give it to you, but I will *show* it to you."

Valerie's throat tightened. "What?" she said.

"I'll show it to you. You put me in a vehicle. I have a map of California. I give you directions."

"We don't have time —"

"No choppers. I can't direct you through the air. Roads only."

"You're out of your fucking mind."

"No, I don't think so. I want a day out, Valerie. I want to see the sky. I want to see anything that isn't the inside of this place, even if it's just for a few hours."

"You can't possibly think —"

"Don't waste the time you were so quick to remind me you don't have. Or *she* doesn't have, whoever she is. I'm making no other conditions. You can have me chained up, bolted to the roof of a Humvee, guarded by an entire SWAT team for all I care. But I want to experience *not being in here.* This might be my last chance, and I don't intend to let it go by."

"You're lying," Valerie said. "You don't have the location."

Katherine sat back in her chair. She, too,

looked tired. But relaxed. Completely at her ease.

"I'm not going to try to persuade you that I do," she said. "I'm not going to try to persuade you because I don't have to. I'm all you've got. We both know that."

"I can't make it happen. For God's sake, just give me the —"

"Who's McLuhan? FBI?"

"Yes."

"He can make it happen."

Valerie hesitated. Could he? More important: *Would* he? It was hopeless: no matter the calculations her rational self was busy with (mainly, whether Katherine was lying), her nonrational self simply insisted: You have to do this. You have to do this because if you don't, Nick dies. To which, amid its chaos of second guesses, the rational self replied: He could die anyway. He could be dead already for all you know.

"Don't think about it," Katherine said. "There's no point. There are no games here. I want what I want. It costs you nothing. Well, virtually nothing. Bureau gymnastics. A great deal less than the value of a life, at any rate, back in the utilitarian moral world."

Valerie burned. Every second of deliberation was an unaffordable luxury. *I want to see anything that isn't the inside of this place, even if it's just for a few hours.* She could neither stop the doubt nor ignore the fact that she had to proceed in spite of it.

"You're thinking about it," Katherine said. "I told you: don't. That's a waste of time. You can come at it from any angle you like, but it won't change a thing. You give me this or you don't. If you do, I get to feel like a human being for a few hours and maybe a woman doesn't get raped and tortured and murdered. If you don't, maybe you've cost her all that just because you're worried I'm smarter than you. You're telling yourself you've got a choice, but we both know that's a lie. In your heart the decision's already been made."

Stop. Stop. *Stop.*

Valerie was out the door without even being aware that she was in motion.

In the hallway, McLuhan looked at her from under his dark brows.

"Well?" he said.

There was no thinking, now. There was only whatever she could put between Nick and his death. There was only love.

"There's something you have to do," she said.

42

Detective Will Fraser lay on his bed, naked. He was exhausted. Seventeen hours today, same as yesterday. His body had begun sending him abrupt bulletins that he wasn't as young as he used to be. The night before, he'd come home so whacked he'd fallen asleep at the kitchen table. His daughter, Deborah, had come downstairs for a snack in the small hours and found him. She was home for summer break from her first year at Michigan and now seemed completely nocturnal. Jesus, Dad, she'd said, go to *bed.* Will had been dreaming of his own father, who had died two years ago. In the dream, Will had been in the hospital, trying to resuscitate the old man, screaming for doctors, all of whom seemed to have vanished. In fact the entire hospital was deserted. He'd woken, at Deborah's shaking, in a fragile emotional state. He'd been so confused he'd thought for a moment Deborah hadn't *left* home for college last year, that *that* whole thing had been a dream, too. He was overcome with love for his daughter, and put his arms around her. What a good girl you are, he'd said. Her leaving had hit him and Marion hard, not just her absence, but its testimony to their no longer being young, to life thinning out a little, to the gradual subtraction of precious things. When Will had woken and found his daughter near him, it had felt like a gift from God. Deborah had said: Holy moly, are you *drunk*? But she'd hugged him back anyway, laughing, and the sound of her laughter and the feel of her in his arms had all but broken his heart.

Now he lay on his bed wondering at the passage of his time. He was forty-four years old. How the hell had that happened? It seemed only yesterday they were driving home from the hospital with Deborah newborn, Marion looking both exhausted and strangely renewed. The pregnancy hadn't, strictly speaking, been planned, but as soon as Marion had told him he'd known he was ready to be a father. Ready only in the sense that it was a deep confirmation of an instinct that had, up until that moment, been vague: he was a family man. There was the Job, of course. There was the Work. But the true center of his being demanded the warmth of flesh and blood, the intimacy of home. Love.

He knew where these thoughts were coming from. The case. Valerie and Nick. Ever since it had become apparent that the victims were connected to Valerie, Will had been filled with a ferocious sense of the madness waiting for him if anything happened to his family. He'd gone through contortions, bribery, bullying, cajoling, to get uniform cover at his home when he was on duty. Thank God Deborah *was* home for the holidays. What would he have done if this was during term time? Roped in the Detroit PD? Pulled her out of school?

Nick had been taken. Imagine if it had been Deborah, or Logan, or Marion. It was unthinkable. He would lose his mind. Part of the reason he was working himself into exhaustion was, naturally, desperate loyalty to Valerie, for what she was going through. But part of it was simply shameful gratitude. That it hadn't happened to him. He wasn't proud of the feeling, but it was there nonetheless.

Marion came out of the bathroom wearing nothing but high heels.

He was astonished.

"Right, Mister," she said. "Listen to me.

Enough with this broken-balls nonsense. I'm going to give you the best fucking blow job you've ever had."

"What?"

"You heard me. You don't have to do anything but lie back and enjoy it. I'm hot and you have been *medically approved* for action. It's completely psychological and it has to be nipped in the bud. Enough is enough. Now give me a goddamned kiss."

"Holy mother of God," Will said.

"Leave God out of it," Marion said. "This is going to be all the Devil's work."

"Isn't this your show?" he said. The TV was on, muted. *Orange Is the New Black,* to which Marion had become addicted.

"Priorities. Now shut the fuck up and let me perform this incredible selfless act."

She kissed him, slowly. Ran her fingernails *very lightly* over his cock, the method they both knew was infallible. Will had a brief, nightmarish image of a diagram of his balls, felt the ghost of anxiety and tenderness for his parts, the way the doctor had said: It's nothing. I can do this procedure in my sleep — but Marion knew what she was doing, and after the first few kisses, when she slid her leg over his and he felt the heel of her shoe graze his calf, his body took over.

Afterward, he said: "Jesus Christ."

"I think I might have been a hooker in a former life."

"Thank God for reincarnation."

Onscreen, two of the inmates were getting into an argument.

"You know I said it was a selfless act?"

"Yes?"

She took his hand and slid it between her legs. She was wet.

"It's possible I lied about that."

Onscreen, a prison warden poured herself a cup of coffee.

Will lifted Marion's wrists above her head. Kissed her nude underarm.

Stopped. Froze.

"Fuck," he said.

"What is it? Is it your balls?"

"Fuck," Will repeated. He leaped off the bed.

"Jesus, Will, what's the matter?"

"Nothing. Stay there. Just . . . Holy shit."

He pulled on his discarded trousers and hurried downstairs. His laptop was on the couch in the living room. He could hear Marion coming down after him. He opened the screen and selected the footage from the Katherine Glass trial.

"What are you *doing*?" Marion said from the doorway. She'd taken off the heels and

490

thrown her pink terry cloth robe around herself.

"Sorry," Will said. "Just . . . I just . . . Just hang on a second."

He fast-forwarded. Backed up. Went forward again. The public gallery. Seconds. Two minutes. The faces he'd gotten sick of seeing, though he knew now why he hadn't been able to leave it alone.

43

He called Valerie from his car. Voice mail.

"Val, it's Will. Listen, the footage of the Glass trial. I thought I was nuts, but it turns out I wasn't. There's a girl in the public gallery. She's there every day. I cross-checked with the Bureau's profiles of prison personnel and ran the names through DMV. Melody Lomax. White female, twenty-eight years old, no arrests, no priors. Check your in-box for the photo. She's one of the guards who brought Katherine down to see us at Red Ridge. It's six years on and she's gained some weight, but it's definitely her. No coincidence. Local blues say she's not home and she didn't show up at work today, but I've got an APB out and I'm driving up there now. Search warrant's coming. She's not far from Red Ridge, so call me back when you get this. Stay strong, kiddo."

It was after three A.M. when Will pulled up outside Melody Lomax's bungalow on the outskirts of Garston, a small town of just over two thousand souls, ten miles west of Red Ridge prison. The homes here were plain, but solid enough: whitewashed exteriors and short, dusty front yards, some shingle, some grass. Blue-collar territory. There had been a steel plant, but it had shut down a decade ago. The place had the look of a struggle for reinvention, a community still trying to work out whether it was viable.

The local sheriff's deputy, Remmick, was waiting for him, a square-built young guy with a mustache that would have been at home on the face of a seventies porn actor. Will struggled to suppress his irritation: it's a stakeout, moron. You don't show up in a marked department car. Then he considered the size of the place. There was probably no alternative.

"No sign?" Will asked.

"Nope, nothing."

"You know anything about this girl?"

"Never heard of her. What'd she do?"

"Maybe nothing," Will said. "They send the warrant?"

"Sure did. Got it right here."

"Okay, can you move your car a couple of blocks over? If she shows . . ."

Slight embarrassment from Remmick.

"Oh, sure. Right. Yeah."

Assume the requisite information had been passed to Katherine by Melody Lomax. (So much for the genius code-breaker — although even thinking this Will had to concede the quality of Katherine's performance.) Lomax would go down at the very least as a conspirator or accessory to murder, but the real prize, obviously, was whomever she was getting the information *from.* Face-to-face? Would he risk that? It galled Will to think of the hours that had gone into the bullshit with the material Katherine's lover had sent. The whole fucking thing designed to get her into exactly the position she was in now. I'll show you the location. Thank God Valerie wasn't alone. Alone she'd be a sitting duck. McLuhan — Will had a vague respect for the agent's grinding dedication, his apparently joyless commitment to getting through the work — wouldn't go without a team. Valerie would've railed at the delay (as would Will, had it been Marion in Nick's place), but McLuhan was dispassionate. It was too easy to mock the slaves to protocol. Times like this, you needed them. God bless you, Vic. Keep her alive. Keep her *alive.*

But where were they now? And why hadn't Valerie returned his call?

494

The choice: wait and hope that Melody showed — or go in now?

By the time Remmick returned, Will had made up his mind. However remote the possibility, it was conceivable Nick was being held *here*. A basement? Jesus fucking Christ.

"Let's go," Will said. "Put on your gloves — and in any case, please don't touch anything."

"What are we looking for?"

"I don't know yet."

Under flashlight illumination Will picked the lock on the back door. The warrant allowed for forced entry, but he wanted their visit invisible if and when she came back. If she was in face-to-face contact with Katherine's guy (Eugene? Jesus, could it really, seriously, be *Eugene*?) she'd be more valuable as the subject of a tail.

The door opened straight into a small, untidy kitchen. Not quite a health hazard, but there were dishes stacked in the sink, unwashed pans on the stove, and a day-old pizza box on the Formica-topped table. The swing-top bin was at maximum capacity. Twenty-four hours more without a cleanup and the place would stop looking slovenly and start looking, officially, A Mess.

Nothing exciting to report from the living

room, nor the bathroom. Evidence said a quiet, glamourless single life (no shaving foam or male cosmetics), Home Depot clearance furnishings, and a TV two generations behind state-of-the-art. Incongruously, it seemed, a large reproduction canvas of a Spanish bullfighter, mid-kill. Will was no connoisseur, but it looked like a K-Mart compensation for a complete lack of taste. The first other room they tried was stacked with junk: cardboard boxes with old copies of lifestyle magazines, newspapers, battered shoes, clothes bagged as if for Goodwill, utility bills and credit card statements, a dressmaker's dummy torso, a fish tank with neither water nor fish in it. A lug wrench.

"Weird," Remmick said. Will could feel the thrill coming off him. Small-town deputy. This was probably the most fun he'd had in years. He smelled of brutal alpine deodorant and a freshly starched shirt. Underneath, cinnamonish sweat, not unpleasant. Will imagined a loyal, pale, dreamy wife in flip-flops and a sundress at home in a house only a little ritzier than this one. An unreflective marriage, but not a violent or toxic one. Maybe even love, in an understated way. He was sensitive to love, these days.

He opened the bedroom door. Nothing

out of the ordinary in here, either. The same unloved and unlovely furnishings as throughout. The dark-green carpet didn't go all the way to the baseboards. There were two bookcases, but they held ceramic ornaments — animal figurines, mostly — some of which looked homemade. Will went around the room. It was true: he *didn't* know, exactly, what he was looking for. He thought of the countless times neighbors of crazy murderers said: Jeez, he just seemed like a totally normal guy. In this case, girl. Woman. She seemed like a totally ordinary young woman. Kept herself to herself, but, you know? I mean, there's nothing wrong with that, right?

There was no basement. Nor, as far as they could see, access to an attic space. The garage was empty, aside from more boxes of junk, a push lawn mower, and a half-dismantled vacuum cleaner.

They were passing the bedroom on their way out when something caught Will's eye. Something hard and black was protruding from under the mattress of the unmade bed. He swung the flashlight.

"Hold on," he said.

It was a cloth-bound book. Which, when opened, revealed itself to be a journal. The handwriting was big and schoolgirlish.

Will flicked to a random page. Remmick was at his shoulder. The kid's body heat was close. Will scanned. Flicked another page. Read more. Something *tonked* in the air-conditioning.

"Right," Will said. "Holy fucking shit."

44

It took too long. Any length of time was by definition too long. To his credit, McLuhan didn't make her go through the obstacle course of persuading him. To his credit, he saw the logical necessities immediately, though it was plain from his face that they disgusted him. But he was immovable on the practicalities. It took more than two hours of scrambling: calls to the Bureau; the Justice Department; Warden Clayton, who'd dragged herself out of bed and driven over and had what was obviously a quiet but heated argument with him behind the closed door of her office. For Valerie the seconds and minutes were dry leaves consumed in a fire. Her body pounded, as if her soul were trying to escape. Every moment of her existence was a moment of Nick's existence. The time it took for the wheels to turn was the same time it took Nick to survive whatever wheels were turning for him. What she wanted was to get Katherine alone and simply torture the information out of her. Her fantasy was a confusion of all the things she knew — now — she was capable of doing, and at the same time all the ways every one of them could betray her. Because the bottom line was that Katherine could send them on a wild-goose chase, tortured or not. Eat up more of the time Nick didn't have. The corollary of that, of course, was that Katherine could be *taking* them on a wild-goose chase anyway, now, though it didn't alter their obligation to go through with it. Again, that was Katherine: no choice. Or Sophie's Choice. There was no escaping the possibility — likelihood, in fact — that she'd been planning for this moment from the start. And even *that* didn't make a difference. Face value or not, the Katherine option was one they couldn't afford not to take.

It was after two thirty A.M. when everything was ready. McLuhan commandeered an armored prisoner transfer vehicle and called in a six-man SWAT team. Two local squad cars for escort. With them, Valerie, McLuhan, and Susanna Arden, weapons restored from the Red Ridge lockup. Between them the crew had enough firepower to take down a small fortress. Valerie was aware of some offstage conflict between Arden and McLuhan. She could guess why: Arden looked dead on her feet. Arden, apparently, prevailed.

"No," Katherine said, when she shambled out in her restraints between Valerie and McLuhan. "No chopper." She had the road atlas clutched between her cuffed hands.

"You're not going in it," Valerie said. "It's escort only."

"Are you insane? He'll hear it."

"Not your call," McLuhan said.

Katherine smiled. Took a moment to fill her nostrils with the night air. In spite of everything it made Valerie notice the scent of the land in the darkness and gave her a useless understanding of the earth's indifference to human affairs. Billions had been born, lived, and died, sparks sucked into the infinite furnace, moments, glimpses, nothing. Her life. Nick's. Everyone's.

"No chopper or no dice," Katherine said. "And I'm not riding in that, either. I want a window to look out of." The prisoner transfer van was, naturally, windowless but for the windshield, which was screened from the back by an armored plate. "Otherwise I might as well be in my cell."

"It's not going to happen," McLuhan said.

"Yes, it is," Katherine said sweetly. "And

don't make me add any more conditions, please. It's not as if I couldn't come up with a list. It's been six years since I had a martini, for a start."

McLuhan took Valerie aside, out of Katherine's earshot.

"Just do it," Valerie said. "There are cuff bolts in the squad car."

"Yeah, yeah," McLuhan said. "Listen. The Bureau's tracking my phone. Wherever we are, they'll know. The chopper's coming, whatever she says. He'll hang back, but he'll be there. Anything fucks up, I just want you to know the cavalry's not far. Okay?"

They put Katherine in the backseat of one of the squad cars and cuffed her restraints to the built-in bolt. Valerie slid in next to her. McLuhan and Arden up front, McLuhan behind the wheel. Everyone bar Katherine was equipped with headsets, channel open to the SWAT guys and second squad car.

"Jesus," Katherine said. "The smell of a car. Even a police car. Humble vinyl and stale coffee. Bliss. It might sound ridiculous but this is like cocaine to me. You free people take all this for granted. Everyone should go to prison, just once, if only to make them appreciate everything prison takes away."

"Just tell me where I'm going," McLuhan said.

Katherine opened the road atlas. "This is so exciting," she said. "Get on the 101 and head north."

They'd been on the road less than ten minutes when Katherine said: "Okay, now stay on this all the way to Santa Rosa. I'll tell you what to do when we get there." She turned to Valerie. "This might be the time," she said.

"The time for what?"

"For the other thing I wanted to discuss with you."

"We already discussed that."

"No, remember my words: *one* of the things, I said. There are several. In fact the truth is I can't imagine there's much it *wouldn't* be worth my while to discuss with you. You underestimate the richness of your mind, Valerie."

She nudged the side of Valerie's thigh with her own. Valerie couldn't stop the reflex to pull away.

Katherine laughed. "For heaven's sake," she said, jangling her restraints. "Don't fret. I can hardly jump on you, can I?"

Valerie forced herself to suppress a shudder. "All right, what is it?"

503

"Look at me," Katherine said. "I need you to see my face so you'll know I'm not lying."

Valerie turned in her seat. The freeway lights went over both of them in rhythmic stripes. Katherine's eyes were clear and bright.

"Nineteen years ago," Katherine said, "when I was a mere slip of a girl *of* nineteen, I went to a party in San Diego. Hillcrest, in fact. Hipsters, mainly, even though I don't recall that word being much used back then. Anyway, having not yet shed the skin of woeful cliché, I was dating the bass guitarist of a band called — if you can believe this — the Grits. A very sweet boy, almost as pretty as me, but drearily conventional in the boudoir. Well, as you can imagine, he was on borrowed time from day one."

Valerie glanced up front and caught Mc-Luhan's eyes checking her in the rearview. Katherine had lowered her voice, but she still wondered how much of this he was hearing. Instinctively, she didn't want him to hear any of it.

"*At* the party," Katherine continued, "I met a guy, a different guy. Handsome rather than pretty. The chemistry was instant. He was understated. Like a cowboy, so good with a gun he doesn't have to say much. A little older than me, I guessed, but that only added to his appeal. He played it *awfully* cool, but you know, I was, well, *me*. As you pointed out: my only gift. I was used to guys foaming at the mouth if I so much as glanced at them. Every consummate skill is in danger of disgusting the person to whom it belongs. There must've been times, don't you think, when Robin Hood, nauseated at yet another bull's-eye, felt like breaking his bow over Friar Tuck's head. I digress. The point is, in spite of cowboy's admirable laconicism it was obvious he wanted me. *You* know how that is. I don't imagine there have been any men you've wanted that you haven't had?"

Definitely a question. Valerie didn't answer — though for a moment she couldn't stop herself from looking away. A road sign loomed up: SANTA ROSA 3 MILES.

"Look at me," Katherine repeated.

"Get on with it then," Valerie said, not merely looking at Katherine but staring into her eyes. This time, *Katherine* looked away.

"God, Valerie, you're fierce. I so much wish we'd met under different circumstances."

"We still good?" McLuhan called over his shoulder.

"Yes," Katherine said, leaning forward as

505

far as the restraints allowed. "Another ten miles at least. Then the exit to Geyserville."

She sat back in her seat. "So," she went on in a lowered voice, "I sought out my bass player and told him I had no further use for him. I know that sounds harsh, but to be honest he was lucky I bothered. I was, I repeat, very young. It's extraordinary to me now how long my social decencies endured. I wasn't even particularly promiscuous. I barely ever outright cheated on anyone. Relative to my nature I was practically a nun!" Katherine smiled, as with incredulous but fond reminiscence. "I didn't waste any time after that. I took cowboy to one of the lockable bedrooms. It was strange. He had depth. I wasn't entirely sure how to be, you know? Which of the many masks to put on? Slut? Naughty girl? Princess? Trembling innocent? Hyperventilating romantic? I had the full gallery of faces, the comprehensive range of personae — but unlike every other man I'd ever been with his desire was opaque. I was used to being able to turn on a dime, but — rather maddeningly to me at the time — he seemed not to be wearing his preferences on his sleeve. Fuck, that's two hackneyed idioms in one sentence. I'm sorry. This is what comes of having a prison library full of bad books. One's narrative style suffers. But then one wouldn't expect Nadia Comaneci to launch straight into her uneven bars routine after doing nothing but cartwheels for six years."

Valerie was listening — but only with a frail, distant part of herself. The rest of her was reaching out into the unknown distance. I'm coming, Nick. Stay alive. Do whatever it takes to stay alive. Please hold on. *Hold on, my love.*

"I was wearing a tight, short white Lycra dress," Katherine said. "I know: forgive me! White heels, too, dear God. I can *carry* all white, mind you. With my hair it doesn't shout tragic bombshell the way red or black might. And with eyes this color you want them to do all the work. You want a blank canvas. I tried rich greens for a while but I looked like a goddamned Christmas decoration. Hang on —" She looked down at the map, then leaned forward again for McLuhan's benefit. "Five miles. Then take the country road east toward Castle Rock Springs."

It occurred to Valerie that she still had her headset on. While Katherine spoke to McLuhan, she reached up discreetly and turned the mic off. She wasn't sure why. The part of her that had been listening to Katherine demanded it.

"I think I've told you this before," Katherine continued, easing back in her seat, "but one of the virtues of being the way I am is sexual telepathy. It's all in the eyes. You know this, Valerie: what makes you come — whatever might be going on physically — is the knowledge that your partner is *right there with you.* Knowing what you're thinking. Seeing you, knowing who you are, what you are. Even the Bible admits it: Genesis 4, verse 1: *And Adam knew Eve, his wife.* . . . It's no accident that 'knowing' is perhaps the oldest euphemism for fucking. Shared knowledge of each other, in the end, is the dark bliss. . . . Anyway, to make an unforgivably long story short, it was good. He knew me. We had mutual visibility. What was in me was in him, notwithstanding it rarely saw the light of day. I'd wondered at the immediacy of the attraction. I wondered no more. It was all rather astonishing, though I lay there in his arms afterward like a cat, delighted by the infallibility of my instincts. We hadn't needed to exchange a single word. The Devil is most eloquent in his silences."

She nudged Valerie again with her leg. "You're looking away again," she said. "Are you still with me?"

"Yes," Valerie said, not meeting Katherine's eye.

Katherine paused for a moment. The squad car passed an eighteen-wheeler. Valerie noticed the driver, a large, dirtily tanned guy with dark eyes and a gray ponytail under a Yankees baseball cap. He was singing along to something on the radio. The lives of people who weren't Police. She had the mad thought that if Nick survived she'd quit being a cop. She remembered his fantasy of emigration to Polynesia. *I restore a boat incredibly slowly and you lie in a hammock. . . .* She made an absurd silent commitment to herself: If Nick lived, she would secretly arrange to go there with him. Maybe they would never come back. If he lived, all the world's formerly shut-down potential would be open to them. She would have his child. She felt the certainty in her womb, as if she were already carrying it. Nick's survival would be the license that granted both of them any future they wanted. It was clear to Valerie that as of now she didn't care if she never saw the inside of a police station again.

"As you can imagine," Katherine said, "I was smitten. It had been for him the way it had been for me. That much was obvious to both of us. Consider my heartbreak, then, when, in spite of giving him my number, in spite of saying good night with the same mutual transparency that as far as I was concerned guaranteed the beginning of a new and extraordinary affair, I never heard from or saw him again. Not for many, many years."

"The Man in the Mask," Valerie said.

For a long moment Katherine just looked at her. Then she shook her head. No.

"When I *did* meet him again, we recognized each other right away, though he pretended not to. There was no forgetting each other. There was no erasing what had passed between us that night. But neither was there any erasing the fact that in the intervening years *so much* had changed, for both of us. Besides, the circumstances of our meeting would have made it impossible for him to acknowledge me. I could tell — with the same telepathy that had stamped that first encounter with its imprimatur of collusion — that he would claim not to know me. Not to *have* known me. Like Peter denying Christ."

Valerie stared at her. She knew nothing, except the sense of something vast and annihilating, very close. Katherine's face was like a portal to something infinite. An emptily gleaming hell.

"You know who I'm talking about, don't

you?" Katherine said.

Valerie didn't answer. Katherine's eyes were unbearable.

"I'm sorry, Valerie," Katherine said. "It was Nick." Then she leaned forward and said to McLuhan, "Take the next right. Two miles, then look for a narrow road on the left."

45

Valerie didn't speak for a while. She was almost wholly relieved — because her reaction was simple: Katherine was lying. Lying desperately. Lying *comically,* if she truly thought there was any chance that she, Valerie, would believe her. She was almost wholly relieved.

Almost.

She couldn't help knowing Nick's parents had lived in San Diego for several years, nor that he'd spent summer vacations there, between college and the academy. That she couldn't stop this concession meant something.

No. It meant nothing. It was Napoleon's white horse. Nothing.

But the whole of her world depended on it. The scale of the potential loss made even the smallest scrap of possibility glow, a solitary spark that could burn down the house, the city, the love, the life, everything.

It could burn her away into nothingness. Even in the midst of her vast reflex, denial was the understanding that if it were true — *if* it were true — there would be no recovery for them. Ever.

Katherine's repeated questions about Nick. Written off as the woman's instinct for provocation.

No recovery? Ever? Weirdly, a strange part of her wondered if that were true. Her weary realist, her cop habit of being unsurprised by anything found itself going through the prosaic logic. Suppose he *had* fucked her? What was that except a young guy fucking a young woman he knew nothing about? In itself it was ordinary. It was predictable. It was the most ordinary and predictable thing in the world. He wasn't responsible for what Katherine was, what she became, what she did. She was a hot girl at a party. It wasn't a crime.

But it was a crime if he hadn't told her.

There was no universe in which he oughtn't to have told her.

If it were true then it was lying by omission. If it were true then it was a lie bigger than love. And there *was* no recovering from that. Ever.

What was in me was in him, notwithstanding it rarely saw the light of day.

Valerie's relief came back. *That* was a lie. She knew Nick. What was in Katherine wasn't in him. Katherine shouldn't have added that claim. It was a detail too far. Nick no more wanted what Katherine wanted than she, Valerie, did.

But what had he said when she'd confessed her childhood cruelties to Dalia Poole? *It's what we do. It's what we find our way out of. You can't seriously . . .*

No. It was impossible. Nick wasn't that way, or at least no more that way than the average fantasist, herself included. It *was* nothing. Katherine was lying.

"Valerie?" Katherine said. "Are you all right?"

"Yes, I'm fine."

"You don't believe me." Not a question. "Of course you don't. Why would you?"

"No," Valerie said. "I don't believe you."

"I didn't expect you to." Katherine looked out of the window. McLuhan had slowed, looking for the narrow road. There were trees on both sides. No road lights now. "Proof is vulgar," Katherine said, still peering out. "Evidence is vulgar. Resolution, in fact, is always vulgar. It's only ambiguity that keeps us going. But ask yourself how I know Nick has a birthmark in the shape of a little arrowhead on his left hip. Not visible except in the context of intimacy." Then to McLuhan: "Here. Take the left and pull over."

The land was rural. The trees on the right-hand side had given way to open fields, though on the left their ranks were still dense. Evergreens, as far as Valerie could tell. The sky was clear and black around the swarming stars.

"All right, listen," Katherine said to McLuhan. "Put the following GPS coordinates in your phone. It can't be more than a mile from here, according to the map, but this place probably has tracks all over it. I don't know what sort of building you're looking for." She gave McLuhan the numbers. "That's right to five decimal places," she said. "It should take you to the exact spot, but obviously you don't want him to hear you coming."

McLuhan relayed the information to the SWAT team. "Pull up the satellite view," he said. "I need to know how close we can get."

It took a few minutes. The team leader got out and came over to the squad car, iPad in hand. He was a stocky, dark-featured guy in his midthirties with a look of dense muscle underneath the fatigues. HOOPER, his name tag said. McLuhan rolled down the window.

"Okay," Hooper said, lifting the screen for them to see. "If the numbers are right this is the spot. Looks like a private residence, maybe a farm. Nearest neighbor half a mile away. Two hundred yards from here we take a right. Another hundred and there's what appears to be a long, gated driveway on the left. We're going to have to kill the lights and drop the vehicles before we get to that. I'm saying just about . . . ." He traced the image of the lane with his finger. "Here. That leaves us around fifty yards plus whatever the length of the drive."

"Fine," McLuhan said. Then to Arden: "You're babysitting with the uniforms."

"Jesus, boss —"

"No argument. You stay with Glass and the officers. That's an order."

"Come on, Agent," Katherine said. "You know there's never a dull moment with me. I'll regale you with tales of my excesses."

"And you," McLuhan said, turning in his seat and staring Katherine down, "shut the fuck up and listen. The cover for this little jaunt is a prisoner transfer. As far as the paperwork goes you're on your way to another facility. Understand me: I've already drafted the report of how you were killed in an escape attempt. You've no idea how much I'm looking for a reason to submit it.

You do anything other than sit absolutely still and you will be shot. Believe me, we can make it look however we want it to. I have that on the highest authority. Are we clear?"

"Well that's *me* put in my place," Katherine said. "Were you spanked as a child, Agent?"

"If she sneezes," McLuhan said to Arden, "shoot her in the back of the head."

They left the vehicles as planned, with Arden and the two local uniforms guarding Katherine. Valerie's insides were a swirling emptiness. The night was soft and silent, the stars brilliant as if with a collective delight. Images of Nick in the video clip flashed and collided with the new material, grossly implanted: Katherine running her fingernails over the birthmark on his hip. It was impossible. She could neither accept nor deny it. Only keep suffering the repeated contradiction. It was like being stuck in a dream she knew was a dream but from which she was forced to concede she might never wake. She went through the motions of putting on the vest like an automaton.

At the driveway gate Hooper and two of his team went ahead in night-vision goggles. The intel came back quickly: the building was a two-story house with three access points, front and back doors plus one set of French doors that opened onto a yard at the rear. Blinds drawn. Lights on in two ground-floor rooms and one upstairs. Possible basement, possible attic. A 2015 Jeep Cherokee was parked at the front. A derelict Ford fifty yards from the main building, wheelless, on blocks. No sounds from within. Hooper's evaluation was simple: standard rapid entry and room clearance. Go in hard, fast, strong. Two men at each access, Valerie and McLuhan following as cleared.

"Okay," McLuhan said. "Let's go."

The next few minutes for Valerie were a blur — the sound of the doors busted; the repeated shouts of "Clear! Clear!" as one by one the rooms were confirmed empty: a kitchen bare but for wall cupboards and a small wooden table with an open laptop on it; the smell of bare plaster and floorboards; a camping cot with a rumpled sleeping bag half unzipped; empty water bottles; the dark hairs on the backs of McLuhan's hands; the staircase with several uprights missing from its banister; a bedroom window with a hole the size of a tennis ball in its glass.

There was a basement — a cellar, rather:

nothing in it but utility meters and a few rotting plywood crates.

The house was unoccupied.

Everyone had seen the laptop. Hooper put a man at each exit. He and the remaining two SWATs joined Valerie and McLuhan in the kitchen. The air in the small room was heavy with their adrenaline. She could smell the sweat in the tough fabric of their fatigues.

"What does it say?" McLuhan said.

There was a Post-it note stuck to the laptop's screen, just below the Web cam.

" 'For Nick, hit any key,' " Valerie read aloud.

"Don't touch it —"

Valerie hit a key.

A split second in which every heart in the room stopped — then the screen opened.

On it was the Man in the Mask, sitting at a desk, smiling. Given that the only times Valerie had seen him in the mask he'd been naked, he looked now — dressed in a plain black T-shirt (and presumably trousers) — slightly ridiculous. Like a role-play enthusiast who'd simply forgotten to remove his headgear.

"Hello there!" he said, smiling. "I'm so glad you made it. How's everyone doing?"

Eugene. The smile and the voice. There

was no mistaking it, despite the mask. The same impish buoyancy. Eugene Trent. Or whatever the fuck his real name was. Nick's squash partner. More than a year. All those conversations. All this time.

The room behind him was bare brick, with what looked like tarps spread on the floor. The room from the video clip, Valerie knew. *Not* a room in the house in which they were currently standing.

"I need to see clear evidence that Nicholas Blaskovitch is alive," she heard herself say. It was odd to her. Something in her still functioned, despite her body's state of contained madness.

"Now, now, now," Eugene said. "Let's not have that peremptory tone, Valerie. You look magnificent in that getup, by the way. First things first. Have a look at this."

He picked up the laptop at his end and panned its Web cam left. They saw three monitors, between them showing camera angles of every room in the house they were in, as well as a couple of views of the exterior. Redundantly, everyone in the room looked up and began scanning the ceiling. The kitchen's camera was in the back corner, angled to take in the optimal view. Valerie heard McLuhan sigh. The SWAT guys were silent — and very still. Valerie thought of the scene in movies where soldiers suddenly realize they're standing in a minefield. Like the kids' game of "statues."

The laptop returned to its original position.

"So," Eugene said. "That's *that* out of the way. Now let's deal with *this.*"

He panned the Web cam to the right.

Nick.

As she'd seen him before. Mouth duct taped, shirt open, hands cuffed above his head and fastened to a chain suspended from the ceiling. His ankles were in restraints just like Katherine's, attached to bolts in the floor. Not quite on tiptoe. He could take some of his weight on the balls of his feet. Some, but not all. Valerie thought of how long he'd been in that position.

His eyes were closed and his head hung forward on his chest. The same signs of a beating, but as far as she could tell, nothing added since then. Nothing *visible,* she corrected herself.

Eugene, momentarily out of view with the adjusted angle, now reappeared, holding a bottle of water in his left hand — and a black rubber-handled knife in his right. He approached Nick.

"You seeing this?" he said.

He opened the water bottle and poured

some of its contents over Nick's face. No response.

"Oops," he said. "Hang on. He's still with us, I promise you." He yanked Nick's head back by his hair and emptied the remainder of the bottle over his face, shaking Nick's skull while he did it. Nick spluttered and roared back to consciousness. His eyes opened.

"*There* we go," Eugene said. "Good morning, Nicholas! Welcome back. Say hi to your lady. She's on-screen. Look, over there."

Valerie watched as Nick struggled to focus. Eugene picked up the laptop and brought it closer, turned so that Nick could see it was her. Eugene's hand reached into the shot and tore the duct tape from Nick's mouth. It reopened a split on his lip. Blood welled. Valerie closed her eyes. Forced them open again. His face was drained. She remembered the final phase of the women. The loss of everything, even pity for themselves. He wasn't there yet. But she could see he knew that death was with him, like a third person in the room. Resignation was in his eyes. *It's all in the eyes,* Katherine had said.

"We're coming, Nick," she said quietly. Her throat felt all but closed.

"I know," Nick slurred through his swollen lips. "I know. It's okay."

Eugene leered back into shot. "Nicholas Blaskovitch, back online," he said, beaming. "Now let's get on with business."

"Wait," Nick said.

"What?" Eugene said. The laptop wobbled. He righted it. Nick looked into the camera. "It was the squash," he said. "Turns out this guy can't stand losing."

It hurt Valerie's heart. She felt it as a fracture in her chest. What it cost Nick to joke. Through the fear, through the isolation, through death in the room with him. It was a small victory for him, she understood, for both of them, a communiqué that made Eugene an object of discussion. An utterance that left the intimacy between them untouched. Love.

No matter what, Valerie's inner voice was saying. *Please, God, no matter what . . .*

Eugene replaced the duct tape over Nick's mouth. Moved the laptop to a new position. Set it down on — presumably — a stool or another table. The angle kept Nick in the center of the frame, perhaps ten feet from the Web cam.

McLuhan moved away from her.

"Whoa there, FBI," Eugene said, coming close, his face filling the screen. "You. Yes, you, with the headmasterly nostrils and lycanthropic eyebrows — stand still."

McLuhan stopped.

"Let's not have any nonsense, please. This is a live feed, so, you know, er, *don't.*"

"You're not rerouting?" McLuhan said.

"This isn't a conversation," Eugene said. "Just stay put, dude. Jesus, you look like Christopher Lee. You ever considered acting?"

McLuhan didn't respond.

Eugene reached up under the mask and scratched his forehead. "Okay," he said. "Call the other guys into the kitchen."

"Why would I do that?" McLuhan said.

"Well, for one thing," Eugene said, "I'm miles away and there are no hired goons waiting in the evergreens to launch an assault. For another, this." He stepped back and slashed the knife lightly across Nick's abdomen.

As the blood bloomed Nick convulsed and roared behind the duct tape. Valerie's arm involuntarily covered her own midriff. She felt sickness rising. "Just fucking do it," she spat at McLuhan. "Fucking do it *now.*"

"That's the ticket, Valerie," Eugene said. "I hope the only demonstration I need to make?"

McLuhan signaled to Hooper, and Hooper called his men into the kitchen. Valerie observed Eugene checking the monitors. "One, two, three . . . four, five . . . six. Plus Val and Chris Lee. Good. Excellent. Now, please bring Katherine out from backstage. Don't make me prove I know she's there."

Valerie looked at McLuhan. His eyes said No.

"Répondez s'il vous plaît," Eugene said. "Come on. Don't fuck around." He held the knife up against Nick's abdomen a second time.

"Don't!" Valerie said. "Stop. *Stop.* Yes, she's here. Just wait. *Wait.*" She spoke into her mic. "Arden? You reading?"

"Here."

"Bring her up to the house." Valerie glanced at McLuhan. If he tried to stop her, she thought, there was every possibility she would shoot him. Right now there was every possibility, full stop.

"And all other personnel, please," Eugene said. "I want to see the entire cast and crew. Don't bother leaving anyone, because I'll ask her when she gets here. And if it *isn't* the full complement, Nick's next cut won't be foreplay. Please understand me. Do you understand me?"

"Yes," Valerie said. "We understand you."

McLuhan turned to her. "Stop this," he said. "Valerie . . ."

Eugene raised the knife to Nick's throat.

"It's okay," Valerie said into the camera. "Don't hurt him. She's coming."

"You're not in charge, Val, I know," Eugene said. "But you've got to make sure the Count doesn't fuck this up. All I need — just like you with Nicholas here, is to see with my own eyes that she's alive and kicking. Can you imagine how difficult this would have been before decent technology? What would I have sent you? Morse?"

"Are you en route?" Valerie said into her mic.

"We're coming."

"Bring the officers."

"Say again?"

"Bring the officers."

"Roger that."

"Cool your heels, Count," Eugene said. "We're just talking. We're just leveling the field here. It's all civilized. It's all good. Don't do something stupid or Valerie will shoot you in your monolithic head."

McLuhan couldn't help looking at Valerie. She looked away. Which was all the confirmation necessary. He was sweating. Valerie could feel him making calculations. The SWAT guys were wondering when the cutoff word would come. Her hands were ready. She was ready — for whatever she would have to do.

"Good grief," Katherine said, when she entered the kitchen between Arden and the two uniforms. "This is like something from the Brothers Grimm."

"Hey, hot lips," Eugene said, on-screen. "Long time no see."

"Hello, you," Katherine said. "I can't say I *wholly* approve of the new chin."

"It'll grow on you. And needs must, right?"

"I suppose so. I doubt you'd be as understanding if I'd had my ass changed."

"That's different," Eugene said. "That would be a crime against humanity. Now, what do you say we get this show on the road?"

"Fine with me," Katherine said.

What Valerie did next she did without thinking. She stepped up to Katherine and kicked her as hard as she could between her legs. Katherine went down onto her knees, gagging. Valerie grabbed her by her hair and yanked her head back. She took out her Glock and held it to Katherine's temple.

"Are you out of your fucking *mind*?" Eugene screamed.

The whole room was in shock. McLuhan's mouth was open. His hand had gone instinctively to his holster.

"Just leveling the field," Valerie said. "You touch that man again and I'll do damage she won't walk away from. You think I care? You don't know anything about me, you dumb fuck." She looked past Eugene to Nick. He was nodding his head. Yes. Get your bargaining chips on the table. He's going to kill me anyway.

His courage deepened the fracture in her heart. Forgive me, Nick. Forgive me.

"I'll fucking *kill* you!" Eugene shouted.

"Maybe," Valerie said. "But not until you've gotten what you want, I assume. Now, shall we discuss?"

Eugene's visible rage made him look more ridiculous in the mask. Perhaps he sensed as much. Perhaps, as Katherine had foretold, his pride got the better of him. Either way, he ripped it off his head. The knife's blade flashed as he did it. The gesture seemed to push him past fury and back into calm. It looked like a relief to him to be undisguised, to be confronting the world in glorious unprotected liberty. His forehead was damp with sweat.

"Jesus," Katherine gasped. "Valerie, you're fucking insane. You have no idea —"

"Shut the fuck up," Valerie snapped.

"Everyone calm down," Eugene said.

"Everyone calm down and listen. We're going to trade. Nick for Katherine. Simple as that. A nice, calm, balanced, and most important *civilized* exchange."

"That's not happening," McLuhan said.

"Yes, it is," Valerie said. She gave him a look: Trust me. I've got this covered. I can make this work. He shook his head. But he didn't make a move. He looked exhausted, suddenly.

"Now, here's what needs to happen," Eugene said. "Count, you listening? There's a way of doing this, and it's the *only* way. Just listen very carefully. First of all, whoever's got the keys for the restraints, give them to Valerie. I know you're not going to unlock them yet. They just need to be in her possession."

"Arden?" Valerie said.

Arden, not surprisingly, looked to McLuhan.

"Give them to me," Valerie said.

McLuhan nodded assent. Arden handed the keys to Valerie.

"Splendid," Eugene said. "Couldn't have done it more beautifully myself. Everyone's still calm. No one's hurt. God's in his heaven — all's well with the world."

"All's *right* with the world," Katherine corrected, still struggling for breath.

"That's my girl," Eugene said. "Precision in all matters, especially literary. I stand corrected. Now, in the cupboard under the sink there's an empty plastic box. Get it and put it on the table where I can see it. The cupboard *under* the sink. Do it now, please."

McLuhan hesitated.

Eugene sighed. "Look," he said. "We can do the movie exchange if you like. We can haggle and hedge. You can try negotiating conditions of your own, you can try *stalling.* But I'd really rather not waste the time. Every gamble you take is based on the assumption that I won't kill Nick. And we all know that's not a gamble you can afford to take."

"Fine," McLuhan said. "As long as you can afford the assumption that we won't kill your girlfriend here."

"Okay," Eugene said. "Let's play that out. I do some more damage to Nick. I'm quite keen on the idea of gouging out his eye, actually. Not least because I think he'd suit an eye patch. So let's say I do that. Crazy Valerie gouges out Katherine's eye, tit for tat. Then I break Nick's leg. Valerie retaliates in kind. And so on. War of attrition. You're the good guys — or at least Valerie is. Sooner or later she won't be able to stand it. Sooner or later she'll shoot *you.* I know what she's like. The woman has passion. I have passion, too, but I'm willing to gamble Valerie'll crack first. Do you really want to play that game? I'm pretty sure Nick doesn't."

"Just get the fucking box, Vic," Valerie said. Her Glock had drifted away from Katherine's temple. She could tell McLuhan was starting to think she *might* turn it on him. Would she?

Yes, if it came to that, she would. Her look told him as much. *I'm quite keen on the idea of gouging out his eye, actually.* There was nothing she wouldn't do to stop that from happening. In the moments since seeing Nick on-screen she had left a great deal of herself behind. She was in new terrain. It was as if an entire cumbersome apparatus had rotted and fallen away from her, freeing her limbs. She felt curiously light and free. There was literally nothing she wanted, now, except to hold Nick in her arms, alive, safe. All other considerations were rescinded.

McLuhan retrieved the box from under the sink and set it on the table.

"Good," Eugene said. "Now everyone, one at a time: cell phones in the box. Don't make me trawl through the logic again. No one has to die. Just follow the instructions.

531

You can keep your weapons if it makes you feel happier. Count, you first. And don't do it *painfully slowly,* as if some alternative strategy might pop into your colossal head at any moment, because it won't. Valerie, vigilance, please. Every cell phone. Headsets, too. Do it now."

McLuhan, looking like he might vomit, deposited his phone in the box.

"Empty your pockets," Eugene said. "All of it, into the box."

McLuhan nodded to the team, and one by one they complied. Including Valerie.

"You're not going to come out of this," McLuhan said. Valerie wasn't sure to whom the remark was addressed. Eugene or her. Both of them, she thought. She didn't care. It was wonderful to have all your cares reduced to a single necessity.

"Okay, good," Eugene said. "Now, Valerie, take the box — and Katherine — and the two of you step outside the kitchen door. Leave the door open and set the box down on the floor. Stay there. We're all good. We're all happy. No one's lost an eye. See how this works?"

The compressed energy in the room went up a notch as Valerie followed the instructions. But no one moved. She was terrified that one of the SWATs or uniforms was going to do something stupid.

"All right," Eugene said. "You and Katherine just stay there for a moment. Count? You with me?"

McLuhan moved back into view of the screen.

"What now?" he said.

"You noticed the car on blocks down there, right? Please observe. Just give me a few . . ." Eugene hit some keys on the laptop. "And, three, two, one —"

The wrecked car exploded.

Not a *huge* explosion, but big enough to take the Ford's roof off. The sound seemed profanely loud in the quiet landscape. Valerie watched the light from the subsequent burning tinting McLuhan's face. Everyone in the room had flinched, involuntarily, backed to the corners. One of the officers was down on the floor.

"Be still, my ducklings!" Eugene sang. "Be still, be *still.* That was just a demonstration. Everyone be still. I can't stress how important that is. Now, listen up. Listen very carefully, Count. Look at the kitchen doorframe, please. See the four little red lights?"

Valerie saw them herself: red, winking indicators on four tiny units fixed flush into the frame. Without the lights you wouldn't notice them, and the lights hadn't been on when they entered the house.

"Valerie, Katherine, be very still, please," Eugene said. "Count, those are motion sensors, just switched on by my own fair hand. If you glance over at the window to your left you'll see four more there. You with me? There's a second explosive device in the cupboard *above* the sink. Considerably more powerful than its younger brother. Feel free to check. It won't go off unless you go near the door or the window. Those sensors are, well, *awfully* sensitive."

"Open it," McLuhan said to Hooper.

"Are you fucking kidding?"

"I repeat: It won't go off," Eugene said. "Not with my beloved still so close, I promise you."

Hooper, with visibly trembling hands, reached up and eased open the cupboard above the sink.

Eugene wasn't lying. No one had thought he was. As well as the explosives, a second laptop, displaying a digital countdown. Just less than twelve hours.

"Jesus fucking Christ," the officer on the floor said.

"Now, we're fully wired up here," Eugene said. "You've got a few hours to sit tight — but the sensors will disarm when the counter reads zero, and you'll all be free to stroll out without a care in the world. All you have to do is stay put. What do you see on the shelf below, SWAT boy? You can remove it. It's perfectly safe."

Hooper pulled out — delicately — a hefty paperback. *The Complete Works of William Shakespeare.*

Eugene smiled. "You'll have to share, I know, but I didn't want anyone to get bored."

Katherine laughed, arms still wrapped around her middle.

"At the risk of truly *giant* redundancy," Eugene said, "any attempt to interfere with the explosives will be fatal. The counter will skip to three seconds. Just long enough for each of you to make his peace with *Le Grand Peut-être,* before you're on your way to meet him — or not, as the case may be. Breaching the sensors will, on the other hand, cause *immediate* detonation. I'm well aware you might have a bomb-disposal guru among the SWATs, in which case I can do nothing but wish you the very best of luck. Oh, and don't think of shooting out the floor or the ceiling. In fact, don't think of doing anything in the hope that I haven't already thought of it. Everyone clear? Find a comfy position and settle in. Valerie? I'm not going to tell you to leave your weapon, because I know you won't, and we'll be back into the war of attrition. Bring it along, with my blessing. You won't need it. You and Katherine can now make your way to the Cherokee parked out front. The keys are behind the left front wheel. The tank is full and there's a cell phone in the glove box. I'll call you in two minutes to let you know where you're going. The phone, naturally, will take my incoming calls only. Katherine, I'll see you shortly. You look fabulous, by the way."

46

The cell phone in the glove box was ringing by the time Valerie and Katherine got in.

"Put it on speaker," Eugene instructed. "Take a left out of the gate at the bottom of the drive. Two miles and you'll come to a T-junction. Go left again. Four hundred yards, you'll find a pull-off with a black Chevrolet parked in it. The keys for it are in the driver's doorwell of the Cherokee you're in right now. Switch vehicles. Keep the phone."

Fuck. McLuhan's and Arden's training would've forced them to note the Cherokee's plates. Eugene wasn't taking any chances, confiscated cell phones notwithstanding. Valerie was thinking: Six years he's had to plan this. Of *course* he's not taking any chances. To plan this. The murders, the packages, the goddamned ciphers. Cassie's abduction had been nothing more than a device to raise Katherine's code-breaking stock. The abandoned car tip-off, Eugene's absence from the cabin, all architected. It had never been about the killings. It had been about getting Katherine Glass *out.*

"So who's been feeding you?" Valerie said to Katherine.

"I'm not talking to you," Katherine said. "My cunt is *killing* me. I think you might have *broken* it."

"Don't even joke about that," Eugene said.

"Come on," Valerie said. "You might as well tell me. Was it Clayton?"

"What makes you think anyone was feeding me? I'm a genius."

"Yeah, you're a genius. But you had the information all along. Who gave it to you?"

"No one important," Eugene said. "No one who'll be *missed,* that's for sure."

"Nick's got a nice cock," Katherine said, holding her midriff, bending forward to ease the pain. "I can see how good it must be for you."

"Hey!" Eugene said. "I'm *right here,* for Christ's sake. Jesus."

"No dice," Valerie said. "It was a nice try, but since your boyfriend's seen him in the Bay Club locker rooms we both know where *that* information came from. Why on earth did you try that? It couldn't possibly have helped you."

"What can I tell you?" Katherine said. "I'm prone to mischief."

"I told you," Eugene said, laughing. "I told you she wouldn't buy it."

"She bought it for a while," Katherine said. "You should have seen her face. It was priceless. *All that love.* Valerie, you looked like someone had eviscerated you. *Christ,* I feel sick."

"All right, all right," Eugene said. "Slow down, you're almost on the Chevy. And yes, I'm tracking the phone."

Once they'd changed cars, Eugene directed them northeast. He was keeping them off the freeways. Roads without cameras.

"I realize you'll accuse me of cliché or something here," Valerie said. "But how exactly do you think you're going to get away with this?"

"Oh, Valerie, come *on,*" Katherine said. "Seriously?"

"We're smuggling ourselves out in specially designed giant cans of tuna," Eugene said.

"Valerie's thinking that even if we kill her, and poor handsome cowboy Nick, our faces are all over the news. We're *known.* Nowhere to run, nowhere to hide."

"Yeah," Valerie said. "I'm not as bright as

you two, so I still think in the old-fashioned ways."

"Don't knock the old-fashioned ways," Eugene said. "They've stood the test of time. They still apply, ninety percent of the time."

"But not this time?"

"Not this time," Katherine said quietly.

"Take the next right," Eugene said. "Head toward a town called Cobb. But you're looking for a turnoff to your right, half a mile before you get there."

"The thing is," Katherine said, "you underestimate the power of resources. Of money."

"His money," Valerie said. "You must be worth it."

"Trust me, Val," Eugene said. "She's worth it."

"Thank you," Katherine sang, as if she were receiving her change from a cashier.

"So you have an out," Valerie said. "I have to assume you're leaving the country."

"Valerie," Eugene said, "no one can take your necessary assumptions away from you. They're your right as an American. The trouble is we *love* this country. We're suckers for the life. I'm not talking about democracy and Guantánamo. I'm talking about Tylenol ads that tell me when pain strikes I *deserve* the best drug on the market. I'm talking about cheerleaders with missed periods and the dirty-sweet smell of Mc-Donald's. Born-again Christian porn stars and biological warfare. Texas. *Texas,* glorious Texas. A pocket full of down-home maxims and a shotgun over the shoulder. This is a country that always says more than it means. Giant, glamorous, and inane. It's irresistible. It's our element."

"This is all great," Katherine said. "But you know, I would *really* fucking appreciate these cuffs coming off."

"Not while I'm driving," Valerie said. "And by the way, I'd like to hear Nick's still alive."

"He's alive," Eugene said.

"Prove it, or I'm pulling over."

"Jesus, Valerie," Eugene said. "We still doing this?"

"Like I said: I'm old-fashioned. That was a dandy speech, but it doesn't alter the math. Let me talk to him."

Eugene made a noise akin to a teenager *finally* giving in to the umpteenth demand that he get off the fucking Xbox and tidy his room.

"Nicholas," he said. "Wake up your ideas, man, you're a shambles. Your lady's on the horn. Talk to her. Tell her you're peachy."

"Shoot her," Nick said. "You know the way this goes."

"Hey!" Eugene cried. "Don't say that! Fuck. We're cooperating here. What's the matter with you, for Christ's sake? You'll have to excuse him, Valerie. He's had a rough day. The important thing is he's still with us. Unmolested. Pretty much fresh as a daisy, in fact. Or a globe amaranth, if you prefer. Now, heads up. You're about fifteen minutes away. Take a left at the road marked 'Amner Lane.' I'm hanging up for a moment, but I'll call you back in five. Valerie, don't do anything insane."

47

Nick's arms were blood-locked and his ribs ached. He suspected at least one of them was broken. It hadn't taken long for the struggle reflex to burn through. The cuffs were solid and the ceiling and floor bars to which they were attached were bolted to the concrete floor. There was nothing he could do. His face felt like a hot skin mask. His immobility was terrible. It worked continuously in him like an insatiable fever. As far as he could tell they were in a domestic basement, long since set up as Eugene's tech HQ. Aside from the workstation and swivel chair, monitors, two desktops, three laptops, and a stack of slimline devices Nick couldn't identify, the room contained only the expected boiler and utility connections. Bare brick walls and the tarps on the floor. A small electric fan heater nestled under the desk.

Eugene had just hung up from the call to

Valerie. He took another cell phone from his pocket and dialed.

"Melody, where are you?" he said wearily, to what was obviously voice mail. "This is the fourth message and you're now *two hours* late. I'm worried about you. For heaven's sake please call me back. I need to know you're okay."

Eugene hung up and returned the phone to his pocket. He moved to reattach the tape to Nick's mouth.

"Logistics, logistics," he said. "But for want of a nail, best-laid plans, et fucking cetera. Jesus, there's no end to it."

"Don Lewis?" Nick asked. "The night-club. Bullshit?"

"I'm afraid so," Eugene said. "It's amazing what failed actors will do for cash. I needed a *little* rationale for my cry for help. Now, what sort of gymnastics do you think Valerie's contempl— Ah! Wait. Fuck." He'd noticed something on one of the monitors. "Melody, you *shopping bag* of a female . . . Christ. *Finally.*"

Nick could just — barely — discern the image on the screen. A dark-haired woman in jeans, denim jacket, and ridiculously high red heels, tottering toward the house. Eugene had cameras angled out into the grounds.

"Excuse me a minute, Nicholas," he said, reattaching the tape. "I'll be right back."

He returned, a few moments later, with the young woman. Her dark hair was in a tight French braid. Her short nails were deep red. He was back on the line to Valerie.

". . . Stay on Amner Lane until you hit the fourth turn on the left. Take that, then another mile you'll come to a gravel track on your right. There's a 'deer crossing' sign directly opposite, so you can't miss it. Over two cattle grids, fifty yards, you'll come to a metal five-bar gate, which is open. Through that just follow the track between the trees until you see the farmhouse. I'll be watching for you. Instructions to follow when you're through the gate. Katherine? All well with you?"

"Yes. Apart from boredom. Valerie's sulking."

"Good. I'll see you shortly. Hanging up now. Back on the line in two shakes of a lamb's tail. Be good, girls."

As soon as he'd ended the call, Melody said: "It's my goddamned phone. I don't understand it. The home screen button's been . . . You know, like for weeks now I have to press it like five or six times before it comes up. And then I get this fucking thing, you know, like the red lightning flash thing? That just means charge, but I tried charging it and nothing. Just *nothing.* I don't know if it's on or off or what —"

"I told you," Eugene said. "It doesn't matter. You're here now."

"And then when I left I realized I'd forgotten the shoes. You know you said to bring the red shoes?"

"I did," Eugene said. "I'm a victim of my own erotic whimsy. But you know how fucking hot you look in them? It's your fault."

Melody's face looked pouchy. She was staring at Nick.

Eugene went to the desk and picked up a large military knife. A seven-inch blade, bottom edge serrated. He stood behind Melody and reached around to put his hand between her legs. "Girls later," he said, kissing her ear. "This one's a necessary exception. Do you want to start?"

Melody was trembling, breathing hard through her mouth. Eugene undid the buttons on her jacket. Smallish breasts in a red lace bra. A slight ripple of fat over the waistband of her jeans. A deep navel holding a well of shadow in the room's bare bulb light.

"Shouldn't we wait?" she gasped, as Eugene's hand popped the buttons of her jeans and slipped inside her panties. Nick observed the panties were black, didn't match the bra. In the mad clarity of his state, he had a sense of her as someone who would always get something wrong, some detail that spoiled a strove-for effect. Her whole life was like that, Nick thought. It was there in her eyes. "I mean for Katherine?" she said.

"Oh no," Eugene said. "She won't mind a little foreplay. She won't mind us getting warmed up."

It seemed a long time to Nick that the two of them stood there, Eugene caressing her, Melody opening and closing her eyes, going in and out of some darkness in herself.

"What do you want?" Eugene said. "Tell me what you want."

"Oh, God," Melody said, closing her eyes. "I want . . . I want to . . ."

"Yes?"

"I want to —"

She didn't get to finish. Eugene flicked his arm out and drove the knife deep into her bare abdomen. Hard, fast, buried all the way to the rubber-grip hilt.

Nick watched her face open into shock. Her eyes were soft and dark. With her suddenly yawning mouth they formed three portals of darkness, as if someone had shot three huge holes in the moon.

Eugene's other arm locked around her throat as he drove the knife in a second, third, fourth time. She barely moved. The red of the blood and the white of her flesh was terrible, the colors of a stale Christmas. Nick wondered who she was.

Eugene released his hold and Melody's body slumped to the floor in front of Nick. Her collapse released the slightly sour smell of old denim and the tang of blood. Someone's daughter. Someone, somewhere, would have this news brought to them, eventually. In spite of everything it gave him a small, distinct feeling of the open American spaces, hours of television, pointless arguments and festering bitterness, the unknownness of millions of lives, all their crammed repetitive details shrunk to nothing by the scale of death. Strange thoughts, given his own death, so close, so close.

He looked at Eugene.

Eugene wasn't, at that moment, looking at him. He was staring at the body at his feet, with its slowly expanding puddle of blood. To Nick it was as if a mask had gone from Eugene's face. There was a new, essential nudity to it, revealing something basic, a delight that, however briefly, blotted out everything else, all the play, the intelligence, the nuances of character. Eugene looked like a child mesmerized by something wonderful. This, Nick thought, *this* was who Eugene was. It gave him an understanding of all the architecture required to protect it, the elaborately and meticulously constructed personality. It gave him a glimpse of the *effort* that it must require, for Eugene to appear so easy in his skin. It seemed impossible to him, and yet here Eugene was, revealed. All the games of squash, the cold beers, the tales of sexual conquest and mishap. All of that was wrapped around this center, like a galaxy around a black hole.

Eugene looked up at him. "Phew!" he said. "Thank God *that*'s out of the way. Can you imagine *fucking* her? I deserve a medal. Well, not me, but the boys at Viagra." He went to the workstation and opened a drawer. When he turned back to Nick he was holding a pair of night-vision goggles. "Okay," he said, with the generous smile Nick knew so well. "Now, if you'll excuse me, I have to go and kill your lady."

He was dialing as he left the room.

48

When Katherine undid her seat belt Valerie took her right hand off the wheel and reached for her sidearm.

"Relax, Valerie," Katherine said, wincing and clutching her belly. "Thanks to you I've got fucking stomach cramps. You really shouldn't have done that." She leaned forward and rested her head on the dash. "If I throw up in here, it's your fault." She breathed through her mouth, from which a little saliva fell. She looked, Valerie was forced to concede, as if she might be about to throw up.

"Holy moly, Valerie," Eugene's voice said, "you've got a lead foot, woman. Look where you are already! Were you *trying* to get pulled over? Oh, wait — maybe you were. That's you, you minx: always thinking. It's no wonder Nick loves you."

Valerie was at the "deer crossing" sign. She hung a right into the gravel track. The first of the cattle grids rumbled under the wheels. She thought: one more cattle grid, fifty yards, gate, house. The trees on either side came right up to the edge of the track. If Eugene had lied . . . If there was another vehicle swap . . .

"I have a confession to make," Eugene said. "I wasn't entirely honest with you about the fair warnings."

"You didn't send the postcards?"

"I sent empty envelopes addressed to the gals," Eugene said. "I dropped the postcards in the trash by hand. I can only imagine your hours of dreary rigmarole with the dear old U.S. Postal Service. I'm dreadful, I know. My sincere and shamefaced apologies."

Katherine was doubled up now, her hands moving up and down from her knees to her ankles in a rhythmic self-soothing gesture. "I suppose this is what getting kicked in the nuts is like if you're a guy," she said. "Except I bet this is worse. Guys have a much lower pain threshold."

"Stay focused, Val," Eugene's voice said. "There are potholes."

Katherine groaned. As if on cue the car dipped into and out of the warned-of potholes — and suddenly Valerie's instinct tightened. She couldn't say why. There was only the slightest shift in Katherine's aura, a minute adjustment to her bent posture and a suspension of her breath — but it was enough. Simultaneously it flashed in her mind that she hadn't checked either vehicle before they'd gotten in. The whole operation had been designed by Eugene. Pre-designed. For Katherine. Which would mean —

It happened fast. Katherine's hands came out from under her seat holding a gun.

She got it to perhaps the level of Valerie's knees before Valerie jumped on the brakes.

Katherine's pitch forward jammed her up against the dash. Valerie's hearing filled up with the sound of the shot, as if sound were a solid mass surrounding her.

But she wasn't hit. Even in the blur she'd felt the bullet's impact in the driver's door. Katherine still had the gun in her hand. There was no time. Valerie — still restrained by her seat belt — lunged and grabbed the pale wrist, wrenched and slammed it against the dash. A second shot went through the Chevy's roof. Valerie smashed Katherine's hand harder — and the weapon dropped from its grasp. It hit the hand brake and slid down next to Valerie's foot. Katherine was trying to get her feet under her. Valerie's free hand flailed for the seat belt release. It

seemed a long time before it popped free —
but when it did it was a blissful liberation.
It let all the adrenaline flow free.

Valerie punched Katherine in the throat.
Grabbed the back of her head and slammed
it into the dash. It was very satisfying to
hear Katherine trying to force breath
through her windpipe. The cell phone had
fallen in Katherine's footwell and, since the
jolt had lost the open connection, was ringing again.

Valerie retrieved the second gun and got
out of the car, raced around to the passenger door. Katherine, dazed, was trying
to do something with her arms. Valerie
opened the door and pulled her out by her
collar, choking her further. It seemed almost
comical that Katherine was still in the Red
Ridge inmate fatigues. She was making
small sounds, her mouth opening and closing, her beautiful face crimped into confusion. It looked to Valerie as if Katherine had
bitten into a delicious-looking cake — only
to discover it was filled with something rotten. The smell of the trees was rich around
them. Dust kicked up from the track swayed
in the headlights. In spite of herself a moment passed in which she looked Katherine
in the eye. Pain was there, yes, but outrage,
too. Fear. Valerie could see the woman try-

ing to fight off the idea that this was her death. It gave her a shot of euphoria, to see that for all her talk, for all her fireworks, Katherine Glass was terrified of dying.

She took out her Glock.

Shoot her. You know the way this goes.

It would be so easy. Shot trying to escape custody. Katherine Glass, gone, forever. The world would not mourn. The world would be relieved.

The gun felt so simple in her hand. A small, pure, heavy instrument, a one-dimensional personality with a single, disinterested function. Valerie's finger tightened on the trigger.

Was it only the thought that Eugene might be close enough to hear the shot that made her hesitate? Was it the desperate calculation that there might still come a moment (in the nightmare of moments swirling ahead of her) when Katherine alive would be more useful to her than Katherine dead? Or was it the smear of dirt Katherine's white hands had picked up in her fall and the lock of hair that had come loose from the ponytail? Was it nothing more than Katherine's status as a living human being she had it in her power to kill?

She kicked her, hard, in the side of the gut, and as Katherine doubled, dropped to her knees, flipped her over, adjusted her grip on the Glock — and smashed the weapon into the back of her head.

The cell phone was still ringing. Valerie picked it out of the passenger footwell and laid it on the ground.

Come what may, Nick, she thought. I love you. *I love you.*

Then she hammered the phone's screen with the butt of the gun until it was silent.

She dragged Katherine's unconscious body into the trees. The physical contact — Valerie's hands under Katherine's arms — was, if anything, even more bizarre without the woman's kaleidoscopic chatter. Her weight surprised Valerie. Katherine had the short upper body and long legs twenty-first-century women craved, but the suppleness wasn't without density. She unfastened the restraints, wrapped Katherine's arms around a tree, refastened them. She had thought of putting her in the Chevy's trunk, but her inner logistician said otherwise: if Eugene got past her (if Eugene killed her, she rephrased — no fucking nonsense, Valerie), that would be the first place he looked. She tossed the car keys deep into the darkness. She wanted a gag — but there was no time. She would have to bank on

Katherine not coming to and making a racket anytime soon. As an afterthought, she threw the keys for the restraints even farther into the darkness. Let Eugene deal with *that* if he killed her. She supposed he would shoot through them. Ah, well.

She looked up between the interlaced branches overhead. The sky had lightened. This was the magic hour filmmakers allegedly loved, light burgeoning from cobalt to mercury, eventually peach. It was only under the trees that the darkness was complete. She picked her way through the undergrowth to the edge of the gravel track. Safety off. The second gun tucked into the waistband of her jeans. Her simple human self was grateful that she was wearing her favored footwear, a brand called Teva, something between a sneaker and a hiking boot. Maximal mobility, grip, spring, comfort. She spared a mad moment of pity for the days when female cops wore feminine clothes. The lightness of being hadn't left her. There was still only the one thing that mattered: holding Nick, alive, in her arms — even if they only had seconds to share it.

Second cattle grid. Fifty yards. She kept low.

She could see the open gate up ahead. Maybe thirty or forty feet beyond that, the farmhouse, a solid pale building set in a front yard of weedy concrete, meadow grass growing on either side. She'd have to skirt the open space. Cut around behind the first row of trees. Then only fifteen or twenty yards to the side of the house. No visible cars. Presumably parked around back.

She quickened her pace. Just shy of the gate a second narrow track at right angles from the first. Barely big enough for a vehicle. It startled her as she passed its opening. The raw space was like a presence. The air in there felt cold. Maybe it went down to a stream?

It didn't matter. She ignored it, passed through the gateway, and veered to her left. Not random: to her left because the most basic instinctive machinery said keep the gun hand — the right hand — between you and the house.

A little more than a minute, perhaps two. She was hot, breathing hard. Her hand was wet around the Glock's grip. But she was level with the side of the house. A fucking *big* house, now that she was close up. There could be a dozen rooms in there. No lights showed. Pray one of the doors is open. Can't afford the sound of a broken window. Can't afford *sound,* period. He hears sound and he kills Nick.

(If he hasn't already. The size of that reality was like a tidal wave she knew had reared up behind her. A wall of dirty water a thousand feet high. She could feel the chill of its shadow on her back. She wouldn't turn and look. She wouldn't.)

She straightened. There was nothing left now but to cross the open space to the house. Come what may. I love you, Nick.

It was what she said to herself instead of a prayer.

She had taken three quick, running strides out from under the cover of the trees when the first shot hit her in the back.

It felt like being *kicked* in the back. She was still wearing the vest, but the force of the slug was enough to knock the wind out of her and send her sprawling onto her front. The ground hit her face with an abrupt taste of turf and pain detonated in her nose. She was aware — even in the moment of impact — of the Glock's cold mass in her right hand. She hadn't dropped it. She had to turn. Get her elbow under her. See him.

But there was no oxygen. Her lungs had emptied. It was as if the gun were nailed to the ground. The air was quicksand. The roll onto her side distended time, stretched seconds into minutes, hours, days.

Too long. Long enough for Eugene to break from the trees, night-vision goggles up on his forehead now, giving him the look of a giant insect loping, upright. Long enough for her to see him smile, raise the pistol, fill her vision, and fire a second shot into her thigh, just above the knee.

49

"Where is Katherine?" Eugene said. He didn't sound angry or urgent. In fact his tone was suave, intrigued.

Valerie was at the end of what felt like a very long ride, dragged by her hair through the farmhouse kitchen and along a corridor to the open door of the basement, where Eugene kicked her down the flight of dusty wooden stairs. He'd relieved her of both firearms. Her leg was a mixture of sensations. It was as if a horse had stomped on it and the stomp had started a fire made, impossibly, of ice. The pain took her right up to the brink of passing out. She could feel unconsciousness there next to her, like the edge of a warm, dark lake she could slip into, so easily, so soothingly. But every time she rolled back.

She opened her mouth to answer Eugene, but the pain halted her for a moment. She turned on her side and vomited. She saw, for the first time, the body of the woman in the corner, facing away. But the French braid reminded her of someone. Through the nausea, it came to her. The moody guard from Red Ridge. She even remembered the name: Lomax. Christ, was that all it was? The simplicity of it disgusted her.

"I repeat," Eugene said: "Where is Katherine?"

"Let him go," Valerie spat, "and I'll tell you."

She had met Nick's eyes just once. Long enough to say: Whatever happens, I love you. Thank you. I'm glad we're together. Nick, still silenced by the duct tape, had returned the look. Then, of all things (and yet of course), winked. I know, Skirt. I love you, too. She had smiled.

"Let him go and you'll tell me," Eugene said, as if weighing it up. Then he stepped over to Nick and pulled the knife out of his belt.

"No!" Valerie screamed. "Wait!"

Eugene jammed the blade into Nick's left shoulder. Nick writhed. Fish on a hook. Eugene twisted the blade. The sound of Nick's sealed-in scream tore through Valerie. "All right!" she roared. "I'll tell you. Stop it, goddamnit, you fuck. I'll tell you."

Eugene withdrew the blade. Nick

screamed again behind the tape. He looked at Valerie, shaking his head: No. Don't. He's going to kill us anyway.

She knew that. This was the endgame. The only thing it was possible for her to win was a quick death for her and Nick. A quick death. Together. At least together. One night, years ago, lying close in bed and talking about death, Nick had said: I don't mind how I go, just as long as I'm not alone. I'd like someone there with me, even if it's a complete stranger. Someone to say goodbye to. It hurt her to remember this, and yet at the same time she was glad. He wasn't alone. She had given him that, at least.

"She's in the trunk of the Chevy," Valerie said. "On the track between the first and second cattle grids. I shot her, but I don't think it'll kill her."

"Thank you," Eugene said. "In that case I'll take a look. It's a shame to forgo what we had planned for you two — where the devil are you off to?"

Valerie had begun dragging herself toward Nick. She wanted to touch him, even if it was just to grab hold of his ankle. Together.

Eugene stomped on the wound in her leg, ripping a cry from her throat. "Oh no, no, no, *no*," he said. "None of that, if you don't mind. Christ, you're positively medieval.

Now, who wants to go first? More painful for Nick to watch you die? Or for you to watch him die? Decisions and imprecisions . . . Oh well, I know what Katherine would want." He raised the gun and aimed it at Nick's face.

At which moment a peculiar thing happened. Simultaneous with the sound of the shot, some small fragments popped out of the top of Eugene's skull in a little spurt of blood.

His knees went from under him and he collapsed onto them. He seemed to stay like that for a long time. Long enough for Valerie to note the strange look of vacancy, one eye rolling back, showing almost all white. Long enough for her to see the gun drop from his hand. Long enough for her to think he was trying to say something.

Then he fell forward onto his face, one arm twisted under him.

There was a bullet hole in the top of his head, and the fair buzz cut was dark with blood.

She followed Nick's gaze, turned, looked up to see Will Fraser crouched halfway up the basement stairs, Smith & Wesson still trained.

"I fucking hated that guy," he said, taking out his phone.

50

It was hard for Valerie to communicate all the information she needed. She was afloat in pain. Red and black nothingness kept coming close. And through all of it she was straining for the sound of sirens. She wanted to surrender to the soft currents of confusion. A siren was a winged female creature whose singing lured sailors to shipwreck on the rocks. A siren was a beautiful woman. Katherine was a siren. And yet a siren was what she wanted. Why did they call them sirens?

Somehow, she managed. Will passed on the location of the house where McLuhan and his team were watching the bomb clock tick down. Two disposal units would be dispatched, one there, and one here, since there was every possibility Eugene had rigged it such that both sets of tech hardware were involved. Vaguely, Valerie imagined headache for the squad. Imagine *that* job. Every day tiptoeing through a mine-field. Every day.

"Katherine's back down the track," she said. "Cuffed to a tree near the Chevy."

"Got it," Will said. "Jesus, I leave you alone for five minutes . . ."

When the tape was removed from his mouth and his hands and feet freed from the cuffs, Nick couldn't stand without Will's support. Will laid him on the floor next to Valerie.

"Hey," she said, laying her hand on his chest.

His lips were swollen. "Hey, Skirt," he slurred. "Remind me later there's something I need to ask you."

"I'd have been here sooner," Will said. "But that crazy girl . . . Jesus, if she hadn't come back to her house to pick up a god-damned pair of shoes . . . You know it's one of Katherine's guards, right?"

"Yeah," Valerie said. "I know."

Nick and Valerie entered the world of the hospital, the white world of beneficent drugs. The bullet had missed Valerie's femoral artery but chipped the femur and ripped through a ligament. She'd be in the hospital for at least a week. And reliant on a crutch for a while after that. Two of Nick's ribs were broken and the knife wound was deep. "You'll get patched up," the doctor told him. "But there's a lot of damage to the muscle. You might need help reaching a top shelf, possibly for the rest of your life."

"I'm retiring," Nick told him. "And emigrating."

"Oh yeah? Where?"

"Polynesia."

Nick called Will to come see him.

"Listen," he said. "I need you to get something for me from the apartment."

"Holy shit," Will said, when Nick told him what it was. "Don't you want to wait until you guys are out of here?"

"I'm done waiting," Nick said. "She gets shot too often."

Later that evening, an orderly deposited Nick at Valerie's bedside. She was on the phone to McLuhan.

"Well," she said, when she'd hung up, "at least we know now who he was."

"Who was he?"

"Ethan Muller. Of the *banking* Mullers. His family cut him off years ago — *bought* him off, I should say — but he's still worth about two hundred million."

"That's some buy-off."

"Cheap at twice the price, according to his father. He tried to rape his sister when

566

he was thirteen. She was nine. The old man's glad he's dead."

"So am I."

For a moment, they looked at each other. So much that didn't need to be said. Death had come so near, for both of them. Neither of them would have thought they could be any more close, and yet their shared survival had stamped something on them, a new certainty where they had thought they had certainty before.

"You didn't remind me," Nick said.

"What?"

"You didn't remind me there was something I wanted to ask you."

"Oh, yeah. Sorry. I had just been *shot.*"

"I wanted to wait and ask you when you were brushing your teeth. I'm not sure why."

He pulled out the small, black velvet box. Opened it.

"Oh my God," Valerie said.

51

One Sunday, three weeks after she'd come out of the hospital (she'd been back at work — desk duty only — for one), Valerie filled up the Taurus at her local Mobil and drove out to Red Ridge to see Katherine Glass.

She was curious. Not morbidly (the job had long since satisfied *that* quota), but out of a strange interest in her own capacity to assimilate the non-assimilable. The problem — if it was a problem — with surviving the sorts of things she had survived was that it opened up new room in you. It invited you into what felt like an elite human activity: understanding humans. So much of what she had never understood had remained impenetrable to her not because it was inherently mysterious, but because she was afraid of it. And now, apparently, she was afraid of nothing. If you were fearless, it was your obligation to do what others were too afraid to do.

Throughout her stay in hospital, and in the weeks since, the thought of visiting Katherine had flickered in and out, then stuck, then become a reliable preoccupation, then a calm certainty. It had a neutral, incontrovertible logic: she *had* to see her because she *wasn't* afraid. She couldn't even say quite why she understood this. Only that she did understand it. It had burgeoned in her like a benign revelation.

Surviving death had made her feel, paradoxically, both young and old. Young because, naturally, the ordinary pleasures of being alive — the simple *fact* of being alive — had been tenderly refreshed; but old because death (with birth) was the oldest human thing, and to have touched it was to have brought some of its ancient imprint back with her into her life. Katherine had, she now realized, *always* seemed old to her. Katherine had touched death from the other side, by giving it to people. Valerie's half-shed moral self still railed against that, but she was already beginning to see that the railing would morph into first sadness, then a kind of clean (and possibly terrible) understanding. An understanding without pity, but an understanding nonetheless. She had begun thinking of Katherine as someone who was doomed to get a particular bit of math wrong, every time. And it was this single mistake that would forever prevent her from . . . From what? Valerie didn't know. But she had an intimation that Katherine thought the same way. Beyond good and evil. Good and evil were the languages we fell back on because we couldn't understand the mistake. In all her dealings with Katherine she'd been bothered by the feeling that Katherine knew something that she, Valerie, did not. Now, having come back from death, she'd found herself thinking maybe it was the other way around — or at the very least, mutual: Katherine believed Valerie knew something that she, Katherine, did not.

None of this was clear to Valerie. She didn't feel, merging with five lanes of traffic in the bright morning (it had rained earlier, and the world had a fresh, rinsed feel) that she had *thought it through.* It wasn't thought, really, that had brought her here. It was something either subtler or more crude. But whatever it was, it moved her with a force of disinterested inevitability.

At the prison, she stood for a few moments outside, smoking a Marlboro and finishing a cappuccino she'd picked up at a rest stop a few miles back. The morning's clouds had dispersed. Now blue sky showed, and sunlight winked on the puddles. She was thinking of the Venerable Bede and Cassie's description of the feasting hall. Drinking and eating and arguing and laughing, fighting and making love. But there was more going on in the feasting hall than that. Katherine Glass and Ethan Muller were there, too, doing what they did. You have to make sure you see everything. All of it, as much as you can. You've got a moment, that's all.

Inside, she went through the security drill. Gun. Purse. All sharp objects. No food, no drink, no cigarettes. The guards went about their business with the same bored diligence she remembered from the times before. The buzzers buzzed, the doors slid open and pounded shut. The place's smell of cramped life and brutal cleaning products was unmistakable. The air was heavy, close, migrained.

In the visitors' room a hard-faced blond guard Valerie hadn't seen before was on duty, along with Warrell, the guard who had accompanied Katherine with Melody Lomax on that first visit, what felt like a lifetime ago. Because her machine couldn't stop what it did, Valerie remembered that on that visit Warden Clayton had told Warrell to take Katherine back to her cell and Lomax to bring her and Will along to her office for debriefing when the interview was over. But in fact *Lomax* had gone back with Katherine to her cell and Warrell had escorted them to see Clayton. All these small things. No matter how good your machine, there were always things it missed.

Katherine sat at the same table, cuffed at wrists and ankles, leaning back in her plastic chair. She looked tired, but her hair was freshly washed, pulled back in its trademark ponytail. For a while, when Valerie took the seat opposite her, neither of them spoke. They just sat and looked at each other.

"I knew you'd come," Katherine said.

It didn't seem strange to Valerie that those were Cassie's words, what felt like a lifetime ago.

"I guess a promise is a promise," Katherine added. "Even to a monster."

"You need to remember what I promised you. I said that if the information you gave us led to his arrest, I would come and visit you once a month until they killed you. Those were my exact words."

"And so?"

"So, we didn't arrest him. He's dead."

Katherine looked at her as if with grudging admiration. "That's the letter of the law, not its spirit," she said.

"As was your so-called information."

"You've changed," Katherine said. "Something's different."

Valerie didn't reply. Katherine was studying her, bright-eyed, suddenly. A childlike excitement. As if her intuition was being proved right.

"It's the strangest thing," Katherine said. "I knew you'd come, but I didn't know why."

"I'm not sure I know why, either," Valerie said. "But here I am. Maybe I'd like to hear your story. The real story, if it's of any interest to you to tell it."

"Do you think there's any hope for me?"

"Hope of what?"

"Redemption. Salvation. Avoiding Hell."

"Honestly?"

"Always."

"No, I don't. It's just that in all the conversations we had I don't think you ever really told me your story. It surprises me, but I'm interested in what that might be."

"You've always been afraid of me."

"Yes, I have."

"But now you're not."

"No. Now I'm not. Just curious."

Katherine sat back in her chair. "I read this thing once," she said. "I forget where. It said that reading a book is a dangerous thing. It can make you find room in yourself for something you never thought you'd understand. Worse, that you never *wanted* to understand. Are you sure you want to understand me?"

"No. And I'm not sure I ever would understand you, even if I wanted to."

Katherine's smile broadened. She took a deep breath, and exhaled into visible relaxation.

"I'm glad," she said. "Now. Where should I begin?"

ABOUT THE AUTHOR

Saul Black is a pseudonym used by Glen Duncan, a British author born in 1965 in Bolton, Lancashire, England to an Anglo-Indian family. In 1994 he visited India with his father before continuing on to the United States, where he spent several months travelling the country by Amtrak train, writing much of what would become his first novel, *Hope,* published to critical acclaim on both sides of the Atlantic in 1997. Duncan lives in London.